*Caracole* ("caper" in English, "snail" in Spanish, and "prancing" in French) is Edmund White's new novel, a baroque invention that is also a high-stepping adventure. Its form curves back upon itself like a snail's shell.

"A devastating panorama of life in a high-powered city where everyone is on the make in one way or another and where the mixture of greed and vanity is evident in most of the practices of love . . . *Caracole* would be my nomination for the finest French novel written in English." —Phyllis Rose, *The Nation*

"Just as Strauss's opera *Der Rosenkavalier* uses a courtly tale of eighteenth-century Vienna to comment on the composer's own time . . . so *Caracole*, ostensibly about a fictional capital verging on the Venetian, parodies fixtures of contemporary New York intellectual life." —*Christopher Street*

"The largest and most accomplished of his novels, and one that will confirm his status as one of the most interesting of America's younger writers." —Peter Ackroyd, *The Sunday Times* (London)

"Sensations pile upon sensations in this dense, swirling book which piles images of sensuality, pride, greed, and lust on every page in the dance-like interactions of its main characters. . . . Elegant, original, and hauntingly evocative." —*The Sunday Telegraph* (London)

EDMUND WHITE is a former senior editor at *Saturday Review* and has taught creative writing at Yale, Johns Hopkins, and Columbia. In 1983 he went to Paris on a Guggenheim fellowship and has remained there as a contributing editor to *Vogue*. Praised by Vladimir Nabokov, Christopher Isherwood, and Gore Vidal, he has been best known for his books about the gay experience, especially the nonfiction *States of Desire: Travels in Gay America*, and the novels *Nocturnes for the King of Naples* and *A Boy's Own Story* (available in a Plume Fiction edition).

CARACOLE

EDMUND WHITE

A PLUME BOOK

**NEW AMERICAN LIBRARY**

NEW YORK AND SCARBOROUGH, ONTARIO

TO
JOHN PURCELL

*The author gratefully acknowledges the help he received from the Guggenheim Foundation.*

"It is so painful in you, Celia, that you will look at human beings as if they were merely animals with a toilette, and never see the great soul in a man's face."

—GEORGE ELIOT, *Middlemarch*


—Parlez donc avec plus de respect, dit la comtesse souriant au milieu de ses larmes, du sexe qui fera votre fortune; car vous déplairez toujours aux hommes, vous avez trop de feu pour les âmes prosaïques.

—STENDHAL, *La Chartreuse de Parme*

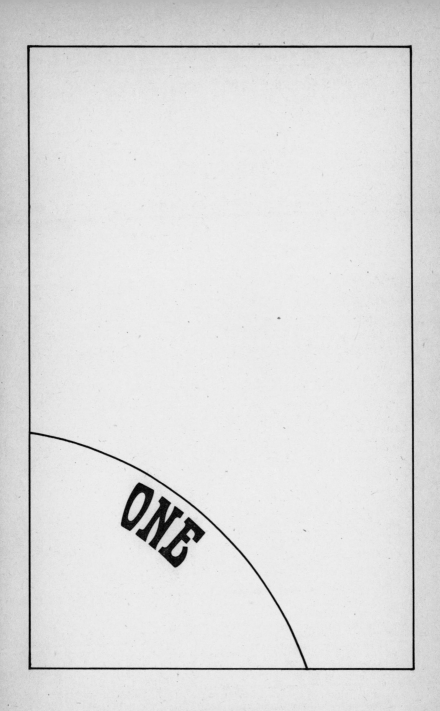

ONE

**G**ABRIEL'S father—a silent, stubborn man, so wary that when asked to go for a walk he would avert his eyes and say, "I'll tell you my answer in a minute"—insisted that in the morning the boy conjugate verbs from the household's sole book, an unglued and incomplete sheaf of pages stuffed between boards the rain had warped, an animal had chewed, the sun had bleached from red to pink. These exercises required Gabriel to shout out every possible form of today's word (its meaning unknown and unexplained) to his mother who dozed, drunk, in the next room, which would have been dark had the shutters not been missing their slats in sequences as irregular as bars of band music the wind blows away on a summer night.

Invariably the historical past was the tense that excited a kind of desire in her. She raised herself on one elbow, turned her enormous face blindly in Gabriel's direction and called for him; the sound of her voice was surprisingly gentle. Once the boy was beside her, he could look around the room and pick out other signs of her former softness, kindness, respectability—remnants, for instance, of family silhouettes snipped out in black paper and fixed to white velvet. Once in a fit she had torn the silhouettes to shreds. Later, she had pieced what she could back together, though she'd scrambled features and assigned Gabriel's long, simple profile (just seven turns of the artist's scissors) to his father's squat neck and placed the nurse's corrugated head (seventy-six minute snips) on her own aristocratic, sloping shoulders—oh, they'd all been turned into monsters.

The six younger children were as scrambled on the velvet as in their mother's memory, which had telescoped the wearisome identities into just two names and just two qualities: Boy (Bad) and Girl (Worse). Gabriel's name, though, she remembered, and she called it out over the unexpectedly short forms of a tense that like her own past had begun and fully ended before the present and, accordingly, had taken on the frozen simplicity of fear or sleep.

Gabriel kneaded her white back with the heels of his hands ("Palms too hot," she'd once grunted) until the skin glistened like pie dough too long on the slab. Conjured out of the shadows, breeding up out of the dirt like flies, came his brothers and sisters, weak blue eyes trained on the domestic mystery of the massage, mouths open to reveal bad teeth and hunger. The children jostled one another, ground knuckles into ribs, jabbed a black elbow into a scabby flank, sending a sibling toppling into the torn organdy duster fringing the bed or hurtling under the lace suspended from the vanity until, caged by cloth, the victim looked out through gray eyelets whitened by cobwebs.

Time for lunch.

He slipped off the inactive volcano of his mother's body and led his younger brothers and sisters, caroming off cracked clay walls behind him, down a maze of corridors to the ancient double kitchen. Past the seven tenantless maids' rooms, home now for bats, rabbits, and grass sprouting up between sinking, tilted flagstones. Past the dim chamber where hundreds of garden flowers had once been snipped daily, frogged, vased, and wafted off to the great hall. Past the mangling room, rollers rotting on their cylinders, chains unthreaded and fused into inverted clumps, the cistern putrid with dried lye. Past the pantry where china and crystal had once been stacked dirty after supper to await washing the next morning, on the theory that servants are too tired and drunk at night to be trusted with it; now the tall cabinet door hung open to reveal shelves, empty save for one upright porcelain menu framed in glazed fleurettes.

In the kitchen he sopped slices of bread in olive oil and garlic and fried them over a campfire he had fashioned out of parts from the defunct stove. He fueled the flame with kindling he'd gathered in the woods. Later, in the early evening he'd fry more bread and, for the sake of variety, slather it with goose fat. The children, snatching the food out of his hand, blew on the hot bread and whistled after each bite. They had no memory of real dinners, real table talk or, for that matter, of polite conversation of any sort; even for Gabriel the family's former grandeur seemed as faint as their cipher on the toppled gatepost.

He wandered in the afternoons down a long alley of trees, once the sweeping approach to the house (which was called "Madder Pink," after the local wildflower), but now lapsed into waist-high grass. Farther and farther from home he'd venture until its portico, still noble if seen from a distance, disappeared below the waving grass. His own heritage interested him not at all. The decline of the family fortunes had happened so slowly—as slowly as the aging of a face—that he could never think of it as a drama. It had all begun eight infinite years ago, when he'd been nine. One day a maid had talked of going, a month or two later she'd gone; one spring the gutters had needed painting, that autumn they were still choked and useless, drawing noisy links of rain across French windows that by winter were paneless, by spring unhinged, fallen lattices confining weeds in squares, grids on grass. The stable hand left and though he promised to return he did not; Gabriel's father emptied the stables one day and for two months the boy's pony, Heart's Delight, still suffered his master to ride him. But after a hard winter the shaggy animal, limping on a bad ankle, looked at Gabriel sheepishly and tottered away from the rope harness.

The real horse he replaced with a stick one, a branch four feet long, wide at the neck and narrow at the tail, something he'd turned into a palomino by stripping off bands of black bark to expose white wood. This mount he named Curfew, after Heart's Delight's legendary sire, and it led him where it would, out beyond the gates, up the foothills and onto Troublesome Mountain. To keep the horse happy Gabriel had to whisper praise in its ear. "My Curfew," he said in a low voice, "has a thick mane and silk tail. He smells like good shoe polish. His legs are wet with sweat. His teeth are yellow as piano keys. His eyes are amber as maple sap. His nostrils are blacker than the insides of gloves. He is brave and trustworthy and obeys no one but me."

Up the steep sides of Troublesome the boy clambered astride his stick. At a stream he dipped the wood in water. On a gravel run he'd dismount and pick a stone out of the imaginary hoof. Slowly they ascended through patches of white lilacs, horsemint, fairy fringe, cow wheat, meadow rue, and stands of laurel, oak and pine.

Just come day, go day.

If Curfew fancied flatland, they'd follow a dry creek bed, the only road that hadn't reverted to undergrowth. On their rounds they picked up two other boys on *their* stick horses, lads who spoke in a way Gabriel found hard to follow. They were sons of the old rural gentry—people who, unlike Gabriel's family, had never lived or studied in the capital, and who, accordingly, retained the out-moded vocabulary of the previous century. One of them had a clay pig, small enough to fit into his pocket; it whistled one dry, low note when blown on the snout. The other knew the names of stones but he was the hardest to understand. Someone's youngest brother he called "the Least One." If he doubted a story, he said, "I don't confidence you." Windows he called "lights" and their hiding place in an oak bole he spoke of as the "plunder room." Where the creek fanned out into a hundred rivulets, this child said, "That's where it turkey-tailed," and if a grown-up showed him special attention he'd ask later, "Why did he much me?" Both of Gabriel's companions spoke in doubled nouns ("biscuit-bread," "ham-meat," "sulfur-match"). Nor did they grasp what Gabriel meant when he said once, "Have a nice weekend." After a while it turned out their families worked every day and the notion of a weekend was beyond their means.

Before Madder Pink had collapsed, Gabriel's father had brought in a dozen dark-skinned tribal families from the South to work the land. Now the fields lay fallow and their mistress dozed night and day in her bed, scarcely moving, conserving her energy in order to achieve what seemed her goal—to get as big as the hair-stuffed mattress. Its coarse fibers broke through the linen net so that when Gabriel rolled his hands over his mother's naked back or breasts he might, to relieve the tedium, contemplate which horse hairs stood upright in their cloth pores and which had been pressed flat, which leaned at unassuming angles and which seemed to be in danger of falling out. Like a growing thing a hair here or there worked its way daily farther and farther out of the bed—a dry extrusion so different from Curfew's silky tail.

Some summer evenings Gabriel went into the woods just be-fore sunset and noticed the light prying dexterously through dark foliage in order to seize and set on fire a single leaf, choosing this one leaf fluttering humbly on a low branch for the day's final, terrifying honors. And at that moment, if he stopped and squinted, the boy could see Curfew's mane ignite and flow, its flow the animal's only concession to the rising winds that were signaling the end to a nine-day hot spell. All the leaves, of course, were pattering like gathered rain blown in irregular volleys off roofs across an empty plaza. A stirring of leaves would start somewhere far away, rush closer, stop, resume, talk in tongues above his head—and the red light on the leaf or mane would solemnly dim; die. Just time to turn around and see the tip of the sun's huge index finger retract below the horizon.

He felt lonely for a second. On the path home the leaves started up again, more anxious than before, a live tree scraped against a dead one, a sassafras brush threw up its hands in mimed despair, a blackbird with an ugly caw showed the unpleasant side to motherhood, a doe lowered her head the better to peer out beneath a low-slung bough at Gabriel, while her fawn, less confident, bounded away through a maze of blackberry bushes. Gabriel feared for a second that the doe might actually charge him, but Curfew whinnied just then and sent her scampering after her child. Even so the boy touched for luck the wax cake hung on a string around his neck.

Where the path turned and broadened just before the woods gave out, he saw that girl again. She had dark brown skin and thick matted hair and now, since she was sitting on a tree stump studying the ground, her hair swarmed over her face like bees suspended outside the hive their queen has elected to abandon. He could almost hear her hair. She was patting a bare foot against the ground, one bare shoulder pitched higher than the other as though she were already halfway into a shrug, but when she drew on her long-stemmed pipe the glow revealed big, widely spaced eyes trained on him. She did shrug then, look away, double the speed of her drumming foot, slap at a mosquito he suspected was there only for effect.

He nodded.

Though she was deep behind her hair she returned his greeting and once again drew a light from the pipe to expose her fat, down-turned lips, broad nose, the baby fat of her cheeks and the sooted satin of her lowered lashes. He took a few steps toward her. Embarrassment, like the burn of gulped whiskey, spread through him; Curfew—this stick toy—seemed ridiculous and he dropped it, hastily kicked it aside. A little whinny of protest . . . he had betrayed his horse for this brown girl scratching her nose.

He smiled at her. Perhaps there was simple friendliness in his smile, but never before had he wanted to be so cunning save in his dealings with his father. With his father, however, Gabriel was always plotting in order not to lose another fight or surrender another freedom; now, he wanted to gain . . . a word, say.

He got it. "Hello," she said. "Want a smoke?" She had an accent and spoke slowly.

"Thanks. Yes." He sat down beside her and she pushed back her hair on the far side of her face, leaving a confessional curtain between them, through which he glanced once. The indistinct line of her profile lengthened as she inhaled the smoke and her chin grew. When she handed him the pipe her paw touched his hand and the heat of her skin thrilled him. It was the heat of another, more intense, shorter-lived kind of animal; it was also, to his mind, an invitation to feel her body all over.

He'd seen her before. She belonged to a family of those tribal laborers his father had imported. Now that they had no work his father had ordered them to leave, to return to the South, but they hadn't. They raided the granary and the dilapidated barn, they shit in the abandoned school house, they stole eggs and even chickens, they ran naked through the fields at night, splashed in the stream, calling to each other in their singsong, raucous voices. On his rounds astride Curfew, Gabriel had spotted their ancient queen, scarcely four feet tall, inching slowly through the grasses, her gold paper headdress catching the rays of sunlight that leaked through the torn umbrella the men held over her. If he galloped toward them, the men, all gold teeth, formed a laughing screen that blocked her from view. She continued her painful progress with just two escorts. He never saw her face, just the glittering hat from which bobbled strips of white parchment on which words in black ink were written. The men grinned goldly, a knife with a red leather grip passed from one hand to another and Curfew wheeled up through the air, rolling eye panicked by a blade either rusting or spotted with dried blood.

He asked her name.

"Angelica," she said, pausing over the syllables as though they were pronounced or stressed differently in her own language.

The smoke from her pipe unfurled lazily in the air until it reached a certain height (second branch up the oak) where the wind tore it to shreds.

If he kept quizzing her, he'd know the foods she'd eaten, the horses she'd ridden, the history behind that white scar brightening the brown web of flesh between her thumb and index finger. And yet the prospect of possessing all this knowledge alarmed him. He wanted to tell her to hold things back or to leave now and appear only at dusk and then just for ten minutes, her mouth sealed with wax, a red thread crossing her lips as a guarantee that the envelope had not been broken open.

She raised a hand to his cheek and he shrank away; looking into her beautiful face he'd forgotten how disfigured his own was. He'd even jumped ahead to some moment when he might know her too well and be bored with her—obviously a fantasy to innoculate him against the more likely possibility she would soon enough disdain him. "What are these?" she asked, touching the acne, the painful eruptions. "Were you burned?"

For a second he considered saying yes. A burn, yes, the sores will heal in a week, nothing really, I'll soon be handsome again.

More likely she was making fun of him, gangly white thing that he was with a blistered face gabbling to a stick between his legs, frightened of deer, son of a man powerless to drive her kinsmen off his own property and of a woman entangled in fouled sheets who lacked hunger but possessed a thirst that couldn't be quenched. To Angelica they must all appear ludicrous. His skinny, shifty-eyed father, whose grain rotted in the fields while he chased his own laborers around the tumbledown hen house in a vain attempt to recover one egg. His fat, pale mother struggling to overflow the margins of her bed, her giant body emblazoned like an old coat of arms with shifting bars of light cast by the missing shutter slats, argent bend sinister in the morning, by sunset dexter: gules. And he must be the most laughable of all, the eldest son, overgrown and dirty, humming as he surveyed his patrimony of weeds, his face showing for him the scarlet shame he was too degraded to feel.

"I must get home," he said, standing and looking at Curfew, writhing on his side under a bush.

Angelica had the cruelty to laugh. And then she actually reached out and touched the mound of bulging muscle below his fly buttons. "Why leave when this is hard?" Her small fingers undid the buttons patiently; she looked up at him. He had not seen clearly the moment when someone else would take up his weapon, nor was he certain it should be handed over to anyone else, since he liked the way it responded to his own touch. When he had fenced with it in solitude he had clenched his jaws shut, widened his eyes, flared his nostrils, expanded his chest, stabbed with rhythmic power and majesty, black knight drawing white blood. Or he thought of himself as the universe, and this galaxy of discharged fluid on his stomach as the Milky Way.

She placed his hand on her cheek and then rubbed against his fingers like a cat. She looked up and whispered, "Sit down." He did.

Many times he'd seen naked women—his mother during the

massage, the laboring women and their daughters at the stream. Their bodies had fascinated him but nothing about them had excited him toward possession, nor did he know they could be possessed.

To be sure, as a little boy he had loved to torment one particular maid by calling to her as he scampered naked through the house. Frail, white, shivering with suspense, he would hide behind the armoire and cry, "Maria. Maria." She ignored him. He called her name again. If she grumbled that she was busy he'd whine, "Something's terribly wrong with my leg. Horrible pain. You must come. I *need* you."

If she rose, sighing, to her feet, then he'd streak to the double doors, close one, hide behind it and wail, "I'm in here. Hurry. I need you." He rushed behind the couch that no one ever sat on in the drawing room and sent up new cries. If she gave up the chase, he shed tears: "Why are you so slow? I'm in pain. Come quick. I need you." As he brushed away the tears he felt his penis quicken, stiffen. On and on he led her through the house in summer, its shutters projecting thin lines of light on teak, silk and tile. Past a startled footman emerging from the drawing room with a tray. Past the laundress whose deafness made her laughter much too crude, given her subtle, puzzled face, as she fed wet linen into the mangle or out on the line over a courtyard white as sugar. Past the music room, its trio of sopranos interrupted voice by shrieking voice as the nude child scampered by. Up the stairs until he reached the balustrade, all his body hidden except his face. He peered down on the bewildered Maria and beseeched her to follow him. His running feet pounded a beat through his bones that kept time with his panting and pulse. Once he was under the water in the tub and could near Maria's approaching steps, his anticipation hurt so much his final laugh of triumph came out as a sob. When she entered the room he thrust his tiny, erect penis up above the surface of the water and laughed himself sick. She pretended to be angry, but she lingered there, smiling with tender complicity. At last she knelt beside him and washed him. She loved him. Once she was his captive he lost interest in her. She became just another servant, like the man who rowed him across the lake or the man who cleaned his boots.

Now the old, almost forgotten pleasure and pain of luring Maria upstairs returned to Gabriel. When he'd been a child the excitement—something like the smell of camphor or the tingling behind the eyes that precedes a nosebleed—had been purer, more abstract. Here, at last, the abstraction had become concrete. It had taken on flesh. He opened Angelica's shirt and her breast released a scent—of clove and of cooking fat, which repulsed him even as he bent closer to inhale it. She pressed her open mouth to his, startling him. He didn't like the slipperiness, and he pushed her away.

In the dark he could see little besides the tips of her front teeth. And he could make out flashes from her eyes; each time she looked up, which she did not do often or for long, he thought insects were suddenly fanning black wings to expose white backs. With the back of his hand he tried to rub away the drop of her spit from his lip, but it still burned him.

His fastidiousness was being contradicted by something else he didn't understand, something invading him as sea mist might roll over the beach, pool between dunes, drop veils of brine over the hair of a fisherman dragging his boat up the sand. This other thing had no name and failed to come together; it was a farfetched constellation some fabulist had drawn over far-flung stars. It stung, then numbed him. It drew on the ache of his penis in her hand, the acne disfiguring his face, the need to seek consolation in what is dangerous. It was as exciting as adventure and as intimate as shame.

She pulled him down to the ground and rolled on top of him. She bit him on the neck and hung on with her teeth. He pushed her away and looked down at his blistered chest. He longed to touch her ear, just once, to touch it with his lips. He was lost to his own desire, lost in the shifting intricacies of her body, losing grip as she gripped more tightly what he could only with effort call *his* penis since now it had become this blunt, greedy child that somehow belonged to her as much as to him. It was between them, an ugly, hungry thing struggling to suck at his pulse, as a leech might fill with his blood or a baby with her milk. She ran her free hand under Gabriel's shirt and across his stomach. The skin rippled and shrank away from her touch—and he thought that this sensitivity belonged not to a boy but to a girl, a mere girl. He was too slender, too delicate, too girlish to support this penis, this monstrous child; its ambitions for roughness, for excitement, were horrifying. He was ashamed. Yet Gabriel found himself rolling over her, their child demanding the pressure of her hand, of her body. He looked down with horror at the glossy black hair bearding her twisted lips below and he gasped; she, too, appeared embarrassed. Her eyes appeared almost all white as she studied her pipe, cast aside and smoldering in the grass. Flecks of tobacco—no, freckles!—marred her skin where the neck joined the torso.

Gabriel's fears gave way to the pleasure of being taken in, of being *housed*. Though he was the one entering her, yet it seemed the gift, the gift-giving, was all hers. She lay on the ground, eyes still trained on the pipe, mouth oddly childish and indifferent, yet her whole body, not just that hairy wound, but her whole body, her head too, all of her was presenting him with a gift.

"Does that feel good?" he asked, moving inside her. He meant nothing by the question. But Angelica seemed startled. Had she forgotten him? Herself? Her eyes lifted from the pipe and flew precariously through the foliage overhead until they settled on him. She looked at him, blinked and nodded with a faint smile, as though she had to be polite and thank the person who'd given her a sedative.

They ended up grappling one another, rolling in the dust,

teeth bared in grins, his loose buckle caught in her hair, her skirt trapped under his knee and ripping as the last spasm shook them.

They were bewildered by what their bodies had done to them. As their breathing evened out they were able to hear other animals scampering through the leaves and an owl hoo-hooing on a distant branch. The smell of the soil thickened under them. His leg felt uncomfortable under hers. A play of shadows masked her face like a badger's; he glimpsed evil, narrowed eyes—no, it was just a thick lock of hair horizontal across her forehead. Her real eyes were lower down, dimmer, vaguer. The little clearing in the woods had seemed the only place that existed a moment ago, boiling and dense, but now it had exploded and was hurtling outward, filling space with dimension, chatter, time, leaving the center forlorn, forlornly tranquil.


Gabriel saw Angelica every evening in the same place. She'd babble away to him in his language with deceptive facility. Somehow she'd learned the latest slang, but occasionally she wouldn't know the word for *bread* or *tree*.

During the day he sometimes saw her with her people, and then she looked like someone else. From a treetop he watched her and three other girls as they gathered firewood.

He couldn't understand their language. But he noticed how Angelica moved out of phase with the others, hanging back until they called her. Then, likely as not, she would forage ahead of the group. Those other girls never stopped talking or eloquently listening. A voice would start on a low note, rise, tap out an accelerating rhythm, swoop up to a point of emphasis, a controlled shriek really, then grind back down to the original, workaday rumble.

All of these exchanges were accompanied by an idiomatic show of raised hands, raised eyebrows, raised lips, as though rising were the difficult slant of talking and listening, opposed to the natural dejection of silence. Gabriel was both fascinated and alarmed by a hard, easy fluency that left no room for tenderness, which he suspected begins in confusion. When they were alone Angelica could be brusque with him, could stare him down out of her cave of hair or flick her eyes nervously up to a treetop in the midst of something important he was trying to tell her. But with her companions she lacked all assurance. Her voice was so low and soft as to annoy them and they glanced at one another above her bowed, murmuring head with amusement or impatience.

Her face was younger than theirs but her body more mature.

One day, as Gabriel was heading out to the woods and Angelica, his father stopped him.

"Here he is," the father said, delivering his son over to the woman beside him. She moved inside a nimbus of cologne that so troubled Gabriel he couldn't make sense of what she was saying, though he did notice she had one eye that wandered and smudges of lipstick on her teeth. As she spoke, traces of her scent, like a pack of nervous dogs, circled him, nipped him or caressed him. He could actually see the dogs, bald and beige, yawning or snapping at the air, their haunches huge as they rose and resumed their leashed circuit, sandy eyelashes lowering on amber eyes. She talked on, lips fluttering over red and white teeth. She paid no attention to the restless animals that stroked him with short-haired flanks and squinted their costly eyes into the breeze.

"Yes," his father said at last, "that should serve you as a warning."

The woman, whom he called "Conception," smiled her two-color smile and gave Gabriel her hand, too moist to be healthy. The adults examined him closely, and Gabriel felt that something dangerous to him might have been proposed had he not cleverly chosen to ignore it. Gabriel rejoiced in his own wiliness. Conception was talking now, haranguing him, and now his father was agreeing with her but Gabriel didn't pay attention. "Yes," he concurred with a meekness intended at once to acknowledge and to mock whatever demand they had happened to make. The woman stumbled off over the rutted, slashed field, Gabriel's father solemn and smooth beside her. In the distance divided curtains were blowing out of an upstairs window of Madder Pink. The panel on the right was ripped in two places close to the bottom hem and as a result it did not stir as readily nor lift as high as the perfect cloth. Conception's perfume clung to his hand and he kept sniffing it with lazy horror. He didn't wait to see if they went into the house.

The delay made him late. The sun was so long down by the time he arrived at their hollow that he couldn't see Angelica, though he intuited her. She had been dispersed into the shifting phantoms of leaves above, her nature as hidden as the massive roots he stepped over and as plucky as the wind strumming those roots on notes too low to be heard. Autumn was infiltrating summer's ranks but only under cover of darkness; it was dark now and cold spies brushed past him.

One of them was Angelica. He caught her and they rolled on the chilled ground, talking all the while. "Feel good?" "Hurry up." "Move an inch to the left." "Stop breathing all over me." "Feel good?" "All right." "Can't you make that thing tighter?" "I could, but I don't want to, your breath smells funny." "There, that's better. See, you can do it." "I can't breathe. I told you not to lie on top of me. There. That's better." "Should I do that some more?" "I guess. Aren't you finished yet?" "Are you?" "I already had two stings. Maybe I'll get a third. I think I will. Yes. Here it comes." "Wait for me." "I can't. There! Hurry." "Stop rushing me. I want at least one sting." "Yours is so messy. I found some of your stuff in me again yesterday." "So what? All right. Don't move." "Is that it?" "Uh-huh." "Then get off me. You smell funny, you really do."

They lay on the ground beside each other, panting and looking at the stars growing like points of frost on the leaves.

Each afternoon Gabriel resolved not to go back to the hollow again and every evening he went. During the day what they had done together oppressed him, like a dream of traveling for hours in airless machinery, feet in grease, cuts of painful light invading the darkness. She herself was an innocent bystander, he knew, as bewildered as he by the relentless turmoil, her frightened hand pressed in his as the terrible chains began to slide.

But when the day started to fade he found himself heading out toward the woods or, if he were already in them, to the hollow. If it rained he was grateful he had to stay home. He wandered through the upper reaches of the house, past missing windows where the elements were rusting an antique wallpaper, blighting the painted flowers, falling on them as poverty falls on the world.

Down the narrow corridor he goes and turns to the right, then ducks into the second room on the left. The light filters through butcher paper glued to the panes, on one of which is written, in a hand perverse with decorative downstrokes, the names of plants, perhaps those a long dead gardener set out fifty springs ago:

> *blush-colored hyacinths, grape and feathered*
> *corn flag*
> *stinking black hellebore*
> *Prince Picoti or July flower*
> *Chilly strawberries*
> *white-flowering swamp bay*
> *devil's bit or blazing star*
> *mountain goat's rue*

This list no longer signifies. Once when he was even younger, it made him conjure up botanical fancies. He'd piece all the names together into a dream of circus princesses nose-deep in boas; of waving maize banners; of a fabulous Straits where the sweet waters had thickened into a giant moor's tripe; or of King Summer's son, plucking a mandolin beside the miniature statue of a listening goddess, her smile suppressed; cold fruit; an emptied inlet, its crater glittery with dried salt, a whale's skeleton beached there like the wind-sateened hull of a galleon; Satan's Pegasus cantering across the wet night sky, evil stars for hoofprints; Angora regrets.

But now these myths, a god's notebook jottings as he wanders the fields listening for romantic motifs he can turn into symphonies —these myths have vanished and left in their place a conjugation of empty sounds, as meaningless as the rain. Here Gabriel rests on a pile of rotting silks and unfocuses his eyes on the cracked ceiling (a fair copy of the flower names transcribed on his face by the light, his twisted mouth a huge *tilde* over an *n* on his chin). He pulls his penis out of the dirty folds of his pants and works it, thinking about Angelica. The silks, worn long ago by a great-grandmother who decided on chastity after six children in five years (a decision cele-brated obliquely in the flower her husband named "mountain goat's rue")—these silks rustle under him, shocked and attracted witnesses to Gabriel's melancholy exercise. He's pleased to have this moment alone to think about Angelica. To submit his red, disfigured face to her gaze every day has required one act of cour-age after another. And stinging her daily has left him no time to relish their fierce pleasures in solitude. Now that she is gone, he can spread her legs and cast her face in shadow. He pulls her head into the light, opens her eyes—no, closes them—rounds her lips, re-tracts them, stains her teeth with red smudges. He places her over him, a black shadow looming against the leaf grisaille above, her face a supposition divined from the explicit hair, elbows and knees staking her down to the ground. Now her pelvis buckles up off the earth, crotch active but buttocks slack, cool, the lips of her sex delicate, coral, easily probed, each hair individual and crisp though the torso and legs have flowed into a melting blur. He kneels over her, young knight with drawn sword above a creature half maiden, half dragon, enameled scales in rainbow-colored ranks serrating into a girl's skin. Now Gabriel and Angelica fall over each other, rolling downhill, and as he rolls he sees trees overhead, then one dead leaf huge on the ground before him, now a flash of snow flung past. Trees. Leaf. Snow. Treesleafsnow.

The woman, Conception, moved into the old school house. She insisted that the roof be repaired, and Gabriel and his father spent two long days inching across it on hands and knees in search of nearly invisible leaks. The original slate had been patched with tarpaper long ago. Now thin brushes slapped foul, boiling creosote out of a small pot onto the places where the paper had worked loose. The woman tended the fire under the pot on the ground below; wrinkling her face and swearing, she threw branches into the flames as though they were live lobsters. She had bound her hair up in what Gabriel recognized as one of his father's old shirts. There was an urgency in her movements and deliberate ugliness in her costume.

She could not abide rest breaks. She drove them on, complaining about the stench from the pot, about the sweat soaking her clothes, about the vast scale of their undertaking, their need to rush before the storm clouds blew nearer. She talked so much about her sweaty body that Gabriel kept picturing it. Today the lipstick was gone, but its absence, like a fermata, counted. She was shorter and squatter, too, since she'd donned low-heeled boots and baggy pants held up by a thick rope. When he got very near her he caught a hint of cologne—yesterday's cologne.

Until now he'd never thought about what he was doing. He cooked the bread in the fat and pummeled his mother and called out the words from the book, but these were just habits. Time was mist, not steam under pressure, and it floated where it would. If his mother had roused herself sufficiently to down more drink than usual, she might shout louder or sleep longer, but later her mood seemed to him no more memorable than last week's weather. It was wet or it was fine, lightning flashed or the sun blazed, his mother dozed or she smiled as she writhed under the lash of a demon she feared but whom only she could see as it arced airily over the room from the gloomy top of the armoire into the shoals of light and shadow rippling over her huge bed. The demon then slithered under the pillow, which she triumphantly lifted. She exclaimed, "Aha! My pet," and grinned blindly around the room at the applause that must have been showering down on her from other, more benign witnesses, their hands clasping their knees with black leather palms, their teeth running like sap.

"Oh, hurry, hurry," Conception called out to Gabriel, who was poised on the ladder as he looked toward the woods. The trees had gone colorless and flat in the evening light, while mauve clouds stroked the sky, as though a bird, after falling in an inkwell, had scrabbled frantically across a blotter. The breeze turned cold.

Gabriel nodded and came down. She stirred the pot with a stick, wrinkled her face in disgust, grabbed his brush away from him and plunged it into the boiling liquid. "Here!" she shouted, thrusting the handle of the brush back at him. Dizzy, he stepped away and the brush fell in the dirt. "No," she screamed. "No!" Like a baby's, her face reddened and shriveled for tears, but the tears didn't come. She kicked Gabriel with her small boot. He laughed as he did when a younger child tackled him. His laughter wasn't meant to mock her. He was embarrassed for her and wanted to treat her anger as a joke. Perhaps it was a joke.

But no, she kept kicking him, falling with every lunge, her breathing as painful and loud as one piece of leather rubbing against another. At last she stopped, doubled up, hugged her legs and seemed to be studying the dirt. From moment to moment a new spasm shook her leg. When Gabriel looked around he saw his father at the base of the ladder, arms folded, face empty. His father raised Conception from the ground, sheltered her in his arms and led her into the school house. Gabriel pressed himself against the wall beside the window. All he could hear was his father's low, rumbling voice. She started shouting and sobbing again. If Gabriel had been forced to live with this woman she would have frightened him. But (he looked around) there was all this land, the woods, the mansion, Troublesome Mountain, and what went on in the school house could be ignored, he figured. He cleaned his brush as best he could, charged it with creosote and returned to the roof. After three dutiful trips up and down the ladder his father came out of the school house. "Just get out of here," he said.

Gabriel smiled and shrugged but his father said nothing more.

Gabriel ran into the woods. Angelica might have given up on him by now. Or she might not have ventured out at all, kept away by the storm clouds. No matter. He longed to see her, to hold her. Not that he wanted to roll around with her on the ground. He wanted her to hold him. A strange last gleam of sunlight, clear and precise, broke through the cloud cover, played over the surging leaves, the supple grasses. Treetops backstroked into the wind. The sunlight burned through the treetops, turning everything lime green. Like envoys of his desire, birds scattered up and away from his running feet, ribbons of song unscrolling from their beaks: "Wait!" they called. Gabriel carried his longing for Angelica inside him; she would lean over its dark waters and stretch a hand toward it.

The queer light plunged the lusterless world into hot sugar water and pulled it up candied. When Gabriel reached the hollow she was still there. The usual rate of talk, of touch, seemed too slow; he needed her now, even while she was talking to him, and he butted his head gently against her side like a calf, then drew back, straightened up, and stared into her face. Finally, in frustrated longing, he lifted her off the ground. She laughed and seemed pleased by the newness, the awkwardness of what he was doing. He carried her around in his arms. Although he laughed too, at the same time he was frowning, as if he were looking for something. She began to slip. He released her for a second, then picked her up again as he continued his search. In his thoughts she'd been motionless, smiling, but now in his arms she twisted and turned, her hot little body filling the tinted air with a hundred gestures until he understood why people might give their favorite goddess eight arms and four faces. Those weren't enough but they did at least suggest the way a girl could crowd a hollow with herself—a pair of arms reaching out to clasp him as she turned her head away in profile, lips lifted, eyes downcast; another two hands to push her hair back from eyes that opened, brightening; two arms to hang at her sides and a face to lower in submission until he butted her side again and moaned and sank to the ground below her, frustrated and yearning; then one more glorious face to swim down toward his, her lips full, her breath fast and shallow, her last two arms pressing his head against her one and only but wildly beating heart.

His father and Conception must have alarmed him in some way as though (yes, that's it) they intended to take Angelica away from him, or him from Angelica, because now the girl seemed specially beautiful. No sooner had he achieved his first sting and exploded inside her than he felt disappointed, excluded, and he began to moan again and ram her with his limp penis. He dared not draw too far back or it would pull out of her and that he couldn't bear. No, he'd rather shrink down to the size of an elf (or a penis) and climb in, wriggling past coils of wet muscle into a sloping corridor leading all the way to the pungent source of that clove scent she harbored, two sacs that filled—veined, whistling— and then deflated, flooding the world with rich but invisible roe. His dream of wandering through her body—past the heart as stately as a frog at night, through entrails more passionate than his own hands stroking her face, restlessly feeling for a new fault through which he might enter her—this dream made him hard again. He dug into her with his sore penis. He pressed his skull against hers; he wanted in there, too. He kissed her; he knew her mouth was another way in. As he became more frantic she turned weirdly calm, but that seemed right. She should be nerveless, she mustn't brace against him, she'd have to dim her fires to a low, steady glow if he was ever to penetrate the magic ring, the hot, magic ring that gripped him, and reach that sleeping maiden who was . . . not Angelica at all but himself. In the end he could only fill her with more of his own white blood, not extract the small, necessary but unknown thing he needed. They heard a branch snap and looked up to see Gabriel's father and Conception watching them. The adults looked at each other and went away.

For two weeks it rained every day. On the seventh day of rain Angelica showed up at the door to Gabriel's house. She didn't ask to be invited in. She and he had adopted a funny manner (it seemed funny to them) of pretending to be younger, more wide-eyed than they were; an adult bystander, regarding them as already impossibly young, would not have understood the game.

"Hello," she said, "I just thought I'd say hello." "Hello," he said back, smiling, gentle, a friendly little kid. Whom were they imitating as they stood in the doorway, shifting their weight from foot to foot, their voices clear, blunt piping? It was a parody of the very embarrassment they actually felt but were too embarrassed to show. A gust of cold wind blew water off the roof, dousing Angelica. She huddled against Gabriel. "Hello," he said again in that nice little kid's voice, "you sure got wet." The game amused her and she piped, without inflection, straight out, "Hello! I'm real wet," and kissed his chin.

"We're such morons," he whispered in her ear through hair netted with mist. "Hello," he mumbled into her neck as he stooped to embrace her.

He pulled her into the house against her will. At first she wouldn't go any farther than the pantry. She just sat on a chair and tapped her foot on the floor faster and faster, her face lowered and eclipsed by hair. Then she became impatient with Gabriel's clumsy way of cooking the bread and pushed him away from the stove.

Lurking in the shadows, Gabriel's brothers and sisters studied her, their faces luminous as toadstools on bark. Hunger at last prompted them to sidle up to her, snatch morsels from the skillet and run off, blowing on their burned fingers.

Soon they became accustomed to seeing her; the youngest child even stole up behind the seated Angelica and touched her hair. And Angelica found herself willing to explore other rooms in this part of the house never entered by either Gabriel's father or mother.

The rain never let up. The weather kept them from visiting the hollow. Gabriel was relieved that the weather had put an end to their exertions, which he now saw as something they had invented that might destroy their health. If living was a small burning (and wasn't breath hot, weren't tears scalding, didn't shit steam in the thunder box on cold mornings?) then surely their coupling turned up the jet too high until the blue flame went orange, blanched, its round glow narrowed into an ominous filament. They had chanced upon a way to burn faster, to escape the normal thermal laws, and one day soon they'd ignite and blow away, a single angel of ash.

Having her here, in his family house, changed her and the house. Now the house seemed like his exercise book—familiar, incomprehensible—and each page or room had been steeped in so many tears of pain or boredom that it meant everything to him and nothing; well-thumbed nothing. She glowed through these dark rooms and he saw them through her eyes. Centuries ago, over there, he'd wasted one summer away sitting in a hot embrasure of oak beside the extinct fireplace, sweating as he gazed out over the zoo of the sitting room: dromedary sofa, giraffe tallboy, hedgehog hassock. And here on these stairs with their ragged runners he'd made descent after stately descent, lampshade for crown, a blanket for robes, his dirty brothers and sisters standing in for dirty peasants. Here was his room and on the dusty shelves the bits of glass he'd collected. One full winter he'd huddled on his bed and watched the one-log fire through these colored spectacles. When he'd held up the green glass the flames had twisted like snakes; the orange glass had set his heart pounding since it was the color of raw mud mauled by horses' hooves; in the blue glass he'd found noble solitude. "What's this?" she asked. "Just some junk," he said, taking the glass out of her hand and tossing it out the window.

Angelica asked him to tell her stories about his past. But when he started to tell her he faltered, in search of a knife for cutting into that tender pulp.

Anyway, Angelica wasn't really interested. She paid attention only when he talked about punishments. "Did he use a belt?" she asked. And off she'd go on a story of her own: the time her mother had beat her for turning her back on a guest, or, worse, exposing the sole of her foot. Or she'd spend hours placing cards in front of him with tragic relish as she pieced together his future out of uninterrupted disaster. She worked with remote professionalism, shuffling, cutting and dealing.

One morning Gabriel took Angelica with him to his mother's bedside. All week his mother had seemed more alert to his touch when he massaged her and to his voice when he recited the verb forms. Her skin, usually as cold and oily as tallow, had even taken on a faint color. Past the pantry, the mangling room, the flower room, the seven maids' rooms he led Angelica, through the great reception hall, its four ceiling entablatures incised with the emblems for Economy (balances and compass), Silence (fish and locked heart), Divinity (triangle in a circle) and Eternity (serpent). They crossed its pink and beige stone floor pooling with rainwater. On through the smaller, second salon, the work of a fanatic of geometry. Gabriel pointed out a portrait on one wall of his uncle Mateo. He lived in the capital. He was a great man, although Gabriel couldn't remember at what, for Mateo hadn't returned to Madder Pink in twenty years or more.

Up the staircase, its curved ascending wall perforated with oval stucco frames, all empty except for one painting: "Girl Searching Herself for Fleas." Angelica solemnly assured Gabriel that the victim could be vermin-free if she would just paint her neck, ankles and wrists in magenta and blue stripes.

They had at last traversed the windowed corridors and open courtyards in the "new" wing and thrown back the successive doors of the old. The number of furnishings (chairs, tables, wardrobes) increased as they neared their goal, just as birds and floating plants become more frequent the closer a ship sails toward land. When Gabriel parted the final pair of doors he revealed the bed; through a fine panel of mesh Angelica could see the great beached body.

Gabriel instantly thought he detected a new order in the mane of hair foaming over the pillows and something very like a smile playing across the mouth. Angelica took everything in with three bursts of vision through her own hair and then resolutely turned her face to the ground. Only by taking her icy hand and poking her could Gabriel bring the girl closer to the bed. "Mother," he said in a voice that cracked, rendering the second syllable on a soprano note. He regained his recently acquired baritone: "This is my friend, Angelica. I want to marry her. I want . . . your blessing."

The amorini twining up the four massive pillars of the bed called with pleasure at the couple through rounded, troubling lips. A squirrel hopped off a branch that had broken through the window, and scuttled across the room and under the armoire. In a distant field a farmer was singing to himself or his animals.

"Come closer," Gabriel whispered to Angelica. "Put your hand in hers."

Angelica darted a glance at him out of the low storm cloud of her hair. "No," she whispered, muffled thunder.

"Yes. Touch her. Tell her your name."

He withdrew to the windows, broke off the invading branch and threw it to the ground outside, where it landed beside a fountain surmounted by a dolphin balancing on a pineapple. A yellow muslin tent of cloud masked the sun. Through the haze he could vaguely see Troublesome.

Over his shoulder he watched Angelica step up on the dais and look down at his mother; Angelica seemed to be a small sleeper inspecting an immense dream. The girl's back blocked his view. He couldn't tell if she was taking his mother's hand. No matter. He felt that from now on the girl would speak for the woman, translating the thoughts that slowly pulsed through his mother's body.

As he and Angelica left they passed Gabriel's father and Conception, who had seen everything through the open doors. They said nothing, but his father was writing something in a ledger the woman held steady for him.

Not once during the next three days did Angelica come around. Gabriel was certain she'd been frightened off by his mother —or perhaps by his proposal of marriage, which he'd never mentioned to Angelica directly.

At first he didn't care. In fact he found the return to solitude comforting. Because of the terrible red eruptions on his face it had been difficult to have someone looking at him day after day. His mother, who was never awake, was easy to love. From the other children he expected nothing; his father and Conception didn't exist. Nor did any of them have to look at him as Angelica had to, if only when she and he were working together to reach their stings. Once he had taken her from behind, but much as he might have enjoyed her warm brown buttocks pushing into his lap and the drizzle of black hair in his eyes, he missed the sight of her face. That was the strangest thing about stinging: it was at once entirely private and entirely mutual until the final moment, when it left him with a stranger in his arms. Now that he was on his own again he had time to daydream for hours and he'd find himself, half dry, sitting in the old marble tub long after the water had drained away, water that he'd patiently hauled and heated. Or he dozed in the middle of the day. Or he rode out on Curfew, although he was afraid Angelica might see him and laugh at him.

But on the third morning he knew he had to see her. He was so lonely. Time, such a comfort only yesterday, today had become the saddest place to sit in. To wait in. To walk in. A hundred times he looked out the window to discover the sun had not moved. The sounds of the house (the settling of floorboards, the thundering passage of the other children)—these sounds, and the sour smell left in their wake, reproached him.

He returned to his room and to his reflection in the broken mirror: still ugly. Until now he'd considered Angelica as something like a servant (her people had once served his) and something like a sister, but her disappearance had elevated her.

That night he couldn't sleep. He heard the wild animals outside, creeping ever closer to the house as it surrendered more and more to the forest. He was so awake he knew he would never sleep again—that this lucid excitement, so preferable to his usual torpor, would last forever. He would find Angelica and take her away from her people and from Madder Pink. They'd live . . . in a city. With his uncle. Yes, his uncle lived in the capital. They'd be happy. They'd never sleep.

As he slipped out he noticed the school house was now rebuilt, complete. Smoke was curling out of the chimney. He listened beside the door. Inside someone was pounding metal on metal. He could hear repeated blows and low, ringing echoes.

He headed out toward Troublesome. Who knew where Angelica's people might be camped? Once a boy he played with had said they didn't live in houses or tents but rather roosted in trees like birds. Another boy, the one with the clay pig that whistled, said they bred up out of dirt at dawn and dispersed into the air again at dusk. Once, perhaps to tease him, Angelica had whispered that after midnight her people slipped through a small hole in the earth and descended into caves redder than Moorish oranges where they feasted on white boys. She'd laughed so hard he thought she'd make herself sick.

The half-moon, a leper's face being eaten away by clouds,

looked down on the woods and the walking boy. With one hand he kept tapping the wax cake around his neck, with the other he pushed back the low branches. The path was one he knew well, but now it seemed longer than usual and slightly changed; once, when he was a child, his nurse had told him how the spirits would trick travelers, translate trees, pile up cairns, plant welcoming lights just beyond a cliff. His foot fell into a hole and he shouted. His shout caused a grey fox, tail low and longer than its body, to glide across the path and dive into a patch of smartweed. When he knelt to adjust his shoe Gabriel smelled something. He pushed aside the twigs to reveal the fox's cache: the putrefying bodies of a weasel and a crow (the bird's feet had been bitten off). The smell, ripe and repulsive, clung to his hand. He couldn't resist sniffing it as he trotted up the hill and across an open meadow, which had turned into a silver flux in the light of a moon breaking free of the ravening clouds.

When he entered the older, darker woods beyond the meadow, he shivered. What, exactly, had become of those clouds? Had they dropped to the earth? Was he inhaling them even now? Would they sing, soprano choirs choking on melody?

Either he or the night had turned warmer. He paused to catch his breath. As the sound of his panting ebbed away it was replaced by the sigh of leaves miles above his head and over there the sudden plop of a falling pine cone. The tree beside him moaned; he touched it in sympathy and shrieked—flesh! A woman, naked, wet —no, moss . . . He hugged himself; he felt his heart pounding under his wrist. Now he'd been decanted into a part of the woods he'd never explored before. The trail had given out, the trees were so high they'd stunted the undergrowth and his way was broad and clear. From a distance he could hear a faint discussion, the spinning of cogs—a brook, now audible, now loud. He knelt beside it and washed his face in it, thinking that perhaps its water would cure his welts, perhaps undo the curse of the black pullet he'd unknowingly offended (such at least was Angelica's explanation of his affliction: "You must capture the pullet, hide it in a black box, feed it blackest dirt at midnight on moonless nights, then rub its egg, which will be pure gold, across your face . . ." He could almost hear her instructing him and see her eyes staring into his over the candle which displaced its vertical bar from side to side in restless chatoyance.

He'd carry her off to the city, which he imagined to be as shadowy and various as the woods, though *its* spires were all peopled.

The moon had risen still higher. He came to a clearing that dimly shone in its cold light. Something . . . *segmented* . . . rustled as it emerged out of a distant ride of trees. Gabriel stood still beside a tree, downwind, and watched and watched.

It was a porcupine leading four of its pups in a straight line toward an apple tree. Slowly and methodically the creatures nosed the fallen apples into a small circle; they seemed so finicky about arranging them. The mother porcupine rolled over on the bed of fruit and wriggled from side to side. When she regained her feet she had speared a dozen apples on her quills. The four pups then took turns rolling in the apples. Now the whole caravan (he could smell the juice) slowly marched off under its ripe, bobbing baggage.

On and on he went, through broad fields, past an abandoned quarry, into a pine woods, its paths slippery with dry needles. He tried to memorize his route so that he could retrace it. Since that task seemed hopeless (turn right at the tall pine) he transformed fear into courage. "I'll never go back," he said out loud, but the words struck him as dangerous and he repeated a spell Angelica had taught him. In his room he had felt so full of energy and resolve that he'd known he could travel forever without tiring; but now he was already worn out and hungry. He was angry at Angelica, as though she were deliberately hiding herself.

Suddenly he came to a knoll from which he saw the camp. A rooster was already crowing, dawn couldn't be far away. A log rolled off a smoking fire and left a trail of fading rubies behind it. In a sudden yellow flare of flames he could see the vague outlines of three huts. Once Angelica had told him that in the South her people lived on islands in a marsh they plied in skiffs. They had fashioned their houses from tall reeds, burnt the dried dung of water buffalo, fished with tridents and suffered the attacks of wild pigs, which could slash an arm off a body with a single swipe of a razor-sharp tusk. She'd also told him, without a trace of shame, that her relatives were skilled thieves; she'd demonstrated her own talent by picking Gabriel's pocket of the things she had, like a magician, planted in them earlier. Here in the North they'd adapted to a new land and made their huts from birches they covered no longer with reed mats but with animal pelts. They ate the barnyard animals they could poach. One of the boys had stolen a rifle and ammunition and trained himself to shoot game.

Their real worry was something Angelica could scarcely explain nor Gabriel grasp—a religious scruple about which of the unfamiliar plants and animals they were eating might be taboo. Owls, for instance, they'd decided were forbidden since they were predators, which linked them to the unholy pelican; nor could her people eat or even touch shoats, related as they must be to their ancient foe, the wild pig; nor could they fish the streams—but Gabriel never learned why. The only other thing that perplexed them was how to orient their huts, since the stars here were new and they couldn't be certain the sun behaved normally; their houses had to face a particular, distant shrine. In no other regard did her people appear to be religious in the least.

A hoarse, hissing whisper filled the air—could the sound be coming from that dog? Gabriel squinted and peered at a lean, murderous-looking animal straining at the taut end of a chain. Yes, the whisper coincided with the dog's opening and closing jaws. The animal must have barked itself dumb. Another hiss and the rattle of another chain—a second dog, smaller and feebler, dragged a chain out of the middle hut. The dogs had picked up his scent. Gabriel had imagined he could slip into a tent, scoop up a sleeping Angelica and spirit her away. But now he remembered the men with gold teeth and the knife they'd tossed from hand to hand as they guarded the old queen.

A man emerged from the closest hut, stretched. He picked up a calabash on the end of a stick and gave it a shake; a soft glow filtered out of tiny holes pricked in the shell, a greenish glow pulsing irregularly. With his lantern in hand he came straight to-ward Gabriel and, just as the boy was preparing to make a dash for it, the man stopped, straddled, lowered his head as though listening to music, then began to urinate—a thick, steaming flow that poured on and on, even as the man yawned and stretched and the stream waggled from side to side, getting the man's thigh wet. At last the water stopped, stopped again, spurted and stopped. The man then rattled the calabash and once again the faint glow brightened; from this distance Gabriel guessed that it had been stuffed with lightning bugs.

At last the man was back in his hut, the voiceless dogs had settled down, the fire seemed nearly extinct. The sky was dark, the brilliant stars confident that night would last forever. Gabriel de-cided to wait for dawn, when Angelica was bound to show herself, to go for a walk alone.

He slept. In his dream they boarded a flying bed with the old queen, who turned out to be as jolly as a sailor on shore leave except when it came to sharing her food, which she hoarded in a box along with bits of broken glass. Guards were trying to drag him off the bed until he explained it wasn't a carpet—

He awoke to find himself being hauled to his feet by two men. It was day. They pulled him violently over the ground by the wrists; when he attempted to stand and walk between them, one of them twisted his arm behind his back until he thought it would snap. His knees melted in pain—and the men hurried on, dragging him behind them past one of the whispering dogs. The dog's eyes were nearly slit shut by the grip of the restraining collar.

They entered a hut and Gabriel was thrown on the hard mud floor. One of his guides planted something—his foot—between the boy's shoulder blades and pushed his face into the earth. His heart beat against the ground and his lungs pressed up against the foot in his back. His wrists burned as though they were still being held. The moist ground soaked his clothes. He tried to will his breath into evening out so that he might hear something above its roar. At last his gasps did subside, and the foot on his spine lifted. A woman was speaking, an old woman. She talked on and on. Gabriel wished he understood her, though he suspected she might not be uttering words but rather one long, million-syllable complaint.

At last he was brought to his knees and saw the queen sitting cross-legged on a velvet cushion, her arm draped around Angelica's shoulder, the girl half-reclining on a horse-skin—ah! he recognized the hide of his beloved mount, Heart's Delight. He hated Angelica, as though she had personally flayed the animal alive.

Her eyes passed over him dully and returned to her lap. A single spot of sunlight, leaking through a chink in the curved roof, concentrated on her hand, which looked thinner and paler.

The old lady was sniffing tobacco she tapped out of a tin can painted with red and black hex signs. She balanced the tobacco on the long, stained nail of her little finger, then sniffed. A look of delicious pain infused her face, her eyes closed to meditate on the itch, finally she tucked her head under her wing to sneeze into her padded sleeve. A moment later she was chattering again. Gabriel glanced over his shoulder at one of his captors, a big naked man whose head was bent in respect. He studied the old woman's mouth, with its single black tooth and white whiskers and the dark lines in the skin that radiated away from it. At some unexpected

moment it smiled and a knowing laugh was shaken out of it. Angelica had lowered her eyes.

"Crawl forward," Angelica said.

"What?"

"Do as I say," the girl insisted. "She wants to touch you. She's
never touched one of your people before."

Gabriel obeyed. The old woman picked up an ivory fly whisk,
and waved its horse hairs around her face and then shook them over
her right shoulder, as though to ward off evil, but jovially, casually.
He could smell the cherry-scented tobacco on her breath. He saw
she was no bigger than a child, a tiny thing he could easily lift and
carry away. It struck him as absurd that the guards, big young
animals, should obey this wizened prattler. Why doesn't each person go his own way, hunt his own food, pitch his own tent?

The queen touched his face with her dry, papery palm. She
patted him. She laughed, as though he were a funny pet. She ran
a hand down his neck and over his shoulder and back to his face.
As she stroked him words, somewhat fainter but no less complacent
than before, worked their way out of her mouth; he could feel them
humming in the bones of her fingers.

"She asked what torture or disease has ruined your face."

Gabriel sometimes hoped that his broken-out skin wasn't really noticeable after all. He had thought he might have exaggerated
it beyond all bounds—out of existence, in fact. But no, the horror
he felt in front of the mirror this old woman felt looking at him.
He couldn't leave home, after all. In the city people would run
away from him. Angelica was not the first of many women in his
life but the first and last. She had been inexplicably kind to him.

"Tell her it's something that happens to men of my people
when they're young. Tell her it'll go away."

Angelica translated and, after another sniff of tobacco, the
woman's sneeze ended in a nod of assent and five more minutes of
unbroken baby talk. As she talked she half stood, sounded now

urgent, now angry. Pointed with her ringed hand, pointed elsewhere with the ivory whisk. Behind him Gabriel could hear steps,
grunts, leather creaking. At last a line of small enamel boxes had
been placed on the faded carpet before her—a carpet whose rose
and thistle pattern he recognized: filched from the green room,
where its bulk, rolled up for decades, had sometimes served as a
rampart when he and his brothers and sisters had played war. He
wouldn't have been surprised to learn that the children themselves
had walked the rug here in exchange for a morsel of food, a lewd
pat or a few grains of tobacco.

"She will cure your skin," Angelica announced.

A silver dish—a finger bowl from some country house or
other, judging from the crest that could be seen sliding under the
water—was carried in; the queen dipped her hand in it and trickled
water over his face. Not water at all. Something odorless and taste-
less that burned and evaporated. The old hands were working
expertly, mixing ingredients from the boxes into a grey-green mud
that smelled of the earth, camomile, rosehips and centaury. As she
concocted the medicine she sighed and chanted in another voice.
At last the medicine was ready. Gabriel was led to a deeper, darker
corner of the hut, where Angelica ordered him to lie down on his
back. He could see fleas jumping in the dirty blanket.

As the old hands gently massaged his face and worked the mud
into his skin he sensed they were opening cabinets of his feelings,
springing open secret panels. Tears spurted out from under his
closed lids. The old woman chuckled; she didn't seem surprised.

She left. For an hour he lay under the hardening cool mud.
Second by second he felt it tightening over his skin. Although he
needed to urinate he didn't dare move. Outside, a dog's chain
snapped and clanked. A mother was talking to her baby. Something
savory—cooking meat and something else—perfumed the air,
though he couldn't hear it sizzling. As he idly attended the mother's
words, it came to him this was the secret language he sometimes

heard his brothers and sisters speaking, something he had assumed was a pig Latin they'd invented. Now he guessed he knew where they went at night and sometimes stayed for a day or more, why they frequently showed no signs of hunger—even how one of the boys had been able to pick his pocket of some new white string. The younger children had melted into this tribe; he had to admit that their own name had become a sieve, the world ran through it, it couldn't retain a thing.

The old woman had been the first person ever to look hard into his face and touch it. Angelica may have kissed him, but she'd closed her eyes. People preferred to avert their eyes rather than look into his face. And the pustules grew, reddened, broke, spread, became quilted on this disc of a face he was obliged to tilt up to every comer, push forward as if it were his finest wheel of cheese, ripe at last. This shame, this *bleu*, he went to inspect in the mirror every morning, each time detecting an improvement, a more normal color—which by noon he admitted was an illusion.

The fleas weren't biting him; maybe they were drowsing too. Far away some older children were splashing in the stream. The mother with the baby had moved and begun to pound something, clothes on a rock, grain, he couldn't tell. The breeze was winnowing the leaves, casting them out in generous arcs, the grain pattering to the stone, the chaff rising in dusty golden clouds, out of which his own face emerged, shining, smooth, the features eaten away.

"Now," a voice from the radiance was saying, "she will—Gabriel! Wake up!—she'll take off the mud." Angelica held him in her arms as he felt his brittle mask being chipped away with a small but heavy hammer. The light hurt his eyes. He started to raise his hand to his face, but Angelica restrained him. The old woman spoke—terribly amused with herself—and Angelica translated: "You are safe now. But today and tonight you cannot look at your reflection or touch your face. If you obey these rules, you can study yourself every day after and your face will be perfect. But if you cheat once while you are here, your face will go back to the way it was."

Gabriel searched their eyes. Was he as hideous as ever? He couldn't find a trace of malice in them. Angelica, in fact, seemed to marvel rather stupidly as her gaze roamed over him. He shut one eye and then the other to squint at the faint curve of his nose, dim radiance of the moon by day. He couldn't tell a thing.

There was nothing to do but thank the queen and rejoice. She held out her hand. Angelica told him to kiss it and he did. The audience was over; he and Angelica withdrew.

That night they were to be married, she told him. All that was required of him was compliance. He had always fretted over every little thing, and every chore, from dressing to breathing, could become momentous as he contemplated it out of the sustained shock of boredom. But now the solace of obedience to these people comforted him as he was led through the intricate turns of a dance by hands that swung him into place, promenaded him, drew him into a circle or flung him twirling outward.

All day and into the early evening Gabriel and Angelica were kept apart. Gabriel was put in the special care of a man who spoke the boy's language with an agreeable flair. With ten other men (boys were kept out) they huddled in their hut, smoked tobacco in a pipe and joked and laughed. The jokes all turned on sexual innuendo, as his guide explained. The word for turtle sounded the same as the word for cuckold, boxes for testicles, fig for vagina, sparrow for penis, sweeping for intercourse. Marriage was expressed in a periphrasis that meant "to the multitude," i.e., going to join the conjugal many; there was another simpler word for marriage, but it was unlucky to pronounce since the dead might hear it, envy the happy couple and cause them to fall ill.

A bullock's lung, clammy and veined, went the rounds and the men drank strong drink from it. Each of them rose to mime a lewd story, many of the plots, inexplicably, involving priests buggered while at their prayers. Gabriel couldn't understand exactly what was being done nor why it was funny.

The other men treated him with kindness; they kept thumping him on the back and feeding him chunks of lamb with their fingers (Gabriel's guide told him to eat only with his right hand). He wondered at their notions of hygiene, since many of them stank, their breath foul from the pale leaves of fermented cabbage they were continually fishing out of a big jar. All of them were naked; only one young man his own age had a whole body. The rest were missing something—an eye or a hand or teeth. Or a foot was withered or a flank scarred (wild pig, no doubt). But the liquor made Gabriel overlook these deformities; it even made him stop wondering if his own face had been cured.

When darkness fell the men led him to the stream, where they undressed him and bathed him. The two who had captured him this morning stood on either side of him and chanted something in unison while an old man with a braided beard hauled water up in a brass receptacle (to Gabriel it looked like—it probably was—a stolen spittoon) and presented it to the four cardinal points, then reversed it over Gabriel's head. He asked his guide what it all meant, but the guide just giggled and shrugged: "These ways . . . beautiful, no? I love the old ways. Very religious." He kissed his bunched fingers with a loud smack: "Very folkloric!"

Drawing him into a quiet, scarcely moving pool (the sky above was the dull silver of weathered pine boards), the men immersed him up to the neck and bathed him all over. Gabriel closed his eyes and relaxed into the cool, sustaining water as hands, small and large, smooth and rough, rubbed his shoulders, his arms, his back, his buttocks. Three little boys had joined the party once the men had left the hut; they now took turns diving to the bottom of the pool and stroking Gabriel's calves and thighs. Gabriel smiled and surrendered; they even patted his sex, which had contracted in the cold water. This was wisdom, he told himself. He who had slept alone, walked out into the world each morning alone, like an old man who'd outlived his family, this was wisdom to surrender to these foreign, possibly dangerous hands (white boy prepared for sacrifice), wisdom to become a lily floating on this motionless, running water, nosed by loving fish, the drowned man saved by his brothers, who were changed by a sorcerer into a school of sea trout. They bore him back to shore on cold, powerful tails—then left him there to revive, pale lad on white sand. His departing brothers plunged seaward, bodies arcing in turns above the water.

Now the men were drying him off with a flannel sheet. He loved the feeling of all these hands pressing at him through the warm cloth. He was drunk and wanted to tell someone (Angelica would have been the one, but she wasn't anywhere around) that he wasn't marrying just her but her whole tribe.

He was becoming human. He said something like this to his guide who smiled (gold molar beside missing incisor) and exclaimed, kissing his bunched fingers: "So good to go to the multitude. Then your broom always busy, boxes open, juicy figs . . . Oh, those figs!" And Gabriel smiled, since to share jokes about sex was some sort of greeting, two men like bird dogs pointing the same grouse.

The men conducted him back to the hut (it was very dark now), stood him in the center and wrapped him like a mummy in an endless strip of gauze, a surprisingly clean, fine-meshed gauze that smelled of dried orange blossoms. They turned him slowly like a top, winding the cloth from his feet up to his head and back down again, leaving an opening for his nostrils but covering his eyes, his mouth, and binding his hands to his sides. Through the double layer of gauze he could see the faint penumbra of a fire and the shadows of men coming and going.

Simplified, made featureless and immobile, he was lifted and carried, horizontal, by four men, the one assigned to his right shoulder shorter than the others, so that he dipped there, and the one on his left shoulder asthmatic. He could detect bobbing globes of flickering light above him—the firefly calabashes, he guessed. He sailed over first one, then the other of the whispering dogs. The path was long and devious and the asthmatic had to hand his job over to a sturdier replacement, one who smelled of garlic and tuberose. At last they came to a point where women's voices and a cold, damp draft welled up out of the ground. Two of his bearers dropped away and Gabriel was carried by just the remaining pair, one on either end, as they began a difficult descent. They labored past rushing water. The singing became louder, individual voices separated out from the treble hum and a single word became obsessive. Deeper and deeper they went, Gabriel's body nearly vertical on the sharp incline. After one last turn and drop he floated, like the wind through poplars, over the singers and smoking orange torches.

He was stood on cold stone and supported from behind by hands. The queen, her voice fainter, wearier than it had been this morning, talked while the men untwisted the gauze, drawing the long thread off their human bobbin. As the last strip of gauze spun away Gabriel blinked and saw they were in an underground cavern. It was a vast room with veined wet walls, many small stalactites and one huge stalagmite, ten or eleven feet long and as ivory as a tusk. On a natural dais opposite him the women stood, their ochre and grey robes ragged, patched, a bit soiled. The men crowded behind Gabriel, all as naked as he. The women had stopped singing and now everything was silent, except silence always is a layering of sounds: the rushing of water far away, the choir of so much breath and so many pulses, the brush of a bat wing against the roof of the cavern.

Angelica was led forward. Her hair had been tamed, drawn back to show how round her face was. Her dress fell from her shoulders to her bare feet; it was the blue of passing sadness.

A skeptic inside Gabriel told him she was still the furry little animal he rolled on top of in the hollow, someone he mildly liked and occasionally feared but seldom thought about except before an evening rendezvous and then, often enough, with anxious distaste.

But the skeptic was shouted down by a great voice in him that called out, "Free me from my self, my strangeness, and the despair of idleness." As he stood there in the underworld he faced a girl who no longer existed as an individual but had become the new law that would rule his days. Together, with two languages between them, they would name and subdue every moment; he would no longer be a lonely sleepwalker, a transparency held up to pale light.

Angelica was obviously the tribe's favorite, and all these people had observed every moment in her short life. Her birth had been auspicious (wild goose against full moon). The placenta she came wrapped in and the milk teeth she later shed—these things had been conserved. She was the youngest and most beautiful flower on this old but only half-domesticated bush, a flower that was now being handed to him. But he was no one. No one had ever looked at him. He was Signore Nulla, Sir Nil. His name had not been inscribed in a book; he wasn't even sure how to spell it. Nor was Angelica trying to catch his eye now, wink at him, smile over the panoply of custom; she seemed absorbed in the changes taking place within her, as though to get married were to give birth.

Two women in dresses identical to Angelica's came forward, one young, the other old; the old one apparently had trouble seeing and someone kept helping her walk. The queen removed her crown and placed over her face the clay mask she had molded from Gabriel's features. The various shards of the mask had been glued together along crude white seams. The brown clay shell and its zigzag seams did not resemble Gabriel since the likeness was pressed into the concealed lining; the exterior looked rather like a coconut crushed here and there to reveal fissures of white meat. The guide whispered in Gabriel's ear, "She is you," and grinned hugely over this good news.

The queen-as-Gabriel approached the old woman in pale blue, who was seated on a stool now. The queen sank unsteadily to her knees and placed her coconut face into the old woman's lap and imitated sobbing, but soundlessly. The woman patted the queen's head, though not with much feeling; her very ineptness as an actress gave her motions a charming rubato in the hesitation waltz of sincerity.

Angelica strode forward like a warrior, slapped the seated woman and then, with outstretched hand, ordered the coconut queen away. As the queen slunk off, bobbing her head in submission, the audience laughed. They laughed and laughed, the pitiless mirth of the tribe.

The queen, now on the other side of the dais, stood in back of the young girl in blue, stroked her hair and hugged her from behind. In this position the patched mask looked like a bear's face that had been brushed through burning twigs, the fire singeing strips of fur down to the pale bone. The bear was fondling the breasts of the girl when Angelica, angry goddess, again drew near, slapped the girl and banished the queen. More general laughter.

"But what does it all mean?" Gabriel asked. He felt he was being ridiculed. It was all a public mockery of his family, his life, his face. The wedding was vaudeville.

The guide explained at length but cryptically and Gabriel feared that what he understood was in the end his own invention. It seemed the rite was a way of showing that the husband must not regard his wife as either a mother or daughter. Or had he got it all wrong and what was forbidden were emotions—the enfeeblement of grief and the snare of love? The guide spoke of "ghosts" and of the "ghost family."

Now the women, smiling, were coming toward him, lifting their hands in welcome. He stood and for the first time his nakedness seemed a pitiful thing. Women were actors armed in costume, men vulnerable spectators.

Some of the other men had arisen at the same time and brought out of the shadows a bed, a narrow string mattress on high legs. The ranks of naked men and clothed women had now blended together and formed a circle around Gabriel and Angelica, who was being undressed. Torch after torch was plunged into a natural pool of water until only one, wedged above their heads in a rock crevice, threw its twisting lights over the celebrants. A small brown bird in a cage was placed on the rock floor beside the bed.

A naked Angelica came into his arms, heart beating so fast as to slow down time; Gabriel folded his wings over her hot body. He could see the other men undressing the women, hands squirming, white robes falling into grey puddles. He sensed the human circle constrict a notch around him like a tourniquet designed to trap blood. The queen (tiny, shriveled priest stripped of her regalia) held his penis in her hand and looked at Angelica, who lowered her eyes and knelt to take communion. From this angle he looked down on Angelica's cascade of black hair, a tiny white button (the tip of her nose) and a mouth pistoning above two shadowy breasts that strained to touch his shins. His mind was above it all. He wondered how he looked from behind, his buttocks tensing then relaxing with each thrust, her small brown hands stroking his white thighs; he saw the caged bird hop from one rung to another and cock its head attentively, looking up; he felt someone's breath on his shoulder; he watched, over to his left, a woman wrap her arms around a man's neck and her legs around his waist, her face dreaming on his shoulder but her closed eyes tightening with each thrust of his buttocks, tensing and relaxing. Gabriel turreted, imperturbable above the orgy, turned to see one man's tendoned hands plundering a wealth of hair; another woman was being fed at both ends, her body held up by a rock between two men who stood above her, each bracing his hands on the other's shoulders, their heads side by side as they peered down into the well their bodies had become. On the dais the old queen straddled a kneeling man who had flung his head back to watch the orgy upside down; the queen, her skin like a baggy suit, crowed ecstatically as she posted in place.

Gabriel drew Angelica to her feet and kissed her blurred wet mouth. She flowed away from him and out onto the narrow bed, her hands lifting in invitation. As he knelt on the edge of the bed he looked down to see his penis jump up with his pulse, a baton beating out fractions of time. The sadness of superiority held him for a moment. A man and a woman seemed to have read his thoughts and, standing on either side of the bed, stretched taut a gauze barrier between Gabriel and Angelica. He closed his eyes and pictured what he wanted to do—to *be*—to her.

His desires were as slippery as a tub of eels. He might be asleep in the sun and awaken to see her stretched out on the sand beside him, legs slightly ajar so that he could easily graze the delicate lining of her thighs and push a finger into that burning dark place. Or she might be sick, weak, delirious and as a fever dream he would visit her. Again, the others must have guessed his thoughts; when he opened his eyes he saw they held Angelica's wrists and ankles to the bed, had opened her wide and rendered her helpless. They looked at him with curiosity. He rose high above her, dark storm cloud rolling in over a tender valley. Someone fastened a black cloak around his shoulder and shook its folds out behind him. The mysterious barricade of gauze had been laid over Angelica's captive body and face. It stirred with her breathing. Gabriel folded the cloth into a bandage over her eyes to blind her and make her all the more helpless. And then, as a mighty lord, he entered her.

No sooner was he in her, surrounded by the kindness of her body, than all his feelings sweetened, lightened, as though vengeance had melted into civility and he had been classicized. Now they were shepherd and shepherdess on a slope above a stream. His cloak and her blindfold vanished, the subterranean stream lost its echo and purled more shallowly. Someone gave them wine to drink and dropped a necklace of flowers over Gabriel's head. Oblivion flowed through him with the wine to meet oblivion rising up from his rocking loins. As he tumbled to his side, Angelica turned on hers, and now they were brother and sister, sleeping far from home under a homespun robe (a robe, on cue, floated down over their nakedness). Angelica was now his friend, they were not really so different from one another; they were twins, not opposites, twins who had found this way to make each other sleep.

In the hush of this moment Gabriel thought they were not a couple but a tribe in themselves, protean parents to a brood of shadows—and under this vision he exploded inside her as the others crowned them with wreaths of gold paper and slipped gold rings on her left hand and his. A second later they were pulled to their feet, the old queen wrung the neck of the bird, dribbled blood over a sheet, held it up for inspection and shouted, laughing, "A virgin!" Children met the bridal party at the entrance to the cave; among them were Gabriel's brothers and sisters, who expertly led him home to Madder Pink through the dark woods, gabbling softly to each other in Angelica's language.

Gabriel slept in his own room all day and into the early evening and dreamed that a whole family of deformed, hungry people were bickering while they traveled through mud. A particularly nasty feud between relatives broke out in a shack where everyone sipped a bitter liquid made from roots. The bitterness made Gabriel spit.

He awoke to find saliva on his pillow and his father and Conception standing over him. His father was grasping a ledger and reading out a list of things. Offenses. They seemed to be offenses, ones Gabriel had committed. The woman was holding up a lantern from the stable and her arm shook either from anger or the weight. She was wearing a chartreuse blouse that sweat had darkened in patches. His father, for some reason, was in riding clothes; perhaps they were the only decent clothes he still owned. The reading went on for some time and the woman was obliged to switch the lantern to her other hand; from this angle it shone red through one wing of his father's nose. Gabriel was looking up at it and saw it through a nostril; the nostril glowed red, a burning red circle. All Gabriel wanted to do was dash for a mirror to study his own face, now that he remembered the capture, cure, wedding—his hand floated up to touch the crumpled paper crown. It was still there. It had fallen in the hollow above his pillow. "By these charges we sentence you," Gabriel's father announced in his drab monotone. He offered the book to the boy, as though the prisoner must confirm the judgment, but Gabriel was too bewildered to read and passed the ledger back. His father and the woman, one on either side, accompanied him outside.

They went into the rebuilt school house. Upstairs the woman opened a freshly painted door to reveal a large metal cage that nearly filled the room. Gabriel was put in and the gate was locked behind him. Then the door closed and he heard his gaolers walking down the corridor, then down the stairs. No light, no mirror, now he would never know. He couldn't hear a sound. Even the night sounds had been silenced. The crack under the door brightened (or was he only imagining a difference?), then dimmed. In the corner he discovered a blanket. He tripped over something that rolled away and clanged catastrophically against the bars. When he recovered it he decided it must be a spittoon, possibly the brass one from his mother's antechamber. Was he supposed to piss and shit in it?

He needed to urinate. But what if there was another receptacle for that? He decided to be systematic. He crawled on his hands and knees from one end of the cage to another, turned, moved a foot to one side and mowed his way back—back and forth. Clumsily he crashed into the spittoon again. Would they hear the noise and interpret it as insolence? Rage? He sat quietly for a long time. He then resumed his scanning prowl of the cage.

Nothing. A blanket and the spittoon, which he decided must be his toilet after all. He knelt beside it and urinated into it; the brass bottom rattled slightly on the floor. He inhaled the pungent odor of his own body. But the room was so dark that, even though he hunched progressively farther over where he thought the spittoon must be, the diminishing stream splashed on the brass rim, then on his trousered knee. He was afraid he'd left a puddle on the floor. He found a wet spot; for some reason he licked his finger, enjoyed the sharp bitter taste; only then did he wonder if they were observing him, adding to their list of offenses.

The thought that they might be watching him comforted him, made this night intelligent. He arranged himself ceremoniously in one corner of the cell, doubling the blanket and lining up the superimposed edges as neatly as possible. It would be his mattress. He was self-conscious and had to think each motion out from the beginning, invent "yawning" and "drinking." This concentration on the habitual rendered his body strange to him and stuffed his mind with instructions; he had succeeded in subjecting the involuntary to his will, a success that surely counted as a failure. Sometimes he feared he'd make even breathing volitional and he'd suffocate in his sleep, his last waking command to expire his expiring breath.

He ran his hands over his face as a blind man might explore a stranger's face. The skin felt almost glassy. One vast bulb of infection beside his nose had deflated. A second brow of welts that had thickened his forehead was gone. His right cheek, which had been scaly, felt moist, and his chin, two days ago a bright red pincushion of scabs, had now turned smooth. Without witnesses, sightless, he had at last become handsome.

Days, maybe weeks, went by in the cage. His gaolers took turns feeding him. They never spoke to him and he was too proud to question or rebuke them, much less to plead with them. They had fashioned the room so cunningly that no light came into it. He was unable to mark the passage of time. The food must have been scraps from their table, the courses all mixed together in a kind of slop and presented in a dog bowl. He couldn't always distinguish what he was eating; he'd pull a bit of raw carrot or a spinach leaf out of a meat gruel. Every other mealtime his father would empty the spittoon and presumably wash it out, since it would come back odorless. His drinking water was served in another bowl. Gabriel could not read their expressions; the light from the open door when his father came and went was too dim. Sometimes the woman wore her disturbing perfume. When she did, Gabriel masturbated to it after she left. He even trotted around the cage sniffing for lingering pockets of her perfume, his muzzle raised and twitching with pleasure, his penis unsheathed. Once he'd thought of dogs when he smelled her perfume; now he'd become one of them.

At first he devised a regime for himself. He reserved a cup of his drinking water for washing his new face. He spent an hour reciting all of the verb forms he could remember. Another hour went to exercise (he hung by his hands from the rungs at the top of his cage). He sought to increase his strength by adding a repetition to every exercise. He confined his masturbating to just four daily periods, spaced out as evenly as possible. Assuming he had two meals a day, one every twelve hours, his task was to locate in his body or mind the fourth hour and the eighth hour after mealtime: these were his scheduled masturbatory sessions, each of which he attempted to stretch out as long as possible. At first he ran through them too quickly. One day he waited too long and had to cover himself anxiously when he heard Conception's approaching steps. He slept in two batches, a few hours between each meal. Sleeping and masturbating were his two pleasures because they were his two means of escaping this cage, of flying out of it on the heavy, wet wings of dream.

He preferred fantasies to dreams because he could steer fantasies, refine them, continue them. He created a woman to be his companion and named her Jane Castle. In no way did she resemble Angelica. She was older than he and taller, forbearing and tender, and her hair was white not as a sign of age but goodness. Their bodies did simple things together. In fact, they seldom got beyond joining hands at the foot of a particular wooded path, strolling up it on a slow curve, stopping under a tree and kissing. No pumping or flailing or moaning—nothing beyond a cool, sweet kiss that went on and on without becoming stale, a kiss that always seemed just to have begun. It was evening. The woods must have been on an island because a late sun was dazzling the water. When Jane Castle turned in profile the light reflected scintillas above her deepset eyes. Her hands, cool but intimate, the arms long and the shoulders touchingly hollow above and below the clavicle—these and her face he could picture, but the rest of her body was a mist. Though he was furiously pumping with his right hand in the cage, on the wooded island his left hand lightly touched her white hair as they resumed their long kiss. Four times a day he met Jane Castle at the foot of the path and four times a day they stopped near the top, her white hair against the sun like silk unraveling from a pod. Her insubstantiality, so solemn and healing, caused him more and more to resent Angelica's body, overly distinct even in memory. Angelica's tapping foot, skinny hips, scorching eyes and beeswarming hair. The way she laughed in a high, nonstop giggle as her eyes were squeezed shut by merriment. The feline roughness of her tongue. Her wariness as she entered an unfamiliar room. No.

No.

No, he couldn't abide the stink of so much real, humiliating presence; better, far better, to sink his face in the silk albino hair of Jane Castle who, he noticed, had acquired the haunting scent Conception sometimes wore.

He stopped exercising. He no longer noticed who brought his food or emptied the spittoon. He no longer washed his face. Sometimes he failed to eat all of his meager meal. His romance became as fragile as smoke.

Now the distinction between waking and dreaming melted

away and the wooded island became his only home, sunset the only hour. He was dimly aware of another self, his agent, who ate and drank, but that person was merely the root and stalk sustaining this last camellia as it dried and turned and stiffened in the silvery light; then the flower refused even this support and began to feed on itself.

Once he dreamed that Angelica visited him. There she was, panting after running, smelling of leaves and clove, her breath sour from fermented cabbage. "Gabriel," she hissed. "They've gone for a walk—I can just stay a minute. Do you have a plan?"

Jane revolved in the sunlight and he turned with her.

"Gabriel! Are you sick? Are they starving you? Here's some food." The apparition pushed a sweaty little packet into his hand. It smelled of lamb. Jane Castle shrank away from the smell. She had been urging Gabriel to give up food and she was especially repelled by meat. Gabriel stood, tottering, weak, between the two women. Jane had turned her back.

"Gabriel! Come closer. Kiss me. Talk to me."

Jane raised a hood of chartreuse silk (so like the fabric in Conception's blouse) and covered her colorless hair. She was beginning to go down the path, which they'd never taken before, on the far side of the hill. Even the sun, which had held still, transfixed, for so long, began to set at last. A cold wind blew up through the trees.

"Gabriel! I can't see you in this darkness. Have you gone blind? Gabriel! Answer me."

Now he was no longer on the island, nor in the cave, but he was swimming toward a voice. It seemed he'd been swimming for hours, maybe days. When he could feel his body at all he felt it as pain. Yet he knew he must make another effort to fight off this sweet drowsiness. He sidestroked toward the voice; the half of his body immersed in the sea was frozen numb. The waterline neatly bisected his body into a half pricked by air and a half coated in cold platinum. Though his mouth was dry and salty, his tongue black, he said, "Yes?"

"At least you can talk. Are you all right?"

"I . . . don't know."

"Listen: do you have a plan for escape?"

He was inclined to reply, "I'll just keep swimming," but that answer required too much breath so he only thought it.

At last he said, "Go to my mother. She'll save me. Tell her to send for my uncle."

Someone outside whistled two long notes, the first higher and longer than the second, as though caressing the name *Castle*.

"That's my signal," Angelica said.

Would Angelica dare to seek out his mother and tell her what had happened? Would his mother hear the girl's voice above the falls that thundered through her brain, the roar in which he, at least, could sometimes discern a small, pale rainbow of assent? He pictured the tiny girl standing beside the bed.

The only thing Gabriel wanted to take with him was his stick horse, but his uncle laughed affectionately at the suggestion and pretended to wipe away a tear of mirth, saying "You wretch, you wretch!" But when Gabriel, after a diplomatic interval, repeated the request, his uncle merely clicked his tongue. What the uncle did want the boy to pack were three things: a gold broach from which all the garnets but four, as dark as old blood, had been clawed; a letter on mildewed vellum ("Your patent," his uncle declared, "or as good as one"); and a miniature in a locket of a woman who looked as though she'd just sniffed a rude smell. "Here is your meager patrimony, my boy," the uncle summed up. "Criminal . . . so little left . . . that *spoiler* . . ."

The other children drew nearer to gawk at their uncle. "Feral sweets," Mateo muttered. "You must say farewell to them."

That seemed an odd thing to do, given that Gabriel had never played with them, that he had never even spoken to them and that they had done nothing to rescue him when he was in the cage. But Gabriel had grasped that his uncle liked family feelings and enjoyed seeing them expressed. Gabriel's impression was that within his uncle, despite his kindness and his dramatic politeness, there was something edgy and cold that demanded the reassurance of tender ceremonies. Or rather, a part of him was truly kind, but that part was elusive, undependable. And yet Gabriel deduced this mysterious kindness (hidden behind the exquisite but false kindness) from a tremulousness in the eyes and a faint smile evoked at unguarded moments by . . . anything: the buzz of a fly in an empty room, a cloud's shadow passing over the grounds.

His uncle had told him that when they reached their destination he would meet other women, women quite different from Angelica, fit to stimulate his mind as well as his body. Gabriel smiled and nodded. He was pleased to discover a way in which he was superior to Angelica and deserved someone better. His need for her body had vexed him, like a hot child held on a lap too long. She owned something he needed again and again, though something which, once possessed, he cared nothing about . . . until he needed it again. He resented her power over him, for she was also a sister, a rival in a game in which she'd been granted an unfair advantage. When he didn't need her he enjoyed pushing her around, shoving her, teasing her. But then the very proximity of their bodies, the panting tussle, would excite him. Though he might push her away, he always ended up by wanting her. Now at last he had found a way to be better than she. He was going away, leaving her behind.

Never again would he live entirely in the present, give up the dignity of yesterday, tomorrow, and some wonderful day and inhabit now like a dog. His brothers and sisters were dogs. They slept in the tall grass when they were tired, lapped water out of the stream, squabbled over food (though they were dirtier and less loyal than dogs). Gabriel's homemade code turned him toward discipline, toward an idealized future where he would behave with the same cool elegance as his uncle. *He* didn't travel with a woman nor did he even refer to one. Perhaps the constant need for women was a rustic vice, a sign of lapsed humanity that he must now shed along with his rags and Curfew. Abstinence must be refined.

Consulting his watch, his uncle said, "Time to leave. Go say goodbye to your mother."

As Gabriel hurried through the maze of corridors to his mother's room, he knew this might be the last time he'd see her. With his hair still wet and scalp tingling, with hands so clean for the first time in years that they felt denuded, as though the dirt had been moleskin gloves, the boy approached his mother. As he stood in the doorway to her room, he surveyed her sleeping bulk. He tried to imagine her rousing herself long enough to write her brother and to give Angelica instructions. Now that he knew about the heroic exertions she was capable of, he viewed her unconsciousness less as a denial of the world and more as a ponderous recuperation of energy, as though she were not a woman but a century plant.

"Mother," he said, perching on the side of her bed. Her face resisted the summons, flinched, spread itself still wider. But now that he was beside her he could detect an unfamiliar blue ghost inhabiting the white sheet over her like the shadow exhaled by snow. He pulled the sheet aside to reveal a dress he had never seen before. The bodice, small stiff cones in rotting velvet, rose and fell on top of her nipples. The torso, stiff with boning, floated up and down with her slow breaths. Somehow she had slit this ancient gown down the back, flattened it and applied it to herself like a bandage to a wound. He pictured the process: her tidal rise, the entranced flow toward a secret storage place, the violence done to the dress (huge hands ripping, ripping in the chinks of moonlight), the recession to her pillow. He lifted her hand and held it in his own. Deep within the cool fat he sensed the bones and muscles that had performed this feat. His hand rose from his side, drifted about, shivered, as though it were a tropical bird his words had blown too far north.

Then he went to the mirror and saw that his face had healed. He was handsome. He had been married.

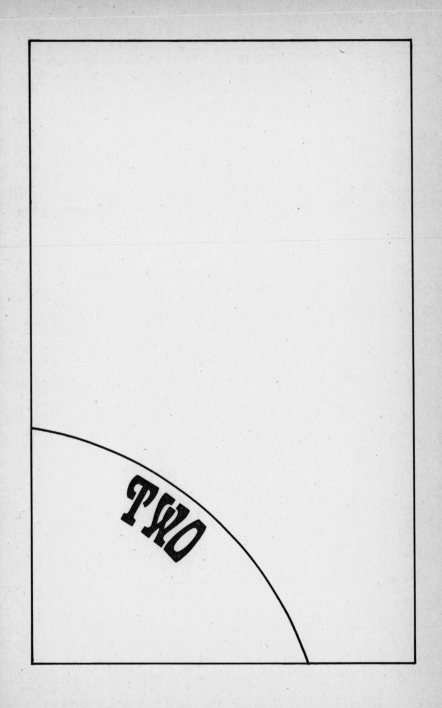

TWO

WHEN Gabriel awakened, he found himself in a bed so clean and sweet-smelling he had to attribute the luxury to his uncle, for only his uncle wore this perfume, only his uncle's linen could feel this fresh and crisp. Arrows of light vibrated on the painted ceiling, flung up off flowing water below or rippling metal cloth. A toffee-dark wood table stood on a polished stone floor by the open window. Like a colt's the table's legs were splayed out under its weight. When Gabriel tilted his head back he looked up at four floating gold sausages, each dangling five nubs—which when seen from a different angle turned out to be the cloud-scaling feet of two putti holding up a crown. These cupids were smirking. They were supported by a crude, worm-eaten upright attached to the headboard—so crude, so thick, that some convention must have declared it invisible, like the hands of puppeteers. A steady breeze bore the sounds of men shouting "Hoy!" on a falling tone.

When he thought of last night, the third night of the trip, Gabriel remembered it as if he'd been drunk—although only briefly, between two sleeps, had a sherry swirled its cloying spiral up the cavity of his chest and licked his black brain with a slow red tongue, and that intoxication had lasted just a moment in one of the many linked caverns of the night. He remembered waking and dozing, his eyes sinking shut into a hand pressed against a jiggling window that looked out on shifting shades of grey and black. He woke, terrified, in a hemorrhage of light, but the light drained away into a small eye that blinked shut and a bell sped off until it was just a faint jingle. Sleep spread his cloak, smiled, doffed his feathers of smoke.

People spoke to him, led him from one conveyance to another, and his bones had a chance to settle in a different corner of the damaged package he'd become. He didn't protest. He had only one job—to sleep though badly wherever he was put. A word or two said by someone down the aisle served as the cue for a dreamed duet between those two fat boys in shorts facing him. The world had no logic, given over as it was to pauses pregnant, then aborted, to wails that signaled nothing and to unreadable scrawls of light on a wet brick wall, whereas Gabriel's dreams cohered, indeed were lunatic with system. His uncle had simplified himself into just a murmuring voice beside him and a hand at his elbow. But the night had so many parts, such panic drawn under a big canopy in tatters, the trip had comprised so much traveling from fear to hope to melancholy, that Gabriel remembered nothing distinct except the silence, the total silence when they'd stopped for some reason in the middle of a field.

The weather had changed. It was hot and from the silent fields was slowly exhaled a rank smell of—he couldn't see it, but he would have sworn it must be red, yes, red clay, heavily manured, a smell at once offensive and intriguing, either fertile or rotten or both. A warm breeze blew across Gabriel's sleepy face. For him, a country boy, this was at last a kind of newness that mattered: new soil. The bubbling silence of heat and growth was baking slowly under the tight lid of a starless night.

Now his eyes strayed over the trembling flash of light on the ceiling. Several "Hoy"s, intoned by different male voices, passed under the window, followed by a vigorous sloshing of water, as though a meaty man were scrubbing himself all over. He saw that one of the gilded cupids was missing a hand.

He had to urinate. The urge throbbed up out of the root of his prostate, through the loosely bagged fruit and along the stiff branch. Each morning's water he studied as an augury or a souvenir, the bitter or scentless residue, attar of his dreams. He looked around. He had no idea where his clothes were hidden. He was trapped here with an erection and an aching bladder. He was pinioned here under a weird blend of shame, anxiety, and lazy pleasure. He dozed off and saw his uncle, the wizard, drain the glass alembic into a pot painted with Angelica's features . . .

"Gabriel—" and the boy awakened to see his uncle beside him, flowing in a yellow robe with enormous sleeves. And in his hands the smallest cup of the blackest coffee Gabriel had ever seen.

Mateo studied his nephew with a troubling avidity. The boy wasn't handsome, which had disappointed Mateo at first, but within a few days he was feeling so much for the boy—guilt and irritable, loving concern—that these tricky emotions had crowded out anything as simple as pleasure in a flattering resemblance.

The boy slept all the time. Mateo would waken him at what seemed more or less normal mealtimes and lead him to the kitchen (not the dining room) where they'd sit on straw stools at the marble-top wood table and eat in silence. Mateo of course knew how to cook splendid dinners of many courses which the two part-time maids, mother and daughter, would come in to help him serve to a dozen guests. But these kitchen suppers for just two, they were a puzzle. He wasn't content to let them be one-dish meals, a stew or an omelette, say. They must have a flair. They must be nourishing. There must be several covers—not only to fatten the boy up but also to set him an example, to tame him: this is how a gentleman eats.

But when Mateo was frank with himself, he had to concede this minimal degree of state was really designed to oblige his own sense of dignity. His brief visit to Madder Pink, the first in years, had shaken him—his sister had become if not the very deity of squalor then the chief shrine to it, and their old house, which over the years he'd described so amusingly and with less and less accuracy to friends, had fallen.

His family, which he'd always fancied to be if provincial at least solid, now turned out to be sordid, violent, nearly extinct. He'd styled himself as a country squire, someone whose sophistication masked a rustic simplicity, who could always return to pastoral innocence, but the pasture had engulfed the manor house, his sister was slowly stifling inside a tomb of her own flesh and her husband had jailed and starved his own boy. Mateo felt his own range of choice constrict into the present; the plush runners of a half-imaginary past and a wholly imagined future had been rolled up and carted away, leaving him marooned on this threadbare patch of now. Once there'd been a comfort in rebelling against a conservative family. Even the sense that one was wicked acquired a halo of blue magnetic sparks when viewed against the black of family certainties.

But now there was no family, he couldn't revert to it, he couldn't even indulge in the queasy luxury of thinking his life had been wrong and theirs right after all. The trip home had aged him. He was no longer the scamp but the father to a new dynasty of one.

Or two. Gabriel made two.

But Mateo didn't want to be the boy's father, exactly. Because he'd never married, never spent any time with children, Mateo had scarcely noticed he was growing older. Naturally, he'd studied every sign of aging in his face and body with the acuteness of the eternal sexual buccaneer, but the years had not resolved themselves into a generation, only a disappointment. He who followed every fashion, hummed every new tune, learned every new dance, spoke and sometimes coined the newest slang, could scarcely feel outmoded. Paradoxically, he had acquired more experience at playing the young man than any literally young man could have done. He'd lost nothing through the years except his looks and a few units of energy, but he was not ready to concede either loss.

These meals, these chores, these vigils with Gabriel made Mateo a little sad. He could see now that so much of the driven gaiety of his last twenty years had been an avoidance of just this nocturnal stillness of two men, one young, one middle-aged, sitting at a table under the bright kitchen lamp—two men pretending not to look at each other, but each bruised by the other's attention, as though they were two closely caged porcupines. Here they were, breathing, their eyelids noisily brushing open and shut, the transit of a fork through the lit air a painful incision, chewing a morbid excess.

They were too much alike to feel comfortable with each other. An insomniac, Mateo would lie in his bed and listen to his insomniac nephew pace the halls, coughing with Mateo's own cough. Mateo's secret was that, despite his bonhomie, he was really a solitary who spent one morning a month in his rooms feeling like a hot rain, an August drizzle running down everything and reviving nothing. Unlike other men of temperament, he took no pride in these depressions. His hours were so carefully regulated and allotted to ordering his house and visiting his friends that he could scarcely afford these hot immersions into boredom.

His childhood at Madder Pink, as vacant as Gabriel's if considerably less savage, had left him unconvinced of his own existence. Perhaps that was why as an adult he filled so many minutes with activity and stuck to his luxuries even when alone, humble as those luxuries might appear to his richer friends. Without this stiffening of ceremony his identity would be so flimsy it might slip off. At least once a month he was forced to remember he wasn't the smiling, puckish boulevardier his friends liked to think he was.

The boy's fearfulness, his suffering, his craziness, frightened Mateo. He, Mateo, was still too close to being just that helpless himself. Giving love (and that was what the boy needed: love)— giving love is like casting a line to someone caught in white water. But they, Mateo and Gabriel, were both swimmers. Once Mateo saw through a crack in the door a violent shadow as of a black wing shuddering. Then there was a pause. Then the shuddering began again, matched by a wet, slappy sound.

Oh.

Mateo felt trapped, guilty, excited, felt he should do something about it. Join him? Make a joke about it, acknowledge it, knock and stop it?

Of course he wouldn't do anything, but this shuddering black wing in the brilliant vertical stripe of light fascinated Mateo and reminded him that the boy had a life of his own, an imagination and a consciousness all his own: a complete mystery. Just as a potato, washed, bruised, forgotten and cast under the sink, will sprout horribly in the dark, rampant with life since it is not only a comically banal vegetable but also a seed, in the same way this boy, under Mateo's spell to an alarming degree, was still, despite his unhealthy torpor, his insomnia, his dead eyes, his silences, his scarred face, his cough in the dark—he was still throbbing with life, at the height of his sexual power, the sickly bird propelled by the mighty thrust of this dark wing.

They were too alike for love to flow through them; perhaps

Mateo confused love with charity. Or perhaps he favored stasis and could only picture love as something conferred by a motionless monarch on an equally frozen vassal. If Mateo had avoided marrying and having children he'd done so, no doubt, partly out of self-centeredness but also partly out of an exaltation of parental love. A father must expect nothing from his son. A father must not look to the child for guidance, for entertainment on rainy days or for confirmation of his own virtues. We esteem something because we have decided not to pursue it; for Mateo fatherhood was precisely this cherished lacuna. He wasn't rich enough or kind enough to have children.

But in Gabriel's case there were other simpler obstacles to love —the boy's very intelligence. Mateo didn't count as an ironist. His comic emphases and pauses, his reversion to inverted commas, his airy, unfinished periphrases (pale yellows shading off to sidereal greens), his acidic formalities—they all were routine, surely. If anything, Mateo considered himself refreshingly straightforward and he had felt complimented once when a friend had said, fondly, "You are a bit of an oaf. Just a bit, a bit oafish."

But the boy ascribed magically black powers to his uncle and, having once discovered the simple fact of irony, now thought he saw it everywhere. If Mateo indulged in a bit of sentiment after a bottle of wine and toward midnight said with a sigh, "I'm getting older and I'm glad to have someone to carry on my name," there was the boy grinning horribly, dirty teeth bared, muddy eyes glittering.

"I'm serious!" Mateo would insist, wounded. The boy's grin widened. He barked a laugh. "Don't you believe me?" Mateo asked.

But this moment was delicate. The boy, till now a worm, had evolved for a second into a snake: alert, fangs flickering. If Mateo insisted on the boy's mistake, he'd be sure to revert back into vermiform humility. The only immediate way to keep alive this lovely malice was to charm it—*not* a wise policy in the long run, but Mateo was interested only in the short walk, the very shortest.

With no fear but with a queasy sense of I'm-sure-I'll-pay-for-this-later, Mateo said, "Of course you don't believe me, nor should you."

Triumphant, the boy cackled with glee.

How did their days go? The uncle, who in the past had pulled the covers over his head, now sprang awake early each morning. Before, he'd taken hours to assemble himself and to construct an optimistic mood for the evening. Now, by contrast, he had to follow a regime in order to set an example. And now (he had to admit) he was playing to an audience: this is how a gentleman behaves. He rises at a reasonable hour no matter how late and drunkenly he went to bed, as though an imperturbable orderliness by day will excuse any degree of nocturnal anarchy. He bathes and shaves without dawdling. Over the coffee he has prepared for himself he reads his mail and the *Little Gazette*. And then? Well, then, he awakens his dear nephew.

The boy had moved out of the airy great bedroom at the front of the palace into an empty maid's room next to the kitchen. He slept on the mattress or, if his uncle made the bed, then in a tangle of sheets twisted around a leg or foot or across his chest like so many dressings over wounds. The room smelled of sleep and sperm and grief. The shade over the one small window was never raised. The monogrammed towels Mateo had placed out on the rack beside the half sink never got used. Their very tidiness looked forlorn.

Mateo made lots of noise in the kitchen. At last he opened the door with his foot and carried in a breakfast tray, which he placed on the bedside table. If he tiptoed away, when he returned the tray would be cold and untouched. Eventually he learned he had to pull the boy up, then swivel him around and plant his feet on the floor. Once he'd created this sagging beanbag copy of a sitting man, Mateo would put the breakfast tray on his lap and leave. He tried not to look too long at the underwear, the palette of a crazed painter obsessed over the years with a narrow range of hues.

Mateo would receive his callers throughout the long morning in his study. Sometimes the boy sat outside the study on one of the two hard chairs placed there for symmetry, not use, and listened to the unending stream of chatter—the mock glee, the mock anger, the whole miniature world of mock emotion shaken again and again into wintry life within the glass convexity of Mateo's conversation, that uncomfortable mixture of ambition and affection. The boy learned that the capital was ruled by another people, the conquerors, who were "obviously" inferior to their subjects and "desperate" for their approval. But to what degree could the subjects mix with their rulers without being unduly "compromised"?

Although Mateo had lived in the city for some twenty years, he still thought of himself as the shunned outsider, the petitioner at the gate, desperate for recognition from his peers, the other nobles of this besieged city. But now his nephew had preempted that role, and Mateo was forced to recognize how much power he'd gained over the years—not real power, for power is simple, but influence, which is devious, wasteful and as likely to promote unforeseen as expected results. Yet influence does produce something, and that was what the uncle knew the nephew was observing. The study was like a smelly laboratory, beakers foaming, lightning dancing over electrodes, glass tubes pumping liquids that turned green in transit. And yet when Mateo discussed influence, sometimes he meant political leverage over the conqueror general, but sometimes he meant nothing more than an ascendancy over one of the dozen reigning beauties every "gentleman" seemed obliged to pursue.

Mateo didn't like his life, or rather he sensed it fell far short of an ideal that he held but didn't dwell on, that engaged none of his intelligence though most of his sympathy. Somewhere in adolescence he'd decided that life should be largely solitary, serious, discreet, unadorned, whereas here he was, compromised, immersed into calls, intrigues, ambitions. From the height of this old solitary ideal that he'd never honored but also never betrayed he looked down on his own worldliness with a sorrowing amusement —sorrow over its pettiness, amusement at its toylike elegance.

He was no good alone. When he went to the country to commune with his soul, his soul stayed in the city. Nor did virtue interest him since he had no dramatic sense of it. That is, he didn't believe in evil. The only thing he could pit against goodness was a persistent intimation of guilt, a floating pollution of guilt without origin or destination, a cloud that destroyed the passages it entered but indifferently, as the wind blows. He always felt guilty, but the cloud never parted to reveal the stark face of evil. He didn't believe that his bad conscience portended anything evil; it was just a weight or counter-weight in the clockwork mechanism that made him tick. He thought of virtue—his chill, solitary notion of virtue—only rarely, as one might glance up at the moon: sharp, distant, sumptuously anonymous.

These observations were peripheral to the panic he experienced morning after morning. He had to find money for both of them. Never had he had much of it, but its absence he'd scarcely noticed since he'd lived in private, that is under hundreds of only mildly curious eyes, eyes that didn't rest for long on the moving target he presented. More, no one had ever been tempted to excavate his personal life, a site that looked so picked over. His secrets were safe (his poverty, his laziness, his hot wet depressions) since he confided so many "scandals" (sexual conquests, romantic defeats, social vendettas) to everyone. In the past he'd sometimes staged a splendid dinner and then lived off the leftovers for a week; now he owed the boy nourishing meals three times a day. In the past he'd usually dressed up threadbare clothes with new scarves; soon he'd have to buy a good winter coat for the boy. He was always at first nights, gallery openings, balls; his name was usually mentioned. Everything he couldn't afford he considered a mere background someone else should provide. In the shabby, animated, indoor life he led, the price of coffee at one café after another or of transportation through the muddy, teeming streets was all he required. Because he was so often asked out, because there were some rich people who courted him, because his prospects were uncertain enough to look promising, he had never reckoned his poverty till now.

Children make everyone conservative. We send them off for instruction in the religion we deride as superstition; we enroll them in morals we regard as damagingly narrow; we prepare them for a life we are fleeing. Mateo superimposed regular hours, regular meals, regular chores onto the chaos he'd always known—chaotic hours determined by obsessive work or obsessive love, meals by formal obligation or animal need, household chores by the sudden announcement of visitors: life by catastrophe. This new order he'd just introduced, he told himself, was somehow enabling; the boy must know a respectable household in order to (here the logic became limp) . . . in order to have, well, freedom of choice, opportunities, all the advantages.

Of course what the boy saw and admired was the chaos. He thought it wonderful that his uncle should still be improvising at his age—they were just alike! And if his uncle indulged himself (the drunken laughing and stumbling through the house night after night, the sudden plunges through the rainy park in a hired vehicle, the glass jars of caviar brought home in iced and insulated bags when the kitchen shelves stood empty), he worked hard to afford these panicky pleasures.

In his years of living alone, Mateo had never noticed his everyday rituals, and if someone had asked him to describe a typical day, he would have been at a loss. But here was the boy imitating not his new sound practices but his old bad habits. Gabriel said he especially admired the way his uncle tucked in work wherever it fit;

any free moment was turned over to making arrangements. No detail was beneath consideration, and to consider them all was his profession, one he practiced sternly in the interstices of his frivolous personal life; he followed a rigorous schedule of interruptions.

Mateo had sought out opposites as friends, lovely calm beings who found his energy necessary to them, but in his nephew he inherited a mirror and Gabriel was as painful as a mirror for Mateo to look at. Every morning Mateo backed up to his real mirror and pecked out of it one sharp, angry glance: still the same. That was all he could see. To love some idle, feebly pulsing blond woman, to stroke that hair and smooth those long limbs was no problem; it was almost a zoological delight. But to love this dirty, sluggish, shockingly vulnerable boy was . . . like loving oneself, which is before everything else an aesthetic problem. If Mateo had surrounded himself with known beauties, old names, professional wits, he'd had recourse to such banal trophies because his battle against himself had been banal. Here he was, up in his forties, still without any of the contentment—or regret—he'd been told to expect. Popular wisdom held that middle age was that time when a man has achieved all that he strived for and has found it empty. But Mateo couldn't indulge in such expensive disappointments. He'd achieved nothing. He was still poor. If he fell ill tomorrow he and his nephew would starve. They'd be turned out into the streets and one great door after another, now opened eagerly at his knock, would stand very still until they gave up and went away. Mateo couldn't wait to get rich, turn famous, ponder new goals, growl with boredom, but now his soul was too tattered to search. And of course he couldn't admit his poverty to anyone, for his métier depended on nothing so much as on other people's certainty that he was chic, carefree. Even the conquerors feared only those subjects they thought possessed secret stores of worldliness, taste, refinement. The mystique of the capital had always been based on intimidation.

But if his new responsibility for Gabriel made Mateo reckon

up his poverty, it also made him aware of his riches. The boy admired him. In his ordinary relations with friends and lovers, Mateo kept everyone so much in motion he never had to submit to their examination. He preferred being feared rather than loved, since fear was easier to maintain. He thought people feared him because he never stayed still, and loved him because he always stayed scarce. But here was this sleepy, whipped boy, as vulnerable as a neck. Here was this boy, staring at him night and day collecting his absurdities like beach glass, his swooping intonation, the solemn little drama he made over his evening drink, his way of memorizing names, titles, promotions, court calendars—all the tattle needed to press into the nest he never finished wattling. How strange to be admired, to have someone else's glance travel over every inch of one's naked soul and linger over a particularly juicy deformity. Mateo had lived so long in a world where almost anything could be ridiculed, where the most useful survival skill was uncertainty and the most dangerous flaw complacency, that basking in admiration struck him as an ominous fattening up for the kill. Oh, he'd handed out so much flattery to others and seen how well even the crudest praise went down, that he was suspicious of anything kind anyone might say to him. But this *mute* admiration, this silent tribute of imitation, was hard to distrust but necessary to resist.

Gabriel listened to his uncle's laughter, which sounded more anxious than ever, a whole birdcage at feeding time. He had been told to "drop in on" the chat Mateo would be having with Mathilda. His uncle had arranged for Gabriel's hair to be washed and cut that morning. The boy had huddled under the white cape while bluebottles flashed through the air followed by cold cloacal seepings over his scalp and down his neck. The scissors snipped the air beside his ear. Florent, the "wig-maker" as for some reason he was called, studied Gabriel in the looking glass. There they were, standing man, highly critical, and seated boy, his drenched head tiny and molted above the great white wings of his cape. Much as he tried to oblige the man, Gabriel could never anticipate at which angle Florent would next want his head. The hummingbird would pivot and levitate off into a concealed smock pocket, and the man's hands, puffed from homely immersions, would tilt Gabriel's skull, but gently, gently.

And now Gabriel, perfumed, scalp tight under less hair brushed fuller, entered the library. He was surprised to see that Mathilda was no girl as he had thought but a woman his mother's age. She was slumped low in her chair, the white of her bodice planting a faint flag in the polished red granite floor. The open window behind her palette-knifed a gob of intense, pulsing pigment onto the stone. Mathilda studied the boy as so much horseflesh; Mateo studied Mathilda. To gain courage Gabriel had told himself the meeting couldn't be as bad as he feared, but now he thought it would be worse. He flashed a confiding little smile at her, but she merely squinted, the better to size him up.

"And here he is," Mateo was saying.

Abruptly Mathilda let her chin sink farther toward her chest. She lifted a foot (should he kiss her boot?) and rested it on the other knee. In pictures she was always shown as tall, composed, head held regally, her face irradiated by those intelligent, unsympathetic eyes. When she'd been a girl she'd had a bad fall from a horse, which had left her with a deformed hip and a limp. Her skin always looked matte, granular, like a sugar cube soaking up water. But in sunlight, now, she was sallow. She yawned, her eyes blinked wetly, she propped her chin on an upturned palm, the fingers tapping a bored little tune. Now she was gripping the armrests and her legs uncoiled and were again stretched straight out in front of her.

"Tell Mathilda your impressions of the city," Mateo said, "while I fetch you some coffee." Before the boy could protest that he knew nothing about the city and had scarcely left the palace, his uncle had slipped out of the room.

Now she was sniffing, audibly sniffing. Was she smelling blood, his, or was she inhaling the bouquet of a wine she might or might not taste?

Outside children were playing, a whole swarm, but many, many courtyards away, their voices crying in an undifferentiated chorus. Distance seemed to have somehow aged these voices, as heat ripens fruit. A cool breeze was blowing past him. Angelica had taught him to avoid drafts since devils live in them. He moved his chair away from Mathilda.

"I hope I don't frighten you," she said without conviction.

"Everything frightens me."

The moment she smiled at his words he realized that sincerity could be turned into charm, that the poorest pumpkin truth might become a carriage that could transport him . . . into Mathilda's favor. The trick, he saw, was to present the most shameful secret as though it were one everyone shared. He resolved to step out boldly into the light carrying it, his shame, in his arms, holding it up, showing it.

"What interests you?" she asked, yawning. "What do you want to do while you're here?"

"Everything and nothing," he said. "You must understand, madam, that I come from a fairly . . . unusual family."

"And so?" she said impatiently. "So do we all. Monster parents, bourgeois hypocrisy, provincial views—I see it all and nothing could be more banal."

"I don't think you quite grasp the originality of my situation." His voice betrayed his anger.

Her eyes widened. She wasn't used to being challenged. Perhaps she was intrigued by this sign of defiance. Just as one gypsy violinist might hear another play a few notes, aching, accurate, across a café blue with smoke, and respond with an exclamation of his own fiddle until in a moment the two musicians have locked eyes and are edging toward one another, their bland expressions belied

by the indignant duet they're improvising, in the same way Mathilda, usually surrounded by a host of ambitious young men, seemed
to have detected in Gabriel someone who could interest her. She
moved closer.

"It could be, I suspect, very pleasant," she said, "to listen to
you establish the originality of your situation."

Gabriel was ready to do anything to make Mathilda like him.
But on the other hand he recognized that only a measure of independence was likely to attract her; he must insist *she* please *him*. For
an unrelated reason (fear of devils) he'd moved his chair away from
her. This little act, which she'd seen as a slight, had given him an
advantage. He suspected she'd do anything to tame him but that if
she succeeded she would lose interest. He walked to the window,
turning his back to her. There were no trees or children below,
nothing but pavement and housefronts enclosing a wide, empty
square. He could hear the children's voices, the splendid hive. He
could picture bees—clustering, wriggling, overlapping—as they
filled and sealed golden cells. The treble laughs and screams had
been simplified by distance into just such a community. For some
reason those voices made him think of Angelica. At night he'd think
of all the things they'd done to each other, the way they'd played
with the fire within them, turning up the wick until the glass chimney charred. He felt that the natural mode of release (if release
could be natural) was to draw one's own white blood, to reach a
sting or two in private; he and Angelica had blasphemed against the
order of things by using each other as fragile means to shattering
ends. Perhaps they had, after all, been invaded by devils, and these
spirits had lashed them into humiliating contortions, making them
monkeys unworthy of the clothes on their back. But of course their
wedding had consecrated their union, if it had been a wedding and
not a dream and if the old woman were a priest and not a demon.

When he glanced back at Mathilda he could see in her eyes the
same sequence of desire that would twitch jerkily through An-

gelica's, a look that would keep changing, not by shadings but absolutely, a series of ever more disturbing closeups of the same subject until it loomed too close and became a blurred abstraction.

She was still seated, of course, when he came over to her and stood beside her. They both watched the blue silk pleat of his pants stretch and fill. They exchanged a funny little glance, incapable of questioning this development but still nonplussed by it.

At his uncle's insistence Gabriel moved back into the pink and green bedroom and the huge bed with the canopy held up by a flight of amputated angels, a bed consecrated to the future and other people, whereas his grubby cubbyhole in the maid's room beside the kitchen safely deleted him from time and society and removed him to a margin that smelled reassuringly of his own dirty feet and stale armpits and unwiped bottom, a cot littered with the crumpled wicks of paper in which he'd twisted yet another letter to . . . well, to a wounded creature of his own imagination, Angelica.

One day he received a note which said, "Hope you're having fun with that wild uncle of yours. Believe it or not, I'll be dropping in on you one of these days. Don't worry. Just for a cup of tea." It was signed with an extravagant letter *A* of which the two sides curled up like windswept hair framing a face barred by mysterious dark glasses.

He hadn't missed her. He hadn't missed anything except Jane Castle and the endless night and freedom of the cell his father had put him in, that absolute solitude to which his cubbyhole here was a mere allusion, a diminution, as one might say that a raised bow suspended over a waiting violin diminishes its silence. To be honest, he had missed having Angelica in his arms, had missed this contraption of wet warmth and twisting muscle he could never quite duplicate, not even with his hand wet or dry, warm or cold, rough or slippery with oil. He'd missed her body. That was all.

Sometimes when he'd spied on her at play in the woods he couldn't reconcile this cool, independent girl with the fiery furnace she'd become when they embraced on the ground. Sometimes she seemed scarcely human, more a kiln for liquifying the stiff ingot he presented into flowing gold. A primitive but obsessive industrial process (up, down, swivel, stop, then on again through the whole clumsy, efficient cycle) designed to melt, then mint, finally mill the mere sovereign he'd turned into. Her face would drain, her teeth would close on his everted lower lip, her voodoo eyes would roll weirdly back into her head, her nails would hang her whole dead weight from his shoulders—and then, once all her vitality was concentrated in her pelvis, her body would heat up, speed up, strip its gears, pause and start all over again at some safer level. She didn't always like him nor he her, almost as though they were both ashamed of so much urgency.

Yet now she'd sent this maddening little note (or had she? she couldn't write and it didn't sound like her—or had she changed?) and he felt he must have her here with him or he'd die. One of these days? "Don't worry," she'd said. Did she mean don't worry she'd stay too long?

A few times his uncle had suggested he go out, run an errand, post a letter, but he'd usually dawdled or managed to fall asleep. This reluctance had been due to his fear of the hectic, unfamiliar world he could see from the kitchen window. Now he had a worthier reason for staying in: he might miss Angelica's visit. What if she came when no one was at home? What if she was desperate— hungry, sick, cold? He slept half the time in the maid's room because it was closer to the front door and the other half in the pink bedroom because it was where they'd live.

Did the doorbell work?

He tested it ten times a day but could never be satisfied it hadn't just gone dead.

Could he hear it in the pink bedroom? Sheepishly he asked his uncle to ring the bell while he listened for it.

"So it's that bad, is it?" his uncle asked with a timid, intimate, worldly smile.

"Yes," Gabriel said, more because he wanted to be worthy of that smile than out of concurrence. "Does it get this bad for you, too?" he asked, having no idea what he meant exactly.

His uncle had just returned from a long evening out. He pushed his old, no longer shiny hat back, the sort of hat he still referred to by the awkward name people had given it in his youth: "eight reflections." He was standing in silk scarf and black cape in the entrance hall under the grimy chandelier with its almost grey chains of crystal and its flyblown lusters, each a specimen slide prepared by time. He smelled of gin and a woman's perfume and an unfamiliar brand of cigarettes. He was like a tray a servant brings out of a room from which one can deduce the activities of the other guests—the half-deck of soiled playing cards, the drained bottle, the dirty glasses, the crumpled note, the still smoking revolver.

"Oh, yes," he said, "I've done my hours of sitting inside, waiting for Her to call."

"Her?" the boy asked eagerly.

"The Eternal Her; the Universal Whoever," his uncle replied, softening the airiness of his remark with the sweet solicitude of his tone, his voice trailing away out of concern. "Did you sit here all night waiting for her—here on the floor?"

Gabriel was about to deny the absurd, embarrassing charge, yet something stopped him. "Yes," he admitted, for it was true. "Yes." He lowered his head.

And then here was the avuncular hand—warm and moist because just extracted from the glove, veined and knowing, a gold band giving a waist to the fat torso of his little finger—here was this hand on his neck, now under his chin, confidently lifting his face back into the light.

"I'm not a monster, you know," his uncle said and smiled, showing the two front teeth that were too large, too smooth, not quite the right color, too innocent of detail to be real, and that always siphoned onto his breath a slight sourness, bitterer at night after a long day of smoke, wine, and the clogged residue of having advanced so many opinions, none quite charitable. Sometimes Mateo wondered if he and his friends were malicious because they'd inherited all the intellectual pretensions of their parents and none of their scope. After all, when the capital had been rich and powerful, the ideas (even the whims) of its nobles had caused things to happen. Now they all took stands—but they were standing on air. Their impotence made them irritable.

"I've sat here," Mateo pointed, "on this very floor and rolled and howled like an animal," and Gabriel knew it wasn't true but appreciated the effort, the invention, as though lying, at least in this case, were a form of politeness. "Howled," he repeated, as though he'd just heard the false thunder rolling in after the fake lightning. His hand dropped and he stared into a single point of brilliance beaming out at him from the heart of the dulled chandelier.

They drank their liqueur together in the kitchen, the room that had, a century earlier, been the studio of a painter who'd found his subject in the silk gowns of society women. "He was my kind of painter," Mateo was saying. "Philistines thought he was one of their own, intellectuals dismissed him for his superficiality, by which they meant his subject matter, the life of the rich. But he was that most delightful of all things—an artist who makes small but daring experiments within an exhausted tradition. No one, of course, gives him any credit, not even now. The vulgar rich think he merely held up a mirror to their ancestors—and that world they now consider démodé, as cold as old gossip. They're even embarrassed to see their relatives in hairstyles so old-fashioned. The intelligentsia, equally vulgar, can detect novelty only if it's canonically avant-garde (usually the last place to look for a real invention). For genius works best with worn-out things, things fingered and faded enough to 'compose,' quilts put together out of the scraps of old sacking, gowns or teatowels. Our man could make his portrait of Mrs. Edwin Smith as the Mother Goddess into a bravura exercise in rendering every aspect of a pearl without ever once dipping his brush into merest grey, blue or white."

When his uncle talked this way (there was an old word for such talk, a word that could be translated "rhapsody") Gabriel sank deeper and deeper into shame and fear, since he suspected this was the way people out there were routinely expected to talk. Just as Angelica's furnace could distill only a few drops of gold despite its twistings and throbbings, in the same way gallons of liquor, years of coaching and hundreds of overheard colloquies had been needed to express this blackest of all stimulants—his uncle's rhapsodic talk.

"But I'm talking about art," his uncle said, that sad, worldly smile brushing across his lips again, "while you're getting more and more depressed thinking about love, about your Angelica."

Gabriel started to deny that he loved Angelica, much less was thinking of her, but he had to confess a desire for her did cross his mind, just as his uncle, although intent on their conversation, still smelled of the woman he'd recently left. His uncle asked him to describe Angelica, and as the boy expatiated on her charm, Mateo nodded knowingly—indeed, almost as though he could picture the girl.

"But I thought you wanted me to love Mathilda," Gabriel said.

"My boy," his uncle protested and shrugged; he smiled, bent over the kitchen table and with chemical exactness measured out a beaker of mandarin orange liqueur, which had been judged not quite fit for guests. Gabriel added, "You're being incredibly nice about my love. I mean my love for Angelica."

"Nice?" his uncle repeated, looking up, blinking with dramatic confusion. Gabriel realized he'd said something wrong. "How can you say I'm being nice when all I'm doing is acknowledging this sweet yoke, these silk fetters, this blessed curse?"

Correction: not wrong after all. *Nice* had been exactly the right springboard his uncle had needed to leap off into generosity and poetry.

This word *love* troubled and intrigued Gabriel. He sensed he could gain an advantage from it or the reality it might represent. But just now "love" mostly seemed to be a pleasant conspiracy he and his uncle were sharing.

When Gabriel had first moved into his house, Mateo had used the boy and his responsibility toward him as a pretext for forgetting Edwige. She was a pretty, nasty little blonde Mateo had been obsessed with for nearly three years. They'd met quite properly, that is comically, at a mock matchmaking. Like everything else in their friendship, this introduction had been ambiguous. A composer, Robert Constantine, who relaxed after his musical ascents into the Alpine mists of passion and number by indulging in a social manner that was flaccid and giggly, accosted Mateo one day and said, "Hey, Mister Sweetie-puss, are you in the market for true love?"

"Naturally," Mateo had murmured, as always embarrassed and flattered by the composer's attentions. Constantine was the sort of insolent fool one would have fled had one not divined his true nobility from his music, those great oratorios for one voice, an ecstatic soprano, accompanied by an always hushed and vast symphony orchestra whispering to itself like a forest wrapped around a small clearing in which a hauntingly tacky band of banjo, accordion and harmonica held forth, smoke rising from the brave campfire in the midst of that chilly wilderness.

Constantine almost never read a book. His last four works had been settings of different passages from the same text. But now he was immersed in an old tale in which two married sisters devoted all their energies to finding a husband for the youngest one, a pursuit conducted through professional matchmakers. His reading had suggested the occasion during which Mateo was to meet Edwige.

Perhaps only Mateo thought the purpose of the gathering was actually romantic. What had Edwige been told? Perhaps everyone, including Edwige, took the evening seriously, as a parody of a form both foreign and vanished yet with a significance open to interpretation. Probably the others half-expected Mateo to make a fool of himself, and Constantine had staged this unfunny buffoonery just to gratify himself. The oddest possibility of all was that everyone —Constantine, the guests, the couple—was more or less confused, and this confusion was due to Constantine's carelessness, his real indifference to everything nonmusical. For if he liked to be silly, this wasn't a strong but an insipid taste derived from his contempt for mere life, that unscored noise, beside which he'd scrawled an insulting ad libitum. Who met whom, what transpired, and how it all ended—these details meant nothing to him, not even when they affected his own fortunes. More sincerely than any monk, he was indifferent to everyday life, which he viewed as a drowsy infant might look at motes in sunlight. Constantine drank too much, squealed with pretended pleasure and played naughty tricks on trusting friends who, unlike him, took themselves perfectly seriously and refused to consider life as just another longish intermission.

And Edwige? She was a blonde who looked pure and still so young that her dissipations merely underscored her beauty, a hollowing of a pink cheek, a smudge of storm-cloud blue under eyes that were clear-sky blue. Like the evening, she herself was ambiguous; she radiated indecision. As an actress she thought she could have everything and capture everyone at once, could play in big, bad crowd-pleasers *and* cultivate the elite. Tonight counted as her first sortie amongst the intellectuals of the capital. She really didn't know how to enter this particular world. Of course she needn't have worried; the intellectuals were thrilled to meet a star even of a minor magnitude and they were already storing up stories about her lack of culture, her infamous politics, her obvious intelligence, her outré but effective white fox coat.

Mateo had actually believed Constantine when he said Edwige wanted an older lover who was intellectual but also sociable. Since this description suited his own most ambitious view of himself, he was sure she'd like him. And yet at the party she scarcely seemed to know which one he was; at least her curtsy wasn't even fractionally deeper when he was presented to her. She asked everyone questions with a charming deference—or perhaps the deference was merely inferred from her practice of keeping her eyes lowered until she lifted them gloriously at the end of someone else's learned or tortured speech, as one might throw open a window in a stuffy room to let in the wet warm night or as an orchestra might silence the rubbishy chitchat of a thousand scornful mouths and commence with the strict measures of an earlier, better century.

Now, three years later, Mateo refused to deny those sublime eyes, but he no longer made the mistake of ascribing their power to Edwige herself. She could not have begun to crack the code of her own beauty. Vengeance and endurance were her only obsessions. She exercised and bought clothes and submitted to facials, diets and daily coiffures so that she—or at least this artifact, Edwige—would endure, unchanged, perfect, eternally tempting to some about-to-materialize impresario.

Her will to endure had nothing to do with acquisitiveness. She had no desire to improve, no program, no ambition; she simply wanted to conserve her patrimony, this face with its almost anonymously regular features designed so as not to distract from those matched curiosities, her eyes. She must endure until chosen. Her genius was waiting, just as her vocation was to wait. Everyone knew who she was and which "quality" she could bring to a role, as a painter knows exactly what this particular alizarin crimson looks like though he seldom applies it. She had a quality, a legend to offer and she must not let it fade or waver out of focus. If the will to endure held her fast, what impelled her forward was hunger for revenge. That hunger—but no, it was a food, something she ate daily and snacked on early and late, something always bubbling on the back burner. She wanted revenge against the managers who'd ignored her, the claqueurs who booed her, the critics who'd been gently ironic at her expense. The social history of a full decade of backstage life had been written onto her memory since it coincided with the history of the slights that had been dealt her.

Her voice was clear and she spoke well although with too few of the greasy, salty inflections of the city to please most of her auditors. They could hear in her voice too much that was foreign, formal, cleaned up: the foie gras of the conquerors and not the pâté campagne of the people. In fact, it was well known that she wasn't a patriot and she was quite content to impersonate the conquerors in their insipid comedies of manners, to dramatize the minor dilemmas of their society women; this very expertise she called her "professionalism" and when one of her rivals—that vulgar Paule —scored a triumph with the mob in a trashy melodrama merely because the wife's declaration of independence from her sadistic husband sounded very much like political defiance, Edwige ascribed the success to Paule's cynicism and the public's ignorance. "She's not an artist," Edwige whispered into the collar of her fox coat.

Everyone remembered something about Edwige's body. A dancer Mateo met at a party said with envy and approval, "But she has the loveliest feet!" And in fact they were very strong feet with a remarkably high instep, which she permitted Mateo to stroke for hours, or which she herself molded when they were alone, as though to make them still higher. Once the dancer had mentioned this attraction, Mateo treasured it all the more, as though it had been taken from him. A masseur whom Edwige had sent him to once when he'd thrown out his back after attempting a new position in bed (tiny pelvic thrusts upward into a waiting weighty receptacle)—that masseur had said, "Edwige has an intelligent body." That sounded right, but Mateo found it disconcerting that her charms had become the coin of the realm.

And of course everyone spoke of her eyes. When Mateo heard the cliché about someone's "meteoric rise to stardom," he said to himself, "Yes, but Edwige already has felt the impact of not one but two meteors, her eyes, which came to this earth from a cold, distant star." This retrospective way of looking at Edwige's stardom and meteoric fall matched her own frozen will to endure as well as her innate dignity, one founded on something as definite and absent as former glory.

She had, of course, slept with hundreds of men in the past ten years, or so he had to conclude from all those knowing smiles, winks and doffed hats that greeted them in the streets (offered, always, he noticed, by the most unredeemed conservatives or their grinning servants) and from a scurrilous ditty one heard everywhere about a certain "lady of *infinite* mercy," yet she denied the rumors and merely smiled when someone whistled the ditty on a deserted rainy street late at night as they were followed, maddeningly, block after block. "Of course people make jokes about me," she said to him, "I am a star."

Love is a progressive illness, one that starts as self-hallucination, an act of parody, and ends as a wholly real, involuntary malady that kills us or something vital in us. Mateo could never quite understand when or why he'd fallen so terminally in love with Edwige, but he suspected that whereas *when* could be answered, at least theoretically, *why* could not. Nevertheless he speculated at such length on his own condition he sometimes imagined that the function of love was to be a *point de repère,* an enigma so bright it distracted attention from bigger fears.

When he tried to tell her how much she was making him suffer, she'd flash a smile as though he'd just given her the cue for a demanding but familiar scene. She accepted the challenge in a serious spirit of fun and delivered all her lines impeccably. "But you offered me your *friendship*," she wailed, crossing the room, turning, extracting one pale hand from her muff, opening it help-lessly, then letting it wilt. "You said we'd be *friends*. Every man in town and half the women want me. They all saw me in that beautiful costume in *A Week in the City*. But you—you promised me friend-ship! That's what I hunger for, thirst for—"

At such moments she looked so fragile, so young, indeed so friendless that Mateo wanted to console her, as though this were the very moment when she'd decide, once and for all, whether life is worth living, whether humanity is good or bad. Although he was exhausted from the suffering she'd caused him, and (since, alas, he ate to console himself) he had become fat with grief, when faced with her distress he couldn't recall any of his complaints against her. His reproaches now seemed gross insults flung cruelly at this inno-cent woman, this spire of helplessness rising in purity against a muddy sky. But then, just as he was about to beg her for forgive-ness, he heard her using a line from her latest adultery farce, and he pulled away.

Her adolescence had turned her into a little old woman, for during those years (such a blur in the telling, at once too full and too constricted, like a severely gathered skirt of deep folds) she'd lived by her wits, drifting from town to smoking, ruined town, taking up with soldiers first on one side, then the other, her talk a jumble of barracks filth in several dialects and two languages. That had been the epoch of the last uprising against the conquerors.

Oddly enough, she'd half chosen that existence. Although she'd been separated from her family against her will, afterwards she'd made no effort to find them again. She'd wandered from town to town, in her hair either a scarlet or blue ribbon, depending on which side seemed to be winning the war. Her wanderings had shaped her.

At certain times Mateo could even hear in her voice the harsh, cynical tones of an infamous bounder named Skeets who'd been her first lover. She'd met him in an army camp along the coast. Skeets had been put in charge of entertainment for the officers on the theory that he knew more actresses than anyone else. He himself loved to emerge in parade uniform and do a turn with the girls at the grand finale. His light baritone was without vibrato, always perfectly on pitch and almost characterless in its purity, as though it were white light rather than a voice, hued and fallible. This singing voice was at odds with his speaking voice, always plummy with innuendo, and Edwige (at that time still known as Mary Ann) had picked up his bitter, vulgar laugh, those low, scornful accents, that withering certainty that everyone, including oneself, was lustful to the point of bestiality and greedy beyond calculation and that if anyone remained gentle and ordinary it was only out of naïveté. Skeets had kept Mary Ann beside him all through the war and together they'd witnessed its horrors. The room beside the emergency room was stacked high with fresh arms and legs just sawn off to prevent gangrene; the floor was shiny and scarlet. They'd seen a friend laugh, turn into an explosion and then look back at them noseless, mouth dribbling teeth. Skeets called Mary Ann "Ermine" because he said she was small, quick, strokeable and randy, and soon that was her name throughout the division. "Ermine," Skeets would say, "I want you to befriend that new officer's wife, you know the one, the prude? I think she'd make a fun playmate for us, don't you? I think she has hidden charms, don't you?" And Ermine was demoted, just that quickly, from lover to accomplice.

She had no older, respectable woman she could confide in. No one even really noticed her change of status. Unremarked, it seemed as natural to her as it was painful. She found herself crying as she scurried off on some seducer's errand for Skeets, but she brushed the tears aside as though they were brambles. Before long, Skeets was lending her out to other officers and over breakfast she and Skeets were comparing notes on their separate conquests, as though they were both men, buddies. He even began to tease her in front of others: "No, Ermine doesn't like big men. She likes them small, square and stupid with just a haze of blond or brown hair on the shoulders and a big ass she can grab on to. That's why she left me—I was too smart, too finely made."

"Shut up, Skeets," Ermine would growl. She loved him so much she'd twisted her own feelings into a shape she thought might appeal to him. She'd begun to wear a drummer boy's uniform, which only heightened the impression that she was his boy. Skeets thought nothing of ordering her out of his tent for the night if he was planning an assignation, forcing her to scurry around to find another sucker, another bed. One night she had to sleep out in the fields, alone, cold. The moon illuminated the silver edges of a cloud shaped like a continent yet to be discovered, a land of dreams. And then the map slid away and the moon emerged. It was just a half-moon, flat edge up, as though that were the cutting edge.

Of course all that had happened long ago. Ermine was now the cold, elegant Edwige renowned for her diction, her "intelligent" body, her collaborationist politics, her white fox fur, her many rich protectors, her bad temper, her considerable but not always reliable talent. She'd fabricated every gesture and pronunciation. When she entered a room she'd pause and preen, turn, pause, preen, turn, pause and preen, before gliding smoothly to a settee and a waiting friend.

If she had to step out of a boat and into a gathering, she'd send ahead an usher from the theater, young and dressed in a simple white cotton tunic fastened down the front with silk frogs, someone whose single job would be to hand her out, to make her otherwise awkward entrance suave. There they'd be, a slender silver boy bending down to pull up out of the water this improbable, windswept girl in a gown the color of palest chablis with a waistband of cassis-dark satin. As a principle she preferred the colors of man-made things to those of unredeemed nature as though she wanted to remind people of the city objects they ate, touched, wore, lived amongst rather than what they regretted having left behind in a village or on a farm.

Before she'd go into a room she'd quiz the hostess about who was where (was Edwige's uncertainty social or logistic?). After she'd "crossed" a whole long room, not merely crossed it but much more effectively crossed it "on the diagonal" and ended up in the most brightly lit corner, preferably elevated slightly on a dais, say, she didn't want to find herself among bores or old, undesirable relatives of the hostess or, just as awkwardly, without a seat.

Edwige felt a physical aversion to Mateo that she couldn't hide and that, once she realized he was in love, she saw no further need to conceal. He had embraced several comforting fallacies. He believed that others love us for our merits and he struggled to prove his to Edwige, whereas the truth is that merit chills ardor. He believed that anyone he loved so well must sooner or later return his devotion, whereas the chief condition for devotion is that it not be reciprocal. He believed that if he insinuated himself into her friendship he'd eventually possess her love, whereas these two sentiments, far from being neighbors, are opposites: affection tranquilizes passion. He'd succeeded in making himself indispensable to her, but in the capacity of *cavaliere servente* he was more *servente* than *cavaliere*.

Just before Mateo had made his trip to Madder Pink and found his nephew behind bars, Edwige had lived with Mateo for a few months. Then she'd insisted on moving into her own wing of the palace, where she had her privacy, even her own entrance, and where she received Mateo only when it suited her. Perhaps his own thralldom to Edwige had made Mateo so sympathetic to his nephew's plight. Certainly during that time Mateo had learned how thoroughly her apprenticeship to Skeets had marked her, for she'd retained a grimness about people and their motives, an outlook that was just, perhaps, but unlikely to see one through the steps of this quadrille one is obliged to dance. She was so scornful about the lust and greed of other people that he couldn't understand how she tolerated her own hankering after revenge. Her degree of rancor, surely, should turn her away from the world. Why didn't she renounce the quadrille and become a spiritual wallflower? He seriously expected her one day to shave her skull and cover her perfectly preserved face with ashes. That she lingered on here in a world she so scorned showed exactly how obstinate she was, since clearly she was pursuing treasures she already could see were rusted, shattered. Never had someone so frivolous—an actress, a celebrity, a woman of fashion—been so grim; she had turned the pursuit of pleasure into a gruesome austerity.

Whenever Mateo suggested they go out Gabriel stalled or played sick or disappeared. When his uncle was near him for hours, he slowly gained confidence, as though his dark side were turning on a sluggish axis toward the sun. They'd laugh and his uncle would transform Gabriel's scraps of conversation, the rag ends of his yeses and nos, into fantasies lavish with invention. To be sure, for Gabriel everything was a strain, an exhilarating crisis, when Mateo was around. Gabriel would lie in his dirty bed, soothed by the dirty smell of his own body, the fingers pressed to his nose familiarly dirty, and he'd daydream of the long night of his imprisonment at Madder Pink and of his crepuscular romance with Jane Castle— then he'd hear his uncle on the steps, at the door, and his heart would sink. A call back to life. Gabriel thought he was being pulled in two opposite directions. He felt the urge to be peaceful (the smell of curled fingers in a warm pillow) but he also had the desire to be powerful (a young man briskly crossing a room hung with lusters under a hundred pairs of envious eyes). Gabriel preferred peace to power. Even his uncle, he suspected, liked peace better. But Mateo had arranged his days and nights so that he had no peace; he was subject to ringing bells, arriving messengers, a cruel mistress who lived just next door in a wing of his palace, the stinging whims of friends, the whining petitions of underlings, the need to call on those with influence or to pacify those to whom one owed too much—a whole self-winding life of emergencies, a clock whose alarm was always ringing.

In a state of peace one surrendered oneself to the lily-pond sluggishness of daydreams. The self brimmed over at its black banks. Power was different. It was both an explosion into the world (I do, I make, Look at Me) and an implosion (I need, I eat, Look at Me). These very transactions—their urgency, their conversions from thought to deed and back into thought—strengthened the ego through irritation.

Mateo regarded the boy's sleepiness as just a temporary reluctance to live, a scab forming over the wound his father had dealt him. Now the boy had a new excuse for not leaving the house, his fear of missing Angelica. Why had this child become so precious to the boy? Was she a souvenir of his past, the only thing he owned? Or did he love her because in this new city she would be even less acceptable than he? Or was she precious to him because he needed something to be precious?

At Madder Pink Gabriel had always known where to find anything he needed. He'd never been anywhere else in the eternity of his childhood. All of the episodes of his past, all his desires had been lucidly graphed onto this Map of Tenderness unscrolling around him; his inner life was entirely visible in the outer world. Each stone, each fallen tree had only to be glimpsed for it to surrender the particular memory it conserved.

But here, in the city, he'd been deprived of this past, taken out of a visionary landscape that had made every memory material and simultaneous, something to be turned over in the hand and inhaled down to its floral or mycelial essence. Now all of his past had been compressed into Angelica's name and face, as though hers were one of those fantasy portraits composed out of fruits and vegetables. Now he could no longer daydream. His uncle was giving him "lessons in conversation" every day. Mateo would challenge him with an insult and coach him in giving saucy or soothing responses. Gabriel showed an unexpected facility, but the tension of these sessions exhausted him.

He waited for Angelica night and day and dreamed more than once of her coming to him, of her face forming like mist on mirrored glass. But she stayed away. Once he dreamed of her assembling herself out of moonlight on stone, out of leaf shadows, out of the breath of cold soil in warm rain, the thrust and clatter of a startled deer breaking through underbrush. Had she come to the city at all? Was she somewhere nearby, spying on him, waiting until he'd been humbled to the lowest, darkest landing before she appeared at the head of the stairs and beckoned him back up into the light?

Or had something dreadful happened to her? She was just a tiny thing. He pictured her robbed, violated, killed, a pitiful brown body left lifeless beside the road, a hand still twitching in the grass, a singed wing on a wire.

Until now Gabriel had scarcely ever had a forethought or an afterthought. At Madder Pink he'd never poised himself above the keys of his world to consider what he might play or how, but rather he'd let his fingers stroll. He had a faint memory of his mother's former health and the family's earlier grandeur, but otherwise he'd felt no layering, no thickness between now and then, thought and deed.

Suddenly everything had changed. He could no longer laze about through his days, letting the world think for him. Now he had to scheme, to call and recall. He recognized, if only dimly, how precarious his uncle's life was, which made his own still more so. He had to be clever. He had to "converse."

They went out into the streets one day, pressing through the food markets, past a wagon piled high with white mushrooms, their stems still gritty with black soil, past the next wagon, in which thin green beans, thousands of them, fanned out in verdant sunbursts. An old woman with a face as fat and white as a church candle sat beating a drum behind her small table of herbs. Her outermost skirt was as coarse as a chimney rug. In the next stall, behind a greasy vitrine, lay a bowl of raw tripe and the rich black mess of spleen; up above, dangling from hooks, hung the feathered or furred carcasses of newly killed game. Ducks lay side by side, plucked clean and wrapped in a twist of red ribbon adorned with flowers. Men in bloodstained aprons and spotless white hats pushed lambs along on overhead metal hooks trolleying down the grooves. The haunting distant shout of "Hoy!" rang out, followed by the sound but not the sight of splashing water. Floating up were the alternately nauseating and inviting smells of cheese—of cheese in molding blue wheels, or in the honey-colored shapes of miniature pigs, or wrapped in soft green plantain leaves, or flung out like camel turds on beds of straw or sealed by a rind formicating with countless black grape seeds, or paddled and braided by a big-bellied man into white balls, each whisked off in a dripping wire scoop by a boy no older than Gabriel, a boy who spoke nothing but the incomprehensible dialect of the city, the language of the Field of Flowers (as the oldest square was called after its rose market), a boy whose buttocks were high and prominent from having spent every spare moment kicking a ball around outside the café his grandmother owned, playing even after nightfall in the soft orange glow of the old-fashioned gas jets that shone through openings cut in lead to resemble roses. The street itself was well illuminated, but since the rose cutouts were only on one side of each lamp, the pedestrian side was dark, obscurely active, as though the pedestrians were the stagehands, nearly invisible, tireless. His uncle told him that the people of this quarter had apparently been able to provision the capital even when the conquerors had held it under siege. No one knew how, but they'd even brought in bales of fresh oysters through enemy lines. In the Field of Flowers the conquerors had never made friends—it was dangerous for them to walk through it after dark. The nobles might be compromised, but the people refused to conceal their hatred. In serving the conquerors, they even dared to mimic their accent.

When Mathilda asked Mateo to bring Gabriel to his very first reception at her house, Mateo assumed she was merely being polite out of consideration for him, Mateo. More than once she'd assured him she knew what it was like to be stuck with a child in their nearly childless world of artists and intellectuals; after all she (with Mateo's distant if affectionate assistance) had raised a child, Daniel, who was now thirty and looked so nearly as though he were her brother that her maternity would have been suspect had not their celebrated, even infamous past together been so well documented. Nevertheless Mathilda was delighted when naïve or provincial people mistook Daniel for her brother or lover, and to increase the confusion she often referred to him coyly as "the darling." This coyness was so unlike her that people expected to catch a sardonic smile and were shocked to see instead the sort of smile people wear when they speak of their pets. What few people knew was that an older child, a girl, had died when she was four. This loss had poisoned Mathilda's joy in motherhood at the same time it had intensified her love for—no longer "my son" but "the darling."

Of course Daniel liked to say Mathilda had less insight into herself than anyone else he knew, a remark with which the astute were slow to agree, since they knew Daniel angrily rejected any criticism, even implied, of this mother he loved—and loved to malign.

They were so close, Daniel and Mathilda, that if they'd never merged entirely it was because fusion was less intimate than reciprocity. To be sure they had their differences, but even their differences were fields of honor on which combat became just another display of fealty. Of course their disputes could be bitter, protracted. Mathilda, the best-known thinker of her generation, a model of independence for nonconforming girls everywhere, found it disappointing that Daniel remained unmarried at thirty.

She respected the conventions. She despised her female admirers and all the other riff-raff that swirled about her, yet her very rudeness was taken as proof of her integrity. In the past, she'd made so many ringing denunciations of the victors—remarks that continued to sound around her—that most people, all those who didn't actually know her, assumed she was still a fervent patriot. She had no desire to invent new forms, to create a new audience; she wanted to occupy the highest chair in the most venerable academy as the first woman—but a woman admitted not as a concession to her sex but simply because she was better than any male candidate. She no longer had a politics (nor even an aesthetics) of innovation. If she'd been an artist, she would have wanted to be the sort Mateo admired, those who make "small but daring experiments within an exhausted tradition."

Although she'd been in the city for nearly thirty years, always seen at events either chic or shocking, in her own mind she'd attended them only out of a historian's curiosity. People (and they were rare) who went home with her after these rowdy affairs were stunned to discover how clean, sumptuous, orderly was her house with its basement given over entirely to a meticulously catalogued library of rare books in mint condition. To be sure, the walls were papered with colorful actor prints exactly as they would have been in any student's or maid's room—but here the prints were forty years old, from the best period, before ugly analine dyes had been introduced, and they represented a complete series by the best folk artists. Moreover, her series had been the subject of an essay by the best critic.

Behind even her most seemingly offhand gesture, one could detect Mathilda's connoisseurship. If she was bored in a conversation with a stranger, she'd deflect his flattery and grope about until she discovered his area of expertise (everyone has one). She'd then proceed to grill him as to what was best. Which were the best stockings? The best vegetables of that region? Best singers? Best philosophers? Best restaurants? If the subject strayed to something more intimate, she'd shepherd it back to her inventory.

In the realm of the best, evidently the best (highest, most conservative, classic, time-honored) sort of relationship to be in was marriage. She herself would not marry again, a failure she attributed to the fear she said she inspired in the men she met or, alternatively, to the sad fact that all the men worthy of her were, naturally, already married (their being married proved their worth). But her son? Yes, he must marry—in a sense "for" her, as a courtier might appear at a boat-launching "for" the absent monarch.

Daniel had very different ideas. In her systematic passion for the best, his mother had sent him to the best school, that is, to the most conservative, the Peers School, where he'd fallen in with the sons of the victors. He'd picked up their cynical politics (which he called "realistic"), their strategic vagueness (a pretended forgetfulness about unwanted invitations, an affected deafness to unwelcome petitions), their imperious manner of sinking from a roar to a mumble, of uttering crucial words (crucial to the listener) through a muffling hand, their taste for ever more extravagant clothes and a corresponding disdain for paying up, their capricious shifts of mood, their blanket approval of any opinion advanced by a friend and blanket dismissal of any idea held by a stranger. Mathilda, whose manner was rigorously plain, the "intellectual" style of the past, overcame her embarrassment over her son's arrogance by

labeling it "foppishness" and viewing it as a curiously patient historical reconstruction of the dandyism of a century ago. Thus her
party-going and his foppishness were both expressions of historical
curiosity—or so she liked to think. This fancy about Daniel comforted her, though it was far from the truth, which would have
forced her, once she'd faced it, to censure him. In fact, Daniel's
taste for fragile, nervous rich girls had led him to frequent the
highest circles, to which, paradoxically, he was admitted only because of his mother's reputation as a rebel against the state. And
Daniel had picked up a taste for love, which meant serial romances,
promiscuity—and that invalidated marriage. Their dispute ended
up being simply an unstated disagreement about what was best. In
her eyes it was marriage; in his eyes it was love, the endless romantic youth of the conquerors, the confident expectation of ever new
joys.

Mathilda always opposed the people she happened to be
among. She would defend whatever was conservative to progres-
sives and argue for liberty on curiously old-fashioned grounds to
conservatives: her manner was to challenge, to question. When
other people generated enthusiasm while discussing a subject they
thought was bound to suit her, she grew restless, squirmed in her
chair, looked about with baleful eyes. She picked at something
imaginary in her teeth as though she needed this preliminary
breach of good manners in order to warm herself up for the real
attack she was about to launch. The speaker became nervous, recog-
nizing she wasn't responding to his words with the customary nods
and smiles, that in fact she was grooming herself like a lioness; he
broke into a verbal run, hurtling over points, scattering notions,
hoping something might appeal to her. At last the lioness focused
on him with implacable eyes. "What rubbish," she said. "I can't
tolerate another word."

And she was off. If Daniel was around, he joined his mother
in the hunt and kill, for their love required ever new victims. If,

for instance, she'd been away for a while, they'd celebrate their reunion with a particularly bloody offering on the altar to themselves they both tended.

Daniel was—not *perfectly* aware, since the awareness was one he grasped without its ever becoming conscious—but *professionally* aware that his own position in the world depended on his mother's, and though he objected to being introduced to inconsequential strangers as her son ("Come, now, that's going too far"), he himself made certain that everyone of consequence knew whose son he was. He even inserted her family name before his own if he was writing someone celebrated. He traveled far from the center (that is, from her) in his daily wanderings, for he relished a whole range of lowlife she would have disapproved of had she known of it—a world of illegal betting and drugs and flashy women, not the nervous blondes he courted but the meatier, darker women he paid, women who took the same drugs and kept the same hours as he. In their dingy rooms in the dyers' quarter, blue with smoke, the walls hung with gypsy shawls, he looked at dishes of herring, garlic and oil without being able to eat them. He talked for hours, at last released from the necessity to seem intelligent, since these women had never heard of his mother. To them he was just another young lord, good-natured if murderously loquacious. "Give you a good workout?" was asked by one whore of another, not about Daniel's erotic performance but about his compulsion to talk. Since he couldn't sleep, he needed someone to share his vigil with. He'd lay his huge head on some woman's naked thigh or welcoming breast and ramble from one childish thought to another. Here he enjoyed at last the childhood that had been denied him.

Because Daniel was Mathilda's child, though a lordly, drawling man of thirty, he was pressed on Gabriel, who in a sense was Mateo's child. The two children must talk. Mathilda's child must take Mateo's child in hand. Daniel didn't like this turn of events. He'd always regarded Mateo as *his* father. He had always been the youngest person at his mother's receptions, thought of as a prodigy until he turned twenty, then a rake, more recently as someone who'd been interestingly ruined by his mother's brilliance, though something might still come from him. Being an only child, Daniel could scarcely think how to help someone younger and resented even the idea of this much-discussed waif. But when Daniel saw Gabriel, so pale and unappealing, so oddly turned out, so incapable of conducting his cane or saluting a lady, so countrified in his way of treating Mathilda's lapdog as an animal instead of as a sort of amative pincushion—when he saw how hopeless it all was, Daniel drew darling old Uncle Mateo aside, very man-to-clubman, and drawled, "Don't worry, old thing, I'll keep a lookout for the poor sod."

Mateo registered a tremor of anger at Daniel's condescension. But he also thought, yes, of course, Daniel will introduce the boy around, start him out on this regime of vanity and nonsense people despise only when they're removed from it through failure, sickness or distance. Daniel will be good for the boy—or bad for him, it all comes to the same thing. No matter what route we took in our youth we look back on it as the only right one to have taken. I was right to have come to the city, to have avoided the inner court, never to have married—although if I'd taken the opposite path I'd have said the same, since we judge our progress from the vantage point we arrive at only by having come this particular way.

To Mateo and Mathilda and Daniel the evening was just another at-home to be gotten through and they sighed when they saw the two servants—aided by a younger brother, always hired for such occasions but getting too chubby for his uniform—edge through the back door, smiling, with an enormous tray from the neighborhood fishmonger of raw, shucked shellfish and boiled crustaceans, all on a bed of crushed ice. Mateo could picture already the black periwinkle shells picked clean and strewn about under three inches of melted cold water, the pink crayfish shells eviscerated and tossed into actually light but seemingly massive constructions, a mandible here, there a gutted thorax poised on an everted tail, huge machines of war abandoned for lack of fuel. As the guests arrived downstairs, one could hear the musicians upstairs getting ready to perform: the unsnapping of instrument cases, the scooting closer of straight-backed chairs, the flimsier placement and replacement of metal music stands, the plucking and tuning of strings, the muffled consultation over the order of the program.

Mateo looked at the reflection of the whole party in the fogged-over panes of glass lining one wall, the abstractions the windows made of them—the image of a blue silk gown filling one square; in another, Mathilda's face, yellow and puffy when seen head-on but in the glass redeemed; in a third a half of lemon into which the snouts of seven shrimps had been stuck; in another, the glow flowing up, up above a shaded lamp crossed and crossed again by the bodies of passing guests, their faces dark except when enlightened by sparks off jewels.

One of Mateo's oldest friends, Walter, was over there talking to Mathilda, and they were both being so true to form he couldn't imagine how they could go on without laughing.

"But this boy," Walter was saying (apparently he was talking about Gabriel), "has an obvious intelligence. You can see a quick wit in those eyes, and you can sense certain profundities. His intelligence is obvious, don't you think?"

Mathilda smirked. Mateo knew that she had so little respect for Walter's own intelligence that she dismissed his evaluations of other people's minds.

"What's your sense of him?" Walter asked, a tiny bit shaken by her smirk. "Do you think he's a *good* person?"

Aha! Mateo thought, now he's cleverly shifted the talk from the metaphysics of intelligence to the mysticism of merit.

"*Very* good," Mathilda said with mock emphasis. Her smirk

had turned into the guilty grin of a kid caught eating sweets before supper. She's so honest, Mateo thought with affection, that even the white lies of social convention embarrass her.

"Yes, that's what I think," Walter declared with new gravity. "It's his *goodness* that shines forth."

Walter's anxious need to take a position on Gabriel—this shy, homely, nearly silent intruder just turned seventeen, this drowsy, suffering boy—struck Mateo as grotesque. And comic.

"But he's not very attractive, is he?" Walter added, just to prove that he'd not been taken in by Gabriel. "Believe it or not, when I was a boy, I was a stunner."

Walter continued to talk about his own good looks, although Mateo knew he'd always been homely, his skin that of the bad sort of redhead; he didn't even have the red hair that sometimes provides a ghastly recompense, the sort of hair that makes one think of a slashed wrist.

Like some transvestites who prefer to draw them in, he had no eyebrows. Had he had eyebrows they would have been raised, for his most constant expression was something between astonishment and indignation. He affected a stutter which was at once humility ("I don't want to interrupt you") and vanity ("My next thought is so important I'm obliged to demand a little silence"). The origin of his stutter (no matter what its function might have become) had been in a written description he'd once read of a great thinker's manner: "So delicate, so honest was his presentation of ideas—and above all so new—that for the first time one felt one was hearing a great mind think, even in the rigorous hesitations of his stutter."

Walter's clothes had once been convincingly academic but in recent years he'd experimented with various worldly fads. Now, out of laziness and indecision, he had reverted to his original scholarly shabbiness without recapturing any of its integrity, since his look was still awash with the flotsam of all these subsequent experiments. He was an anthology of all his earlier enthusiasms—equally true of his opinions.

In his twenties, ten years after the conquest, he'd been a fire-brand patriot. He and his schoolmates would interrupt the performance of an opera and stand up in the balcony and sing out, loud and clear, an entire verse of the suppressed national anthem before melting into the sympathetic crowd. He and his chums paid summer visits to the countryside, collected folk songs and notated the spoken dialect lest it be lost. He later joined the Septembrists, that group of religious radicals who had called for spiritual regeneration and who ascribed the present humiliation of the nation to divine punishment.

The excesses of that movement had led it to founder after the collapse of the Great Return to the People, that touching exodus of intellectuals from the capital into the fields one brief summer. With their soft hands and unskilled muscles, their love of talk and distaste for labor, the intellectuals had trooped out into the country-side, wire-rimmed spectacles glinting in the sunlight, eyes squinting, bodies and feet tightly bound in black. They had come to set out vines or take in sheaves, to share the toil of the People, those sullen subjects of so much speculation, those unwilling objects of so much contention. Within a week the noble experiment had begun to falter. Tight black lace-up shoes were found abandoned in ditches. A scarecrow would be redressed in a black velour hat or broken spectacles. The looseness of urban morals, especially the pedantic licentiousness with which the city women offered themselves to the country men, offended the peasantry. What's more, far from being loyal to the country, the peasants felt attached only to the immediate countryside. Nor did the religion of the Septembrists appeal to them, constructed as it was out of the irrational. The intellectuals kept wanting to stay up all night, drunk on love, rhetoric and wine, flushed with compassion, hands blistered, necks sunburned, but the farmers needed their sleep. Nor did the intellectuals realize they were consuming more food than they were producing until they were unexpectedly greeted not with gratitude but a bill.

A debacle, but to this day an experience Walter referred to with secret pride. Although his thought had evolved far from the mystical ecstasy of that time, Walter was still susceptible to Septembrist words and gestures, the style of hope. Now, of course, his thought (that is, his response to changes in fashion, to the nearly accidental praise and blame he'd received and most of all to the ideas of the famous people he'd chanced to meet)—his thought eschewed precisely the possibility or even the desirability of a vast, warm family of humanity. Any such universal fraternity, he now saw, was sentimental and even potentially dangerous utopianism. Now he argued that power is a pleasure, that society inevitably orders itself into a hierarchy and that any false leveling of distinctions is mischievous. All the same, after a few drinks and in the matey company of old friends, a single word could touch off in Walter a recollection of the aspirations they'd entertained so long ago. Conversely, when some young conservative, convinced by Walter's own arguments in favor of hierarchy and order, ridiculed the Septembrists, Walter grew strangely cold, drew himself up into his spencer or stalking cape or velvet dressing gown or business greys (for his costumes varied daily) and said, "It's one thing to become a pessimist, as I have, and to anguish over it as I do. It's quite another thing to exult mindlessly in these gloomy conclusions, young man. I suggest you embrace some illusions before you lose them."

All nuances were legible tonight to Mateo, since he happened to know almost everyone at Mathilda's reception. He had heard so many stories about each person that he could view everyone in relief, lit by the playing flares of gossip. For in their little world they'd made each other into local deities, each assigned one virtue and two vices, a mission and a grudge—and each was seen as having been bred out of a fantastic mismating. Though they all ridiculed each other, they still found each other imposing or fascinating, oh, quite the best man for that, no one equals her in that department.

Of Walter, for instance, whose lies generated so much outrage, they all said, "He's completely absurd and completely lovable." If an outsider chuckled over Walter's mythomania, anyone in his circle —Mateo, Mathilda, Daniel or a dozen others—could be counted on to say, "He may exaggerate, but he's unfailingly kind and generous. A fool? Perhaps. But we like him so much. He's so likable."

Whereas other people wavered in and out of focus, subject to shifts in resolution and clarity, the inner circle had stencil-black outlines. Most other coteries were below theirs, a few above, some too patriotic, others just puppet salons for the conquerors, some allied to the theater, others to the court; in some birth outweighed talent, in others money was the only entrance fee. The group around Mathilda was politically astute though inactive, endowed with the glamour of the long-past Septembrists though now anything but hopeful as to the possibility of human redemption, artistically sophisticated but unproductive, intellectual but not scholarly, greedy but not rich—middle-aged, shrewd in manipulating influence and dispensing favors, confident, complaining.

Though they all saw each other almost nightly, each denied that he was the least bit social and in any event each would have preferred belonging to a more exalted group. Walter's open house and Mathilda's musical evenings attracted each member with mechanical regularity, but since they were all individualists, uncommitted to any group and caught up by the romance of solitary pursuit (reading, writing, meditating), none would promise even an hour in advance to show up. Every appearance seemed accidental, certainly spontaneous, almost begrudged.

Now the musicians were ready. Everyone went upstairs, sweets were served and the concert began.

Gabriel found the musicians admirable. Their instruments seemed so small and breakable, but such big sounds came pouring out of them. He wondered what would happen if he scraped a bow across the strings—would the same full, plangent voice come forth?

The heat of the room, the sound of the long, low knocking radiator hissing under the built-in window seat and blasting his calves, the smell of evaporating brandy swirling around the huge snifter he held, the sight of the various preenings and posturings the audience used to demonstrate listening to music—head thrown back, eyes squinting and dimly sighting distant glitter; suppressed, seraphic smile; mad, silent chuckle, the fiendish private joke of beauty—all of these sounds, smells and sights swayed around him. Most fascinating was Walter at the piano. His nostrils flared and his breath surged dramatically, almost as though he were ill. His eyes fixed on a single point in space, and Gabriel kept trying to surprise what he was staring at. None of the other musicians, who had been hired for the evening, displayed these interesting mannerisms.

Although other people were beating time with fans or fingers, smiling placidly or frowning with exaltation, Gabriel felt ready to sink into sleep. He'd eaten only one shrimp, and it was his first. His eyes, so accustomed to the dim maid's room, hurt now from the bright lights, the smoke, the alternating blasts of heat and cold. After so many weeks of lying in the foul comfort of his bed, a whole summer of sloth, here he was, scalp stinging from the brush, his haunches hamstrung by the unfamiliar tightness of fashionable trousers.

Mathilda was eyeing him. She'd filled his glass more than once, each time caressing his elbow or knee, applying pats or pressures to each vulnerable folding joint. He felt so odd that he was convinced he must look odd, and he longed to see himself in a mirror.

After the concert was over (Gabriel couldn't believe how long it had gone on and he wondered if anyone else had noticed), everyone gathered around the musicians with refreshments and congratulations. Walter complained about his wrist, which he claimed had stiffened up, had hampered his performance of a particular triplet, but everyone assured him that only the most critical ear could have detected this fault. "No, listen," he admonished them, and he demonstrated two ways of playing the figure, and even for this briefest performance he felt obliged to dilate his nostrils, breathe noisily and fix his eyes. He sounded like a seal.

Downstairs a new group had arrived. Gabriel could hear their low, cultured voices and flights of stagey laughter. Once they'd found drinks they wound their way up the stairs. Everyone froze except Mateo, who rose and went with all the humility and simplicity of love to Edwige's side.

"I despise her," Mathilda whispered in Gabriel's ear, "as I know you must." She rolled her eyes. "I'm sure you have tales to tell, except you're far too gentlemanly. Only you country gentry know how to behave properly. In the capital it's a lost art. Just look at the four women fending for themselves at the punchbowl, the men puffing smoke into their faces, and the dear, deserving musicians ignored completely. Not that a single intellectual here knows a thing about music. Their horrible braying and whinnying, that's reserved for books and court gossip, whereas music requires a minimum of knowledge, which they can't muster. Is there anything more loathsome than an intellectual?"

Mateo (who was now leading Edwige and the other actors in her group to the window seat) had warned Gabriel about Mathilda's anti-intellectual tirades. Mateo had told the boy he must protest, insist on Mathilda's superior intelligence and the brilliance of her circle while conceding she was too good for it. But Gabriel was afraid of getting something wrong, so he just took her hand between his.

Mathilda shuddered with pleasure. Emotion made her voice go thick. A few moments later a curious patch migrated across her forehead, while a brighter rash suffused her neck just above the high-buttoned collar. Her hand felt so small and precise and boned with such fineness that Gabriel admired her for the first time as an animal. He lifted her hand, as just now he'd seen his uncle lift

Edwige's, and kissed it, his lips (in violation of the convention) actually touching her skin.

"We're providing them with enough gossip for weeks to come," Mathilda murmured. "Has your uncle been giving you lessons—no, I'm sure you could teach us all."

Yet something caused her to rise and almost stumble away from him, awkward with self-consciousness. Gabriel felt confident that he'd found the clue to her approval and that he'd have a chance to use it again. No one was as smart as Mathilda, that was obvious. Luckily, he had no points to make. By touching her, by putting their two bodies into contact, he'd shifted their exchange onto a more shadowy plain where she was less sure of herself. Most young people (there were only three others here, he noticed, two men and a woman) apparently wanted to win the attentions of older people in conversation but were unwilling to make love to them, or so Mateo had explained. "It's such a small price," he'd said, with a melancholy, sheepish smile. "It can even be an unexpected pleasure. Even if it fails, just the attempt is flattering, a little adventure, something the older person can later confess to her envious friends. It's an action, a deed, whereas hours of talk—no one at my age remembers even the most dazzling conversation. I'm not saying you're stupid, my boy, but it will be years before you can equal the splendid gab of these sumptuously silly talkers. Whereas as if you so much as kiss one woman or hold her hand, you'll have made an unforgettable impression."

After this first experience, Gabriel could see the wisdom of his uncle's advice. But Mateo might have been surprised by Gabriel's real *appetite* for pleasing others. After so much time alone—growing up in the woods or by the side of his sleeping mother, later lunging after Angelica, coupling with turbulence, finally wandering through the twilit choirs of his love for Jane Castle—after so much time alone, Gabriel hungered for society. He gathered that people feared and courted the members of Mateo's and Mathilda's circle.

Yet at the same time those who were young and attractive (attractive, apparently, because they were young) had a natural physical advantage over their elders. It seemed human flesh lost its value with age. The bargain to be struck was between young beauty and aging power; for the youths, the deal was to obtain the biggest loan of adult power in exchange for the fewest contacts with their young flesh. If Edwige was the most desired woman here (the most dismissed, despised) she'd won her eminence by becoming famous while still young and beautiful. She had brought together youth and power.

Gabriel let his eyes float over her. She was unwrapping candied chestnuts and feeding them to her friends. Mateo had seated himself on the floor at her feet with his back to her. Her hands were too sticky to touch him but from time to time she bent forward to kiss his hair. He laughed, but not with the booming splendor of his public laugh, that coloratura display so eccentric it suggested to the naïve that he was crazy but to the initiated that he was from the court or close to it, a wonderful, splashily plumed specimen from the rarest aviary. Now his smile was that tender, aching smile of the neglected child on holiday. Gabriel had never seen his uncle look so vulnerable or so sweet. In the dim maid's room, Gabriel had always imagined his uncle to be a master of women, a robust tenor overpowering the soprano, singing right into her sprayed face, his own massive chest swelling against hers, his clarion voice vibrating even in the fillings of her teeth. Heroic couplings between grimly ecstatic adults—that was what he'd imagined.

But here was the bewitching Edwige, pulsing and fading like an angel who keeps forgetting her own name, while his uncle sat at her feet with his little-boy smile molded out of pleasure and fear, his face drained of worldliness, as though worldliness had been nothing but tiny and unlikely adjustments of facial parts: a veiling of one eye, a basset-hound droop to the cheeks, a screwing up of the mouth into a blend of scorn and charm—a whole compressed poem of sprung rhythms that could be relaxed only by new and sure feeling. Sincerity took years off him.

Mathilda's son Daniel was at Gabriel's side muttering something. Bruiselike shadows gave a badger mask to Daniel's shifting gaze that looked here, there and grazed Gabriel's eyes only in passing. "Yes, Mateo is hopelessly smitten, isn't he?"

Gabriel saw Daniel's sad smile, which rhymed with the one Mateo had worn that night when he'd said to Gabriel, "It's that bad, is it? You must really love Angelica." This personal torment of love was also a worldly conspiracy, as if only gentlemen—leisured, refined, susceptible to the sadness of the floating world—could feel it and acknowledge its signs of isolation and suffering in one another.

"Of course Edwige is a beauty," Daniel continued. "Just look at her. Exquisite!" And he almost kissed his fingertips before letting his hand fade away.

Once Gabriel and his uncle had called on Edwige in her wing of their palace in the middle of the afternoon, and the boy had been kept waiting in the dark hallway while Mateo performed his commission. But through the half-open door he'd seen Edwige in her chemist's smock waving numbered strips of paper in the air amidst warm gusts of heavy scent. Later his uncle had told him she mixed her own perfumes. It was her hobby as well as part of her profession. That was why when admirers sent her flowers she gave them away to the maids almost instantly. Now, even in this crowded room swirling with smoke, food and bodies, Gabriel imagined that the rich perfume he was smelling belonged to Edwige; it was one of her finds.

"Of course she is exquisite," Gabriel said, "but is she really so much more beautiful than other women one sees on the street every day? I have an untrained eye, but I'm struck again and again by fair strangers I see in the crowd and I want to follow them. I keep wondering why they're not celebrated, sung about, written about.

Some of them are even more beautiful than Edwige. But perhaps men of fashion like to compete for the same few women, precisely because the competition vouches for their desirability. Perhaps a more spontaneous response to the beauty everywhere around us would produce some sort of social vertigo."

"Bravo, you *are* clever," Daniel drawled, "no wonder my mother dotes on you, as do I, as anyone sensible would, but eloquent as your argument is it's complete rubbish, don't you know, for just look at Edwige, not my genre, mind you, she's almost common, and strip away the clothes and those suffocating perfumes she cooks up and she'd be colorless—but as an *artifact,* damn it, she's exquisite, one in a million, inimitable."

Gabriel, who'd never in his life spoken so well or so much as now, was breathing heavily from the effort and stupefaction at his own performance of a "rhapsody."

Back at Madder Pink he never thought that just talking could count as an event. Time, talk, weather sifted over him and if one day he discovered snow on the sill or words on his lips he paid them no mind. Soon they were gone, replaced by rain and laughter or sorrow in sunlight. No history, no turning points, nothing beyond the urge to eat, couple, sleep or hee-haw. But precisely because his moods went as unnamed and unnoticed as the nervous knitting of the air, they were incomparable. He stood astride his stick horse halfway up Troublesome on a late March day and felt the wind chill him, digging through his nearly fleshless body to his bones, his chest an aeolian harp. A moment later the wind died away, the hot sun distilled its chartreuse out of last year's dead leaves and this spring's violets and chives. There was no way he could tell anyone about the exhilaration he felt when the wind blew colder and colder and then a returning concourse of wild ducks was sighted above a grey sheet of water. The birds landed in drove after drove. How could such a moment be set in a sequence beside any other? The moment, say, when he had seen the setting sun impress its seal on the tattered parchment of a birch tree. Or those stuffy, hot after-noons in the attic when his body, thrown naked, long and white on the pile of rotting silks, was scribbled all over by sunlight passing through the lists pasted on the windows.

Gabriel felt certain that here in the city there must also be just such bowered, valueless moments to be seized. He believed that every passing woman had a place and a body to offer—her own scent, even if it were just the smell of the mildewing fiber mitten beside the tub or of the angry tomcat locked behind the spare-room door. But these women (Mateo called them "these charming daughters of the people") didn't mean much to any man in Mathilda's salon because they had not found their price on the exchange.

"But I think (maybe I'm *presuming*)—" and Daniel lowered his grey, almost black lids over the badger mask of his deep-set eyes "—I presume to find in you someone who admires intellect more than glamour."

"For me the intellect *is* glamorous," Gabriel said, quoting something he had once heard Mateo announce. "I'm quite star-struck by your mother, for instance."

"Oh, really?" Daniel affected surprise. When he rested his elbow on the mantlepiece he had to lean forward. He propped his chin on his closed fist, but the angle of his own body robbed his posture of the insouciance he craved. A prop was necessary, and Daniel found one in his vest pocket: a voluminous pale grey hand-kerchief, so sheer the lights of the room shone through it. He waved the handkerchief limply about his face before letting it sag to his side, where he held it, just as one might forgetfully let a splendid bouquet of almost black red roses dangle upside down in one's hand. "Really? Mathilda?"

"But perhaps I'm annoying you by mentioning my admiration of your mother, which in any event I suppose is abstract enough." Gabriel allowed what he fancied to be a thin-lipped diplomat's smile to season his words, but since his lips were full and guileless, the smile conveyed only the simplest sweetness, which disarmed Daniel. He pulled himself up from his awkward slouch over the mantlepiece and, flinging his surprisingly heavy and nerveless arm around Gabriel's shoulder, trailed the grey gossamer of his ducal handkerchief across Gabriel's chest.

"Annoy me? Annoy me?" Daniel asked with feigned astonishment. "You could never annoy me, dear boy. And your admiration of Mathilda is only an echo of ours for you," he lowered his voice, "and for dear Mateo, of course."

Gabriel smiled at the successive explosions of innuendo, especially the way Daniel had decided to turn Gabriel's attraction to Mathilda into something safe and social by reciprocating it with the admiration of mother and son for nephew and uncle, the symmetrical acknowledgment of one domicile by another. However, Daniel's hesitation just before he mentioned Mateo had suggested what? A new downgrading of the uncle, given the nephew's sudden splendor? A rejection of Mateo from the tight little family that Daniel, Gabriel and Mathilda were about to form? Or just a frightening reminder that he, Daniel, had the power to include or exclude anyone he might choose?

What Gabriel perceived as menace was actually only Daniel's fussy little bow to respectability. Daniel was mildly shocked by the alliance that seemed to be materializing between his mother and this skinny boy. Daniel, whom Mathilda had raised to embody the respectability she never ceased yearning for yet had always been obliged to forfeit in the name of truth, had become, without her suspecting it, simply and wholly respectable. When he visited the best tailors, bought the best shoes, frequented the best wig-maker, drank the best wines and courted the best girls, he never squinted at them. All along Mathilda had been attributing the irony of the foreigner to her son; she hadn't noticed he was just another resident. To be sure, he'd picked up her tentativeness, the reluctance of the bridle-shy if avid connoisseur, but unlike her he never doubted the values of the marketplace. His manner of quizzing someone through his glass wasn't skepticism, only more arrogance.

New people came up and brought new drinks and new gossip and somehow Gabriel was revolved out from under Daniel's arm and away to the side of a tall old woman whose glasses had been spattered by a mist of white drops—dried paint, probably. She was wearing a dress of a coarse cloth striped at the hem in ocher and grey. It was the very fabric that the women in Angelica's tribe wore but Gabriel could tell that this lady—her eyes timidly questioning him from behind their wedding veil of white paint dots—wasn't a tribeswoman. Only wealth could have preserved such innocence in someone so old. He could picture the men in Angelica's tribe. There was nothing individual about their looks or ways. But in the city some rich people became more and more eccentric. They ascended the years as though they were scrambling up mountain trails, and from the highest ledge they looked out heady with innocent anticipation. Their innocence and their scruples, their shying away from every exigence kept them skittish with youth. As Gabriel talked to this old woman he kept imagining an elegant foreleg lifted high, eyes pressed back, a beautiful long face wincing as though in response to an unplaceable smell.

Gabriel surveyed the room. The skylight was patched with mist. The musicians had edged toward the door; they looked uncomfortable. They were metamorphosing back from performers to servants, but right now they were still amphibians, half guests, glasses of champagne empty in their hands and deliberately not refilled. They would surely leave if Walter weren't addressing them with such fervor. He seemed to be reliving a recital from his past, for he kept fingering the air.

Mathilda was relaxed on a sofa. She was letting two men, literally at her feet, take turns telling her stories. One of them, who sat on his heels as he listened, would rise as he spoke until he was kneeling. When silenced he deflated back onto his haunches. She looked bored. Her eyes sagged, then started roaming. Her mouth fell open and she breathed through it, asthmatic with boredom. When she caught Gabriel's eye she cocked an eyebrow and even shrugged. He was considering going over to her when some word uttered by the kneeling man, now nearly upright with speech, must have caught in the floating mesh of her attention, for like a spider she was suddenly beside him, coaxing him, prodding him with a sticky pad at the end of a jointed black leg.

When Gabriel stepped into the next room, looking for the toilet, there was Edwige, pressed against the wall, her eyes gleaming in the half-light. Yes, that powerful scent was hers.

She took his hand and led him into a small toilet filled with mirrors of every shape winking and burning on every shelf. She locked the door and bent over into the complication of her skirts like one of those performers for children who lean into a bandbox to change hats, voice and character, but when she straightened up she had shed everything.

Every inch of her body was firm and blond and young, her pelvis bones creamy under the skin as she walked toward him, the chevron of muscles between her breasts looking overdeveloped, as though her breasts (cool, cuppable, culpable) had once been heavier. With every step her shoulders twisted, mobile, the clavicles as hollow as a child's though there was nothing childlike about the impeccably waxed legs and the perversely clean cleft. She drew close and whispered, "Pull it out. Play with yourself."

She returned to her shed dress and stood beside it. She adjusted a round mirror on one shelf and cracked open a mirrored door to her right, not so that he could see her but to multiply her own reflections. Only once did she regard what he had produced at her request. She nodded approval and blew it a tiny kiss.

She entered herself with a varnished, colorless nail, then the whole, fragile finger. Two fingers, after a while. Her stance was wide. Her lower lip pouted but her face never went calm, as Angelica's would. Edwige was performing. He could see her small, almost blue lower teeth glassy in a sea of saliva. Her free hand roamed her body without purpose, smoothing her flanks, rubbing then squeezing her breasts, fluttering up to her neck like a moth to flame before tumbling and idly grazing her legs. For a moment, this hand, too, wanted to get inside her, but then it gave up and went back to her breast. She reached for a mirror on a flexible extension and pulled it out away from the wall. She angled it here and there as she observed her breasts, finally her face. A lovely side gleam floated across her skin and up the wall like the touch of someone blind. Only the fact that she turned in profile and, waving a fluent procurer's hand, sketched in with a salaam the seraglio curve of her back—only that flourish, and the fact that she was here at all, convinced Gabriel she was still aware of his presence. A drop of sweat drew a wax stroke down the lithic smoothness of her side. Her open mouth, the drop of sweat and her two sticky fingers moving in and out of her body were all that suggested an inner wetness to this dry, shapely vessel. Now her hand was crowding her nipple up toward her face, but she was looking at him. The thinnest layer of fat casing her thigh jiggled with her exertions. A wisp of her hair, gathered up off her neck, shook free and caressed her shoulders.

Gabriel was nothing but eyes on stems. He was an arrow flying toward the target she'd made of herself.

Now she appeared to be reaching a sting. Her body was coming up with jerks and spasms. As soon as they shook her she rushed to integrate them. But despite these corrective artistic measures, she was soon doubled over by the pain of pleasure. Her hair was a mess and she was panting heavily. She finished with a funny little whine that was his first clue she'd ever been a child. She leaned against the door. Her features were crumpled, her breathing rapid. The way this sexual power had shaken her free thrilled Gabriel, and it was into her dishevelment that he emptied himself, three milky arcs spurting through the air.

Gabriel rode home beside his uncle. They didn't speak but smiled politely whenever their eyes met. The city was crowded with tourists who'd come to celebrate carnival, its original religious meaning long since forgotten but the event maintained as a commodity. In the past, when the city had been powerful, all the world had been brought in to entertain the citizens; now the citizens entertained the world.

As Edwige had brushed past him, she'd murmured, "I promised your uncle I would never lay a finger on you. Nor have I," and she smiled, cryptic and malign. Gabriel wondered if he'd betrayed his uncle; more pertinently, would his uncle *think* he'd been betrayed if he found out what had happened.

Gabriel had learned that these strange encounters, when people sting one another, are the highway most people travel. Once he and Angelica had imagined they'd invented these exercises, dangerous, possibly, to their health, but now he could see they were merely universal.

Despite the guilt he felt toward his uncle, he knew that something wonderful had happened to him, but what, exactly? And he sat back in the cushions as a group of revelers, costumed in white and masked in black, held high a torch and drew a trim white donkey across the street. He imagined he saw Angelica in profile, that he glimpsed those full lips, that broad nose, that inconsequential chin, but someone stepped forward to block his view.

The interior lapsed back into obscurity and Gabriel felt very old and feeble and rich, as if he'd already led a whole life, although he was on the edge of this densely figured fabric called "life" woven, one gathered, out of the homespun of duty and pleasure's sweet silks—a flag or cloak until washed and laid out as a shroud. Perhaps the layering of this long evening, its many parts, the one shrimp downstairs and the music up, the encounters with Mathilda, Daniel, and . . . ah, but Edwige *was* incomparable, Daniel had been right.

Gabriel tried to guess what her skin must feel like, so smooth, as though pleasure were best achieved through an adult woman who has retained the glabrous purity of infancy. He almost fancied that if he kissed her infant mouth it would taste of milk.

Passing lights flared, rushed and scattered over the soft drum-roll of equally spaced streetlamps. Gabriel smiled to realize that here he was, after all, coveting Edwige, just as any beau might. Perhaps he wanted her so much because he hadn't had her yet. What drew men out through the streets and into other people's drawing rooms in search of this gyrating torment housed in a frail, amused girl?

The torment might last only a moment, but he dreamed of it as eternal. Perhaps he coveted eternity or wanted her smile, her arched eyebrow, the instant when her hair slid free of its topknot and washed over her shoulder, or then again the earlier moment when she had walked over to him (how did eternity walk?) to whisper filth in his ear.

His uncle shifted in his seat. He sat forward and a passing light shone through his ears, turning them bright red. Gabriel could see a soft halo of fuzz dusting each helix—and then the light veered off and what was left in the dark was the startling after-image of two scarlet tulips and the sound of someone sighing and sniffing, a furry, uncomfortable presence, sighing and shifting and sighing.

Gabriel recognized that his uncle doted on him. Still better, he was *known* to dote on him. They'd become an after-dinner story, one introduced just when the talk had become so scathing something sweet was needed, an entremets of charity. Gabriel suspected that this love between them was as genuine—that is, as compromised—as any other sustained feeling must be. No, they were not like a dessert but like a slightly flawed entertainment, two beasts costumed and posed in a tableau vivant for other people's edification.

Naturally, the embarrassed animals will paw at their paper crowns, refusing to cooperate.

All the same, Gabriel sighed with relief that he'd acquitted himself so well at his first reception. He smiled. "Reception" was an old-fashioned word, Mateo had told him, frowned on by the etiquette book of twenty years ago, but favored by Mathilda over "evening" precisely because the forbidding formality of the outmoded term gave her something stiff she could soften as she chose, as in the sentence: "At my receptions I like to see just a few old friends."

And here he was, entering into his uncle's world, already armed with an opinion about Mathilda, his uncle's oldest friend. He, who'd never had any friends beyond his stick horse and the neighbor boy who tooted on the clay pig, could suddenly see the charm of belonging to a "circle."

His uncle had told him how important all these people were. They were all frightfully intelligent, ambitious, hardworking; commerce, law, philosophy, history itself got shaped by this lot, but all their efforts (the growing pile of annotated books, the silent exchange of silent gold bars after the scrawl of just two initials)—all their labors must be ignored at a reception, where the professionally prepared food, the amateurishly performed music and small talk worthier of a girl's school than a great salon constituted the only three possible diversions. "After all the undesirables, unsuitables and *insortables* are sifted out," Mateo had told him, "there's nothing left to talk about; the price of exclusivity is this *punishingly* trivial tone." Of course, once a decade Mathilda might raise a hand for silence and turn to the minister of interior and ask, with immense gravity, "Sir, tell us, is the government going to fall?"

Now, in the sudden frail spume of distant fireworks, Gabriel imagined he could see such historic moments frozen in a dim flash.

His body was relaxing after the day's exertions, and he yawned wetly, hugely, until tears splashed from his eyes. But elsewhere his consciousness crackled with the minute waltz of an excitement that was nearly contentless, the merely recuperative function of an exhausted nervous system. This phantom energy—silent explosions of grey fireworks along the horizon against which whiter smoke was drifting—attached itself to Edwige, and Gabriel spun with her across marble. Or the energy raced, like digits clenching into a sum, until it caught up with Mathilda. He was holding her hand, her fine-boned hand, as her lordly son dropped his immense grey handkerchief over this scandal or sacrament . . .

The boy slumped against Mateo and dozed on his shoulder. No one had ever trusted Mateo in quite this way. He'd slept with one woman after another for more than twenty years, buried his head under slippery whore's sheets or in the fragrant linen of great ladies, reached out in the middle of the night to embrace scrawny gamines or full-fleshed matrons, awakened to hear a blackbird squawking within a cage in the maid's room or the approaching *chink-chink-chink* of embossed silverware on a tray being borne toward his regal bed by the maid herself while the only signs of the mistress (bathing behind the door) were her intermittent hum and cast-aside robe foaming over a blue chair—oh, he'd known the sleeping proximity of all these women, but with all of them he'd been as much an enemy as friend, since love does not obey the usual laws of amiability but feeds on conflict. Two lovers are never quite at peace. The world grants every woman the right to turn to her lover one evening after the guests have left and to say, "It's over. I'm afraid I no longer love you." Though he may cry and plead with her and win a week's or a year's reprieve, she has already passed sentence, no matter how long the execution is stayed.

Conversely, if a great lady takes a chemist's son on as her lover, the world may sneer at her choice, but if she persists it quickly becomes her *legitimate folly.* The circle surrounding the lady steps back half a pace so that the newcomer can wriggle in; after some shuffling the young man is absorbed. Years later, if some visiting dignitary, unfamiliar with local society, comments on the loud voice and hearty manners of the great lady's lover, people will smile and say, "Oh, he is rather impossible, isn't he, but don't we all have our *demon lovers*. And though we might hide them from the world for a while, they always insist on meeting our friends, and in the end they do."

Mateo had lived in the capital long enough now to have seen more than one demon lover emerge, in some final senile metamorphosis, as the guardian of the *gratin* against a whole new crop of parvenues. One of the most frightening men in the capital—a lion of almost ninety who might appear for a moment after the opera in his cape and boiled shirtfront surrounded by a cortege of the most famous names—this intimidating curator of exclusivity started out as a stable hand mucking out stalls. He was promoted first into the house and then into the mistress's bedroom because of his looks —especially his large hands and his slender neck sheathed in nearly translucent skin and the way his cheeks, though by no means full, shook with each step he took—a freshness made still more raffish by the precocious shadows under his clear green pupils—all of it now scoured away by time and replaced by an immense thatch of dyed eyebrows above rufous eyes in black craters and still redder cheeks rouged by broken capillaries, the horrible health of the ancient drinker. He was the vigorous old huntsman whose hangovers made him all the more irritable in his defense of social heights that he himself had scaled so arduously half a century ago and that only a few doddering wags still remembered had once towered so coolly above the lowlands of his youth—origins they cruelly alluded to when they said that if his lordship liked horses so much it was because he'd learned them from the *bottom up.*

But if all these improbable changes had been accepted because they'd been transfigured by passion, what could Mateo think of this much milder claim the sleeping boy beside him was so passively asserting? Precisely because Mateo was thought to be incapable of gaining any advantage from this alliance, the world rewarded his disinterest with a smile—but a queasy smile. For an affection that required so many sacrifices made everyone uneasy. What was Mateo getting out of it? Their praise, presumably, which they obligingly doubled, but until now Mateo had always seemed impervious to praise.

He knew he had his friends fooled or at least puzzled. And he smiled and forgot to wonder what rewards he was, in truth, seeking.

If the boy had been a girl, a pretty adolescent girl, the public response might have appeared to be the same though it would have been entirely different. People would have rushed to congratulate him on his magnanimity in order to hush amused suspicions no one dared to voice but by which everyone felt titillated. How often Mateo himself had seen a slender, long-haired daughter, her nascent breasts and chaste, athletic body veiled by the sheerest summer dress, glide up to her grizzled dad and make him wrap his hairy paw around her waist. How often Mateo had seen this moment and envied such an entirely respectable violation, one that garnered the smiles of every witness. He smiled and thought of Gabriel's Angelica . . .

But a boy? Far from being a consolation, a boy could only be competition.

The boy, shuddering from the evening's exertion, twitched and threw his head back slightly. Examining this face, which he was looking at upside down, Mateo was struck by how ugly and vigorous the boy was. The character lines bracketing his mouth were deep and looked soiled. His forehead was greasy and picked up the passing lights. His lips were full, almost pulpy, but seen from this angle they looked disagreeably sexual. Now his lips were moving. He was muttering something and he was sticking his face fractionally forward. He looked like one of those boys from the Field of Flowers who get into violent arguments with customers. Usually Gabriel wore as meek an expression as possible around his uncle, but occasionally Mateo caught a glimpse of the true hostility within this stranger. Mateo liked having an influence over other people, he enjoyed the game of trading favors and coercing courtesies, but tyranny dismayed him because he kept vividly imagining the rancor that must be below his vassal's servility. With Mateo his nephew played the boy, but as the jutting, ugly mug suggested, Gabriel was already a man—a striving, tormented man.

If Mateo wandered into Gabriel's empty rooms—the squalid maid's room on the airshaft, not the soaring pink chamber on the canal side of the palace—he picked his way through the cast-off clothes, the cast-back sheets, the downcast gloom of such intense sexual loneliness. If two men are not lovers, they can only acknowledge each other's yearning with embarrassment and confusion; and if real tenderness forbids shrugging off someone else's need, then one can only pace around outside the barred door, ready to knock but unwilling to enter.

But of course the boy was competent to satisfy his own longings. He was thriving like a weed in Mateo's hothouse. Now he was breathing with his mouth open, but more penetrating than the smells of wine and shrimp and a garlicky pâté in his mouth was the cold lakewater smell of someone young and healthy. At times when Mateo heard the boy urinating he envied him the force of his piss. To the boy, pissing was surely nothing, just one more dull mystery, but to Mateo, listening, it was the sound of animal vitality.

Not that the boy actually had much energy. If Mateo dragged him around town—in and out of the noisy, jostling carnival crowds, through treeless squares in which human voices took on a hollow ring, deep into the oldest, narrowest streets over which tall, mean houses hunched, shouldering out the light—two or three hours later the boy would be exhausted from their threading their way around dawdlers, over bridges and down passageways too narrow for a couple to walk abreast, into shops or upstairs to ancient warehouses or down into cellars recently whitewashed and tricked out to appear "amusing," although the smell of backed-up drains and the inexplicable crepitations of beams five hundred years old undermined any attempt at trendiness, in the same way as a tart's dead eyes betray her stylish scarf. But the boy's very weakness only threw his deeper health into relief. Gabriel pushed his vegetables aside, drank too much of the Mandarin liqueur, never breathed fresh air, but even so this weedy exuberance had made him sprout an inch taller in six months, forced the urine out of his body in an urgent jet and gave an achingly straightforward vibrato to his low tenor voice. And this fresh smell of cold lakewater to his very breath.

Mateo had always looked young for his years, or so people had said, partly because they liked him and honesty forbade them from finding him handsome. More concretely and believably, over the years many different women quite independently had told him what smooth skin he had. "It's like a woman's," one would remark with envy, even reproach, as though his skin were unattractively narcissistic. He would touch his own back or stomach or chest but he could never feel what they were feeling. He was doomed to find himself real and thrilling only in a woman's arms. He could seldom stay hard while masturbating alone, yet everything in him sprang alert to the touch of a woman—almost any woman.

Then one day the women had stopped mentioning his smooth skin (he'd been thirty-three or thirty-four), but he hadn't noticed the absence of the compliment, which in any event had always perplexed him, until some time had gone by. Then he'd rubbed his hands over his body, but he hadn't been able to detect a difference. He'd shrugged.

He started to notice other slow changes. The hairs on his chest became more numerous and grew longer, then some turned white. When he let his beard grow in, it came in ginger, black and white. His eyebrows grew longer and assumed crazy windswept postures; finally he started trimming them. The hairs inside his nostrils began to poke outside and he trimmed them. One horrible day he discovered a light sprinkling of hair on his shoulders. Another day Edwige said, with open disgust, "It's ridiculous bothering to groom yourself at all when you insist on letting those hairs in your ears sprout like that."

Her disgust echoed his shame, for he felt ashamed of every sign of age. Young men he was introduced to started calling him "sir." The lines around his mouth became so deep that when he shaved he had to put his tongue in his cheek so that his razor could reach whiskers in each furrow. Although he'd often slept with women his mother's age when he had been just a boy, he'd done so as a bright rose chevalier, an emissary from a world all silver, and in bed he'd enjoyed the uncomfortable pleasure of admiring himself through their adoring eyes. Since, however, he preferred adoring to being adored, he preferred girls his own age and, as he aged, he courted girls who were younger, much younger, finally young.

He'd always regarded old men with disgust. In his twenties he'd announced to everyone he was terrified of growing old, but he was so obsessed with this eventuality when he was still so ridiculously young that his friends assured him he was just making up things to worry about—and their assurance, offered so often, had at last convinced him he'd never grow old. This exaggeration of his misgiving had inoculated him against his fears. Once he became immune to age he began to see old men as morally deformed, as a race apart, and their age as a punishment for their flaws—lack of charity, sympathy, optimism, fairness or enthusiasm. "Look at that old fool," he'd mutter with real scorn, and he relished the giggles or sneers of his young friends who, like him, became indignant at the impertinence of an old fool even daring to enter their presence. Conversely, "young" was an accolade. "He's a fine young architect who is having problems finding acceptance" or "Young people today are no longer taken in by that sort of bunk" were typical sentences he uttered.

But this strategy of scorn didn't work for long. By his late twenties he was imagining his youth would end in his thirties, and he sought, with intermittent panic, to find someone with whom to spend the remainder of his days, the grey remainder. This notion of marriage as an expedient against the loneliness of old age was desperate enough to attract him—and to repel him. No wonder he'd never married. Now, of course, he smiled at his assumptions that had sustained this "catafalque" view of matrimony. Now he could see that people didn't stay sealed in marriage, embalmed for eternity; they drifted in and out of it, and even well within it they knew more turbulence than peace. Marriage wasn't a tomb but a limed, noisy dovecote.

Nor were old people content to lie beside each other every night. The old, especially old men, longed for the young, for young female flesh, which they approached with reverence when permitted to, and with rage or crass bartering lust when pushed away. Old lovers deserted each other through death or disease or strange visitations of folly, divisive new pursuits, or the driven whim to travel, to travel, to travel to ever more exotic places, as though if only they moved fast enough they'd make time run backwards and they'd grow younger. They entered temples or took up new languages, wore green beads over their shoulder-length grey hair, moved with suspensefully slow stealth to the dull chiming of stone bells in public parks. Or they stayed together and ate each other alive, their senile rancor more gripping than any pleasure. No one younger knew what they were quarreling about, and this failure to comprehend robbed the young of all interest. Day after day the ancient warriors screwed on their rusty armor and crossed the same dull blades. Such familiar rage exhilarated them to the point where they felt immense and didn't notice how age had belittled them.

Or they stayed together because they had nowhere else to go, and, besides, their children expected them to, needed them to maintain constancy; without it, the children's prospects of their own old age would have become too distressing and they wouldn't have had the heart to go on. But becalmed, disabused, the old woman privately looked at her old man with complete comprehension and no sympathy.

Mateo could find no consolation in age beyond the occasional example of someone old who'd willed himself into furious optimism. The blearing eyes of the old, their failing memories, their spotted hands—oh, but all of these losses were already happening to him, as the dark wave hangs over the swimmer; his own night vision was going quickly, his memory for names was fading, the freckles that had appeared on his hands last summer hadn't faded. His weight had always gone up and down but now he suspected it would stay up until that final dwindling. He often thought these days of how he'd look if he were a savage without ways to groom himself, repair himself: toothless, covered with white hairs, cicatrized with scars of every disease he'd ever had. He knew he'd be, a few days after death, a repulsive corpse, for without his false front teeth, without his fashionable coiffure, without the constant trimming and shaping of all these suffocating hairs and nails, without these tailored jackets that gave him shoulders and a waist, after a week of neglect in the grave he'd exhale at last the putrefaction he'd always known was within him.

Far from diminishing, his lust was growing every year. Not exactly a physical pressure in his groin, if that's what people meant by "lust" (the word confused him as all simple words did), but a craving for (yes, that very same old man's craving for) young flesh. Each embrace, he told himself, might be the last. He was on the point of undergoing exile into that other tribe, the lesser one, the old. One more night of love, which he'd approached hesitantly, gratefully, shamed, and which he'd consummated in triumph, his confidence momentarily restored, his body touched by youth, redeemed by it, explored, affirmed—one more night of love had been granted him. Once more he'd hoodwinked a young woman into thinking he was suitable, even a catch, a member of her own tribe, not a pitiful refugee from the other side; her gift had not been given him out of charity.

But it was a gift he needed more and more often, to the point that his scheming to get it proved to him he really was now on the other side. At a party, when the girl of the moment slipped away, he'd exchange a cold glance with another aging beau. He'd inventory his rival's assets and defects—how thick his hair, how thick his waist—not with a half-humorous admission of their shared predicament but with enmity. When she returned they, the two old parties, would resume their bantering, but only as a way to keep her entertained. They tacitly acknowledged that a staged but affable conversation would display them at their best to her.

He recognized that some of these girls resented him when he wouldn't play the disinterested father and listen to their problems, fan their aspirations, and demand nothing in return. But they didn't understand that he hadn't achieved the neutered serenity they attributed to him. The paternal palm placed on the juvenile thigh was itching. The young assumed desire died by middle age except among the perverted few. They were disgusted by advances from their elders as though to cross the generations were a form of bestiality. "After all, they *have* each other," as the young said (as Mateo had once said).

But Mateo, when happy, still felt young and after a long drunken evening with a young woman he'd mold out of her smiles and nods a new young face for himself. He'd become her ideal if somewhat sketchy companion, a shadow in evening clothes, a slice of white smile in a face nearly featureless. Her very exuberance tonight (quite genuine it seemed) established his own worthiness, for just as a great ballerina can only execute her meditative, cantilevered adagio when supported by a self-effacing partner, so this girl's thoughtless smile could be elicited only by a man as young and nearly as handsome as she—true or not?

And then, by accident, he'd glance at himself in a mirror, the haggard, rumpled face, the belly a comfortable, shaming slope, the attentiveness he was giving her more like drooling than courtship. This rude reminder disqualified not the genuineness of the girl's enthusiasm for him but her taste. Or he felt again he'd played the eloquent impostor. Couldn't she tell that the world assumed her only motive for being with him must be money?

He even preferred it when he knew a girl did hope to gain something from him, for then he could take comfort in the candor of her duplicity. Otherwise he kept wondering when she'd become disabused of whatever illusions had made her find him attractive. Not that he had any money to proffer, but he did have favors to bestow. A straightforward trade of influence for intimacy was worldly, fair, even (if seen in the right light) cheerful. And he was scrupulous about fulfilling his promises. But even in such transactions he wondered how She, the Eternal Whoever, saw him. The next day did she sigh and say to a girlfriend, "Not half as bad as I'd feared"? Or did she say, *"Damn,* but it was gruesome, not worth whatever the old bird may or may not cook up"?

And even these fears were prophylactic, he had to admit, for he knew perfectly well women still loved him. Not one he desired desired him at first glance, perhaps, but women weren't that way in any event. "If you let a man, well, *in* you," one of them had explained, "that's no joke, you have to trust him. As much for your health as for your heart. And remember, sperm are cheap but eggs are dear." And she went on with bits of biology, all perfectly true, but no woman thought of them when seized by passion. Yet they were tender vessels, women, easily broken, that seemed evident. Could they tell right away that he knew how to handle them?

And this lick-lipping, suffering, sleeping boy on his shoulder, would they love him, too? Would this big nerveless hand, flung like something dead on the seat between them, find its way into vessel after fragile vessel? For that was the amazing thing, these women who seemed so superior, so much cleaner and cleverer than men, these women whose hair was shinier, whose skin was softer, whose wits were sharper, who seemed so self-sufficient—they did let these men into them and into their narrow beds with the ironed white cotton sheets, and not out of compassion but passion. They love us and seem to need us. He thought of Angelica again and smiled.

Once Mateo had dozed off in a compartment across from two women, his mistress of the time and her friend. As he lurched into and out of sleep, he half glimpsed them nestling together, chattering and laughing, and he sank blissfully into the downy warmth of being with such admirably *prepared* creatures. One of them sneezed a tiny sneeze, and the other produced a clean white hanky that her friend pressed to those slightly inflamed, nearly translucent nostrils, that narrow and perfectly straight nose generations of brutal male ancestors had bred for by selecting small-featured wives. Later they seemed to be talking about the tribes; one of them hummed a snatch of folk music with scholarly attention to detail. Perhaps she'd been a Septembrist, yes, that must be it. Recipes, politics, the way to revive old sachets, coming musical events—they were so at home in the world, almost as though they were adequate to it.

If there were any wisdom (and there isn't—there's everything and nothing to be learned) it would consist of learning to fall freely. For we are in full, flaming descent, but we move so slowly we imagine we can hold on to certain things (at least this friend, at least this moment). If we fell faster we'd call out in panic. But our speed is slow if constant and some things and people are falling at the same rate; relative to them we don't seem to be moving at all. But then something we are holding (as Mateo was holding his sleeping nephew) accelerates and slides out of our grasp—and suddenly we glimpse blackest, rushing night through the gap.

For Mateo, the trip back to Madder Pink had opened just such a gap—but now the boy, still asleep, was stirring, he was grinning (Mateo saw the smile upside down) and he was murmuring something, a name: "Edwige."

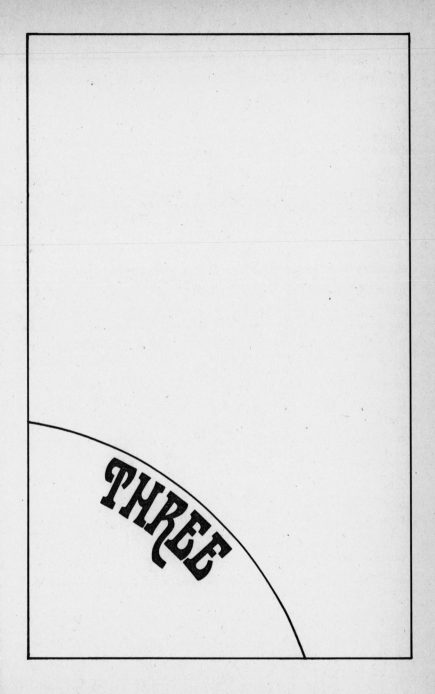

THREE

**G**ABRIEL became Mathilda's lover. From his first meeting with her he'd understood that she wanted him, and her interest in him so flattered him he assumed he must want her as well.

Two months after the first reception he'd attended, she invited him to her house by the sea, a vast rectangle on a hill above a small harbor town. They traveled four days, directly south, to reach it. Halfway there Mathilda said, "If we went inland here we'd arrive at Madder Pink." Gabriel felt an anxious urge to flee, to fly to his mother's side. The next day they passed through the swampy lowlands where the tribes had originated. He wondered if Angelica had returned to her birthplace. Then they entered another country, once a colony of the capital, now, of course, ruled by the conquerors.

Although winter had already come to the capital, here it was still, eternally, summer. The rooms, closely shuttered against the afternoon sun, were appealing because of their sumptuousness and comfort, but Mathilda justified the luxury by discussing her house as though it were a museum. Every chair was different, each wood back carved by a different folk artist in a slightly different style. Some of the furniture was antique, as were many of the rugs scattered everywhere about, one oxblood and covered with seablue flowers, another with faded red grapes on green vines. She told him the story of each rug and each chair with such vehemence that he concluded her wealth embarrassed her. She had to pass off its rewards as research.

She was nearly as tall as he, much older, richer and more intelligent but also lonely and craving intimacy. In the late afternoon, after she'd exhausted herself talking and explaining, he suggested they take a nap. Swifts were piping in flight outside the high windows; their cries were circling, careening closer, then veering away. The geranium-filled courtyard below baked in the sun, as he could see through the tilted slats. She nodded and even blushed. He found a blush strange in such a great lady.

His uncle had advised him to take his time in all the unfamiliar maneuvers of love. "Move slowly," he'd said, "do everything with deliberation. If you don't know what to do, do nothing. If you lunge about it's always a failure."

Gabriel took off his shoes and stretched out fully dressed on the bed. Mathilda seemed timid. She didn't speak a word, though several times her face lit up and her lips parted, but no sound came out. A red patch migrated across her face. She lay beside him on the bed. Far below, waves broke on rocks and sizzled up the beach. She stood and paced to the window and looked down at the courtyard. Light cast horizontal lines across her breasts, which were rising and falling rapidly. She left the room and was gone a long time.

When she returned she paused by the door, her face somehow

lengthened, as though reflected in the long narrow back of a spoon. Her voice was pinched as she said, "Don't feel obliged to pay court to me. Think of me as a friend."

"Come here."

"What?"

"Come here, lie down beside me."

She did, looking as though she'd been pushed out on stage without knowing her lines. He kissed her and tasted a bitter, copper taste in her mouth and found her awkwardly large in his arms. She was also sticky with sweat.

"No, I must bathe," she whispered. "The trip, the dust, I'm not, ha! prepared."

And Gabriel, who'd been so awed by this lady, knew she meant, "I'm not good enough." He could hear her saying the words inside her brain; they were just as distinct as if she'd said them out loud. Many times at her receptions or over dinner, he'd felt he could read her mind. The words she was *saying* were richly and surprisingly scored, made intricate by the elisions and shocking reversals of her thought, but her feelings were supremely simple. Sometimes she thought: "You're not worthy of me." Once when he confided his impressions to his uncle, Mateo said, "Whether she thinks you're worthy or not, the fact she's measuring you at all reveals her interest."

Now he undressed her and he could hear her nearly simultaneous hope and shame circling and shrilling in her brain like the swifts. Her very eagerness excited him, as though he were a surgeon undressing a wound. The part of his mind that remembered she was his uncle's friend clouded over, while that part brightened that found her to be a path leading him on. He sensed that she didn't want to look at his body or have him look at hers. To be sure, she wanted to feel everything he might excite within her body, but she wanted only to kiss him and stare into his eyes, even to caress his cheeks with her palms, as though to concentrate their gaze.

All right. He understood. This would be the usual in-and-out but they'd pretend it was mental telepathy, the communion of discarnate souls. The idea made him smile a lopsided smile, which she picked up; she kissed his smile with a feverish burst of energy. Outside birdsong traced pastry-tube spirals up and down the tiers of air. When she fell asleep, he pulled back the sheet and studied her body. Her nipples were bigger and darker than his mother's and the hair crept farther up her belly. Where her hip had been crushed in the fall from her horse so many years ago the skin looked as though it were covered with white silk floss—the scar tissue. In clothes she looked fat, but naked she had the grandeur of a goddess.

They spent a week alone. She changed completely around him. She became at once his mother, cooking for him, washing his clothes, and his child, letting him tell her things. At night, late at night, they became children together, laughing and running along the beach under a moonless and starless sky so clouded over that the surf registered only as a shock in the sand and a warm flash of foam bathing their feet. In the distance they could see the curiously ecclesiastical lighthouse built two hundred years ago by an architect who'd only done churches up to then; it didn't revolve a lamp but rather stood, brilliantly floodlit itself, like the last chesspiece on the board.

She liked to watch him as he performed his little afternoon rituals—the way he brewed his tea, poured it out, and carried it up to the roof with his strangely awkward movements. He touched everything a bit gently, as though he feared breaking something. And he walked across floors as though they were very slippery.

Mathilda burned after ten minutes in the tropical sun, but she exposed herself to its rays daily as if swallowing a nasty but necessary medicine. Her hair lightened and in the dark she looked more than ever like the goddess of wisdom whose chief attribute, her intelligence, must be visible to the faithful, capped by a copper dome. The sea breezes and waters washed away the stale smell of study and talk and misted her over with salt. He nibbled at her ear and tasted the salt. He liked the fresh taste of salt. One day they lay on the roof, which was pierced by two chimney pots, beige clay tunnels wearing grey clay pots. The swifts hurtled past in full cry. He felt that he, too, was growing more handsome, at least stronger and healthier.

She told him about all the other, earlier men in her life. "With someone as young as you are," she said, "I should cut my list in half. You have no idea how *long* these years have been."

Gabriel, who never thought about age, only power, was mystified by her smiling but pained deference to his youth. Once again it occurred to him that youth might count as a kind of power.

She smiled; she was relishing the poetry of playing the older woman. She wasn't slightly, embarrassingly older than Gabriel; she was profoundly older. She seemed to enjoy her mastery over him.

One afternoon, as she was still undressing, he flung himself naked back onto the bed and said, "Why don't you rape me?"

"What? What did you say?" she asked, chuckling, her questioning tone incredulous and amused.

"Rape me. I've always wanted a woman to rape me. I won't move at all. I'll just lie here. Tie me up if you want to."

"No," she said, still smiling but her pupils contracting with excitement and her full dark nipples stiffening, "I'll hold your wrists."

He couldn't resist bracing his feet against the floor and pushing, squeezing up into her, but his efforts were as minimal as he could manage. She was flying over his body like death floating a shroud over the wounded soldier, her eyes luminous, proprietary. Or he was the white slave boy and she the dusky empress, sovereign over this slender, helpless harem of one. He imagined barebreasted female janissaries peeping out at them through palm fronds, and that excited him too.

As the days went by his very specific sexual requests pleased her, gave her instructions to which she could comply, and directed her attention for the first time in her life to the simple mechanics of making love. No longer was love-making an exalted form of speechless speech. Now she could look at what they were doing. She could impersonate his fantasies and receive his praise for her performance. What else in her *could* he praise without seeming impertinent? And she, who had everything to give him, had felt until now that he wanted nothing or that he didn't know enough to appreciate what she owned.

The swifts one evening sounded as though they were taunting each other across the courtyard, lined up into two teams, loud, louder, followed by a dwindling away to a single soft voice—and then the full heroic chorus once more. All day Gabriel and Mathilda had lain on the roof of the palace. Both of them had gleamed and sweated and smiled, eyes closed into the cloudless sky. They looked like votary figurines dipped in silver and set out to dry.

Mathilda told him the story of her life. Since she was such a celebrated woman, since her political and intellectual views had made her the "conscience of her generation" (Walter's epithet), Gabriel thought that later, possibly, he could turn her confidences into electrifying gossip.

Not that she herself was free of calculation. Unsure of her personal appeal, as though her charm were too close to see, she had to focus on the more distant powers she wielded. One evening, after a supper she'd made and they'd eaten alone in the high-ceilinged kitchen, Gabriel fell silent. He was melancholy. The kitchen made him think of Madder Pink, which in turn reminded him of his mother.

His silence alarmed Mathilda. She thought he was bored with her. She'd been wrong to love a boy who could scarcely read. He'd come here with her because his uncle had ordered him to. He didn't even like her. She was, no doubt, a tedious old bore in his eyes.

And she stood and paced through the whole habitable floor of the palace, touching the curious mystical beasts carved on a stone cathedra, straightening a carpet the wind had flipped back, trying to calm her panic. For she had seldom let herself love anyone and had assumed she was inoculated against any new outbreak of passion. But Gabriel had reached her through an unexpected approach —her sense of family loyalty. She had a very small family that was, moreover, so unworthy of her as to make her own brilliance appear self-created. She'd had to fashion a larger, better family of friends for herself, and amongst them Mateo had long ago become her brother. A rather incestuous brother, at the beginning, though now they were more rivals than lovers. Gabriel, by extension, was her nephew, a homely, almost illiterate nephew who seemed, however, quick-witted enough. True, he wasn't handsome, but his eyes appeared to drink in everything. He also had an utterly irrational "remainder" of sexuality, as one might say of what's left over after any proper figuring has been done. Gabriel should be afraid of her, and he clearly was, yet even that first day when she'd met him, he'd presented her with the stiff fold in his new trousers, which he'd pushed toward her as he stood beside her chair. Now, although he cringed and nodded and pretended to endorse remarks he couldn't fathom, he nevertheless had a sexual confidence that couldn't be factored in. Perhaps confidence wasn't the right word, since confidence can be diminished.

She pictured him pawing his food into his mouth. Imagining this humble act moved her, drove her back to the open doorway. She leaned against an upright of the frame; he was still sitting at the table. He had tears in his eyes. He lowered his head. The tears flowed quietly down and fell in drops from his nose. He wasn't sobbing. His body wasn't shaking. The tears were just dripping hotly.

She imagined wrongly that she was the cause of his tears. Although she was overcome by remorse she also crowed mentally over this proof of her power. He loved her. She'd wounded him. She'd make it up to him.

She sat beside him and held his limp, hot hand, but she couldn't make him look at her. She wiped his eyes with her handkerchief, but these silent, hot tears were unstanchable.

His silent tears made her believe he was the loneliest boy in the world. She believed that she could console him. She alone could dry his eyes by turning off the secret spigots of his bitter heart. "Oh, Gabriel," she whispered, her hand resting on his shoulder, still so slight, the slight shoulder of a boy not yet fully grown.

And she whispered a litany of all the things he meant to her and all the things she could do for him. "You may not know it, but I'm very powerful. Even the court fears me. No matter what your ambitions are, I can help you realize them. Trust me."

He was deep in the cave of his isolation, listening but incapable of speech. If he'd been able he would have assured her she had nothing to do with his grief.

Mathilda said, "I know you must feel overwhelmed by this world you've been dragged into, but just give me the chance to help you. You've given me the gift of your completely innocent trust; I'll give you fame and power—and my love, too, if you want it."

Her heart sang out the words as her lips pronounced them. Irony, spleen, arrogance, doubt and contempt had been the pentatonic scale she habitually thought in, but the eloquence of love had devised a new mode for her.

Back in the city Gabriel spent more and more time with Mathilda. He'd always assumed he had no ambitions except to fill his stomach and sleep in a warm place and feel himself inside a woman. Now he was forced to recognize an urge in himself to risk whatever he might have gained. He became more and more nervous, and though Mathilda fussed over his skinniness, the dryness of his skin and hair and the circles under his eyes, he sat up later and later drinking with Daniel or roaming the great dimmed metropolis. He could never finish a meal. He could scarcely sit through a conversation. From Daniel he learned new bad habits of condescension so at odds with the politeness his uncle practiced.

From a curious angle of vision Gabriel observed that his very irritability made Mathilda love him all the more. She called him her "porcupine," an allusion to the jabs he gave everyone, and soon enough this name she shortened to "Pine," and eventually formalized into "Mr. Pine," as though to complement her way of calling Daniel "The Darling"—the only two bits of coyness in an otherwise uniformly saturnine nature.

One reckless sycophant (and there were always new ones courting Mathilda) overheard the nickname and even pretended to have read the "works" of "Mr. Pine," a remark that assumed she knew no one but brevetted thinkers such as Walter, men who produced "works" that essayed a grave reexamination of a universal ("Man," "The Good," "Justice") and that began with a deliberate misreading of a classic and arrived through a turmoil of paradoxes at a respectably despondent conclusion, one that stood out as "mature" when seen against the glittery optimism the author had professed in his youth and still secretly hoarded.

Suddenly Gabriel could better understand why Daniel had never broken with Mathilda. When they all three went to the opera, everyone looked at them, exactly as though they were the performers. Although the audience comprised primarily the conquerors and their collaborators, Mathilda justified her thrice-weekly attendance on the grounds that opera was the highest form of their own culture and a sort of tinderbox in which the coals of rebellion were being blown into glowing life. Daniel snickered openly at what he dubbed the "tinderbox alibi."

Gabriel couldn't grasp the issues and anyway sensed every position was irrelevant in the face of a tyranny as absolute as it was agreeable. Revolutionary fervor struck him as simply a hostage to a bad conscience and a substitute for a rebellion the poor were too feeble to organize and the rich too compromised to lead. When Walter or Mathilda or Daniel started staking out political positions for themselves, Gabriel yawned. He considered this activity to be empty, late-night oratory, a mock dispute whose only function was to test and strengthen the coherence of their friendships: moral fire drill.

But what was much more real, though never mentioned except in unconvincing complaints, was the stir Mathilda and Daniel created wherever they went. Why didn't they talk about the coup of a dazzling entrance at the opera, about the politics of a bow, the strategy of politesse, the tactics of the nod, the ostracism of a conspicuous cut during the interval, or, conversely, the first intimations of peace suggested by the raised lorgnette? That was all the power they knew or could exercise, perhaps the only power concrete enough to be exercised voluntarily by any individual.

Three nights a week Mathilda, Daniel and Gabriel attended the opera, shown to their box by an usherette who, under the new rules, had shed her uniform for a tailored black dress. After she unlocked the box with the key dangling from her belt, she always refused a tip with a smile and the inscrutable comment, "There is no service," a formula that made no immediate sense but that apparently elevated her to the dignity of a hostess or state functionary. Mathilda liked to arrive early, a habit she ascribed to her "bourgeois anxiety" over punctuality precisely because the splendor of her jewels, the commanding position of her box and the number and quality of the bows she collected from the stalls proved her rank to be far higher. To confess to "bourgeois anxiety" hinted at an appealing modesty—and concealed her real motive, which was to see and be seen. Although she presented herself as a withdrawn, morose intellectual, she had an infallible sense of theater.

Tonight Walter had seated himself beside Mathilda while Daniel and Gabriel stood behind their chairs. The "boys" (for Mathilda called them "my boys") were both elegant in the latest mode. Now that Daniel had taken him to his tailor and *chemisier,* Gabriel could recognize how dowdy his uncle looked and how absurd he himself must have appeared at that first reception last fall. Indeed his uncle no longer counted much for Gabriel. Mateo sped here and there, calling on old dowagers (including some of the most eminent) and he was known to have bedded a few of the great beauties of his generation and the next. But where exactly did he rank?

Everyone agreed Mateo had superb manners, but courtesy rendered so unfailingly seemed more a compulsion than an honor. Once Mathilda remarked to Gabriel in the curtained secrecy of their bed, "If your uncle ever discovers the nature of his crime, he'll become monstrously rude." She portrayed him as someone so hounded by an inexplicable need to make it up to everyone that he'd ended by displaying a suspect courtesy matched only by his suspect compassion. "Not that I'm suggesting his virtues are vices. I'm just saying they're not uncaused. Maybe that's what charm is. After all, he's the most charming man alive."

The charm didn't bewitch everyone. To some people he seemed meddling. Worse, his clothes and quarters were shoddy, his "evenings" overattended and understaffed, his conversation too full of schemes, connections, bargains and, above all, effort. Since he liked everyone, he invited everyone, on the utopian theory that the lion would lie down or at least drink cocktails with the lamb. Guilt and poverty made him not nearly exclusive enough. The richer, more capricious people whom Gabriel was meeting through Daniel smiled weakly whenever Mateo's name was mentioned. Once Gabriel overheard his uncle explaining some bright new undertaking to a titled dandy Mateo had accosted just as he was leaving a shop. Although they'd been introduced several times, they didn't really know each other. Now Mateo feverishly presented his proposal, but out of nervousness he blustered and resorted to so much deference he gave the paradoxical effect of seeming condescending. At last the young lord simply shook his head, vexed and bored, and said, almost sadly, "Oh, Mateo," and hurried away. If only, Gabriel thought, Mateo were as slow and deliberate in conversation as he tells me I should be in bed, then his words, so often dismissed as chatter, would reveal their true intelligence. All he lacks is gravity. His terror of boring people has made him seem silly.

As he surveyed the audience from Mathilda's box, Gabriel wondered what would happen if he saw Angelica here. What if she, too, had acquired a soul since their last encounter?

For Gabriel was so ashamed of his half-savage past at Madder Pink, the nearly pulseless stupor of so many years, that he despised Angelica, too, just a bit. He felt that since then he had been instilled with a soul, and it was this soul, like a swallowed reducing worm, that was making him nervous, skinny, difficult. He liked being difficult. He wanted to be a knife cutting through the soft butter in his sleepy head.

And Angelica? He imagined he saw her dusky face and black hair and brown shoulders, square emeralds traced in diamonds choking her neck like a terrible punishment reserved for royalty. She vanished, and he didn't see her again. If he found Angelica, she might be the same furry brown animal as before. Or, just possibly, she might have evolved as rapidly as he. Now the lights were dimming and the hall with its many tiers was illuminated (in that second before the curtain went up) only by the pale blue windows inset into the doors of each box and by the glow swimming up off the orchestra pit like the effulgence of drowned treasure.

Mathilda felt Gabriel's hand warm with youth on her shoulder and she liked this moment of complicity. She looked over her shoulder and smiled, but she was shocked by the glimpse she caught of the boy's haggard face with its skull-like thinness and cratered skin and the deep lines around his mouth. He was aging so rapidly that soon they'd be contemporaries, she thought with nasty satisfaction. When he was naked his skinny boy's body was mismatched with an old man's head. His body was truly young, his legs and chest were still hairless and his pelvic bones too prominent and wide for the emaciated torso growing up out of them like the first shoot from a buried bulb. And then, above, was the incongruous face so deeply lined with character and suffering, a face almost comic with suffering.

All the better, she thought, smiling. If he was dashing, then other, younger girls would take him away from me and I'd have to kill him. And she smiled at this thought in turn, for she was such a literary creature that most of her experience had been lived through characters in books or on stage, tragic vivid beings whose strong emotions she'd avoided out of fear of plagiarism. And yet she'd learned and felt everything either in violent novels or through still more violent operas; the only emotions she could name, recognize and reproduce were the violent ones. As a result, she smiled ironically or with embarrassment at all her impulses toward expression, but there was no impulse that wasn't operatic in its irrationality and grandeur. When other people perceived her as being guarded, even sour, they mistook her choking back of instinct as contempt for instinct. All she truly condemned were murky or dilute feelings; the great, rare feelings she believed she'd release some day, some day.

And she lifted Gabriel's hand from her shoulder and kissed it fervently just as the curtain rose with a force that fluttered the paper blossoms glued to the unnaturally smooth tree on stage. The stalls were irrigated with spilled light. She felt that this half-educated irritable boy behind her with the voracious sexual appetite and bizarrely earthy sexual manners was, well, a genius, yes, some sort of genius.

She could already picture him ten years from now in his study, the oriental carpet littered with books, papers and a jumble of flaking casts from the antique, the air almost poisonous with tobacco smoke and dust, the intoxicatingly unhealthy smell of mental labor. In a corner, wearing a stained flannel dressing gown, his head wrapped in a turban caked with unguents, there would be her genius, reading, reading in the dim light, irrigating the furrows of his rich mind with the spilled light of the ages. She'd be somewhere nearby. Yes, they'd be living in her mansion above the harbor, where the conquerors would have exiled them for sedition. At last she'd be rid of the curse of worldliness which she'd always worn as unhappily as a falcon wears its leather hood. She and Gabriel (the soprano's voice was floating higher and softer above the agitated strings) would be exiled lovers, doubly exiled since they'd remain aloof even from the villagers, since they'd turn night into day and keep their hilltop mansion ablaze all night as they pursued their studies, their mental labor. If they staggered down the hill for a visit one evening, the old village women, sitting on their balconies, would cluck their tongues in disapproval of these pale, ugly, almost dirty foreigners blinking behind green wire-rimmed spectacles, their appearance the result of neglect, peculiar health fads and exhaustion.

If Gabriel had been handsome, Mathilda thought, he would have become a fool, exposed as he most certainly would have been to the world's blandishments. The tenor had entered. The overhead lights caused his body to cast a shadow the shape of a wishbone.

The thought of Gabriel's abandoning her awakened a murderous rage within Mathilda. If emotions were electric, her eyes would have been casting sparks as they raked the audience, searching out some possible rival. The duet had begun and the lovers, in a literalization of ecstasy, were slowly being cranked up and up, on a platform, as the lights shifted to indicate a slow processional into the gothic vault of night. Since Mathilda had almost memorized this opera she awaited its events with complacency but her own response with suspense. Would it work for her tonight? Would she believe she was hearing and seeing the sounds and sights of her own nobler nature—a nature not in isolation but affiliated to a society finally worthy of it? For she was quite reconciled to her permanent disappointment in actual human company, or at least she had restricted her expectations of happiness to just one other person—to a duet. But within the magic realm of art, at least, a chorus could make harmonious comment on the couple's tragedy and a sextet could orient half a dozen separate psychologies into a sliding, gliding flock of flying sound.

Again she kissed Gabriel's hand. "Mr. Pine," she whispered. Gabriel suddenly looked at Daniel, who'd gone pale at this display and staggered a step backward so that only his huge nose remained lit by the glaucous "moonlight" cast up by the stage. Gabriel stroked Mathilda's hair with one hand and with the other reached up to squeeze Daniel's shoulder. Daniel's look of pain had been replaced by impassivity. He looked as indecipherable as a desert sheik. "Shockingly silly music, isn't it?" he whispered. "Gorgeous humbug."

After the performance Mathilda gave a midnight supper for the singers. She loved their placid, meaty self-satisfaction, the technical ways in which they expressed their vanity. She loved their fussing over drafts and lozenges, their resorting to throat sprays and raised fur collars even in stifling rooms. She loved the complete good will with which they competed in their recollections of great performances (usually their own) and the way they broke out into muted glorious solfeggio to illustrate those points, mouths suddenly a huge red O trembling at the edges, eyes crossed, massive breasts deflating visibly. They never seemed to grasp the refined emotion they instilled in their listeners and in reply to a sensitive eulogy a diva would light up and say in her resonant voice, "You liked that one, huh? It is kind of cute, isn't it?" And, swathed in ermine and pale, perfumed chins, she would wrinkle her nose in the kittenish way she'd once admired in a vaudeville soubrette. "Radiant dumbbells," Daniel called them.

Because Mathilda was a connoisseur in search of the best, she was content to huddle backstage with the tedious stars, these men and women who never followed styles but conformed to the isolated and eternal modes of opera. When one of her intellectual sycophants would attempt to draw Mathilda into a detailed dissection of the opera, its history, its conventions, its ambiguous political status as bravura rebellion for oligarchs, she'd hold open her hands to indicate pennilessness and say, "I can't discuss it. I just like it." This failing (a *happy* failing—she was smiling) was congruent with her automatic impulse to play the aesthete among moralists and the moralist among aesthetes. With Daniel the dandy, she was always preachy; with her opera singers, she was the brooding thinker; with thinkers she was operatic; with Gabriel she was, wonderfully, herself, if that meant someone in love with a shared future she was too shy to mention.

Gabriel went off into the night with Daniel. They got as far as the Grand in one vehicle, which they dismissed, then they mounted the stairs, crossed the gleaming marble lobby, and scurried down the back stairs and into a smaller, waiting conveyance.

This one took them deep into a quarter where dyers were still awake and at work, stretching skeins of green, brick-red and golden yarn across their shops in lamplight the color of a callus. Here men with swarthy faces dressed in white looked like moonlight draped over shadows as they glided away from a whitewashed wall out of a low, dark door. Smells of cardamom pods and rice in milk drifted through the open windows like a narcotic, and Gabriel inhaled them, leaning his head back on the cushions, his body as quivering and bony as a baby bird's beside Daniel's aquiline majesty. For Daniel, in spite of his lordly, drawling ways, his arrogant languor, was robust with energy—or so Gabriel thought.

Suddenly gates parted and in an unexpected glare and bustle

they were greeted on three sides by a household of women streaming out of flung-back French doors, clucking and calling to them. As Daniel descended he pretended to be fussed by such a welcome, but Gabriel could see he was pleased. "There, there," Daniel murmured. Smooth brown arms chiming with bangles reached up to stroke Daniel's back and to grab his long pale hands with the nearly purple nails and to lead him and his skinny little friend inside.

That night they smoked opium and Gabriel drifted off into a dream in which he slowly, slowly floated down in a balloon onto an old bridge lined with shops where everyone, shopkeepers included, was engaged in a perfume-sniffing contest. When he awakened a dull pain throbbed in his temples and his mouth was so dry the tip of his tongue stuck to his lips. He'd been undressed by someone and wrapped in a full, unlined cotton robe in which he felt small and clean. A breeze flowed in a window, even though they were deep into December. The strangely warm night was blowing back curtains. Whenever the breeze died down he could catch the disturbing scent someone had burned into the sleeve of this white robe, a scent he imagined must look green when held up to the light but gold when light shone through it, a scent that would evaporate away if left unstopped for even an hour.

Night after night Gabriel went with Daniel to this house in the dyers' quarter to smoke opium and to dream. Mathilda refused to comment on these expeditions. Sometimes Daniel didn't smoke but took something else, a wobbly black cake lucent as jelly and served wrapped in bamboo leaves. After he ate it he became more and more talkative and in his corner Gabriel would drift off. For a moment there would be such silence in the whole house that Gabriel could hear the sudden thunder of a snapped-open fan or the leaf-crackling sound made by a rustling silk gown.

But behind a screen or perhaps in another room altogether, Daniel was becoming excitable, exuberant; he was laughing at dazzling connections apparent only to himself. The women understood nothing but the most rudimentary words in Daniel's language yet they followed his rambling ecstasies with a chorus of sighs and giggles and low throaty sounds, the cooing sound nesting birds make. They liked this talkative customer who waved away the delicate dishes they submitted to him but who spoke to them—even sang—with such rapture. In their language the short, swallowed vocables that meant "yes" sometimes sounded like "no" in Daniel's language, and Daniel came to enjoy the way his free-form arias were punctuated by a sobering chorus of "no . . . no . . . no," each word delivered with a downward jerk of the chin and a furrowing of the brow, as though a pleat had just been taken then ripped out. If their negative assent, delivered so placidly, suddenly struck him as funny, he'd fling himself back and roar his great lion roar of a laugh. The ladies would obligingly shriek, hold their sides, rock with giggles and wipe tears away with their sleeves, all the while pointing at him and whooping as though to designate the improbable "it" in a children's game turned monstrous. He dubbed this place "the House of Negative Assent."

As Daniel once told Gabriel, the most admired quality in the otherwise decorous culture of the quarter was "wild high spirits" or "going over the top" (depending on how the succinct two syllables of their term were translated), by which they meant the hilarity of these exhausting—and fabulously costly—all-night banquets. Gabriel's sleepy smile was a false rhyme to this hysteria. In his room he whispered to himself, "No . . . no . . . no," and he fell into a dream in which he'd been ordered to sing in an opera he'd never heard but he acquitted himself well, due to the golden cloak conferred on him by a sad, laughing god.

When he woke, the house was cold and silent. December had reaffirmed itself. "No . . . no . . . no," he whispered, the way an old man talks to himself before anyone else is awake. He looked up at the stars through the stirring curtains. Each star was named after a slain hero and Gabriel could name them all. He heard—then saw—something beside him. He watched a grey and white parrot with a black beak step sideways along the sill, then flutter to the floor with a squawk. The bird, cross as a farmer come to town, walked stiffly away from him, stopping to peck at the first pale grains of sunlight that were piling up in magic abundance all around him. Gabriel wondered if he were still dreaming.

Gabriel spent his days with Mathilda. They drank tea together, she read and he pretended to read. Surely she must have known his head was cloudy and aching, but she never murmured a protest against his nightly jaunts with Daniel. Three months went by this way. Then spring deepened. At dawn, cartloads of flowers rattled past the all-night revelers who were on their way home, the erect gay heads of the flowers just peeping over the wood sides of the cart. In the market he saw baby lamb, baby asparagus and, later, wild strawberries. Gabriel even swore he heard a flock of lambs trotting past the House of Negative Assent one night or dawn, but Daniel laughed and coupled the lambs with Gabriel's dream of the grey parrot. Gabriel found himself in tears as, starched and correct in evening clothes, he paused on a landing on his way out and caught the scent of freesia. He buried his face in the bouquet contained in the round silver bowl. Every day new birds, vegetables, smells, flowers arrived in the city as though to summon him —but to what?

He kept some of his clothes (the funny, inelegant ones) at his uncle's house as a half-hearted pledge he'd return, but now he was virtually living full-time with Mathilda and Daniel. He felt comfortable with her. He liked her. On the nights when he slept with her, he'd often reach in his sleep for the warmth of her body. He understood now that the world regarded them as a scandal, so different were their ages, but when they were alone Gabriel thought of Mathilda as a sister.

She'd hired him a tutor, someone who attempted for two hours before lunch every day to make him pursue a rational course of study, but soon enough they became friends and would spend the whole session gossiping about their adventures of the night before. The tutor, Hector, was short yet always stood tall and inclined slightly backwards, as though someone had just thrown cold water in his face. He used a vocabulary of precision, words and phrases such as "rigorous," "systematic," "on the contrary," and "think again." These expressions, joined to his startled look and short black hair, which he was always wetting and brushing straight back, made him seem much more alert than he actually was. In fact he was absentminded, romantic and impractical. He loved Gabriel's stories. As Gabriel recounted something amusing, Hector would stare at him solemnly. Then, after two seconds had elapsed, he'd blink, his lazy smile would dawn gently and he'd say, "You're beyond belief, Gabriel."

Gabriel noticed that whenever Mathilda dropped in for an instant Hector became starchy and precise. If Gabriel denigrated an author, Hector would say acidly, "The author is not being judged." He'd pinch his mouth and say, "That just won't do." Sometimes he'd even put on his glasses and stare over the tops at his charmingly inept student. Then Mathilda would laugh and say, "Don't be too hard on him, Hector, I beg of you," and she seemed half-serious in her reproaches. She could make even a highly intelligent victim look like a fool in public debate, and she certainly applied demanding intellectual standards to herself and strangers. But with her "boys," Daniel and Gabriel, she eased all strictures. She found the feeblest things they said wickedly amusing and ascribed to their dull remarks a depth that she, in exegesis, invented.

Her own brand of brilliance was based on doggedness, a wrestling with what everyone already knew until common sense yielded up something strange and new. Out of loyalty to her son and lover she found in their banalities her own sort of penetration into the obvious. She was always grinning and chortling ironically or slapping her thigh in high intellectual comedy no matter what they said. Gabriel understood that she required an intellectual for a lover and had fashioned one for herself out of the leavings of her own imagination. He was too fastidious, too cold a realist, to deceive himself about his own meager gifts, but he was also too content with their love to disabuse her.

Having once overcome the passivity and inertia that had subdued him for so many months, Gabriel now became addicted to uncertainty. He was restless. He went out prowling at all hours. In the mirror he watched his own face become more and more wizened and he convinced himself he liked this precocious old age. In truth he feared what was happening to him. He feared that he was hurtling through time faster than everyone else around him. He'd moved without transition from the spots of puberty to the wrinkles of old age without a moment to enjoy an ordinary youth. But the decisive way in which his wrinkles forbade an ordinary youth also pleased him—at least something had been settled. He'd have to be a clown or a genius or an axe-murderer, since he couldn't be one more tepid, unexceptionable man of fashion.

From Hector, his tutor, he learned indirectly how the world looked at him. Some people said Mathilda had been unhappy for a long time with Daniel always underfoot; although everything was still outwardly peaceful, an explosion was inevitable. Others said that she had been simply lying in wait for a new lover, alert in her saturnine cave, but that Daniel had mistaken this long abstention as abdication. He'd come to believe a contract bound them, a kind of matrimony, and that they had a clear if unspoken and unspeakable agreement never to fall in love with anyone else.

Mathilda had half-sensed Daniel's misunderstanding and done nothing to set him straight. It served her purposes to have him always at hand. He still lived with her. He squired her about. He listened to her develop her new ideas. He met new people, tested the waters of new salons, took up new follies, slummed on some nights and climbed on others—and he came back to tell her every-thing about everyone. His catholicity made her niceness possible.

She was so well known that like a monarch she couldn't go anywhere unnoticed. Like a monarch she wouldn't have wanted to. But she craved news of the town. As a connoisseur she sought the best, and she also knew that in a world as capricious as theirs the best sometimes coincides with the latest. Daniel kept her up to date. She could sort through the debris and find the one or two novelties she might want to collect. Titled, dowdy and intellectual friends her own age were always astonished by her knowledge of the popular culture of the young and the poor. A new game, a new sport, a new dance, a slang word, a drug, an invention, a club, an outbreak of religious frenzy or a revival of old political hopes—out of the messy, indiscriminate night's catch Daniel brought dripping to her feet each morning she could swoop down to collect the single small shell she fancied.

Gabriel could sense that Daniel was trying one way after an-other to get along with him, his mother's lover. At first Daniel had set himself up as Gabriel's father, the older, more worldly guide to the boy's career in the capital. He'd even said, "You can trust Mathilda and me to steer you right. Frightfully easy to meet the wrong sort. After we've 'finished' you I'll present you to the loveli-est heiress in town and your fortune will be made." A few weeks later, as the permanence of Gabriel's position in their household became obvious, Daniel drew Gabriel aside: "I must warn you, I'm even faintly annoyed you haven't figured it out on your own—but you've fallen without a squawk right into Mateo's and Mathilda's trap. Don't you want to break free of them, meet some younger, and, well, more *amusing* people? Surely you're not interested in their solemn sort of culture, are you—Walter's dreadful banging at the piano, or Mateo's own sort of high-culture hustle, or in Mater's taking everything back to first principles, where they're least likely to bring a smile to anyone's lips. Why not pull free of all their elbows-out washerwoman sort of striving and let me introduce you to some lovely, empty-headed debs who are dippy precisely to the degree their fortunes are solid."

Gabriel only smiled at these sallies, resorting to the sort of sad smile reserved for unfunny jokes desperate people crack at their own expense.

Mathilda hastily threw up the fiction that both Gabriel and Daniel were "her boys," but it was a shelter that protected her alone. At night (sometimes only at dawn) Gabriel slept in her bed and Daniel turned back on the landing to descend the stairs. Daniel slept less and less. He even bathed less. He'd always been a fastidious dandy, quite capable of seizing and tying one ascot after another until one finally folded and billowed in the right negligent way. Once Gabriel had witnessed a servant emerge from Daniel's dressing room with a stack of twenty discarded ascots—"our little failures" as Daniel confessed sheepishly. But now he wore the same clothes day after day and forgot to shave or bathe or have his hair trimmed. Because they were the only clothes he owned he was still decked out in fripperies, bits of gold jewelry, wonderfully soft, muted fabrics, but given his dirtiness they looked more squalid than more ordinary things in disarray might have appeared. "A gold necklace on a dirty neck is not a pretty sight," Mateo remarked to Gabriel—waspishly in order to avoid sounding sad.

Daniel lost weight and the badger mask of circles under his eyes became bruise-black with fatigue. His hands shook. Since Gabriel was also nervous and thin, they both laughed one evening when Walter complained about how unhealthy they looked. "Walter," Daniel drawled, "don't you see we're just like two bored adolescent girls. Brats, we're bored brats indulging ourselves, complete brats, in chic austerities." And if Gabriel laughed it was because Daniel, in his usual lordly way, had just brayed forth to a third party a truth they wouldn't have dared acknowledge to each other.

A rumor was circulating that Daniel was courting a woman in the viceregal palace.

After the opening of an opera Mathilda had commissioned, she offered a midnight supper to the performers, who were of the second rank since all the stars approached had refused to memorize a score that they felt would never enter the repertory and that, moreover, was treacherous to sing. The performers, subdued by the half-hearted applause but unable to complain because of the composer's presence, tucked in; no one said much. Mathilda, over-dressed in a black gown, which she'd had made for the occasion and which looked right only when she stood, kept pacing about, wondering where Daniel was. The black feathers, folded over her breasts, stirred with her rapid turns. He was the one who'd encouraged her to patronize music, which secretly he saw as one more step away from the radicalism of her past, toward an ambiguous artistic milieu where she could meet rich conservatives and even melt in with them without ever really noticing the transition. Mathilda had thought that, given his musical enthusiasm, he'd surely help her celebrate even a fiasco. She found his absence alarming but pretended she was merely vexed.

"How can he do this to me?" she whispered. The centerpiece, an ice sculpture of a rose in honor of the opera's name, was melting visibly in the glare of candles. The evening was uncomfortably warm. Late spring was here, and the heat, which always signaled the end of the Season, rendered this event all the more unfashionable. "It all feels like a gardenia gone brown," she complained to Gabriel. "I wouldn't mind if Daniel were here. We could all have a good laugh. Why didn't Mateo come?"

Gabriel returned to the composer's side and plied him with questions just as his uncle would have done. He knew that if his eyes, which he was making as round and fascinated as possible, strayed for a second to the pacing Mathilda or to the doors that didn't, wouldn't open, he'd spoil the compliment of his attention, and the composer would return to his supper and chagrin.

At last the double doors flew open (the cheeses were being removed and a petal of the ice rose had just noisily fallen off) and there stood a swaying Daniel, greasy hair sticking up on one side, his shirt torn, a two-day's growth of beard bringing out the menacing adult male in this exquisite who usually did everything (at least outside the boudoir) to deny his age and gender. Three tribal girls from the House of Negative Assent were with him, propping him up, their saffron silks, usually glimpsed in firefly dimness through half-closed shutters, looking tawdry and vulgar in the glare of hundreds of candles. They were giggling and cooing like a kettle about to boil and indeed when Daniel broke into a huge cruel laugh the kettle blew and the dark-skinned girls raised high their screams of merriment. They made Gabriel think of hired mourners, shrieking and tearing their clothes on cue. "Daniel, at last," Mathilda said. "We're all about to go upstairs, where I hope to persuade our guests to treat us to a reprise of the evening's—"

"Rubbish," Daniel said. "Absolute rubbish. Opera is theater, after all, and there's no court of appeal for theater. A flop is a flop." He went up to the composer, who'd risen in protest. Daniel placed a heavy, dirty hand on the man's shoulder, which was thickly padded (his hired evening clothes). "Sorry, old man," Daniel said, "but your opera, let's be honest, was consummate rubbish."

The girls didn't understand what was being said nor who anyone was, but incomprehension didn't inhibit them. They strode around the room examining everything—curtains, rugs, furniture, even the flatware—as though it were for sale; all the while they called back and forth in their loud, penetrating language—Angelica's language, Gabriel thought with a twinge. The singers had lowered their heads and were scrutinizing their empty place settings, pretending not to have heard Daniel, with whom they were in agreement. The composer said, "Sir, I'm not aware of the musical training that enables you—"

"Too boring," Daniel muttered, yawning, his mouth thrown open as wide as possible, "too utterly predictable, your pique, m'dear. Shallow academic pastiche; *The Ice Rose,* indeed—I suppose you meant *rose* to be a verb as in 'my gorge rose.'"

"Madam," the composer said, turning to Mathilda, "I'm desolate but I must take leave of your fête." He reached for her hand to kiss, but she slowly placed it behind her back.

"I'm afraid Daniel, in his tactless clubman's way, has told you the truth. What's the sense of going on pretending?" she asked, taking her son's arm. The singers, in response to an operatic scene, were now staring frankly, and a few were even smiling. "I'm afraid the future of your work is no more solid than . . . that!" And she pointed to the centerpiece, its petals nearly melted away by the heat of the room.

Daniel laughed horribly at his mother's remarks and the girls he'd brought rushed to his side and whooped with professional amusement. Gabriel in his corner couldn't quite read these events. Was Daniel laughing at the composer's pretentious failure or at his mother's hungry bid for unanimity with her son? Gabriel had heard more than once about the bloody sacrifices Daniel and Mathilda liked to heap up on the altar to their own love. Was this just such an offering? Or had Daniel come here tonight to humiliate his mother?

"Madam," the composer said, his eyes flashing with anger and pride but his trembling mouth already admitting defeat, "I'm desolate that my humble efforts have failed to satisfy such a discriminating Maecenas."

"Hold your bloody sarcastic tongue," Daniel said, quietly murderous. "Discriminating enough to recognize a flop and a cad. You'll not have another chance, not in the great world. Perhaps some girls' school may sign you up to do them if not an ice rose then a sludge thistle but your dreams of real fame are melting away, yes, seem to be quite runny before your very eyes."

Daniel's mouth was dry and a white line had formed on his lower lip as though to mark how high the tide had risen.

Mateo had found Angelica a tiny apartment, just a room really, with one window from which, if she stuck her head out, she could see the Tower, the Assembly, the Grand, the park, even an edge of the Palace. It was high on a hill in a quarter famed a century ago for its bohemians but now turned into a white, pink and green rookery for kept girls and impoverished, heavy-drinking foreigners, a place where shops on a few of the main streets sold cheap curios or expensive suppers and where the languages of every corner of the empire rang out in late-night hilarity. But if tourists crowded the squares, the twisting back streets were reserved for the residents, for their miniscule grog-shops, the greengrocers' stalls and the five-table family cafés where only one main dish a day was available but that one at a song—literally, sometimes, a song and a quick scrape on a fiddle from someplace over the sea, a fiddle bordered in mother-of-pearl, its neck as thin as a hungry cat's.

Angelica loved sitting by her window or better yet stretching out on the love seat under it and gazing up into the evening sky that darkened slowly but inexorably. There she'd lie, dressed for the night except for her shoes and dress, but her underthings, nails, hair, and maquillage all in place and impeccable, and in this clean, anticipatory moment she'd dangle one washed, depilated, creamed and stockinged leg over the sofa arm and listen to the night sounds. Downstairs was a garden restaurant. The waiters were eating their early supper before the customers arrived. The chef was complaining about the new system for posting soup and salad orders; one of the waiters seemed proud of himself as he told of how he'd gambled away all his tips after closing the night before.

Next door lived an old man and woman whose open window was almost adjacent to Angelica's. She couldn't understand a syllable of their language, but there were few enough syllables to guess at, since they seldom spoke to each other. But every morning very early, soon after daybreak, the old man, dressed in blue coveralls, went off on some sort of job. If Angelica knelt and peeked through her keyhole she could see the woman standing in the open doorway facing her old man, who was already in the hall, his back to Angelica. They just stared and stared at each other with wordless devotion for a full minute, then another, not touching except with their eyes. The woman's hands sometimes worked her apron as though she were wringing it dry. She would look at the man with an extra intensity, and her hands would work. They grunted something and the man walked away. The woman watched till he'd turned on the landing and started down the stairs. Then she angrily struck a tear from her eye with her knuckle as though it were a cinder and closed the door behind her.

Angelica envied them.

But she had her own old man, of course. Her Mateo. He was a bit trickier; their love wasn't so simple. When she'd first met him he'd been kinder to her than anyone she'd ever known or even heard of, although she'd been slow to recognize the kindness. She'd been a frightened half-wild child running through the immense, shadowy capital with a desperate message from Gabriel's mother, a plea to Mateo to free her imprisoned son. Gabriel's mother had given Angelica a few coins for the journey and a scrap of paper; on one side was the message, on the other a map guiding her to Mateo's door. But the very first night the money had been stolen and on the second Angelica had somehow lost the paper. She'd retraced her steps, even crawled on all fours looking for that scrap of paper. At last she resolved to go on with nothing but her smile and wits to guide her.

One man would hand her over to another, and they'd all swear they were heading to the capital, but they never were. At first she didn't mind. She liked all the attention, the fanciful compliments, the long hours of travel, the strange sights, the powerful drink. Along the way she teamed up with a small fair girl her own age named Chrissie, and they each felt safer with the other nearby, although such security was illusory. One night she and Chrissie were squeezed between two big brutes who stank of garlic and stale sweat. Another night she and Chris were pushed out of a vehicle after they'd dozed off beside a randy shepherd and his fat, homely son. The two girls curled up in each other's arms and slept beside the road until the dew drenched them awake at dawn.

In a village of mud huts they were taken in by an innkeeper who became enamored of Angelica. Chrissie, consumed by both envy and jealousy, turned so tirelessly belligerent that Angelica finally, one drunken night, fled the village with a passing group of soldiers.

They secreted her in a dark cubbyhole where one soldier after another visited her. There was just a bit of light by the arched entrance when the heavy leather curtain was pushed back. She'd see the eyes of a soldier, eyes the color of the sea just before a storm; when he lifted his cap the blond hair beneath was pressed down into a sweaty, brown cloche. Another one had immense black pores in his nose and teeth that seemed outlined in green. Most of them were already hard by the time they unbuttoned their trousers. If she propped herself up and caught their eye and stared at them reproachfully in the lapse of sunlight as they came in, they'd sometimes feel sheepish, especially if they were very young, and they would kiss her cheek as a brother might when told by his parents to welcome a little sister home. One stroked her hair. Another patted her like a good horse. A few of them opened her shirt and kissed her breasts, but she came to dread these stabs at making love since the perpetrators took longer than the others and expected her to murmur her gratitude. Some soldiers laughed noisily with their mates in the queue just outside the cubbyhole, and one fat, bearded captain kept the jokes coming even when he was on her, in her. "I told you to let me go first, you farts. Now it's stretched out and with this sweet little sausage of mine, I can't feel a damn thing. Might as well be shaking my pinky in the breeze." He smiled down at her as though she too should appreciate the witticism. When he saw her look of hatred he rested more of his cold, sweaty weight on her.

Eventually she'd reached the capital, barefoot and in rags. A candle merchant named Maurizio, up from the south with a shipment of slender tapers overly scented with coriander, took a liking to her. Without touching her or asking anything he offered to spirit her through the city gates in his candle bale. Since she had no papers and no money, nothing but Mateo's name to go on, she'd never have gained admission otherwise. The candle merchant seemed to recognize Mateo's name; he even treated it with deference. A pretty redhead with chiseled features and bow legs and glasses that flashed with the fire of intelligence, Maurizio seemed embarrassed by his rosy skin and the delicate modeling of his face; he spoke with the deliberation of someone far older, going so far as to risk incoherence because of the dry, elderly sounding locutions he used ("Be that as it may," "They're six of one and half dozen of the other," "As different as chocolate and cheese"), so at odds with his blushing, dewy beauty. After her terrifying encounter with the soldiers, which had left her too sore and bloody to walk, Angelica had found that when an attractive man approached her she wanted to vomit, though she never did. To avoid the nausea, she kept her eyes trained on the ground and became as modest as a practiced ascetic. The girlishly lithe merchant she scarcely glanced at; when she addressed him she stared at his dusty left boot.

Her induced shyness was precisely what attracted Maurizio. She appeared to be even less assertive than he was. He offered to smuggle her through customs at the risk of losing his irreplaceable documents. Once they were safely in the city he took her to a house in the dyers' quarter and there his aunt let her bathe and sleep. Over wine Maurizio told Angelica that the reason he spoke so deliberately was that he'd stammered as a boy until a celebrated actress, whom he'd visited backstage, had befriended him and told him that he must think out each sentence fully and say it mentally before ever opening his mouth. The method had worked and had given him the unexpected advantage in business of seeming far older than his years and much more serious than his looks suggested. He still felt grateful to the actress, whose name was Edwige, and visited her occasionally. He should despise her, since she'd become the plaything of the conquerors whereas he was an ardent patriot. And Angelica? What were her politics?

"I'm just a woman," she said.

The candle merchant and his aunt laughed. The aunt said, "Forgive me, my dear, but you're a girl, almost a child, not a woman. You're also from one of the tribes, to judge by your looks and accent, and in the eyes of the conquerors your tribal status is all that counts. They don't see you as a woman, unless as an object for their soldiers to abuse. No better than a salt lick set out for cattle to lick, one and all, for cattle to lick into lovely, dwindling shapes until you're all licked away."

The woman was so accurately and poetically evoking what had just happened to Angelica that the girl's smile faded and her eyes drank in her wisdom.

The next morning they led her to Mateo's house. Angelica resolved that if she stayed on in the city, she'd cultivate the merchant's aunt (Maurizio himself spent little time in the city and when he did come to town he was always involved in political meetings). She caught a hint that he, Maurizio, carried messages between bands of patriots. He said, "You, so young, so innocent, you could help your country. No one would ever suspect you. But of course most tribal people feel as oppressed by the patriots as by the conquerors. What are your politics?"

"Give me time," Angelica said, too proud to admit she had no idea of what he was talking about yet flattered that he sought her aid. Just when she'd felt that she had nothing to offer anyone, this man seemed to need not her body but her cunning.

When Mateo opened the door and saw Angelica for the first time, he thought she was one of those dirty and aggressive children who hold up a drugged infant, its eyes sticky with flies, and whine for alms. He hated his mornings, which were inwardly anxious and only apparently lazy, to be vexed by bill-collectors, by florists or caterers or tailors he'd failed to pay, by provincials or foreigners he'd met the night before at a reception and to whom he'd made rash promises—all those who reminded him of how powerless and impoverished he was. He needed a whole day of conjuring with himself to raise his spirits as a magician might cause a lady to levitate: time, concentration, endless pots of coffee and flattering notes from friends and admirers. If by teatime he'd dispatched and received a dozen messages, if his mantelpiece had been snowed under by a sudden avalanche of crested invitations, if he'd condensed his dispersed matutinal fogs into a simulacrum of a human being, then he could welcome with warmth a stranger, even a poor stranger.

It was all a question of momentum. In the mornings nothing moved, nothing flowed, the realm of the material comically—humiliatingly!—resisted the impulses of the spirit. Bathing, shaving, dressing were each an ordeal, partly because he had an almost limitless amount of time in which to do them and, quite secretly, he half-feared that once he was ready for the day the day would turn out to be empty. He misplaced things, an almost terminal fatigue beset him, he'd feel close to tears on the toilet as he contemplated the gross, failing bellows and mulcher he was attached to, his body. In the morning his body seemed older, heavier, hairier, less acceptable than at any other time. It had not yet been redeemed by (or at least subordinated to) his birdlike prolific chatter.

His preferred mode was beneficence, but on some mornings he stung himself awake through petty rages. He'd detest everyone. The young would be kept waiting, then given lectures on their manners. If Walter dropped in he'd be liberally peppered with freshly grated scorn. "Oh, you're so *mean*," Walter would squeal, thrilled at the attention. Walter had such an uncomfortably *baggy* sense of himself and his friends that he delighted in the tight-fitting costumes of sadist and masochist, so neatly reciprocal, so brightly plumed. Like Mathilda he had a taste for society but no gift for it. That both of them passed for social leaders, Mateo grumpily observed, had more to do with their persistence than skill. Or with the general debasement of public life under the conquerors.

Mathilda's fame as a thinker, earned and deserved, would always attract new people—luckily, since she was perpetually in need of recruits. She drove away most of the old people with her rudeness, her moodiness, her unreliability, her arrogance. In fact her only old friends were Walter, Mateo, and her son, at least the only ones she saw regularly, and even Mateo was becoming less and less faithful—he'd even failed to attend the premiere of *The Ice Rose*. Of course she had hundreds of acquaintances in every corner of the empire. Mathilda never needed to change her ways; she would never be humbled through rejection or isolation. This constant change of cast even suited her habit of regarding life as research. For just as she used Daniel to spread at her feet his night's haul each morning, just as she justified the luxuries of her mansion in the South as ethnographic trophies, in the same way she looked on new acquaintances as specimens to study. If someone invited to tea for the first time said something clever, Mathilda had the shocking habit of vigorously nodding approval while looking at Daniel, as though to say, "Well, haven't we stumbled on a gold mine here!" Once Mateo had tried to explain to her how many ways in which she was being insulting (treating the guest as entertainment; applauding his tricks as though condescension were praise—praise, moreover, directed to *Daniel*, as though the guest himself were subhuman and communication wasted on him; praising him in such a qualified, menacing way that he would know lower grades could just as easily be handed out next time).

The fact that Walter maintained open house suited and attracted all the aging intellectuals in their circle, people who craved company but who considered making engagements and carrying around a little black social notebook the height of foppishness. They haughtily turned down invitations for a week from now, even three days from now, until every hostess in town had dropped them. Their remaining social option was the permanent one: Walter's house, which he kept open out of a genuine simplicity, a democratic love of good fellowship he'd acquired in his twenties as a Septembrist. Democracy also informed his judgments about people. He just happened to find the rich, the famous, and the titled "amazing good sports" or "terrific talkers" whereas the obscure came under fire for their "standoffishness" or their "shyness—always a form of egotism."

Walter had other blunt but stunning arrows in his quiver. For instance, he had a waggish way of treating the oldest, frailest philosophers as though they were rakes and heartbreakers. "Oh, you coquette!" he'd shriek. "Don't pretend you didn't happen to notice the tears in that poor girl's eyes when you snubbed her. Beast!" And, shouting, Walter would stamp and point at the innocent culprit, who feared he actually had wounded a young person. The philosopher would be even more confused by the role Walter had cast him in—and terribly, terribly pleased. For just as every great pianist imagines his true genius lies in the kitchen, so every thinker fancies his forte is the boudoir. The fact that this talent has gone undiscovered until now only makes him all the more blushingly eager for it to be detected.

At Walter's house some oafish bit of mummery was always under way. His immense wardrobe of unsuccessful "looks" and lapsed fads could provide all the fancy dress any number of masquers might require, so long as no one was too squeamish about coffee stains, blisters of dried egg or specks of loose tobacco. Whether pounding the piano or prancing up to the door dressed as a doge or doll, whether accusing intellectuals of carnal excesses or reducing four trustees from the museum to kittens all in pussy costume, complete with long tails, miaowing their way through a "comic" quartet penned especially for one of his evenings by an equally silly but far more gifted Robert Constantine, Walter could always be counted on for some new absurdity.

Mateo was the least willing to jump through Walter's hoop. Once during a party Walter rushed up with a paper heart held to his sleeve and asked, "What do you guess this symbolizes, Mr. Pussycat?" Mateo coolly replied, "He who gets slapped." Walter's grin faded and he started bawling, "You're so *mean,*" an alarm designed to provoke curiosity in the other guests. Walter was so pleased that Mateo had delivered one of his acerbic *mots* at his reception that he didn't care it was at his expense. Moreover he claimed he liked it when Mateo turned "disciplinarian."

Of the "vices" in himself Walter alluded to with such pride, no one, not even Mateo or Mathilda, could be certain they weren't fabrications, no more real than his getups. He frequently mentioned his three-hundred-pound "dominatrix," a "housewife in the *banlieue,*" someone he would hire to trample on him and shave his entire body. But he seemed suspiciously alive to the humor value of a perversion one rather thought the adept himself (at least) would take seriously. Had he been so scholarly as a youngster that he'd neglected to cultivate any interesting twists in his character? Did he know how to attribute bizarre tastes to other sere "pussycats" because he'd had to trick himself out in just such inventions? The irreality of Walter's eccentricities led him to peculiar insights. He once sat beside the twelve-year-old daughter of his oldest schoolchum, a girl who'd been raised in the strictest seclusion and by the most old-fashioned governess, and whispered to her, "I'm sure you have the capacity to be very *cruel* to a man."

As it so happened, his intuition was dazzlingly accurate and the girl shook all over with the ecstasy of self-discovery—a physiological response her horrified parents interpreted as the normal revulsion to an abnormal insinuation. They hustled her out and broke off relations with Walter. One afternoon, however, the child returned on her own to show Walter the drawings she'd just done at school. "But can't you draw any better than that?" Walter asked with trembling scorn.

"Then you'll have to draw them for me, you filthy, ugly man," the girl hissed. Walter sat down, delighted, docile, and did her homework for her, as he was to do for weeks to come, enjoying the most perfect contentment of his life.

In fact he had surprising powers of concentration, given his social extravagance. Tucked in among the many calls he received and the few he paid, he managed to write curious tracts that were more praised than read. He was always just finishing a new one or racing off to a corner of the empire to read one to some learned society or other. Since his works were too concrete to interest philosophers, too general to attract politicians and too colorless to intrigue artists, no one believed they were addressed to him. Unread, his works inched their way across the shelves. The only people who actually consulted them were critics who saw no reason not to like them, particularly since Walter was such a good host, so influential and so highly regarded by so many other thinkers. Young provincial teachers also read Walter in public squares on hot afternoons during the long summer break and blamed themselves for not being able to stay awake for more than a page or two. Why? The sentences were short, the words clear, the tone sober, the conclusions modishly pessimistic. If the continuity sometimes seemed sketchy and the logic elusive, a provincial could only blame himself and this wretched, sleepy town where he was slowly becoming as moronic as his drunken neighbors, shouting through the night, all night, every night.

Mateo had been enraged this morning by an unannounced visit from Walter, who had just dropped off a copy of his latest title, issued no more than six months after his previous work. Mateo thought it unfair that he, too, wasn't a writer who could place on friends these impositions called "books," these liens on busy people's time and thoughts, these thefts one was expected to greet as gifts, these week-long monologues by nonentities one wouldn't let go on in person longer than three minutes. Walter hadn't left more than an instant before a timid knock announced the arrival of this beautiful beggar child.

Mateo was about to say "The lady of the house is not in" and slam the door when the girl muttered, "Your sister at Madder Pink sent me."

Mateo feared his sister was dying or dead and tears gathered behind his eyes as he led the girl down the dark narrow corridor walled at the far end in warped glass, a slimming mirror he always consulted when he needed to feel hopeful. There he was, slim again, with a miniature storm cloud of hair beside him, or perhaps it was a moving squadron of bees deserting the bagged and burned hive.

The child told him about Gabriel jailed in the cage his father had built, about the wicked mistress and the dozing volcano of a mother who'd finally erupted when Angelica came to her bedside and told her of her son's plight. Angelica sullenly confessed her loss of the letter Gabriel's mother had sent him.

"And you? What relationship do you bear to my family?" Mateo asked. Angelica's mouth flickered into an uncertain little smile and her huge eyes softly touched each object around her as though her eyes were hands.

Instantly he recognized that despite her almost undetectable accent and her fluent, colloquial choice of words, she could say far more in his language than she could understand and her vocabulary, like ice on a spring lake, was just sufficient to the swiftest passage. He also knew instinctively that she was hungry but would refuse food if asked. He put bread, cheese and a knife before her. Then he excused himself and left the room, since he guessed she might be superstitious about eating before a man or an infidel or a stranger or by day or who knows what, they have a million rules.

Later, realizing she was dropping from exhaustion, he told her he'd be much obliged if she'd stay the night; he might have a few more questions for her in the morning. He drew her a bath, showed her to her suite, and closed the door, then began to fear she might not know how the old-fashioned faucets worked and would leave the water running till it flooded over. Well, there was no going back in there. He could tell she was as proud and apprehensive as she was ignorant.

As she was lovely.

As soon as he'd seen her he'd thought of a cat, one that would lift its chin to be nuzzled while its lids drooped shut over gold eyes, its breath just the softest pulse of air, its mouth a welted black seam, the insides of each ear so pink and floral one expected to see a stamen rising in it . . . Later, its hunger could be heard in the creaking mews that followed each opening of its jaws by half a second, as though only the back of the hinge was rusty. When hungry the animal paced across a human lap, leaning its skinny flanks into anything solid, pausing to knead bread—no difference, really, between its way of asking for supper or sex.

The next day her embarrassment about how to behave in such a house made her angry and she huddled in a chair in the kitchen hiding behind her swarm of hair and tapping her foot. Mateo prepared breakfast for her and left her alone with it. He peeked into her bedroom. She hadn't turned down the sheets; he could see the dent in the coverlet her slender body had hollowed out. Later he could smell tobacco. She was smoking an ornamental ivory pipe that had been gathering dust on a shelf of bibelots for a decade and a cannister of sweet flake nearly as old, certainly stale.

The week before, he'd happened to attend a dull reception, which he'd gone to only because the host had said with ill-mannered gaiety, "Name your day!" And because he, Mateo, sometimes romanticized life among the unfashionable. There he'd found solace in a young couple so mismatched one had to assume either ambition or a taste for rather specialized *cochonneries* must unite them. The young man seemed to be almost entirely constructed. He'd been a street urchin, a scrappy little fighter; now he was a poet and a dandy, but he'd made a boutonniere out of selected simples from his past. Although he was as attentive and well-groomed as a dancing master, he liked to allude to his hooligan past and fit into his polished speech rough expressions.

She (her name was Flora) belonged to Angelica's tribe but was some sort of princess, in any event bejeweled, well-spoken in several languages and dressed and made up with attention to detail. Her escort spoke about poetry and then, somehow, moved on to a comparison of Mathilda's and Walter's thought, neither of whom he knew personally and both of whom he referred to by their last names alone, as though they were already dead; Mateo had an unpleasant vision of seeing their names on tombstones.

Flora glazed over during the young man's disquisition. She pulled a mirror out of her purse and examined every pore of her face with unpartisan attention. She even bared her teeth and studied them. She lifted her upper lip and checked her gums. Next on the inventory were her nails, then her rings and bracelets. Satisfied with her own appearance, she sat back, looking much older and fatigued, and took stock of every other woman in the room.

Mateo thought it so odd that the boxer-dandy had chanced to mention Walter and Mathilda. People often spoke of Mathilda, of course, no surprise there. But the two together like that? "I know them, you know, they're both friends of mine, dear friends. I could introduce you to them."

Mateo could scarcely believe his own foolishness, the way each sentence he uttered compounded the folly. When he'd first come to the capital twenty years ago, he'd always been promising strangers favors. He hadn't even had to like them. If he was near them he thought he must like them; proximity was his most sincere form of affection. Over the years he'd learned to censor this impulse even if he couldn't eradicate it. He knew his own standing had been kept artificially low by his lack of exclusivity. Too many people of all sorts grazed in his salons. Mathilda didn't like meeting new people. That was a job for her son. If Daniel liked someone new, if he kept seeing him, bringing back intriguing reports, then maybe one evening Mathilda might come along, unannounced, to some place neutral, a café, say, or a Sunday concert in the Palace grounds. And if that went well she might stay on for supper. Later she'd most often say to Daniel, "Oh, I *certainly* see what you mean, but he's not my kind of thing, you know. More yours. But you're so brave. You go everywhere. You're getting to be a social omnivore, aren't you?" Pause. "But you don't really *like* him, do you?" Her eyes flicker into flame, a pyre Daniel ascends. "No?" Laugh. Daniel burns. "I thought not. I knew you couldn't." Imitating a high-pitched voice: " 'The sixteenth century is the *matrix*'—what a silly little man."

That was Mathilda's way of meeting new people.

She certainly wouldn't attend a reception if she thought she'd be stared at by—or introduced to—nobodies. Once when Mateo did introduce her to an attractive but unremarkable provincial couple, he later lied to Mathilda and told her they were breathtakingly rich. "Ah!" she said. "Now it comes clear. Rich! They weren't just agreeable provincial bores. I see now." Another time Mateo had invited her to dinner with a celebrated painter she'd known since her adolescence. As the painter nervously told in too much detail about his recent sketching trip through the mountains, Mathilda sank into anthracitic sullenness. After coffee Mathilda said to Mateo in a noisy "aside," "Why'd you invite him?"

"I thought you were friends," Mateo muttered, blushing at her rudeness and humbled by her anger.

"Well, we are, were, but . . ."

"I'm terribly sorry," Mateo said, suddenly angry at having to apologize. Later he realized she disliked the painter because he'd known her when she was still a society twit, before she'd remade herself into an intellectual.

Now the boxer-dandy was saying how it would be the crowning event of his whole life, such a profound honor, if he could ever meet Mathilda. Mateo noticed that a minute ago he'd been rather cruelly dismissing Mathilda's ideas; the honor appeared to be purely social, just as a composer whose concerts people doze through becomes galvanizing only when he's on hand as a name to be pronounced, ever so casually: "Marie, you know Bob Constantine, don't you?" Marie's eyes widen then drop a veil as she registers the name and suppresses her surprise.

At the possibility of getting on in the world, even the dazed Flora had sprung back into action. "You know Mathilda? I love her thought," she purred. "I think she's so chic and so brilliant. I'd be frightened to meet her. But when? I'm a wonderful cook if you like spicy food. How about all of us, you, Mathilda, us, our place tomorrow? Seven o'clock? Drinks first? Isn't this thrilling, darling?" And she turned to her refined ruffian of a lover, who playfully jabbed like a prizefighter in the general direction of her voluptuous breasts bursting out of her white piqué décolleté gown.

Mateo had cooled their ardor but kept their card tucked into his blotter. Now he realized in one great simplifying intuition that he could get Flora to look after Angelica while he, Mateo, made the trip to Madder Pink. Flora had exactly the sort of glamour Angelica would admire and imitate—and that would serve the child well if and when Mateo brought home that nephew of his (Gabriel —that was his name). Both children would need instruction, of course, new clothes, tutors, dancing classes, visits to the wigmaker (where would the money come from?). He hoped he'd like Gabriel, whom he'd never met. But the girl, Mateo sensed, would be specially difficult, since her understanding of the language was imperfect and she was set apart from them by several social classes and half a century. Sweet, though. Sexy. Bright, no doubt (if Mateo liked someone he called him or her "bright," intelligence being a quality he was incapable of measuring and didn't really believe in).

Flora eagerly agreed to the assignment and came to spirit Angelica away on the morning of Mateo's departure. Flora in a day dress was too blooming, too scented, too colorful, and looked almost comical as she came walking through the smart crowds below Mateo's windows. Amidst all those muted greys and duns she looked like a bright pink hibiscus with its red throat and crepey petals—the sort of flower, the sort of woman, a child might happily draw. When Flora came in she studied the portraits of Mateo's friends lining the hall walls and seemed to be memorizing the names so that she could repeat them later to her intellectual lover. Homework done, she went to the slimming mirror at the far end, tugged at her skirt, which had ridden up her hips, produced an atomizer from her purse and sprayed herself all over, lifted her long black hair with a deft gesture as though it were a sheet of fresh pasta she was folding into a box, and shifted the whole sleek burden to her other shoulder. Now she was ready to meet her little charge.

Angelica in her bare feet, cotton pants and ripped, dirty shirt emerged from her room and looked suspiciously at this jangling, perfumed lady who was almost ceaselessly spiraling in place, like a rope trick, dealing with the alluring problem of her hair, laughing over something Mateo had said and touching his sleeve coquettishly, asking a bewitchingly naïve question: "Mateo, Mathilda? Your names, so similar . . . are you brother and sister?"

Mateo laughed, said no, and Flora laughed, too, swooped down to the child and hugged her. "Aren't I a great silly? What will your uncle Mateo think?"

Angelica didn't crack a smile. She looked as though she was the member of a sex quite distinct from Flora's with her wide, unplucked eyebrows, her breasts jiggling freely inside her blouse, unlike the bound, shaped mounds Flora had molded for herself. Angelica's hair was wild, her face devoid of color—no highlighted cheekbones, rouged cheeks, painted lips. Just a simple kid's face, almost a boy's, except it was too round, the cheeks too fat, the mouth too full to be male. Flora broke into her native tongue, which she spoke with many more hand gestures.

Angelica frowned as though remembering a forgotten tune. Then she smiled for the first time and replied. Mateo excused himself, saying he had packing to do, but from the next room he could hear the two of them jabbering as Angelica gained confidence, even laughed. Half an hour later he found them side by side on the sun-faded black-and-gold-striped silk sofa in the grand salon. Flora was pushing Angelica's hair back with both hands and cocking her head to one side to judge the effect. It was through Flora that Mateo learned Gabriel was "married" to Angelica, whatever that might mean in the girl's parlance; a pledge of friendship, perhaps, or a solemnization of primitive animal functions.

When Mateo returned from Madder Pink with the bedraggled, weakened Gabriel, he thought it best to protect the boy from the demands of his "marriage." Mateo instituted a regime that progressed from complete rest to nearly complete rest. Meals and the occasional bath were Gabriel's only duties the first few weeks. His nephew even rejected the noble pink bedroom above the canal in favor of a maid's room, as though just now the demands of sunlight and flowing air were too strenuous for him. At the same time Mateo kept Angelica—well, somewhat ignorant of the truth. He had Flora tell the girl that he and Gabriel were traveling, had gone, yes, on a long trip through the mountains. Best way to mend the lad's shattered health.

Angelica seemed only mildly curious about her "husband's" fate. When Mateo dropped in on Flora one afternoon, he found the girl startlingly changed. She looked older. Her hair had been cut and straightened; it was held in place by a white gold hoop. This coiffure gave her a forehead, ears and a neck, all of which she'd lacked before. Makeup had made her eyes still larger, elevated her cheekbones, lengthened her nose, thinned her lips and somehow made her weak chin stronger. What before had been just a tiny blank space under wild hair had now taken on definition, become dramatic. In record time she'd also acquired a ridiculously affected manner in crude imitation of Flora. She greeted him at the door with, "Mateo, darling," and a spiraling, undulating walk, her hand plucking imaginary threads from his sleeve. But she was like an inexpensive guide who has learned a travelogue by rote and cannot sustain interruptions, for once she'd greeted him and led him into Flora's sun-drenched sitting room, she lapsed back into foot-drumming shyness exacerbated by her lack of a hair-hedge to hide behind.

Flora filled in for her. "Oh, we're having such an amusing time together. Every day we go shopping for hours. I think our Angelica has an unsuspected talent for shopping." Mateo smiled. Flora protested, "But I'm serious! She's very systematic. We're putting together a basic summer wardrobe for her now. And we have our daily makeup sessions. Her makeup today—sweet, isn't it—we call *capriccioso* because it's *entirely* free-form."

Mateo sat beside Angelica and with some ceremony said, "You're very beautiful." She looked so happy that he thought such pleasure was worth whatever it might cost him. Curiously, when he later drew Flora aside and she gave him the bills, the amount was surprisingly small. The shopping had been mostly looking. Nevertheless, Angelica modeled her few purchases for him while Flora kept up a rapid commentary in both languages that managed to lend dignity to the event, while very quietly, very subtly she smiled at the whole thing in gentle complicity with Mateo. Angelica made her entrances in one costume after another until she'd exhibited the four she owned. She turned and posed with modish *sprezzatura* until, in the midst of showing the third ensemble, she suddenly shrieked and clasped her ears and dashed off to find the missing gold earrings and narrow Martian sunglasses.

Mateo felt guilty joy in the flattering attentions of these two dark, groomed beauties. He'd spent so many years among the strong intellectual women who populated his official circle (meeting other softer, more yielding women only singly late at night) that he found himself lacking a manner to deal with such charm.

The two tribal princesses made him feel so important—the ludicrous comfort our grandfathers knew, Mateo thought, deciding to relax his moral diet just this once and give himself over to the deep-dish pie of their cooing and chirping: a blackbird pie! His opinion of every detail (what did he think of this antique gold brooch, two hornets imbibing a drop of honey?) was sought so earnestly that he had a glimpse of the irresistible lure to self-importance women had once represented for men . . . Did still, no doubt, in small-town marriages. In Mathilda's seaside town once on a hot, starless August night he'd walked past a blazing window and looked in to see a father eating a big dinner of several steaming dishes at midnight while his wife and daughters stood and watched him with anxious devotion. He'd been so fat that his shirt had bulged open between the two middle buttons to expose a little *lucarne* of pale, furry flesh.

Day after day Mateo dropped by Flora's on his way elsewhere to pay a call on someone or to pick up tickets or to leave his card on a lady he didn't yet quite know. Whereas in the great world he realized he seemed buffoonish to his elders, eccentric to his contemporaries and forbidding to his juniors, when he was with his tribal princesses he knew he was being looked at as a norm of civilized behavior. Until now, he'd always come in on conversations at an angle. He'd always been the one to make the oddball, funny comment or to scandalize everyone with a paradox that turned over a rock of convention to expose squirming, unsuspected life. But the princesses, far from marveling at his pronouncements, memorized them. He who had been the jester was becoming the king. At home Gabriel was silently imitating him. At Flora's the princesses adored him. He who'd learned to listen and occasionally to comment was now having to speak. Why not?

Why not?

He told himself he was protecting his nephew by concealing Angelica's whereabouts. Nor did she express any eagerness to see the boy, even though she now knew he was living with Mateo and recuperating from his ordeal. Once she slipped under the door to Mateo's house a note for Gabriel: "Hope you're having fun with that wild uncle of yours. Believe it or not, I'll be dropping in on you one of these days. Don't worry. Just for a cup of tea." In imitation of Flora's way of signing herself with an *F* that looked like a morning glory closed for the afternoon and drooping over a fencetop, Angelica had devised for herself an *A* composed of her new straightened hair with just a bit of bounce at the ends and her new squint-thin sunglasses. She prided herself on the jaunty wording, lifted from one of Flora's conversations.

The next afternoon, when Mateo stopped in at Flora's, he invited Angelica to go for a walk with him. She seemed sad. When he asked her what was wrong she said, "In another year I'll be fifteen and in my country that's when a girl has, you know, a big party . . ."

Mateo could well imagine that what she was calling a "party" was in fact a foul orgy or human sacrifice. He'd once read an anthropological study of her people, although he'd gone vague on the details. "Don't worry, my dear," he said, putting an arm around her waist. "I'll give you a lovely party."

"Will you dance with me? If I were having a fifteener back home, I'd be all in white and my father would dance with me."

Mateo produced a beautifully pained smile at the word "father" only as a civilized reflex; privately he was delighted, and even felt an incestuous stirring in his crotch. "Of course I'll be your father." He pictured the two of them waltzing across the polished marble floor of the ballroom in his palace. A good time to open the room to the public again, he thought, and to remind them all of the quality of my stuccos! Automatically, a guest list began to assemble itself, clusters of names floating closer as raised shapes he could read by touch and also as tastes (sweet, solid, salt, pepper, acid, bland) that he'd have to compose into something savory, subtle—not his usual chaotic smorgasbord.

As they were approaching Flora's door and about to go up to her eyrie, they passed one of those museum trustees Walter had introduced to Mateo. The old goat screwed a monocle into his eye, doffed his claret hat to Angelica and, when Mateo glanced back, gave him an obscene high-sign. Why, Mateo thought, I suppose we do look like an improbable couple made plausible by lust, *my* lust; we're either father and daughter out for a stroll (genre scene) or, given the complete disparity in our coloring, we're bounder and exotic dependent (filthy postcard). "Angelica," Mateo said as they began their ascent, she four stairs ahead and burningly conscious of his eyes on her narrow hips, "your little note to Gabriel was thoughtful but I'm afraid it's thrown him into terrible turmoil."

She looked back with a stricken expression. "I—" she went pale and swayed on the narrow step.

He rushed up behind her to steady her. "There, there. No real harm done. But could you see your way, just for now, to maintaining a nourishing silence? We must think of the poor child's fragile health."

Angelica backed up slightly against Mateo, who was now on the same step. She looked over her shoulder at him. "Whatever you say, my dear," she whispered huskily. Mateo started to protest (but I'm only thinking about Gabriel) when suddenly he had his arms around her and she was twisting toward him, her mouth opening to his, her tongue muscular and hot, her tonic natural scent of clove reaching up powerfully through the unpleasant jasmine perfume she'd dabbed herself with. He hadn't realized how hungry he had been for a sweet human body in his arms until now, and he feasted and feasted on her—his mouth feasted, his groping hands feasted, the whole trembling length of his body pressed to hers feasted. It seemed that he could reach down through her mouth or up through her cunt to her winedark, richly bathed, majestically beating heart. She turned her eyes to one side and up as though she were reading something just over his shoulder, but when he glanced back he saw nothing there except the bottom of the next flight of stairs. Like his nephew so long ago, Mateo wanted to be in this strangely absent woman, to live inside her, but whereas Gabriel had half-feared her as a savage and had invented a treacherous thermodynamics of the female body and a faulty hydraulics of the male—had, in short, reduced their meetings to occasions of perilous physics and mortal shame—Mateo saw her as a provincial miss, a dusky naïve, the fictile soubrette whom (yes, of course) an older, worldly woman had all along been grooming for his—(ah, yes) his attentions.

And yet Mateo himself found something dangerous about this girl. He was an Infamous Seducer and yet he felt he had no experience behind him, no method to fall back on. He must pull each act of seduction out of his very body. If he'd been more honest, he might have admitted that all seducers feel innocent, that their professional innocence is what makes them seductive. At a certain moment in any long, drunken evening, anyone in his circle was capable of saying, "You know, under all this I'm really very innocent." Yes, but the *all this* has become a considerable carapace; were it to be pierced, would searchers find this celebrated innocence cowering within? Even the coarse, automatic way of alluding to innocence is only one more proof of how well-traveled the road is, that road called "sincerity."

Mateo was not shy or unsure of himself. No, but he'd been punished for a long time by Edwige. His body had been starved by her, even while she'd fed his imagination.

After he'd met her at the absurd matchmaking session organized by the composer Robert Constantine, Mateo had fallen solemnly and irreversibly in love with Edwige. Love is the least sociable of the sentiments, the most isolating, since not even the beloved is interested in it. In that way love is like death, which the living treat with respect so that they need not think about it. Once death is looked at in the eyes, one follows, against one's will, the hooded figure through the streets and out, out beyond the town walls. And once one lies down beside love, one can never rise again. The voices of duty, of friendship and authority, sound fainter and fainter, a bit like the shouts from the boat that the drowning man hears as indifferent whines. Mateo had been in love twice before, but enough time had elapsed since those two sadnesses for him to have forgotten them. So, after years of abstention, the addict forgets the sweats, the anxiety, and remembers only the cold wind along the midnight beach or the swelling stamp of friends dancing in the café, or the lyric panic of the flame, the spoon, the eyedropper.

How had she, a stage beauty who couldn't even spell, subjugated him? She, of course, had nothing to do with it—yet another way in which love is unsociable since, like god, it is a first cause, not shaped by events. It is at once the most artificial of sentiments and the one that feels most like a force of nature: unremitting, doctrinaire. Impatient friends say, "But you've just gone and talked yourself into it," forgetting that what begins as a game can end in tragic seriousness. Or they say, "But she's an idiot!" as though love were an award for intelligence.

Of course there is one good thing about love (lovers pride themselves on it and admire it in each other): the lover cares enough about at least one thing to love it. In a world of saurian indifference, of bet-hedging and planning for a future one wants to be secure since it can't be happy, the lover dares to risk everything on a loser, himself. Mateo loved Edwige, which meant he looked at her with unwavering fascination. He loved her perfect body (her "intelligent" body as the masseur had said).

According to the letter of the law (a law she had codified), they had never been lovers at all nor had she misled him even for a second. On the contrary, he was the one who'd misled her by telling her she could live in his palace, she could have her own wing, he'd expect nothing, they'd be friends, nothing more. She'd made him swear to friendship, which he'd done smilingly, as one smiles while counting to twenty at the start of a game one is sure of winning.

But he hadn't won. She had indeed moved into the east wing, the five little rooms above the shuttered and shrouded ballroom. The wing had been added three centuries after the body of the palace, which had been built by a bellicose family who'd abandoned the premises soon after they'd encased the facade in rose and sea-green stones, leaving behind little except their name, which had designated it ever since. This name had associated the palace in the public imagination with a distant branch of the family who'd been far more illustrious in rank and deed—who, in fact, had led the heroic but doomed resistance to the conquerors thirty years ago. A hundred times Mateo had explained to people that his own family was unrelated to the original owners, who, moreover, should not be confused with their admirable (and now extinct) collateral branch. But just as language over time fuses distinctions and thereby becomes impoverished and efficient, in the same way popular legend, moving in the opposite direction to the accounts of professional historians, flattens narratives and forges them into weapons. Mateo knew that his palace, its current disrepair only serving to heighten its romantic appeal, was revered by more and more ardent patriots as a symbol of nationalism. The fools were even looking to him—or to Gabriel!—as the last heir to a great tradition and the next leader of its revival. That he was (and would always remain) blissfully indifferent to politics did not deter them.

In their religious way, they claimed to see a meaningful sign even in his indifference. "When he changes heart," the people whispered, "that will be a signal the revolution is finally about to begin."

Edwige initiated a melancholy reign of chaos over the palace. She had done nothing until now but appear in tidy comedies that audiences, made up of the conquerors and their collaborators, arrived at late and left early after gossiping from box to box. She suddenly decided she was ready for something more . . . artistic. She accepted no new roles, starved herself, slept all day, and roamed the palace by night. She wore strange costumes of her own devising, patched together out of things she'd found in the attic or at the flea market. And she disoriented herself through drink and dormitives. This new epoch had begun with the ambition to seem interesting (to catch the interest of some more daring impresario) but had been pursued with the somber restlessness that leaked over from her long quarrel with the world. She was too relentless to be eccentric, too bitter to be capricious. All night long she'd pace the corridors. Sometimes at three or four in the morning Mateo, in Phrygian nightcap and cotton gown, would stand in the silent ballroom—with its shrouded chandelier, flaking stuccos and sinking marble floors—and listen as Edwige dragged a trunk from one side of the room above to the other, back and forth. There. Now. She was doing it again.

All through that winter as fog rose off the canals and snow traced in ermine the black forms of pleasure boats, as warning buoys clanged in the entrance to the harbor, Edwige looked across the canal at an old countess who sat behind closed windows with blue shoulders exposed to the cold in the mandatory décolleté gown of the last century, while, out of sight, her hands and feet were plunged into warmers servants kept stoking with hot bricks from the kitchen fireplace; all through that long, monotonous winter when the city seemed to be haunted by the flat, unresonant tolling of the bell called "Mother" and by ghosts vaporizing off moss-bearded steps or escaping foul, sealed-over wells of braided marble in empty courtyards, Edwige, inspired by the disciplined decorum of the unknown countess, pursued her nocturnal efforts at self-transformation, as though she were a larva slowly metamorphosing herself inside the palace into a moth with immense white wings separated by the slenderest black body, like luxuriously blank pages enclosing a velvet bookmark.

Edwige judged Mateo nicely. She seemed to know that the less kindness she showed him the more enamored of her he'd become. A more affectionate or careless woman would have let some warmth escape if only accidentally, but Edwige was avaricious in measuring out her smiles with calipers and her nods with a transit. If she hadn't been living under his roof, he might have been able to forget her. Or at least think about her less. But he had a superstitious credulity about sharing the same roof with a woman; by moving in she'd become his wife. If he had always kept women at a distance before it was because he was so susceptible to them. Just as proximity had once been his deepest feeling and a stranger close by had had more influence over him than an absent friend, just as he would still eat and drink anything in sight and his only method of moderation was to maintain an empty larder, by the same token his only way of taming love had been to keep it out of reach.

Once Edwige pushed past the door, she broke through the membrane housing his heart. That's what he meant by superstition, for he could only take literally the expression "We live together."

In a *roman à clef* by one of his friends, he appeared as a fool "head over heels for an actress who was usually heels over head— but not for him." He found himself quarreling with every single description in the book. The writer (whom he'd dropped, not out of anger but contempt, of course) was obviously someone on whom everything had been wasted. She, the author, had shown him as a heartless, stylized creature suited only to play a minor role; where he saw in himself nothing but trembling nuance and anguished compromise she saw smugness and compromise. Even his conversation, which he knew was his highest art, an organ toccata scattered across contrasting assemblages—this conversation she'd transcribed as nothing but shrieking high notes for a fife! In describing him, she'd even lifted a line from someone else's poem: "Vain, flippant, unfeeling monster."

But what had caught his attention was that one line about Edwige. Had Edwige's adventures while she was already living with him become common knowledge? How much did the novelist really know? Which escapades was she referring to? Were they ones he already knew about or had there been others? Heels over head . . . he bitterly resented the cozy little way in which she discussed sex as a familiar, titillating object rather than as the strange, embarrassing improvisation it really is.

Mateo was "intellectual" only because fashionable people were supposed to be. He far preferred the witty bantering of Edwige's visiting theater friends. They'd drop by before rehearsal or for a midnight supper after a performance and Edwige, wafting her perfume testers through the air in her bedroom, would keep up her side of the wisecracks, the gossip, the lore. Or she'd spring up and do a two-minute "bit" with one of her girlfriends, a pitch pipe-perfect evocation of a show Mateo had seen and forgotten.

The other actors treated him with a certain deference because Edwige had told them he was an intellectual; they respected intellectualism though they had no desire to slow down long enough to cultivate it. They caught fire only from each other, and Mateo, whose knowledge of the commercial theater was limited, never could tell exactly when they were quoting or when they were inventing speeches. Whereas Mathilda's opera singers had a clear, proprietary sense of how to feed and care for the Voice and could comfortably anticipate the moment three years from now when it would be bright enough for that coloratura role or sufficiently darkened for that mezzo part, actors had no such confidence about their "instrument" (the body? the voice? the interpretive intelligence?). Nor were achievements as easily recognized in the theater as in the opera house, nor was the repertoire either as static or as good. Edwige, unlike a diva, had to choose her "vehicles" with little advance knowledge of whether they'd "work." For her the line between her art and her personal life was far less clear than it was for singers. When Mateo pointed out all these disadvantages to her, Edwige shrugged and said, "True, but the ambiguity of an actress's life is the same sort of insecurity we all feel every moment. The serenity of the singer isn't very lifelike, is it?"

Her logic was impeccable, but an air of anxious defeat did hang over her circle. One actress had memorized an extensive vocabulary of gestures and poses (the top of the right forearm pressed to the brow with a clenched fist and the other arm dangling straight down, hand open, the left foot advanced and flexed—all this symbolized Rebellious Fortitude). No one, alas, knew this language, and all of her efforts had resulted in only two unpredicted glimpses onstage of an implausible but noble plastique. Another actress had studied dialects of every sort and could "do" old mountain women or garrulous cardsharps or over-refined ladies who changed all their $r$s to $z$s in imitation of the conquerors. But she, too, had only had two opportunities to use this knowledge. Tumbling, singing, dancing, memorizing the classics, walking a tightrope, playing with a medicine ball, these ladies filled their days with earnest but superfluous chores.

Edwige had added to her other pursuits the ambition to be original. She should never have been an actress, since, although she could perform brilliantly, she had neither the insouciance to wait out the long spells of idleness in the theater (or rather *out* of the theater) nor the docility to submit to the orders of an impresario. She wanted, again and again, to be chosen, as though at each audition her entire value was on trial. If not chosen, she would plot vengeance against these new enemies; if chosen, she would plot vengeance against these new enemies—for how dare they have judged her! Even the text she resented, and she and one of her friends accordingly were preparing an evening in which they'd inverted and cut up a lamentable sex farce written fifty years ago. The epicene rejoinders, which had once sped swiftly by in a flood of naughtiness, now loomed out of the frieze at disturbing angles. "Alone, at last, my perfect pet" was slowed down to an ominous, sinister pace in which all the sadness within her Edwige could never acknowledge was given plangent expression.

Mateo couldn't think about anything except her. He'd stand in the cold ballroom and listen for her. One night a bird flew in through a broken pane and flapped past the empty ceiling panel out of which an improvident ancestor had slashed the Allegory of Age and Youth to sell to strangers. The panicky sound of the wings and the bird's mewing cries illuminated his own desperation. Edwige would let him stay for hours in her apartment but every hour marked a new extreme in her exasperation and his abjectness. Although she maintained a strict decorum and solemnly gave him her hand to kiss when he arrived and departed, she enjoyed teasing him in the interim. If her tongue drew tears she merely chastised him: "Darling, if you can't take a joke . . ."

He had supper with her one night and he became drunk while she remained sober. The more he drank the less he wanted to leave her. Her supper consisted of all the half-peeled, half-baked vegetables, the decoctions of raw egg and wild thyme honey, the bran puddings and sesame-seeded fruit soups that she regarded as healthy. She could never arrange for a smooth, invisible flow of courses in decent dishes. Her broken crockery and the haphazard presentation was the homage she paid to her mess hall youth as the daughter of the regiment and her subsequent years on the road as a performer. The meal did get served, he drank his coffee, she her tisane, the clock struck midnight, a servant cleared even their cups and liqueur glasses—but still he didn't leave. Edwige stagily suppressed a yawn, turned up the lights—but still he didn't leave. She even alluded to her busy morning tomorrow, but he uncorked himself a new bottle of wine. He noticed that she began to shake with rage or nervousness as the hour of one approached. Finally she stood, held out her hand for him to kiss and said she must retire, but he could see she was glistening with sweat, her yawn was out of anxiety not sleepiness, and her eyes shone with panicked alertness.

He knew that at one something would happen. He refused to leave, although by now she'd gone grim with anger. Then there was a loud pounding at the door. When she didn't answer the door flew open—and there stood four of the boatmen from the canal station next door. She'd asked them to come up after they got off work; she was to be their last fare of the day. If Mateo had left even as late as midnight she would still have had plenty of time to repair her toilette (or dishevel it). Certainly she could have kept secret this bizarre encounter. Mateo described a florid bow and walked out past the burly, middle-aged men with their barrel chests and shoulders hunched over from a life of pulling oars.

Mateo was swept out by the force of his own gesture. When he was down the dark hallway he glanced back to see beyond the open double doors Edwige, cold with anger, standing motionless in profile, head bent, wearing her aquamarine silk dress, her long hair swept up off her neck, although a few feathered golden hairs were floating free. They seemed to be moving slightly with static electricity. Mateo thought of cotton candy, of the way it suddenly crystallizes thread by glittering thread in the whirling basin around the heated, sugar-filled cone. The four men—all good family men, whom Mateo had known for years, one of them having ferried him about every midnight ten years ago during his romance with the Black Venus, another the father of that poor child with the deformed leg—the four men looked embarrassed but ready to serve.

Once he was downstairs in the cold fog pooling between buildings and curling around him, he walked and walked through the early morning streets. He'd felt triumphant about discovering Edwige's secret, but now the excitement had flickered out and he was alone, exiled; he'd seen something he wasn't supposed to and she was angry. She might leave him—which made Mateo chortle at his own stupidity, since she'd never been with him. She'd only lived under his roof. It occurred to him that just as childless women of a certain age sometimes courted pregnancy, so unmarried men in their fifth decade begin to dream of establishing a household. At this point his "family" consisted of just one member: Edwige. And now he'd driven her away with his jealous prying. Now she'd never let him watch her again while she took a bath.

His night vision was so bad that were it not for the white stones that bordered the steps going up and down bridges he would have plummeted long ago into a canal. He heard a high-pitched cry and saw something white coming toward him. He put the two clues together and came up with a hysterical woman he knew (they called her "the Ugly Duchess"); he opened his arms wide to receive her flying embrace and said in warm welcome, "Stella"—and a seagull squawked past, nearly brushing him with its wings.

Later, lights emerged out of a fog near the palace gates of that other woman—what was her name?—who in fact was so proud of her thousand-year-old name, despite the fact that her only illustrious relative had been the one who'd betrayed a patriot leader. Her uncle had wanted to improve his memory and had hired the penniless Great Patriot to teach him his mnemonic method. When the lessons didn't go well, the disgruntled patrician had turned his professor in to the authorities. The seven years of imprisonment and trial that followed, the "confession" the wardens extorted through torture, the prisoner's subsequent disavowal of it, the judgment, the sentence, and finally the execution by burning in the Field of Flowers near where boys play kickball and greengrocers hawk their vegetables—all that had resulted from the noble student's gripe. Silly woman. Silly heiress to a silly family. But he doffed his cap and bowed at the illuminated sphere that welled up out of the watergates to her palace, lest she find him rude.

He stumbled through the dry square where they sold old clothes outdoors, a place that looked so parched and deserted on Mondays when the merchants folded their tents and one could study the facades. Mateo always felt so dry in this square, as though it were a hundred miles from the sea in a dusty town on the plateau. No one fashionable lived here, although one of the palaces bore the name of a patriot family that had refused office under the conquerors and had become so poor they now took in boarders, or so people said. Tonight only one light glimmered at the other end of the square, on the route to the post office. Like a bat Mateo listened for fine changes in the tune of his own echoing steps; when the notes squeezed up a quarter tone and became louder and less hollow, he knew he was approaching a wall. He'd memorized every inch of the paths he usually took—from the Tower to the Grand, or from his own house to Mathilda's—but if a child left a ball on the pavement or a workman tore up some stones to repair a sewer, Mateo sometimes fell, certainly stumbled.

Now, in a darkness that was ply of grey over ply of black, rag heap of shadow against bone pile of lamplight, Mateo wandered nearly sightless, opening his arms in greeting to a gull and bowing toward a garbageman's scow, which he mistook for the departing Mocenigos (ah, yes, that was their name). Just as time and the salt air were eating away the filigree of marble balustrades, in the same way night was effacing the visible. But against this murk, so demanding in that with each step he had to make a few new navigational guesses, discard others and revise all, he could see in haloed profile Edwige and her four boatmen. He saw the golden hairs stirring on the nape of her neck and he imagined dipping a paper wand into them and collecting a twist of spun sugar.

After a few days went by he sent Edwige a basket of hothouse fruit. She invited him later in the week for tea. Her other guests spoke nothing but their own language, which Mateo happened to know. Edwige and Mateo shared the burden of entertaining these excitable foreigners with their wasp waists and tongues, their punctilio over their own culture and their simultaneous contempt for and adoration of the smart set in the capital (a social map they'd drawn in somewhat idiosyncratically, so that they placed Walter, who had once lectured in their university, at the exact center of things, whereas they imagined Mathilda was Walter's disciple, a relationship he himself had suggested during a visit to their land).

Edwige didn't smile at Mateo once or address him directly but the hard work of coping with these guests (distant relatives of Skeets, Edwige's first lover) brought them closer as the hours trudged by.

Now that Mateo knew she craved violent sex and even hired boatmen to beat her (for one of the boatmen had been persuaded to tell Mateo everything) he resolved to win her through brutality. One evening, when she gave him her hand to kiss, he twisted it and brought her howling to her knees. "Bitch," he growled.

Two seconds dripped two drops of eternity into the room. Edwige blinked, rubbed her wounded hand, then she burst out laughing. She staggered to her feet, tried to slap him but almost choked on the laughter that came heaving up out of her. She calmly wiped the tears from her cheeks with smoothing fingertips, almost as though she were rubbing in a night cream, but then a new spasm of hilarity would shake her and she staggered over to the small table by the window and leaned on it for strength. (Remember this bit: onstage, portray "weak with laughter" by leaning weight on table, she thought.)

The lover is a figure of fun to the beloved because he never understands her but she understands him all too well. When Edwige recovered she sat him down beside her, patted his hand as a grown-up daughter might pat her senile parent, and said very quietly, in a calm voice, "Even if I do have *un gout raffiné* for certain excesses (I always like a thrashing when I'm getting cramps, it's a remedy I learned that year I worked in the circus), even so, I don't want to have my oldest and best darling friend twist my hand like some playground tomboy with braids in the middle of the after—" but she never said "noon" because a wild spume geysered up out of her and she went on to wet a big linen handkerchief clear through with tears of malicious merriment.

Mateo tried to smile sympathetically with this laughter at his expense, but his smile felt like vinegar on his lips. She howled and twisted and he averted his eyes, almost as though she was revealing too much of herself (convulsive laughter like birthpains, friend looks away in embarrassment: use this bit, she thought). What he thought was that if we love someone, anything she does seems sexy, even her erotic shortcomings seem to be new enticements. If we're not in love, then and only then do we seek perversity in bed, which we'll accept only from strangers. A friend is neither a lover nor a stranger, hence useless—or comical—when he casts himself in a sexual "role" (for Edwige's way of studying every moment as a stage possibility was beginning to infect Mateo's vision as well).

He would decide he must reconcile himself to friendship and nothing more with Edwige and he'd begin to take all the steps needed to reorient his feelings. He wouldn't see her at night when wine and the intoxication of his own chatter would persuade him she must *secretly* return his love. He'd ask her to perform little errands on his behalf, the sort of commissions any friend and no lover would give. He'd see her for lunch, but only with other people. When he ran over to see her he'd make sure he was dressed in his old moth-eaten dressing gown. He'd tell her about his sexual adventures with other women and ask her advice.

She responded to these changes in an unexpected way. She didn't notice his deshabille since she never really saw him anyway.

She refused to do errands for him, but she would have refused a friend if she had had one. She didn't observe that he was avoiding her at night; moreover, she would visit him whenever it suited her. She had never liked his dinners, since she hated being imprisoned at a table for hours of talk, especially cultural chat of the sort Mateo's friends produced. What she liked was running in during the aperitifs and kissing him with quivering, locked-eyed intensity before rushing off: mysterious domestic scene. She absolutely refused to give Mateo advice about other women. She became very irritable one afternoon and said, putting down a perfume tester and pushing back the enormous white sleeves of her chemist's smock: "But, darling, I know so few women. I have no idea what, or even *if,* they think." Another time, when she was screwing diamonds into her ears and Mateo was lounging on her bed and discussing a conquest he hoped to make, she said, "Am I so old and ugly that you dare to discuss other women with me?"

Not that she wanted him, but she wanted him to want her; she found it indelicate of him to abandon his picturesque, hopeless love for her. Naturally she felt free to discuss her beaux with him. In her descriptions they always had such strange, even unappetizing problems; what she always neglected to mention was that they were, without exception, mortally handsome. Sometimes she'd bring a beau by. Mateo could see the sure signs of a massive, perfectly shaped body under the expensive tailoring. Or he'd recognize in her escort the small, exquisitely modeled features of the conquerors, heads that looked as though they'd been given a few extra turns on the lathe. Edwige took on an eerie innocence with the beaux she liked and she'd smile at everyone else's remarks with benign, myopic dignity; she and the beau gave the impression of monarchs visiting a state institution they didn't care to understand all that well. If she was really infatuated, she'd lace an arm around Mateo's waist, lean her head on his chest, look out at the beau and say, fondly, "Isn't he wonderful?"

She could never quite let Mateo go because he loved her, and his love she admired. Also, he gave her good advice about her career, or at least advice. Her career was the subject she could never exhaust but that exhausted everyone not in love with her. And finally she too shared his clownishly old-fashioned and never-mentioned respect for the home, the hearth, the household. With Mateo, she half-believed she'd at last found a home. If she didn't wholly believe in him or it, that reluctance was due to her wanting to settle down with someone younger and more handsome. And of course it was also due to the wild, bitter, damaged part of her, the war-orphan part, that didn't believe in homes at all.

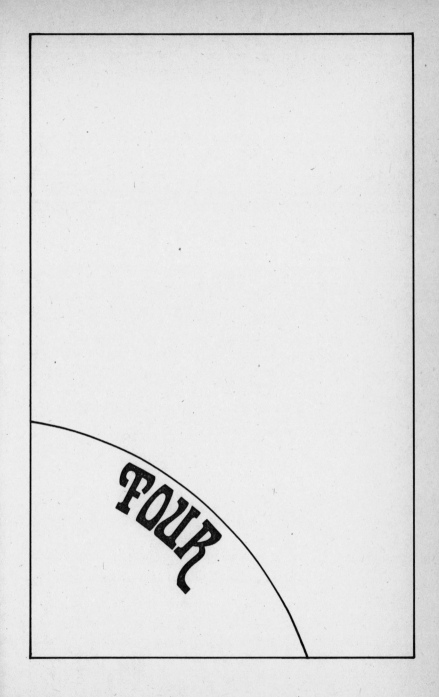

FOUR

**G**ABRIEL saved Mateo from Edwige. When the boy was brought back to the capital late that spring and moved in with his uncle, he was so pitiful, so stunned by suffering, that Mateo devoted all his energies to him. Mateo never had a moment to think, "How much love will I give this boy?" The boy's demand absorbed all his uncle's supply. If the simple phrase, "We live together," had given Edwige complete power over Mateo, Gabriel's moving in had conferred on him the same authority—the absolutism of domesticity.

With this difference: Edwige didn't really want Mateo's devotion, or she wanted only part of it part of the time, whereas the boy greedily took everything offered him. Whereas Edwige had to keep Mateo at some distance lest he expect too much from her, and even banned him from her wing of the palace for days on end, the boy, being Mateo's nephew and ward, never questioned his claims or his uncle's bounty. Mateo had felt for so long that the terms under which he was offering his love to Edwige were suspect. What a relief to have the boy doubt neither his motives nor his right to love him. All along Mateo had known how disposable he was to Edwige. She was surrounded by admirers of her beauty, just as Mathilda never lacked for admirers of her intellect. Whether Edwige spent a week or a month with one man or another, whether she wept bitter tears over a third, could be seen as moves in a game as absorbing as it was inconsequential. For Edwige the options of romance were dimensions of frustration; they were unavailing distractions from the failure of fame to visit her. No wonder her very restlessness would cause her from time to time to sweep every last chessman off the board.

But for Gabriel, at least during the first few months of his stay in the capital, Mateo had brought him forth from the dark and lured him back into the light. A delicate operation, the ascent out of the underworld, and especially delicate for the one who was dead but now must live again. Just as a deep-sea diver must not be hauled up too quickly, lest his lungs burst, in the same way Mateo had slowly to raise a half-reluctant, half-eager, all-fearing Gabriel into the world. The solemnity of this task outweighed the interest Mateo took in Edwige's sex sprees and restless romances. Mateo's limited time, energy, money, wit, food, had to go to this bedraggled child who would starve otherwise, whereas the imperious, irritable Edwige would scarcely notice if one more costly bouquet was flung at her feet or not. Mateo traded in one obsession for another, his jealousy over Edwige for his resolve to save the boy.

Although she often spoke of friendship, Edwige had few friends. Her only confidant was a fey girl who'd be be fat when Mateo saw her one time and thin the next. Her natural appearance seemed to be fat, since fat gave her two puffs of sadness under her eyes, which provided just the right degree of somberness against which her antic humor could glow. When she was thin, she wore her thinness like a costume. She'd suck in her cheeks at the door, toss her head back and lead herself into the room. With her Edwige would talk about men, casting, food and clothes; in addition, with her Edwige was working up her "experimental" playlet, a project the friend collaborated on out of loyalty alone since she didn't understand a word.

Such a friendship demanded little. They'd go to an audition together if they both happened to be going anyway or they'd take tea together at the Grand after a rehearsal or before a performance. At lunch neither of them would ever eat much (in contrast to the truly enormous quantities the friend would consume late at night if she was on a binge, but that wasn't exactly the same as "eating"). They'd split a salad and even that they'd be careful not to finish: "We'll each leave a *leaf,*" Edwige would whisper, tucking in her chin in a headmistressly way and looking at her friend over the tops of nonexistent glasses. When one of them was touring the provinces she never wrote the other. At the beginning of an affair with a man the two women let long silences develop—which contrasted sharply with the nightly conferences they held at the troubled end of an affair.

Now Edwige decided to befriend Gabriel. Her vanity and her pretensions to eternal youth kept her from wanting to mother the boy. Besides, her kind of careless, wisecracking affection picked up in army camps and backstage (the two great sites of transience) would scarcely have suited a mother.

Gabriel's obvious attraction to her (the bulge in his pants always seemed to find her as though it were a magnet and she due north) reassured her. He took her for someone more or less his age, she assumed, although she was considerably older. One of Edwige's misgivings was that only in the virtually childless world of artists and aging statesmen she inhabited could she be taken as "young."

She was afraid that if she was ever placed beside a genuine youth, her own claims would fade. She knew that her skin was sleeker than any adolescent's, that she'd retained the litheness of a swimmer and that she could "play confusion" more convincingly than anyone less confident, but she also knew that in a lineup with real teenagers she'd give herself away. The two creases circling her neck (the "necklace of beauty" as women had once called it hopefully) were now ineradicable as was the coarsening of the skin at the elbows, and she'd lost the touching tremor that had once caused her hand to shake in company, an avowal of terror that had so embarrassed her back then that her face had always gone scarlet with anger and shame—yet another beguiling "turn" she wished she could have "kept in the act." Her voice wasn't thin enough, her nose not small enough, her eyes not nervous enough, her cheeks not full enough, her clothes not unfashionable enough to be truly youthful.

And yet Gabriel seemed to take her as some sort of contemporary, perhaps an older sister. When Walter would pay a call and, after purveying all his gossip, begin with the obligatory "intellectual" part of the visit ("Recently I've begun to speculate on the meaning of treachery"), Edwige would glance at Gabriel and make a horrible face, rolling her eyes back into her head until only ghastly white crescents showed, and letting a string of drool unspool out of her palsied lower lip—such a sudden and shocking transformation that if Gabriel didn't burst out laughing then he was sure to a moment later when she turned herself into a squinting, nodding, self-improving lady who had only one little tic which caused her to bare her gums like an angry capuchin monkey for a mad moment before lapsing back into the polite homiletics of her nodding. Or if Gabriel was imprisoned at the dinner table with Mateo's motley guests Edwige would breeze in to blow kisses all around and to swoop down to whisper, "Better thee than me," into Gabriel's burning ear.

In the fall, three months after Gabriel's arrival in the capital,

Edwige was cast in the biggest part of her career, and she won the role through Mateo's intervention. Until now she'd courted but ignored Mateo's advice, although she'd been grateful for his confidence in her talent. But one evening at Mathilda's, Mateo met a playwright who had earned a fortune with well-crafted melodramas that flattered audiences by serving up last year's Intellectual Issue as a garnish tucked around the meat and potatoes of suspense. His newest effort had been done in response to his impresario's challenge: "Write me a play in which the heroine is silent in the first act, nude in the second, and smothered to death by feathers in the third." That *donnée* somehow linked up in the playwright's mind with recently fashionable cant about madness being a form of higher wisdom—to result in *The Priestess*.

The playwright had chanced upon his "problem" (for it was a "problem" play" as he gravely explained) while reading a book of Walter's. That the book actually ridiculed the madness-is-wisdom equation had completely eluded the celebrated reader, nor was Walter eager to correct his mistake. The playwright could broadcast Walter's name to the thousands of people who attended his plays and read the program notes. Privately Walter could later dismiss the playwright as a fool "whoring after the multitudes." Because the playwright met Mateo at Walter's salon, where the tone was clubby and men and women of power routinely exchanged favors without much fuss, he responded with a breezy "Yeah, sure" when Mateo said, "You know, I think Edwige would be perfect as the Priestess. For one thing, she's one of the few women in the theater who could dare to undrape publicly every night. For another, she's my mistress—and she's been driving me crazy at home. Please help me out. Take her off my hands. Shall I send her around tomorrow at noon?"

When Mateo told Edwige of this rendezvous, she was not at all pleased. She angrily rebuked him for mentioning "undraping," would have had a fit of apoplexy had she heard his claim that she was his mistress, and did go into a fury about the private audition, where she thought she'd be asked to undress and even *unbend* for the writer—but in spite of her better judgment she kept the appointment and got the part. She was treated with all the respect she demanded from men in her profession, a demand that didn't keep her from paying men outside it to degrade her. The playwright, in turn, had been impressed by Edwige's alliance with the world that most despised him, the intellectual.

The night Gabriel went to see Edwige in *The Priestess,* few intellectuals and fewer courtiers were in attendance. Most of the audience was made up of rich merchants and their wives goitered with pearls and howdahed with diamonds, but for the frail boy, still weak and dazed and yearning for his smelly bed in the maid's room, the assembly wounded him with its brilliance. When Edwige, playing the catatonic priestess of a suppressed cult, sat mutely in the witness stand onstage during the first act while the prosecutor instructed the jury about her crimes against "civilized people," Gabriel kept wondering when Edwige would make her entrance. At last he recognized her under her makeup and looked at her with new sympathy. He, too, was an enemy and outcast of society. Never had "Mom," as he called her to vex her—a name Edwige let pass precisely because it sent him into gales of laughter, proof of its absurdity—never had "Mom" looked so serious or so attentive. Although she said not a word every eye was on her face, across which emotions traveled, as warring armies might pass over a strategic island in a condensed version of its history.

When the curtain came down Gabriel thought the play was over, but once he understood that Edwige would appear nude in the next act, he felt a strange excitement break out all over him, for night after night he'd locked himself in the toilet and masturbated to the anthology of images he'd put together of Edwige: Edwige doing her experimental playlet ("Pet Perfect My, Last at, Alone"); or Edwige waving perfume testers as she sat like a rain goddess within the white storm cloud of her chemist's smock; or Edwige being handed out of a boat by a liveried usher from the theater— or out of a vehicle by the doorman at the Grand, her cynical smile tipping up on one side while the enormous pale gauze brim of her crownless hat sliced over her eye on the other side and two yipping white dogs, which she'd borrowed for the afternoon because they set off the black fur hem to her dress, scampered daintily at her feet. In every sequence Edwige was finally stripped bare by his imagination and Gabriel, like a learned doctor who paces around a spotlit table on which the narcolept lies, had been nothing but a traveling, flashing monocle in the dark. Once in his fantasy he'd had her waken just as he'd reached a sting and she'd flown sobbing into his arms. He'd gasped—and outside the toilet a floorboard had creaked and, horrified, Gabriel had looked through the crack to see his spying uncle, flustered, retreating on tiptoe.

Gabriel had heard Edwige say that during the audition and throughout the rehearsals of *The Priestess* she'd never once taken off her clothes. That had been a point of honor, of rather quixotic honor for the management, considering that the whole city was flocking into the theater precisely to see the moment when the mad Priestess would re-create the secret orgy with which her people solemnized a marriage. The Priestess, after stripping nude, would narrate to the jury the entire ceremony—or some such gibberish. No one cared. Just as people were willing to endure opera plots about armed goddesses on horseback because one sublime aria described the hiding place of the gnome's gold, in the same way audiences were content to wade through the playwright's anthropological and philosophical fantasies (summarized by the prosecutor, someone who by the end of the play would have gone mad himself and become the priest of the cult who would offer Edwige to the throbbing winged embrace of a randy god disguised as a swan)— content to suffer through all this nonsense in order to see her superb blond body. When Gabriel saw it he forgot who he was and where he was and became nothing but eyes caressing her body. Where is her body hair? was never a question he asked himself since everything about her beauty was so highly finished that he accepted it all as incontestable. Like a mortal who lights a candle to see she has been sleeping with a god, Gabriel felt that for months he'd been giggling at home with a goddess whose divinity was revealed only now before this throng. The courtroom was being converted through lights and strange rustlings into a nocturnal woods where the jurists became either entranced forest animals (the bespectacled, bewigged judge on his bench was now an owl on a branch) or the naked orgiasts. Blue, ghostly, Edwige held aloft what during the trial had been her cloche hat but now had reversed and turned into a foaming skull goblet. With a start, Gabriel realized the playwright had fulfilled all three of the impresario's commands.

Just as children never question what happens around them but accept heinous deprivations or bizarre luxuries without a blink, in the same way Gabriel found it unremarkable that his uncle's mistress had turned out to be a divinity. In one old song that Walter loved, a father who learns he must sacrifice his son sings, "Make thee ready, my dear darling, for we must do a little thing," and the child responds, "Father, I am all ready. Father, I am all ready." Exactly this simplicity marked Gabriel's sudden conversion; the most dazzling religious moment of his life was merely "a little thing." In the dressing room as Edwige laughed and drank champagne and fussed over her wig and reprimanded the humble prop man for that third-act gaffe and received her friends with kisses (that like certain plants live on air alone), as she cleaned her face with cream and joked coarsely with a braying but ever more scornful and blithe Skeets, even when she reappeared after a ten-minute absence bathed and dressed in a close-fitting dress and with her golden hair woven into thick plaits piled high, a look wonderfully at odds with her savage splendor on stage, never once did Gabriel feel it would be anything short of sacrilege to say a word to her.

At last, on the way out, she threw an arm around his scrawny torso and said, "What did you think of your poor old mom? Did I spook you?"

"Yes," Gabriel said, startled by his own answer—and he took her other hand, kissed it and turned away.

An insensitive woman would have teased him or made a fuss or cackled to draw attention to the tribute she'd been paid, but Edwige merely smiled and left in an aura of perfume she'd concocted especially for this occasion. Gabriel felt he was like the moon, visible only when lit by the sun; when Edwige left he went into eclipse.

After the great war, just after Edwige had been Skeets's little "Ermine," she had drifted to the city; the courts had been burdened with old men accusing each other of treason and the conquerors had brought chaos with them. In the cafés their soldiers ate oysters and beefsteaks while the citizens starved themselves fat on noodles or thin on a soup in which some kindly stranger's carrot had lingered for a moment. One night Edwige was so hungry she sucked the corner of the sheet on the bed she happened to find herself in, hoping to extract nourishment from the starch. A weak sleep would seize her and wrap her in its heavy warm arms, as though sleep were a mother pulling its child out of a tub into white towels. This heaviness would alternate with an effervescent lightness, and then Edwige could feel her eyes glow. In the grip of exaltation she'd rattle on to everyone, expending her last energy on the voiced air being siphoned out of her lungs. She could only think of a cat she'd owned as a child that had run in circles, its eyes starting from its head, foam flecking its lips, until it lost the last bit of flesh clinging to its frame and died, a limp swatch of bone and fur. In the midst of desperation her impossible, cruel job was to stay handsome. She would trade the use of her body for the use of someone's washbasin and soap. Every day she watched her merchandise—the size of her breasts, the sheen of her skin, the plush of her hips—dwindle through attrition. She knew that a bit of bright ribbon in her hair or a wide black belt or a flash of nonsensical silk would enable her to attract customers, for even the lowest man harbors a fantasy. She had nothing to sell but a laugh, a droll wink as she stepped out of her shift, the temporary berth her body could lend someone, and the draft of a poem that began, "Once a man met a girl . . ." She had to pretend to a coquetry she'd long since ceased to feel. She had to wink and then look away, glance over her shoulder then disappear around the corner, pause to fix her garter as though she didn't know she was being watched. Since she had become skinny and desperate, most men turned away from her, as though real human want were a talisman to ward off the evil spirit of desire. Even so, she did sell herself from time to time—for a bowl of soup or a place to sleep or a pair of shoes that she made fit her by stuffing newspaper in the toes. Her luck she could only attribute to the fact that in an open city money must move, like a slow lava flow, and in the absence of genuine goods to buy it will go to purchase a dram of human fluid, an erg of human warmth, a dyne of human touch.

One night a red-faced, mushy-mouthed man took her back to his luxurious apartment in a palace that had been quarried out of the marble ruins of an ancient amphitheater. Although the barred windows were hung with cobwebs and the rusticated stone walls outside had sprouted weeds, inside spotless modern luxury prevailed. Her client treated her very decently but almost as though he had a chore, perhaps a pile of laundry, to do and nothing should distract him. With a bachelor's fussiness he bathed her, dried her, reclined her, topped her, dressed her, paid her, showed her out, all the while mumbling half to her, half to himself and never once looking her in the face. His name was Douglas.

Now, all these years later, the great Edwige as the Priestess had acquired one admirer more persistent than all the others—that same man, Douglas. At first she thought he remembered her, too, but soon she was satisfied he didn't—a relief, since she felt her reputation was like an old roof, always springing leaks. She'd slept with hundreds of men and the only one she'd ever turned down had written that spiteful, overly successful song, "The Lady of Infinite Mercy." Douglas came night after night, sat in the fifth row on the aisle, and shamelessly pulled out his binoculars when Edwige stripped. Basket after basket of his roses filled her dressing room. Once he persuaded someone who knew Edwige to invite her to a midnight supper at his palace after her performance. Edwige went. Nothing had changed in the intervening years. Through an open door she even glimpsed the very room where the skinny, big-eyed Ermine had lain back athwart the bed, knees wide, while the fussy, mumbling client had sat on the floor and pulled her, this hungry food, to his licking, lapping mouth. Now he bored her but he had amusing guests to help her while away the hours after the play during which she slowly came down from her excitement. He even invited Mateo to dinner once. Douglas invited all of her out-of-work actor friends. On her birthday he gave her a large midnight supper party.

On the Feast of Health, an ancient holiday that commemorated the sparing of the capital by the plague, he had Edwige and the entire cast of her play ferried out on a flower-covered barge to watch the fireworks.

Once he said to Edwige's fat friend, after he'd poured out a small fortune in these baubles and elegant diversions, "I wonder what I'd have to spend to hold Edwige in my arms for just an hour?"

The friend laughed, tapped him on the knee with her fan, and said, "But you had her ten years ago for the cost of two green apples, and you never looked her in the face and couldn't wait to see her out."

When the friend reported her snappy reply, Edwige was furious. "You silly pig," she said, "you don't give a damn about my reputation, just so you can keep those gums flapping." The friend shrugged, more wounded than she showed but less than the words might have warranted had they been pronounced by someone outside the theater.

Just as an otherwise responsible person will play games with his health, since the threat of sickness gives him an itch to scratch, a persistent irritation he can persistently worry, in the same way Edwige's life—made up of long dull stretches of waiting for satisfactory roles and, when she was working, long dull stretches of acting —required the mild anxiety of risking and defending her reputation. Whether she was sought for a role or not and how she was reviewed by the critics were so beyond her control that she liked to distract herself with this other hobby, this gardening of her reputation, in which she could make some sort of effort by weeding a nasty patch of rumor or sowing pretty seeds elsewhere. In a city that idolized either the tentative beginnings of youth or the absolute mastery of maturity, Edwige, who had been around far too long to seem new, could only hope to become a sacred monster. Now, while enjoying her new celebrity as the Priestess, she should be quietly rewriting the past and fashioning a new version of her "private life," which is an actress's most public representation of herself.

An actress, of course, cannot ever be as respectable as a society woman, nor would it be good for business if she were. But neither must she seem sordid, a cheap pleasure boat for hire. Rather, she should trail behind her a full, colorful legend eyed with raffish scandals and rayed with splashy heartbreaks, everything romantic, smart, urban, tinged with a sadness best conveyed by a brave shrug as she walks off, whistling, into the foggy night. During her years as the daughter of the regiment and later as a mudlark in the conquered city, Ermine had sometimes used her body as a welder uses his torch, melting the hearts of man after man in the white flame of—not her lust, for she was too cold, too determined, too bitter to be lustful—but her determination.

All of those big brown hands on her white thighs, those hard-breathing faces swimming down through the darkness to sob on her nearly fleshless chest, all those voices wrapped around a cigarette telling their secrets in the dark as they lay beside her . . . Strangely enough, she remembered those years as the best, her time of independence. Even now, when Mateo would rope her into more than two social evenings in a row or Douglas would wangle more than one acceptance out of her in a week or her impresario would force her to dine with a rich provincial angel, a kind of wildness in her would feel endangered, a wildness she felt was as central to her art as it should be peripheral to her reputation. Feeling trapped, she'd answer an obscene letter from a fan, arrange to meet him, and submit to his most feverish advances in the little room he rented above the taxidermy shop, a room suffocating with the smell of ammonia and carrion. Or she'd drift into the dyers' quarter and Mateo would see her at dawn returning to his palace. She'd be drugged, her eyes wide and unblinking, face licked clean of cosmetics, hair wild and pushing back the ice-blue silk hood of her cape.

She'd tell all these men fake stories about herself. She'd invent for herself new names, accents, histories, professions. Dissimulation was her method of feeling her way into new characters. Like all artists she knew how to decant private obsessions into other terms —in her case, characterizations of people she'd observed. Without ever questioning the equation, she'd learned from Skeets to link sensuality with stupidity. "He's too stupid to care about, but he sure is great in . . . in a pinch," and she'd laugh her low laugh and pat her lap.

One of the characters she'd invented for herself was "Clara," the twenty-year-old farm girl with the peasant's braids, the loud voice and the comical gullibility. In spite of her resolutions, Clara was convinced every time to wriggle out of her cheap, handmade dress and straw shoes. Clara believed every declaration of love, no matter how halfhearted, and with village candor she pledged her troth to every rake. She slapped her thigh when she laughed, she refused wine with a suspicious wrinkling of the nose, and she expressed wide-eyed enthusiasm for the carnival, that tiresome festivity that had been extended another week almost every year until now it ate up a good six months with preparation, decoration, celebration and recrimination. Clara lived with her "uncle" and from time to time Mateo would be cajoled into playing the avuncular spoilsport in order to create a spicy farce that Edwige calculated would heighten the transports of her suitor.

Mateo knew how to play this role so believably because he was playing it in all seriousness with Angelica. Flora had helped him to find a tiny apartment for the child and Mateo had carried a bag of the new clothes he'd bought her up the five flights of rickety, windowless but freshly painted stairs. Angelica's delight in her own little home delighted him. Among the members of her tribe few smiles were ever exchanged; the normal way of wearing the face was impassively. But from Flora she'd learned to cock her head back as though she were letting the wind stream through her hair and to smile and smile.

Now she paced sullenly around her room, touched many things, straightened a few, fussed with the shutters, bounced on the love seat and, in the midst of her inspection, she remembered Flora's advice, "Don't forget that sunny smile" and she smiled— but this time the real joy beating in her heart suddenly struck a spark and her smile blazed with real brilliance. She flung her arms around Mateo's neck, nibbled his ear and said, "Oh, Teddy, I'm so happy." Just as Mathilda had renamed Gabriel "Mr. Pine," Angelica had nicknamed Mateo "Teddy," a choice she never explained but that he suspected served to make him hers, a friendlier velour version of himself.

Despite Mateo's celebrity as a womanizer, in his opinion he'd never been an efficient worker in the vineyards of love. He'd always taken too much time to prune, to plump, to sniff, to taste—he'd listened with sympathy to too many stories, lent advice and (when he had it) money, written stern letters to landlords and beseeching letters to employers, carried packages to a lady's friends or relatives in distant towns, and performed hundreds of small commissions. Whereas some seducers kept a list and moved with steely purpose from one arbor to another, crushing everything they encountered, Mateo lingered, hesitated, caressed. Unlike some seducers, he loved women—not their abjectness, not just their bodies, but their company. Whereas many if not most men preferred talking with other men, Mateo preferred everything about women, including their conversation. He'd shop with a woman, carry her reticule, hold the ball of wool, lick the bowl, walk her dog, comb her hair. One male friend had once confided he didn't like to spend too much time with women because he was afraid of being feminized by the contact; other men pretended to complete ignorance of female pursuits. But Mateo, the true lover of women, wasn't concerned with his own dignity at all. He lost himself in this pool of femininity and hoped he'd be buried surrounded by women.

Now with Angelica, this "delightful daughter of the people" as he would have called her, he was constantly pleased, if pleasure is defined as mastery over a small range of small surprises. She'd prepare an inept, burned little supper while he'd nap. And he'd be charmed by glimpsing through drowsy eyes the melodrama she was making—the way she leaped back from popped grease, cursed, nursed her wounded hand, bagged her newly shaped hair in a bandana, hummed a tune, tasted a broth with wide eyes and puckered mouth, respiced. The conqueror aristocrats he knew were so subdued, which was how he liked men to behave, but in women he relished the pure uselessness of florid response. Just as in Mathilda's mansion above the harbor town he admired the ardor of the anonymous craftsman who'd decorated a wood chair with a carving of a mermaid, in the same way he admired the posturing Angelica brought to cooking or cleaning or sewing, gestures that required so much attention she forgot the task at hand.

What he didn't do was make love to her. She fully expected it and even seemed wounded by his coolness. Flora assumed they had long since been lovers and would reproach Angelica for her bad housekeeping by saying, "With such a man, the joys of the boudoir are not enough." (Flora was especially keen on Mateo, since he'd finally arranged that little supper for her and her lover with Mathilda and Daniel.) Even Mateo didn't know why he hung back from touching Angelica. If he'd searched his mind he might have said, "But would she trust me if I were like those scores of soldiers who abused her?" Or he might have cited his unwillingness to compete with his own nephew, although the boy seemed to have forgotten Angelica.

And then Angelica became pregnant. Flora told Mateo and suggested he arrange for an abortion. With great solemnity he sat with Angelica on the love seat before the single window. The evening sky was clouding up and a strong wind insisted on the mood of intensity. But Angelica shrugged and said, "All right. Fine," over and over again. Mateo thought she was overdoing it.

He went with her to the doctor's and brought her back to her little home. Flora nursed her. When she awakened the next morning Mateo was beside her bed and said, "Angelica, it must have been terrible."

"Not so bad, Teddy," she whispered. "About a tablespoonful."

Mateo's solemn mask slid off and he laughed. He laughed and laughed. After living for so many years close to complicated ladies, he found Angelica's directness hilarious. Afterwards, solemn again, he tried several times to talk about "her loss," but although she nodded because she thought he wanted her to, he could tell that his words puzzled her. The only thing she really experienced was a feeling of relief. She thought of all those soldiers who'd invaded her. Now she was done with them. The nausea she had felt whenever she looked at a handsome man went away. The knife had scraped her clean.

Although Flora served as an interpreter between the two languages and helped Angelica to pick out breezy, up-to-date expressions and gestures, nevertheless Mateo kept noticing gaps in the girl's comprehension. He could guess how indignant she'd be if he proposed to teach her; accordingly, he asked her to teach him her language. Day after day he'd sit beside her on the little love seat and she'd help him decode a religious book written in her own tongue. Part of her problem, he now saw, was that her vocabulary in her own language was small; if it had been sufficient to her savage past, it would not be adequate to her civilized future.

Unlike his father, who had preferred easy conquests and slept with his mother's maids, Mateo had always courted bluestockings, beauties, well-known actresses or social leaders. Perhaps because of his own sinking status, that of a newly poor member of old country gentry, he'd needed the strong updraft of recognized names. Now for the first time he found his nearly total control over Angelica erotic in a new way. In the past, he'd known the pleasure of seducing proud, independent women. Now he knew the more stirring if less involving joy of owning another human being. Why he of all people—so polite, so kind, so eager to assuage suffering—should need to feel masterful in order to feel desire puzzled him. The men of his generation had struck their parents as powerlessly effete, yet even with their extreme affectations they'd nevertheless given proof (at least to one another) of masculine dignity. To be sure, they were no longer like their fathers, who'd written poems to Woman and seen Her as either Good or Evil. No, they didn't believe in Evil or even evil and they professed to be in search of individual women, nuanced, side-lit beings who could serve as companions to men. Nevertheless, Mateo and his male contemporaries had referred so often to female psychology that they finally made it come into being. "Like most women," "as a woman," "because she is, after all, a woman"—these were the remarks that invented distinctions. It turned out that the game of conquest, of mastery over women, required some sort of gender difference, but not any *particular* difference. Men were content to concede some of their prerogatives to women (and all of their responsibilities). What they couldn't surrender, however, was this sense of difference dividing the sexes—a difference that constituted almost all their worldly wisdom, a knowledge as detailed, as confidently held and as false as a phrenologist's. Blondes were lusty and brunettes more so, virgins ached for it and dowagers begged for it, women were practical or scatterbrained, delicate or thick-skinned, hysterical or in steely, sinister control, scheming but not ambitious, ambitious but not disciplined, disciplined but not inspired, inspired but not driven, driven but not visionary, visionary but impractical and back around again. The accent shifted, now plucking one syllable, now another, but wherever it moved it made a resonant break. Sometimes Mateo thought that precisely because men and women now lived more or less the same lives, these imaginary differences were being imagined more intensely. Or sometimes he thought that since the conquerors had shut down the theater of public life and driven everyone into fantasies, the only remaining place where power could be exercised was through love and sexual intrigue. Perhaps the importance they granted love was proof of their impotence, not because love was an escape from responsibility but because it became interesting only when all other forms of expression had trickled dry. Sex was the game of chess retired generals played.

The women of his generation had done everything to live up to their new eminence. What a relief, then, to find in Angelica a creature who spoke his language with some difficulty, whose transition into civilized society was partial and possibly reversible, who was young enough to be his child, even a child of his thirties, whose color and scent were exotic, and whom Flora was inducting into feminine graces as dated as they were foolproof.

Mateo's anguish over his body and its disgrace became less acute when he sat beside Angelica, since with her he was no longer striving to be an equal (equally energetic, presentable). With her his superior cultivation was assumed, just as she was assumed to be more beautiful. When she sat on his lap or twined a slender brown arm around his creased neck and fallen shoulders, she was seeking, not conferring, approval. All his life he had preferred cherishing to exhibiting attractions, and his sense of his passionate self was as a surround of admiration. Now age and Angelica had clarified his function. In a painting he would no longer be represented as one of the two interlaced nudes but as a gold cloud of knowing engulfing a woman, just as in the flowing dark the slightly parted lips of living shell concentrate light on the couched pearl.

And yet he held back from sleeping with Angelica, even though he knew his hesitation confused her, indeed embarrassed her. Her body, through even that briefest pregnancy, had taken on a bit of flesh. Her narrow hips were fractionally rounded, her already full breasts still heavier. Despite her ripening, he still didn't make a move. He told himself that at his age he'd learned that the preliminaries are more pleasurable (because more subject to personal variation) than the brief and straightforward act. Or he argued that this confusion of avuncular and amorous roles would diminish in piquancy if ever resolved.

But the truth was that with both his nephew and Angelica all his power over these peculiar children derived from his forbearance. Although Gabriel felt that he was gaining a soul from his uncle, in fact he was being instilled with guilt. What he called a soul was guilt. At Madder Pink he'd awakened every morning with no regrets for yesterday and no fear of tomorrow; no wonder his sense of time had remained rudimentary. But in the capital what had been staccato became legato through shame and anticipation. He was always trying to stave off the anger his uncle never expressed save through a raised eyebrow or a faceted question ("Are you sure you want to accept that invitation? Do, do—but my life should prove a cautionary tale against social promiscuity. Mind you, it's better to err in the direction of generosity. Better for your soul. It's *never* better for your reputation."). One such sentence—with all the anxiety it generated, delivered as disinterested advice, but containing an obscure directive—forced Gabriel to scan everything he and other people said or did for clues. Experience was no longer an engulfing wave but an elaborate meal whose recipe must be reconstructed by guesswork.

In the same way, by never concluding the sexual bargain with Angelica, Mateo introduced an anguish into her merriness that made her whole being more ductile. If he'd bedded her right off, she would have flung herself with relish into the part of the fussed, clucking young mistress on a budget, wheedling for trinkets, daring to take liberties, hovering over his health as though his health were their missing child. Mateo would have reproached himself for such an abasement. By forbearing he'd made her edgy, self-doubting, a cloudy sky under which colors discovered their true hue.

Or so he assumed. The truth was that soon after he established her in her room she began to "see" other men, as she would have phrased it. For instance, Felix, a blond man with a facial scar and small dead eyes. Although he was twice her age he acted like her contemporary since he hummed the same tunes, was equally bored and had the same idea of conversation as alternating jokes and silence. He lived just across the way. He'd recently been released from prison, where he'd served a two-year sentence for theft. Or there was the delivery boy from the pharmacist whose single fantasy was to stride about in undershorts massaging his erect penis through the cotton fabric while she squirmed naked on the bed "begging for it"—a scenario that demanded a strict interpretation by the performers and that he rehearsed her in again and again. Or the pharmacist himself, who supplied her with pills to excite her and pills to calm her in return for her compliance: she had to put on a dress and veiled hat and sit opposite him on a straight-back chair. They were strangers, traveling. Stealthily he extracted his already sockless foot out of his shoe and burrowed it up her dress and between her thighs while they each continued to read a newspaper. The papers trembled but they never lowered them.

Felix the blonde was the only one she spent any time with. Mateo had forgotten how heavily free time weighs on the uneducated. Mateo, her "Teddy," devoted almost every evening to Gabriel, although one night Mateo had put on his evening clothes, including the cylindrical shiny hat he called "eight reflections," and invited her to dinner and dancing on a barge hung with paper lanterns and garlands of flowers, the drunken Saturday night solace of shopkeepers, a place where Mateo could be certain not to encounter anyone he knew. When he'd returned to the palace he'd found his nephew obsessed with longing for this bewitching girl who all evening had swirled across the dance floor in Mateo's embrace, her eyes unnaturally brilliant, her chatter incessant and scattered, almost as though she'd swallowed a handful of stimulants. Mateo had known a special sympathy for Gabriel and felt half tempted to tell him Angelica was here in the capital, but his better judgment prevailed.

Most of the time "Teddy" was paying his calls on the rich or the celebrated, an activity Angelica couldn't quite picture, but that she equated with Flora's shopping. Alone, Angelica would visit Felix and share with him some of the pills the pharmacist had given her. Felix would press her for details about Mateo's palace (he was planning a robbery) but she couldn't supply them, since she'd been invited in only the first time she'd met him, and that visit she could scarcely remember, so frightened and exhausted had she been. Mateo had not yet become her lovable Teddy with the slightly sour breath, the booming, operatic laugh and reckless gestures; then he'd been just an old man in a shabby yellow silk robe who had refused to share a meal with her, who subjected her to an insulting purification in a big marble tub and who had doubly insulted her by failing to share her pillow. Now he still held aloof but Angelica had decided he must be beyond the age of bedtime pranks, although he still seemed to hear faint erotic echoes of the original boom when she sat on his lap or let him waltz her around the barge under the flower-drenched canopy. She knew that whatever she wanted she could get out of him, but she treated him with a delicacy and respect she'd felt only once before, for her grandmother; in Teddy she found less dignity than in her grandmother but more sweetness. Mateo thought that Angelica feared him, but that fantasy he'd invented to disguise from himself how infatuated with her he'd become. She didn't fear him, she only feared the power over him he'd granted her and hoped she'd be worthy of it.

She knew that he was far worthier than Felix but Teddy left her alone too much and she had to fill her time somehow. She liked to "party" with Felix; they'd swallow their pills, drink wine and read aloud the latest episode of an illustrated romance. Although Mateo attributed her rapid mastery of the language to his own lessons, her progress was entirely due to her wanting to grasp exactly what had happened to "Vanessa" when she entered the lightning-struck castle. She and Felix discussed each character for hours, their speculation given license and color by the pills they'd assimilated.

Felix was also an enthusiastic masquer. Before his sentence he had been the president of the Golden Boys, one of the many carnival societies in the capital, organizations zealously but amateurishly monitored by the conquerors for signs of political subversion. Felix still owned all his past costumes, although the balding velvets and tacky fringe and slashed silks seemed less gorgeous to Angelica than to their owner. One evening he dressed her in a high, starched white hat and a peasant girl's wedding dress. He decked himself out in the groom's traditional embroidered sash, white boots, hairnet and jodhpurs, and together they drew a white donkey, symbol of a prosperous union, through the night streets just as palest fireworks began to go off.

Now Angelica entered the tragic, novelty-wracked life of the city poor, those clever, unhappy denizens of the capital who'd rather attend the public ball that opens carnival and live on coffee than sit down to a big family meal on a farm. Now she found herself dancing with strangers, caught up by an army of devils who handed her over to a choir of angels, who led her up, up, through the dim, crowded tin hovels stacked one above the other on the hills surrounding the lighted bay. There, in a wind scrubbed clean by sea-salt, she paused to watch fire-flushed paper offerings float up, up, up the dangerously dry mountain face as whatever pixie or demon who happened at the moment to be breathing his rummy breath down her brown bodice beheld the rising red globes reflected in her wondering eyes.

She had to hear a song only twice before she'd learned the words, had to see a dance only a moment before she'd joined in. Big blond figures, parodies of the vaguely grinning conqueror general and his chinless wife and drab, defeated daughter, teetered past, animated by men on stilts who spun their dolls around, curtsied them—and then ducked out from under them and scrambled off to join other dancing clubs on other hills. The abandoned effigies were trampled under by masquers too anarchic to care in any organized way about desecrating these particular images. Now a band of penitents, weeping and singing, marched past to the beat of a bass drum as slow as a dinosaur's pulse. A half-ton reliquary was passed from one exhausted squad of six bearers to another. Those who'd been relieved drank water, splashed their faces, staggered off, indifferent, into the crowd, their bare legs wrapped in strips of white cloth, glimpsed here and there beyond the swirl of cloaks and skirts.

Angelica had long since lost Felix and the white donkey. She'd snaked her way down the hill and back toward the bay. A long-haired, bearded man walking past held a child in his arms and pretended to be gobbling her tummy as she squealed with delight. Four teenage boys were carrying something heavy, swearing. For them this piazza was not the theater but backstage; soon enough, at some private ball or other, they would uncover their prop and "go on."

Day after day Angelica swam downstream with the masquers. Many of them, like her, were "foreigners" (as the people of the capital called even their fellow countrymen if they were from another town). Such foreigners often took her for a native and asked her for directions, which often, proudly, she was able to give. She was learning the capital's brisk way of saying yes with a hiss, as though this response were cause for irritation, of counting out change with airy impatience, of talking loudly over a shoulder and laughing while queuing up and rudely brushing others in the line with her purse, of spicing her conversation with such expressions as "even so," "in short" and "that is to say" even when they meant nothing.

She slept for an hour or two whenever she was tired, sometimes at home, often she knew not where, and she'd melt off into a sleep that matched her fondest version of the afterlife, lulled by someone equally drugged who was strumming a guitar or genital by a dawn window as sunlight twitched brighter degree by absolute degree like a penis pulsing erect—which often enough she was also staring at these mornings or evenings, her cheek couched on some hairy thigh whose hair was softer to touch than it had looked to be. She became an expert in all the varieties of home decor and plumbing, of other people's lapses and strictures, of their varying notions of hygiene and romantic chatter. No one ever asked her for her story, but she asked each man for his and got it. For the most part the stories seemed so sad that she never suspected half of them had been made up to impress her.

She loved the way the city seemed to be a rich wave bearing her up, a wave so salty she couldn't sink, and there was always, just at the right moment, something to eat or drink being pressed in her hand, or fresh sheets being turned back. Pleasure—dancing and dressing up and drinking and making love—had become a job she and all the others were good at. She had no more need to fear hunger or rape or the cold, and she thought in the past she might have unknowingly solicited those miseries because now, no matter how high she was flung, there were always hands to catch her. When she first learned that city people paid money for cut flowers she'd laughed at such folly, but now she saw that she was a similar commodity, something most people had for free or didn't want but that some people were willing to pay for. The carnival was a costly, useless setting for an equally useless person. It had so many contests, required such elaborate preparations, followed such a detailed schedule over so many weeks that its very complexity obscured its essence: its uselessness. In its flickering, multitudinous warmth Angelica suddenly found herself walking with a white knight and a unicorn. Just as she bade them good night she wrote her address with a dull pencil on the skin of the white knight's powdered palm but she was too drugged to keep her numbers small. She ran out of space for the final two. "Can you remember two?" she asked. "Can you remember the two? That comes at the end." He laughed and promised he'd remember the two, and then he disappeared into the fog, which embraced him with its shaggy bear's paws, pressing him against its massive, melting chest.

One evening she found herself in the dyers' quarter in front of the house where the candle merchant's aunt lived. She knocked and was let in. The aunt was alone and served Angelica an apple stewed with vanilla and cinnamon. They sat in the whitewashed kitchen with the brass pans hanging over the fireplace and a rush broom in the corner. A pile of small, rotting apples was sitting on the sill just outside the window, infusing its fragrance into the breezes that floated in.

Day after day Angelica went back. She told the good woman all about the adventures she'd had since she moved to the capital. From the woman Angelica learned that the patriots looked to Mateo and Gabriel for leadership of some sort, since their family had always been linked to the cause of freedom and their palace had been the home of a great patriot ancestor. Angelica met other patriots at the house, although they never gave their names. She liked knowing people and she enjoyed shocking Mateo with her extensive acquaintance. Every time he was puzzled when she saluted a flower girl near the Grand or a waiter at one of the big shellfish restaurants on the grand boulevards, she gloried in her popularity.

One evening Maurizio was at his aunt's. He and Angelica went out for a walk through the city. Angelica was pleased to be seen with such a girlishly handsome young man wearing a rebelliously scarlet waistcoat. She listened to Maurizio's low deliberate voice as he talked about the growing spirit of resistance in the city. At every corner another gloomy old palace inspired him to a new flight of eloquence, for here he saw the original meeting place of the Mystic Order of Companions, there he saw the first guild hall in the land, here he found traces of the Great Fire, there the very spot where a great patriot had given his life. As he talked, Angelica wondered how his full lips would taste and how his skin would smell. She doubted whether he'd have a smell. She looked at his slightly bowed legs and imagined him kneeling over her, then sitting back on her stomach and placing a hard, small, red penis between her breasts. When she stood next to him on a bridge she smelled the coriander scent of the candles he sold—ah, he did have a smell after all. He asked her if she would be "willing to work for the revolution," and she said, "All right. Fine."

Mateo had reduced his holiday duties to just three—the governor's public ball in July and two smaller, much more select balls. One was held at the beginning and the other at the end of the original three-week-long carnival season as it had been until the festivities had ballooned out into a six-month public menace, the ideal dissipation of political energy and the perfect distraction from the continuing oppression of foreign rule. Or so Mateo's liberal friends liked to think.

If Mateo and his circle disliked carnival, their distaste was due to the standstill traffic, the servants who disappeared for days on end when they won (or lost) a costume contest or drank too much, the thieves who looted houses under the guise of a midnight ruckus, when the Lord of Misrule declared a particular palace ripe for chaos. The sad thing, Mateo thought, was that everyone, himself included, wanted to live in the new century, but no one could afford to. The conquerors had taxed the city dry, stripping it of almost all its wealth, replacing its solid gold crown with a party favor of metallic paper, substituting a cardboard horn for its call to arms and dancing barges for its merchant fleet. Patriots spoke of "legal resistance," and the "struggle on the level of culture." One leader, a popular poet, had called for the creation of a void, a silence around the victors—but the success of this strategy had promoted only the further disintegration of resistance. The conquerors might have preferred popular affection to silence, but for them the capital had its *eternal* charm, its *eternal* gaiety; it remained the perfect spot for a honeymoon, and under such a lavish coat of local color they scarcely detected the rot. The workers still sang, the boatmen still sang, the kids in the street still sang, even the courtesans sang; song seemed to be the usual lilt of the city, as humor was the flavor of its speech. The conquerors liked to compare the way the palaces looked now with their appearance in paintings centuries old—and the almost total resemblance reassured them.

Writers visiting the capital churned out travel essays about the childlike joy of the people, their cheerful patter, their natural facility as musicians and mimics and poets, their picturesque affection for songbirds, the shameful decay of their palaces, their generosity and fire in love—and all these observations obscured the volatile politics of the moment. Most of the victors back home, when they thought of this city at all, thought of its whores. Wives became uneasy when their husbands went off on trips alone to the city and men nudged each other and winked when they were assigned there. Typically, one man would say to another, sketching in large, imaginary breasts with his hands, "The women there are very *intelligent.*"

The conquerors perceived the citizens of the capital as foreigners, that is, as a totality. Paradoxically, this very stylization served the purpose of subjugation, since the conquerors' preconceptions inadvertently molded the behavior of the conquered. The people of the capital played up to expectations and were applauded—or resisted and were ignored. Folklore drew in the crude image of the plucky, vain, excitable man and the frivolous, spendthrift woman —portraits that precluded discipline, cohesion, purpose.

The conquest itself had so shattered everyone's confidence that patriots either denigrated or overpraised the national character— but in either case they made the mistake of assuming there was such a thing as a national character. They brooded too much on style. Long before the conquest the city's autonomy had been preserved more through cunning than might and its pride in its diplomatic finesse had led to an overestimation of its apparent resistance to incursions. As merchants, the people had long ago found it expedient to tolerate every religion and nationality, but this cosmopolitanism was cynical and disguised an essential parochialism, an interest in nothing but the four hundred families who had always ruled the city. The triumphant pageants they staged about themselves for themselves had camouflaged the decay of their ships and the emptiness of their coffers. When an ally had lent them a vast sum to rebuild their navy, they'd spent it all on a huge, brutally ugly marble barge placed in the bay beside the old customs house, a folly doubly foolish in that the architect had miscalculated the depth of the water and the stone decks were swamped at high tide. Moss carpeted the slippery prow. Useless. Dangerous. Expensive. Ugly. The marble barge symbolized the ineptness of the city even in its pursuit of caprice.

Once Mateo had confided to Mathilda his suspicion that Angelica, his little friend, must be sleeping around with various anonymous masquers.

"But how old is she?"

"Fourteen."

"You *are* vile," Mathilda said. "The poor child. You really do see your own bestiality in everyone, no matter how pure. She probably doesn't even know how babies are made."

Mathilda liked to make herself mistress of any possible wardrobe of female identity, especially when the subject turned to female sexuality. All of the hundreds of separate remarks she'd made over the years to Mateo had been consistent: "Women mature very late sexually, and in any event never like sex as much as men do. If a woman is drawn inordinately to sex, she's either a member of one of the tribes (in which case it's all right) or she's deranged (and should be pitied). Whereas men need a sexual relief almost every day, women never need it, and the longer they do without it the less urge toward it do they feel. Male excess is a physiological oddity but counts as a moral failing. Men are able to separate sex from love (a tragic knack), whereas for women sexual passion is tolerated only because of amorous devotion."

In fact Mateo had found that though she was too dogmatic, her indefensible and inconsistent version of women's sexuality had served him as a useful guide in the seduction of respectable ladies. He'd always courted women's sentiments, never their senses—and had discovered that among respectable women, at least, the sentimental quickly turned sensational. He liked to say that if he could make a woman laugh he had a "sixty-five percent chance" of bedding her. Coached by his years of placating Mathilda, Mateo would drape a fraternal arm around a woman's shoulder and chuckle with her about male arrogance—and end up by letting a dangling hand, ever so fraternally, brush her nipples.

But Angelica was younger than any woman he'd ever known since he himself had been an adolescent and his terror of appearing outmoded to her led him to underestimate the continuity of human experience. He was certain that the young were fundamentally different from everyone else. For instance, if Angelica were an adult then unquestionably her flashing eyes, melting kisses, lingering touches would indicate an aroused appetite; he would have taken her on the spot. But since she was so young, he wasn't sure he could trust these signals. Also, she was so dependent he feared seduction might be a betrayal of the rules of hospitality.

And then one night, unannounced, he let himself into her room and saw her fully dressed on her straight-backed chair, her newspaper raised to conceal her face while a preposterous man opposite her was corkscrewing his naked foot up her skirt, a smudge of newsprint on his nose where the paper he was holding had fluttered against his sobbing face—and then two quite different shrieks, a whoop from her, the groan of a decelerating engine from him. They looked up to see the invader. Mateo gaped for a second only, then bowed and said, "Madam, you know how very poor my night vision is. This room is too dark for me to see a thing. I'll walk around the block while you provide more light—if you will be so infinitely obliging to my infirmity." He left. Behind the closed door he could hear hissed recriminations.

When he returned he found a shaken Angelica, alone. He held her, patting her on the back, saying "Oh, well. There." They lay beside each other on her bed, fully dressed, and he assured her his love for her contained not one jot of lust until he noticed her sobs had modulated into little moans and she discovered a short, fat erection in his tight-fitting trousers. In an instant they had undressed each other.

They were both smiling that little incidental smile that in highly conscious people accompanies a strong emotion—grief, shock or horror—and that, far from invalidating the emotion, ennobles it by paying it the tribute of an awareness full to the point of irony. There are two sorts of irony, the cheap kind that disowns experience and the expensive kind that acknowledges it; this was the expensive kind. They could both see the humor in their situation, the neat way in which this dénouement clenched the farce that had gone before. They were also smiling (if the valises of their smiles were to be fully unpacked) because they liked the people they were becoming.

Mateo kissed every inch of her body, the boyish hips, the breasts with their black nipples and the two moles on the left side of her neck like buttons of hardened wax that had run down the candle from the dark flame of her hair. He lay beside her and played with the nipple nearer him, the right one. He sucked it and when his mouth wasn't on it his hand was. He didn't bruise it or bite it. He treated it with tenderness but also with constant, childish attentiveness, almost as though he were an intelligent but obsessive dog which is either fetching its favorite, much-chewed stick or staring at it, ears up, eyes fixed, nostrils working. Mateo wasn't violent; there wasn't even the slightest hint of violence in him. He was afraid of loving her. He sometimes felt he had a restless lake of love ready to flow into any welcoming channel but equally ready to retreat. The years hadn't managed to kill off his love, which remained as ardent as ever, but they had taught him reflexes enabling him to draw quickly back at the first sign of hesitation someone else might give. He'd learned to say, "But she'd never do, because she's too young/old, smart/stupid, rich/poor," but this knack at finding fault was a recent acquisition, in no way a poisoning of the lake itself, which remained pure.

Angelica thought he had a wonderful wet, full mouth and even the trace of sourness in it she'd long since come to find fascinating, although initially it had repelled her; now it was his mouth. His fleshy fingers couldn't stay away from her right breast. They talked in bed all night and all the while his hand was pressing against her breast, lightly, smoothly, or circling it meditatively, and the next day and every day thereafter she could feel his hand on her nipple even when she was alone, walking down the street, say, as her white cotton blouse rubbed against her skin. Then she had to smile and this physical ache seamlessly matched her love for him, her need to be with him, as though her heart, too, were on the right.

Her intense but calm, welcoming love transformed him in his own eyes into someone who was . . . worthy. This ridiculously young girl seemed unaware of the ludicrous spectacle middle age was supposed to represent; in fact she, this child, said to him one day, "I hate the way you're rushing yourself into old age. There are lots of steps in between. Take them slowly." The remark was so unlike her that it stood out in relief. It made him trust her more, for it proved she wasn't just living from moment to moment, pivoting in the shifting breeze, but that she had her own orienting device and that in this long migration of their love she knew her direction.

Then, of course, he suspected she was merely repeating some bit of nonsense she'd picked up from Flora. It sounded like Flora. He knew perfectly well that the very sort of canned wisdom we hoot at in a public forum we greet as profound when someone lovely whispers it to us. Then he repented his suspicion; even if it was well-founded, all the same, Angelica's urge to remember and repeat the remark touched him.

And she was right. Middle age had confused him, as an operation confuses the patient. He didn't know if anyone still found him attractive. He was so afraid of exposing himself to ridicule that he preferred to assume he'd already become—instantly and without apparent transition—cravenly old, as though age were a failure of courage.

But when he stood to one side he perceived how shadowy everything actually was. Vague. One day a young man said to him,

"But you should beat whoever did that portrait of you in Mathilda's house. It makes you look sixty!"

And how old do I really look? Mateo wanted to ask.

On some days he slept more than ever before and even sank into short, delirious naps late in the afternoon, but on other days he had more energy than he'd known in his twenties. Some nights he felt short, fat and winded as he staggered home from a late dinner. He imagined that the masked revelers whirling past him didn't see him at all. But now, with Angelica, he felt quickened—in fact, restored to a youth that seemed so recent, so eternal, so natural a prerogative that he half-believed he'd merely misplaced it for a moment. He'd always been the rakish, winning youth, whose irreverence and lust and enthusiasm had all been wrapped in the paper of youth under youth's ribbon. Just as fame permits someone to be terse, since his remarks are sure to be heard, and beauty allows someone to be silent, since there is no danger of a beauty being ignored, in the same way Mateo's exuberance—the leaps and hesitations of his affection and excitement—had needed the alibi of youth. Without it he scarcely knew how to be taken; when he'd lost his youth, he'd felt like a magician whose top hat has been stolen.

Angelica made him handsome again, no longer a character actor, a possible villain with comic touches, but a leading man. When he was away from her he smiled frequently, thinking of her, and for a moment he would have a hard time following the conversation, as though a tropical breeze had caught up with him on a winter street and for a moment folded him in its recollection of sun, palms, sand. When he didn't feel happy he felt anguished. She'd told him she found him attractive, and he'd believed her at the time, for he knew the very young are not yet slavish adherents to a standardized code of looks, and that they make undue allowance for such minor decorative touches as kindness, loyalty, intelligence, strength, humor, courtesy. Or perhaps the men she'd grown up among were even in their twenties as hefty and hairy as he'd become in his forties and she'd been on the lookout for someone *solid* of her own—a frustrating search in a city of painfully slender men, mere pencil marks in a setting that had always been more faithfully rendered by a sketch than a worked-up painting.

Or maybe she just liked him. Plausible as that seemed when he was with her, when he was away his confidence faltered. She'd been mistaken about him, and when she saw him next she'd rub her eyes as though awakening. Or he had been going through a brief, illusory spell of good health and good looks, perhaps, but today the slightest breeze would knock all the petals off the rose.

Some of his fears, he conceded, were talismanic, designed to hold off old age by worrying about it excessively, but some fears were surely justified, for he was in a state of transition. One week he'd hang over his belt, the next his trousers would nearly slip off him. One day his face would be suffused with a healthy glow, the next he'd be grey. Since his beard was nearly grey, if he let any of it go unshaved it aged him instantly.

And then, with a sudden sickened gesture, he wanted to push this overcooked gruel off the table, be rid of this self-absorbed self-doubt and assume his natural age with dignity and realism. But Angelica had tenderly cautioned him against *"rushing* himself into old age." (But how had she recognized his mistake? How was she able to leap ahead three decades to spot the error of her well-fed, satisfied elders, those strangers we like to think are deformed not by having accumulated the usual years but by having criminally joined a corrupt generation?)

He found he was always looking at the hall table for a note from Angelica, and often enough one was there, even when it was long past the normal hour for the post and she had had to hire a messenger. When he read her misspelled letters his heart beat faster and he wanted to read them to someone else—but the only person around was Gabriel, the very person who musn't hear them. So he smiled at the dish when he ate and into the closet when he dressed.

He could picture her face very clearly, not her exact expression, but the brilliance of her newly acquired smile and the "sophisticated" way she let her ridiculously made-up eyelids flutter. When he closed his own eyes, however, what he saw wasn't her face but rather migrating patches of red, gold and orange that pulsed brighter now here now there, and he felt similar spots of warmth crossing his solar plexus, as though miniature dawns were bursting rapturously all over him.

At night they'd lie side by side and, after they'd made love (the girl kept referring to "stings" or something, part of her barbarous heritage, no doubt), Mateo would let his hands travel slowly, slowly, gently, gently over every inch of her back, legs, stomach, breasts. "You know how to tickle well," she said, and he didn't tell her she'd used the wrong verb. In fact he too began to use "tickle" to mean "stroke." He'd go through moments of self-loathing, as when she touched his earlobes affectionately and he could hear her fingertips brushing the bristles he'd trimmed as short as possible. But mostly he liked himself again, liked the way that the events of the day were tucked into the gaps between being with Angelica or thinking about Angelica. He was always tired, in need of a shave, his clothes rumpled—tired and smiling. He knew the romance of the capital all over again, the thrill he'd first felt in living here, in walking casually past monuments pictured in history books, in ringing the bell to a little door recently set into a vast old door made for giants when he called on a lady whose last name joined with a hyphen an ancient family of savants to a still older family of warriors. His mornings, no longer anxious and squalid, were spent in Angelica's room; she would run out to a bakery and buy sugarless apple tarts and he'd eat them while listening to the new sounds of her quarter—the cry of the old man with glass on his back, the different cry of the scissors-grinder and even the frail call of an old lady who sold nothing but tin buttons, ex-voto copies of the golden buttons we are to imagine close the vestments of the dead.

For the first time in years Mateo became impotent. He told

Angelica that he'd hurt his penis. Later he told her he loved her too much. And this second explanation seemed close to the truth. With other women he'd seldom pursued the affair beyond the conquest. Up to the moment of surrender he remained greedy for each one's approval, afterwards indifferent. One woman he'd dropped a month after her capitulation had spat out at him the remark her husband had made, "He'll never stick with any one woman; sex is his profession and hobby and to practice it he must be free." Now that Mateo wanted to stick with Angelica (he didn't say forever only because the years had taught him discretion), he'd become impotent. Angelica applied her mouth to the problem as though it were a purely local breakdown rather than a systemic betrayal; he'd see her black hair foaming over his lap first thing in the morning to no avail.

He blamed her age, her bottomless appetite. He blamed his adulation of her and sought without success to cultivate contempt. He blamed his age. He blamed Gabriel and his own guilty conscience about the boy.

And then he blamed his own career in sex, which had warped his responses as surely as some cultures stretch necks, lengthen earlobes or bind feet, distortions that cannot later be undone, that leave the victim incapable of a normal life. He'd become so specialized in the pursuit of sexual conquest that now when love wanted him whole he couldn't oblige.

Although he was always content to play the buffoon, his buffoonery was an art, a graceful silver-point recollection of the original crude cartoon, a translation of the comic text into another, more refined language, of Pulcinello into Pierrot.

But impotence! It would soon make him a laughingstock.

He rushed into the arms of a prostitute he'd visited over the years in the dyers' quarter. With her, whom he scarcely liked, he regained his potency. Through the thin wall he heard another man's voice—by turns exultant and anguished, fussily inflected, cultured, unrelenting—and he thought of all the ingenious ways an ocean finds to hurl itself on a cliff, no two waves alike and yet all pulverizing. Poor woman, poor cliff, Mateo thought, and he wondered who the man might be. Probably a collaborator; he'd grafted the harsh accents of the conqueror onto the melody of the capital, as though the softest, saddest waltz for strings were to be played by a brass oompah band. When the people of the capital spoke to one another they pitched their voices very low, women as well, but sounded as though they were talking baby-talk, with liquid consonants (no difference between a *p* and a *b*) and a cantilena that gave an odd, haunting music to any utterance. Like a music box winding down, speakers tended to slur and linger over the ends of sentences.

The conquerors, even when they could speak the local language, pitched their voices high, pulled the mute out of the trumpet, blasted tinnily away, made nasty little meals out of any two or three adjacent consonants, especially an *s* and a *k* followed by another *s*.

As Mateo lay in the arms of the prostitute, he could hear outside the window the voice of one boatman singing antiphonally across the water to another, now to a third posted by the customs house, a "lamentation without grief" as the most famous of the conquerors' poets had decreed, he who seemed a pompous windbag in translation but the unique font of wisdom to his countrymen. Outside the narrow ogival window a half-moon was suspended in smoky splendor over the mirror of the bay; bonfires could be seen through the haze, burning on a distant island, the first place in the region to have been settled a thousand years ago but now abandoned to wild grasses and crickets except on this particular day of carnival when one of the dancing societies staged its festivities there.

The boatmen were improvising their songs to well-known words, ignoring their meaning and thereby rendering them all the more poignant, as when the verse, "He rode away," so charged with pathos, rang out with jaunty joy. In this setting, removed from anything he was used to, Mateo was tricked into deep feeling. He hadn't been paying attention to the boatmen, but their words, so familiar, conveyed by music so strange and strangely cheerful, surprised him.

Mateo cried freely and shamelessly and drew away from the dozing whore. He put on her unlined silk robe and sat on the windowsill. The moon looked at him skeptically. All his life he'd questioned each moment of happiness that had come his way and found it imperfect, not quite consonant with his ideal. Every such moment had been a rehearsal for the eventual performance that would be better, more focused, comprehensive.

But now it struck him that the happiness he'd been preparing for had arrived. For instance, he'd always been squirreling away bits of lore about the capital, its palaces and squares and museums and waterways, because he'd been getting ready for the day he'd give a grand guided tour to a young woman who would be in awe of his knowledge: his bride. But Angelica was his bride, the only one he'd have, and she hated his "lectures" and would stagily flutter her hand over her open mouth to indicate a yawn and beg him to shut up. Not that she was without curiosity about the city. Once when he'd asked her what she did with her days she'd said that she walked everywhere and tried to memorize the names of the streets. The modern capital was what interested her, the varnished surface of the new painting and not the ghostly pentimenti of its past. The idea of her walking around and memorizing street names made him smile—how she longed to be a city slicker. Her funny, touching, home-made notion of an education . . .

This was the happiness he'd been waiting for. As though to remind himself, late at night he'd hug her and say, "I'm so happy."

When he slipped out of the prostitute's house at dawn he ran into Daniel, disheveled, black hair flying, nose nearly prehensile, so startlingly bony did it look in a face otherwise so puffy.

"You here, old thing?" Daniel asked.

Mateo smiled weakly, conscious of his gritty beard and creased clothes. He thought Daniel should not have spoken but, at most, simply nodded; the situation was as uncomfortable as it was compromising. "Yes. But, Daniel, you don't look well."

"Neither do—" he interrupted himself, sighed, smiled with an eerily inappropriate grin and came over to lay his greasy head on Mateo's shoulder, which he had to stoop to do. His body shook and the high sound of a trapped mouse came peeping out of his throat.

"What's wrong? What's wrong?" Mateo asked, wondering if this great anguished giant was his son after all. Mateo felt such sympathy leap up within him he had half a notion it must be instinctual. Daniel sobbed, then with improbable rapidity straightened up and smiled. Tears vanished into a grey ducal handkerchief. "Frightfully sorry," he said. "You must think me rather wet." Loud honking nose blow.

They walked through the popular quarter that was already noisy with banter and bartering. Although the conquerors had slowly taxed into extinction most of the city's trade in the things that had brought it wealth—spices, precious metals, silk—somehow the food market still teemed with the vegetables and crustaceans the people loved (servants had written into their contracts the number of lobsters they'd be given to eat every month). Mateo and Daniel sat in a tiny café of five tables, all five painted with shiny red-and-black hex signs. They were the only customers. The old proprietor wore his tribal finery, a painted shirt bordered with ermine skins, dance bells tied to his leg and a valor stick in his left hand. He walked on his toes and set down each miniscule cup of coffee with a conspicuously awkward fuss designed to suggest he was unfamiliar with such humiliating service and would be more at ease hunting —despite his forty years in this very café. Daniel ordered inaudibly with his hand muffling his mouth, refused to look at the old man and stuck his huge long legs out into the narrow passageway so that the man had to climb over them. As he was just clearing the hurdle with difficulty, Daniel came out of his reverie, looked up and muttered, "Extraordinary little man . . ." with bored contempt. Mateo winced with embarrassment; the only extraordinary thing was that the boy's grief had done nothing to improve his manners.

Here they sat, the greasy haggard young man in absurdly fashionable muted plaids inset with irregular stripes of grey leather and the middle-aged man with the grey beard coming in fast and the rosy cheeks—full but beginning to shrivel, like ripe apples that have waited too long to be eaten—his powerful shoulders and barrel chest wrapped in a black cloak he'd obviously donned the night before, the two of them transected by the early morning light that lit up from behind the bodies of men and women on their way to work, bright light that threw a net of gold over someone's fuzzy hair, dazzled off a window and turned the sun lanes between buildings into a full chord of radiance humming with the dust cast up by passing feet. The workers were joking and rushing by and eating as they went and Daniel and Mateo, these rumpled gentlemen who'd not yet gone to bed, felt as soiled as strumpets in a schoolyard. Even their shadowy loves and *original* ways of suffering seemed heavy and overly perfumed in the channels of bright, dusty light.

Drawling as though he were repeating a familiar society scandal to a provincial cousin, Daniel told Mateo of the strange, intolerable split that had developed in his life. "Everyone thinks I'm in love with my mother and that Gabriel's arrival in our household has destroyed me. But the truth is that I almost find their love a relief. After all, Mater is rather heavy going. Madly proud of her I may be, still—" He darted an anxious glance at Mateo to see if he'd be allowed to go on in this tone (the content didn't worry him; it was intended to be shocking). Mateo had played with Daniel from the time he'd been a baby and knew perfectly well how recently Daniel had acquired this accent and manner. By now, of course, Daniel had his new guise under control. Outsiders thought he was the most intolerable sort of lordly snob. They resented his loud voice, his constant references to people by their nicknames (so hard to equate "Bootsy" with the Lady Cathleen), his refusal ever to start at the beginning of a story or to arrive at the end of a sentence, his avoidance of nobodies at a reception or, if he was trapped, his way of lecturing or heckling them in a voice intended to be overheard by other somebodies.

And yet Mateo, dubious as his own rank might be, had always held Daniel's respectful attention. If there were ten people at a gathering, Daniel would watch Mateo. Not just glance at him but drink him in with absorbing eyes, as a lover or peasant or child might. When Mateo said something—often an unsuccessful compromise between the politeness of the court and the erudition of the academy—Daniel would follow every turn of phrase and shift in register with an ebbing and waning smile of fascinated approval, just as a mother will unconsciously mouth the words her child sings at a recital. Daniel sometimes laughed at Mateo behind his back and even impersonated him, but in his presence he still, unwittingly, admired him. A little chat in Mateo's study, surrounded by the piles of his vast, exhausting and pointless correspondence, had always reassured Daniel. Mateo had a way of approving of the boy, of always taking his side and of saying, "But you did the only thing you could have done," or "Exactly right, and too good for him, I'm sure," or "How fearfully clever. Never would I have thought of that—oh, you are sly." With Mateo Daniel seldom lingered over his painfully accumulated mountains of circumstance; Mateo's constant nods and laughing eyes and instant comprehension hurried the boy along. From Mateo he learned to see his life and problems from the distance of summary, of elegant citation, and this very distance was curative; around Mateo Daniel's problems suddenly seemed like regiments that a general advances or retires with a nod.

Daniel veered between feeling too muddled to walk his dog or clean his desk and, on other days, soaring too high, suddenly exhilarated with visions of his own importance. On some days he was grateful if the waiter took a moment to recommend the quail with raisins; on other days he enjoyed snubbing the chancellor. "Can't bear his drivel—after all, Mater has accustomed me to the high table. The chancellor talks so long and says so little—a lot of wash and not much hang-out." Daniel had organized a "chat box," as he called his club, but its only function was to provide him with new people to insult. When someone else presented his views on free trade, the sparrow or paleolinguistics, Daniel would drape himself over a card table, lie face down on it exactly as though he'd been shot while gambling, and groan. Sometimes he'd pull himself upright with effort and, amazed, say, playing to the invisible balcony of spectators, "Just fancy saying, 'On the side of the angels,' whatever that might mean."

Or he'd be overheard, during a closely reasoned philosophical investigation into the twenty-two meanings of the word *mind*, remarking to another dandy, "You must have him run you up a shirt in the new color: *cuisse de nymphe émue.*" Once one of the older scholars in the chat box invited him to "take a dish of tay." Daniel let his monocle fall from his eye and said, "Sir, one takes a walk, one takes a liberty, but one *drinks* one's tea—preferably alone." Sudden exit.

In the true spirit of sadism, Daniel had named Walter president of the chat box, and it was Walter who led the discussion after every presentation. Walter spoke to poets about metrics, beginning his comments, "As a poet . . ." Similarly, he spoke to austere composers whose nugatory, mathematically rigorous half-page scores had never been performed, about his own thrilling if aborted career as a romantic pianist. He said, "As a musician," and stuttered to command attention. It was Walter who, though he was bald on top and grey-brown on the sides, was overheard saying to a flamboyant actress famous for her platinum mane, "I know what you mean. As a blond . . ." And Walter was the one who'd dubbed the club's inner circle of savants, grizzled geniuses weighed down with imperial distinctions, the "Chat Box Pussycats" and devised a cat's paw to be worn on the lapel just below the Rosette of Honor.

Daniel took bitter delight in all this nonsense, for though he was far too well-bred ever to write a line himself or express an opinion, he loved learning things and hearing other people's thoughts. His frustration as a thinker made him ridicule thinking. His grandiosity, which so rapidly alternated with his sense of helplessness, led him to enjoy staging debates between other people that were serious enough to reflect glory on him and absurd enough to keep him entertained. He wanted it all ways at once and got it. He even received some sort of remote pleasure from the companionship of his fellow club members. His dandyism, which had been flung across the chasm between the world of the conquerors' salon and that of the capital's intelligentsia, had ended by becoming a hammock in which he lazed. His mother wanted to be an aesthete among thinkers and a moralist among aesthetes, but that was an opposition that gave dramatic complexity to her ideas, not her social life. Daniel, as he now revealed, was living a social duplicity so complex it had to remain half-secret. He couldn't confess everything to Mateo, who was still his mother's closest confidant, but his old habit of conferring with this benign "uncle" who always sided with him now came back.

He told Mateo that two years ago he'd met Claude, whose father, of course, was the conqueror general. Before that he'd entered the highest foreign circles through school chums. Within their group, for which the division between adolescents and adults was far more real than the barrier between the two cultures, the patriot-conqueror conflict was so familiar as to seem laughably trite. These elite kids spoke both languages without accent. On the streets, wearing their school uniforms, they astonished passersby when they switched in mid-sentence from one language to the other, shouting as they threaded their way through crowds. Without ever noticing the change, they spoke the conquerors' language through a paralyzed facial mask and without a gesture, whereas with the first word of the language of the capital their hands and features thawed and flowed. Observers couldn't help laughing at the contrast, since the conquerors' language promoted a chilly formality, whereas the language of the capital, although equally polite, required a warmth, a physical proximity, to seem idiomatic. In the language of the capital the formal *you* was always collapsing into the intimate form, just as the past tense soon drifted into the present, the eternal present of story-telling. The process reversed itself in the conquerors' language in which social distinctions multiplied forms of address and the conditional and subjunctive shadowed nearly every utterance.

The children of the Peers School had a stronger loyalty to one another than to the warring factions beyond the academic walls. They laughed at every rehash of myths about cultural differences and rolled their eyes when their relatives attempted to warn them against "foreign" contamination. "Why'd they send us here if they were so worried?" the kids would ask.

And it was true that those patriots who had sent their children to the school had already chosen assimilation and all its advantages over patriotic purity and poverty. In some circles of the capital the parents, even after these thirty years, could not bring themselves to receive the conquerors, but to enroll their children in the school was considered progressive. "I can't stomach hearing those voices at my table, but my day is over. We must be realistic—otherwise our children will sink to the level of the tribes. The conquerors already call us 'the natives.'" Pause. "The conquerors would be content to assume our ancient names for us and live in our stead in our thousand-year-old palaces," one old patriot would add to another.

Daniel had become the most convinced, even lacerating, defender of assimilation. To be exact, he never mentioned assimilation but rather attacked any policy that fell short of it. The patriot cause was so splintered, so muddled, so compromised that a keen eye could easily pinpoint its failings and evils. The rhetoric of national autonomy scarcely fit a former colonial power, just as the language of democracy had never been well-suited to an oligarchy. Most offensives against the conquerors (including the war ten years ago) were little more than ruses to engineer self-advancement; every rebel, it seemed, could be bought off. Laughing, Daniel said of one such traitor, "He sold his soul for fifty pieces of gold—and I assure you he was overpaid." Daniel had also once dashed off a cartoon that showed a patriot in picturesque white boots politely asking the guard in front of the general's headquarters: "Whom do I see to sell my honor?" Such jokes, far from laughing treachery out of existence, actually domesticated it; dishonor came to seem a kind of nasty but familiar joke.

Nor were there many pages in the hundred years of history preceding the conquest that anyone could point to with pride. Rather, it was a tale marked by dishonesty, greed, ineptness and above all silliness. In fact, the only thing that patriots could celebrate was a once-brilliant artistic milieu (of which there were no living exemplars), diplomatic wiliness (scarcely suited to inspire popular enthusiasm), unparalleled luxury (spoils), and a tradition of repartee and conviviality (present today almost exclusively among the collaborators). Daniel, of course, wasn't considered by most people to be a collaborator. Far from it. As his mother's son, he was assumed to be at the very least "progressive"—but never naïvely so. No, he was a "realist." He wasn't "sentimental." Although he had never attacked the regime, his disillusioned smile and shrug and the sudden lowering of his eyes whenever the conquerors' policies were mentioned suggested that he'd once railed against them but had now wearied of such futility. If pressed, he'd hold open his hands and stare at his interlocutor intensely: "Do you seriously expect me to rehash all that at this late date?" Against the assumed background of his patriotism his cautious praise of the conquerors ("We'd do well to imitate their discipline") counted as an admirable retreat from puerile jingoism toward a sober reevaluation of the conflict. His favorite word was *provisional*.

By linking foppishness to an eloquent rage in political debate, Daniel seemed a throwback to an earlier century. The intervening generations had caused both elements to diverge, reducing dandyism to a cult of the pretty and aristocratic rage to bourgeois sullenness. The perambulating reader of decorative verse, discontent writ small on his pale brow, had replaced the earlier full-length portrait of the heavily powdered exquisite with a poisonous tongue and a dead black rosebud for a mouth. Although he could be quite nasty in a fight, Daniel sometimes maintained his dandiacal indifference. Once when a patriot accused him of treason for consorting with the enemy, Daniel refused to say a thing but merely lowered his lids and let his face become arctically impassive. Later, when his mother asked him why he hadn't struck his accuser, Daniel shrugged and said, "Ah! I thought of it but I'm too lazy for that." His languor (his motto was, "I won't be rushed") concealed a steely sense of purpose. His casual clubman's style admitted only a narrow gamut of expression (bored to mildly curious) that nonetheless signaled a wide range of response (contemptuous to adulatory). He idolized genius, no matter how eccentric (in that regard he was still his mother's son), but that cult he set a bit to one side, as a gentleman might place a temple at the end of an alley of trees which he'd visit only occasionally on a summer afternoon walk. The working part of his estate, of his life, was politics and society.

Through his old chums from the Peers School he'd met

Claude's brother, a dedicated horseman concerned not at all with the hunt but with the more exciting, still more costly if less prestigious world of polo. Although he was four years older than Daniel, he found Daniel to be perfect company. Daniel was so amusing with his nutty dandyism and his stories of gallant adventures in the dyers' quarter, but he could also be trusted not to bring up embarrassing political matters. At the paddock one morning Daniel had been introduced to Claude.

She had a scattered, hectic manner, thrillingly intimate one moment, sonambulistic the next. "Do you like this dress?" she'd ask him. "It's the dress my mother wore the night she lost her virginity." She seemed almost to be drunk at those moments, except she never had alcohol on her breath. She would lean forward, thrusting her chin out, and leer for an instant before her gaze would slowly detach itself, wander vaguely away, just as her smile faded. It was the same transition an actress might make in a horror play when she collapses, laughing, after waltzing and looks up to see her groom turning into a wolf, his swelling hairy wrists bursting through the silk sleeves and lace cuffs—except Claude stopped short of a scream. She merely looked away. Sometimes walked away. And then looked back with a dawning little smile as though to acknowledge the effect she'd just made.

She had no eyebrows, her hips were too wide, her bust too small, but her features were perfect. Her platinum hair was as startling as the element of magic in a fairy tale, the detail that counts at once as a curse and a reward. Her lower lip was too full; one could see it in the portraits of her ancestors. She didn't dance or dress properly and her command of languages was unusually sketchy for someone of her class and nationality; one wondered why her family, which obviously prized her, hadn't trained her better. She sat too long at the table; she was a gourmand.

She was witty, or at least considered a wit. She stayed up all night, gave herself indiscriminately and cheerlessly in sex, drank too much in secret, and longed to experiment with drugs. It was she who said: "In the capital women are so important that all political questions are settled on the bidet." After hearing how the divinity of a certain shrine in the capital had instantly answered three prayers in a row, Claude muttered, "Punctuality is the one thing I look for in a god."

An older man such as Mateo would have seen right away how her dissipations, so wild and amusing in a girl, would soon enough become coarse and grotesque. Her eyes were big, nearly hypertrophied, and the shadows under them dark enough to remind people of Daniel. She loved jewels and went swimming with her pearls on; she'd stand at the shallow end of the pool with her wrists and fingers, burdened with gold and diamonds, resting on the dry ledge.

Like many society girls, she believed only in people she knew. Figures in history appeared pallid to her unless she was related to them. "But *that* archduchess, silly, was my great aunt," she'd say, suddenly waking up in the midst of an otherwise dull recital of recent events. Or she'd side in a debate over physics with the physicist who'd once been presented to her. "But we *know* Doctor Gervaisais," she'd offer as proof of the soundness of his theories. Villainy or virtue, the sacred or the profane, all such abstractions became concrete only when embodied by her acquaintances, who turned her life into glowing allegory. If an impresario hoped to interest her in becoming the patron of his theater, he would be ill-advised to troupe before her his finest entertainers; the excellence of strangers bored her, whereas the most embarrassing failure of a friend impressed her with its sincerity. "It's not quite there yet, of course," she'd concede, "but what integrity! This is exactly the sort of work-in-progress that needs a chance." Unlike some patrons, who lose interest when a project is criticized, Claude dug her heels in—unless, of course, the critic was also a friend. In that case her feelings were divided but still more intense; nothing excited her more than a family squabble.

Her fascination with her own circle was so exclusive that she scarcely grasped how the world ranked various artists and thinkers. She'd say, leaning forward, almost risking her balance, "I think Paxton is on the verge of showing me his illustrations to Robert's poems," without comprehending that most listeners were unlikely to know either name. She cast important invitations to concerts or galleries into her white porcelain fireplace but traveled to a remote monastic island in the estuary to see an exhibition of her old tutor's pastels of kitties.

She lived on stimulants, which broke the usual social rhythms and made her interrupt herself, interrupt others, skip several steps of formality and rush into instant intimacy or irritation. She placed far too much faith in her judgment, which was alarmingly erratic. Dangerous people intrigued her, especially older men who had once been famous but now drank too much and forgot to bathe and had long since cut their ties to society. She liked to sit up all night in squalid rooms with them and listen to their drunken soliloquies while her bodyguard paced back and forth outside downstairs in the rain. Perhaps the neglect these men tendered her reminded her of her father, the general, and made her feel at home.

Her father, loathed and satirized by the citizens of the capital he ruled, was curiously enough a hero back in his homeland, a man who'd written a series of poetic, even mystic accounts of his voyages to exotic places, books short on information but long on atmosphere and wisdom. All his works were still in print in a uniform edition. His portrait as a young adventurer wearing tunic, fez and dagger was printed on the cover of each volume, with the result that most of his new readers, adolescents themselves, forgot to check the publication date and assumed the author was still young, intense, romantically restless—anything but the obese bureaucrat he'd become. His editors, hoping to preserve his vogue, discouraged him from making public appearances.

In his books he sounded unmarried, childless, intriguingly friendless through some accident of fate rather than a character failing. In each book he found himself in a new country, eternally melancholy, questing, curious about the people around him and especially sympathetic to the local women, who were almost always oppressed by savage customs and in need of a civilized young male friend such as himself. Claude's friends from other conqueror families longed to meet this pale, hollow-eyed father and refused to take her side in any family row she reported. They preferred to whisper to one another, out of Claude's earshot, "Too bad such a noble spirit had to have such a bitch for a daughter. No wonder he's so inconsolable . . ." Of course patriots would have welcomed her complaints, but she was too clannish to be guilty of that indiscretion.

And too suspicious. Her misplaced confidence in some older men who scarcely registered her existence was matched by an almost insane distrust of all strangers and, depending on her moods, some very devoted friends. The distrust was constant but its objects shifted. She'd be in the midst of a party, laughing and joking, when suddenly everything would go sour for her, exactly as though the papered walls of the lamplit room had turned transparent and she could see beyond them a smoking village, weeping women, dying children. She'd cock her head at a strange angle, as if an invisible masseur were making a peculiar "adjustment," and her facial muscles would tighten, her mouth would compress into a frightened line, her eyes glitter with diabolic recognition.

If the attack was a mild one, she'd simply slip away without an explanation and for a few weeks avoid this particular group of friends. Even if she admitted to herself how totally unfounded her suspicions had been, she still harbored a lingering trace of unspecified resentment against the people who'd inspired them.

If the attack was grave, she'd move restlessly about in her chair, roll her eyes, mutter obscenities. Her escort might try to calm her, but she was like a horse that smells fire before its rider does and caracoles anxiously. She'd start to insult the hostess, insist on leaving and then angrily kick furniture or even strike people as she was hustled out. Now there was no reasoning with her, she was gone for the evening, as though demons were breeding like flies out of the filthy corners of her mind. Everyone treated her as though she was sick, nothing more. She'd suspect her brother of laughing at her with his friends, her mother of plotting to confine her to a clinic, her father of wanting to send her home to the fatherland or to strip her of her considerable inheritance from her grandmother. But mostly she imagined her friends were whispering about her.

Daniel found her fascinating—maddening, too, he'd add, as though her malady were an unfortunate subtraction from her appeal rather than (in his eyes at least) a substantial addition to it. For he might have found her schoolgirl enthusiasm for garrulous drunks and her debutante loyalty to her friends insupportable had it not been for this fierce quivering craziness that would suddenly jump her, as a thug jumps a passerby. He'd met her in the paddock, found her intoxicating if silly, then forgotten her until one morning a month later, in a smoky café in the dyers' quarter, she'd come up to his table, her hands dirty, her hair unpinned on one side, her dress rumpled. She'd said tonelessly, looking down, as though someone else were forcing her to make this embarrassing request, "May I sit with you?" He felt that if he'd said no she would have shuffled past and asked the man next to him the same question in the same way. Later she told him she'd had a "rough night"; that was all she'd say.

For some reason she trusted him. The traveling searchlight of her suspicions never lingered on him, not once. Perhaps that he was the son of a famous mother as she was the daughter of a powerful man caused her to see him as a sort of twin. Certainly they had similar stories to tell one another. They understood how parallel their lives had been.

Her father's younger brother, who'd died of his own hand

before Claude's birth, had written tight, hermetic poems, sonnets no easier to enter than a royal tomb, each apparent way only a blind alley for exegetes. Claude, who despised her father's books and found his romantic posturing repulsively counterfeit, had worked up a sentimental kinship with her dead uncle. She'd hold his poems in her hand or mouth like an inscribed scarab she couldn't decode but that she hoped would secrete its clear, bitter juices into her system. No one would tell her anything about him. Once when she asked her grandfather for information he looked her hard in the eye and said, "How do you intend to spend your summer?"

There were no pictures of the uncle in the house, no copies of his books, no letters, and his name was never uttered. Claude thought the memory of her own existence could be just as efficiently erased by the family if she broke rank or killed someone or killed herself. In a bookstall by the river she once found a collection of engravings of "the literary stars of tomorrow," portraits of the now-forgotten avant-garde of thirty years ago, and among the severe young women and stern young men with their ink-black hair, paper-white skin and hyphen-shaped mustaches, she'd chanced upon her boyish, clean-shaven uncle, his smile at once sweet and devilish, as though he was someone saintly who nevertheless took a schoolboy's whooping delight in other people's follies. His right eye was white, staring, the pupil far too large, as though it had been hammered flat, whereas the left eye was mischievous, blue, normal. Apparently he'd been blinded in the one eye as a child, or so she forced her father to explain at dinner, a victory she had to pay for by enduring three successive nights of his angry silence.

Now she equated Daniel with this lost uncle. Not that they looked anything alike nor that Daniel had any ambitions as a poet. In fact, Daniel had no ambitions at all (this very uselessness, perhaps, was his brand of poetry). Moreover, she had no notion how her uncle had sounded or moved: nothing. But Daniel's long-suffering dandyism fused in her own dreams with the image of the smiling uncle and his one acute, amused eye and the blasted white one "trained on eternity" (the phrase was her own invention, something she'd never said aloud, since it was the only poem she'd ever written and she feared it would fade if exposed).

Both Claude and Daniel were caught up in family ceremonies and they'd each been too well trained to attempt to extricate themselves. Claude went along with kissing babies and launching ships, just as Daniel never failed to attend his mother's salons or to present her every morning with his broken adventures of the night before from which she could extricate the two or three shards she needed for the mosaic she was patiently assembling, its design long since determined, only the materials in which it would be executed still open to choice or chance.

But if both children fulfilled their functions on stage, in the wings they badmouthed the management. Their true problem was that the world saw them as nothing but extensions of father or mother, but the Peers School had exercised a strong if silent pressure against voicing complaints of that sort. Only "babies" whined about the drawbacks of too much power or too much wealth. Since Claude and Daniel couldn't talk about their real problems, they grumbled about their allowances. Claude was kept on a particularly tight budget. Her sad styleless mother, whose absence of chic seemed to her compatriots proof of her solid character, never understood that the people she and her husband ruled regarded her and her daughter as comically dowdy. If the conquered had to salute the conquerors, they could find solace in noting that the head that wore the crown had had a bad dye job. Her mother's full, unexercised figure, limp flaxen hair, complexion that couldn't tan but would only burn and peel, her preference for square black accessories and nubby brown fabrics all swept the capital into storms of laughter. If the visual genius of the city had retreated from the higher arts of painting and sculpture, it had done so in order to enter into the popular arts of daily life. The display windows of the chocolate shops observed the change of seasons with a gale of autumn leaves and broken branches all in *feuille morte* shades of marzipan; the papermaker, in the same location for four hundred years, had survived so long through a permanent commitment to transience, suitable to his perishable medium. His latest craze was for papier-mâché spheres, pyramids and obelisks, all sheathed in paisleys stamped on gold-sieved backgrounds. Such costly, silly baubles changed hands every other minute—eggtimers that were crystal eggs hollowed out to contain painted scenery and sand flowing over a miniature waterfall; cuff links that made the faintest allusion to handcuffs; robes and wallpaper that matched, designed for waterside rooms, printed with shimmering silver waves on aquamarine silk. Shoes, jewels, hats, gloves, belt buckles passed over the city to settle here and there for a season like unfamiliar birds blown off course—temporary, splendid. Although the citizens sometimes seemed more a collection of individualists than a polity, everyone conformed at least to the latest styles. If fashion dictated that women must wear voluminous tartan stoles, shopgirls too poor to buy an "original" hurried off to the fabric wholesalers and devised their own, wrapping and rewrapping the yards of cloth until they discovered the designer's trick.

Claude had grown up in this city and had absorbed its tastes; the looks of her visiting cousins seemed so hopeless to her she'd say, "I'm sure glad Sophie is a reader, since obviously she'll be spending her nights alone," or "How clever of Maggie to sidestep fashion altogether." Her parents reminded her daily of the superiority of their own culture ("Back home the only people from the capital are the whores and the maids" or "At least people back home don't smell funny" or "No one back home lives on credit, but everyone here does"). Of course they were willing to acknowledge the beauty of the palaces here, but these edifices had been built hundreds of years ago and seemed more works of nature than mere humanity. Secretly, however, Claude's father hoped she would pick up some of the celebrated sophistication of the city—but not too much.

Daniel had taken pity on this unhappy, reckless girl whose wardrobe struck him as valiant if inadequate. Almost at once he started counseling her against the new pinks, the new costume jewelry, the new wigs, and steered her toward the darkest, softest cashmeres, toward antique gold jewelry and daily visits to a "designer" of severe, asymmetrical hairstyles. Together they'd stay out all night; they took each other to their favorite haunts in the dyers' quarter. She once invited him and a group of five other friends to a "love boutique" where tribal men and women made love for visiting lords and ladies. Seven chairs surrounded a cot under a shaded light. The visitors in Claude's party were bejeweled and swathed in silks, since afterward they would be "going on." Now they sat in their chairs drinking vodka neat, only their hands and knees under the light while their plucked and powdered faces were lost in shadow.

A man and woman came out in gaudy synthetic versions of their tribal robes; they bowed all around, undressed and set to work. Their bodies looked almost childishly small. The spectators were close enough to have stroked the man's rising and plunging buttocks or to touch the woman's breasts or face, but the jeweled hands merely toyed with the iced glasses or nervously pinched a silk pleat. The performers, smiling with gold teeth, paused and gestured good-naturedly to indicate the audience should join in, but no one did. Claude, who'd organized the evening, was struggling to appear blasé, but her hand was shaking and her eyes kept veering away from the spotlit intimacy of these two brown, glistening bodies. She couldn't look long at the woman's grinning face or the man's sweat-slick shoulder or the way his white scalp could be seen where a lock of his straight black hair folded back.

Claude and Daniel locked glances over this squirming, breathing display. The only illumination on their faces was the light bounced up off the bodies of the performers. Claude was sitting on one side of the bed, Daniel on the other and, unblinking, they stared and stared at each other. They saw nothing else and could hear nothing but the woman's feeble, unconvincing moans and the occasional sound of flesh slapping flesh.

A few days later Daniel was posing in the nude for a woman artist he knew, an older woman he'd met through his mother, when Claude, completely by surprise, dropped in. Apparently the two women were friends. The artist never stopped painting her model, the model never stopped posing. Claude strode about the room, chitchatting, passing along news about a sick friend, her eyes grazing nervously across Daniel until she stopped, became silent, leaned against the door with her hands behind her hips. She looked and looked at him. He could feel her looking, even though he didn't look back. Then she left.

She must have realized that, since she'd seen his body before he saw hers, a kind of etiquette demanded that she make the next step. The following day she sent him a note inviting him to a state reception. Daniel attended and Claude insisted he stay on for supper with her family. He did, but her father was so rude to him, pretending not to recognize his family name and responding to each of Daniel's drawled remarks with military briskness, that Claude felt impelled to drink too much. She became sick and had to leave the table just as the flowers were being removed out of deference to the bouquet of an "important" wine her father was uncorking.

Daniel's clothes—his handmade shirts with the concealed buttons and notched collars, his jackets with the narrow armholes and minute silk stitches, his pleatless nankeen trousers and glove-leather boots that pooled around his ankles, the scent of vetiver in his copious grey handkerchief—caused her father to draw back in disdain, as though he were endangered. Certainly nothing could have been more foreign to the father's cult of nature and simplicity, his

vision of melancholy, peregrinating second sons seeking heart's
ease in the mountains and woods or of a beer-drinking peasantry
in tune with the rollicking seasons. Daniel represented languor, the
enervating South, artifice and seduction whereas Claude's father
espoused discipline, the bracing North, harmony with the outdoors
and resistance to blandishments of any sort.

Daniel and Claude were constantly together, either hiding out
in her wing of the governor's headquarters or carousing in the
popular quarters. When Daniel would arrive at her palace in the
early afternoon, soon after awakening, he'd ask to be announced
to Claude's brother. The brother would then escort him to Claude's
bedside and leave the lovers alone. In complete contrast to the rest
of the palace—scented with pine branches and potpourris and filled
with heavy oak furniture, hunting trophies and paintings of stags
and rainbows or of the old mail coach hurtling down a mountain
pass—Claude's room was fashionable in ebony and angel skin and
filthy and smelled of valerian. She woke in slow, irritable stages and
sent her breakfast tray back untouched (the dry whole-grained
toast, stewed apples and unpasteurized milk were her father's idea
of a healthy beginning to each challenging day). Then she and
Daniel quibbled over her wardrobe or tried to remember what
they'd done the night before ("I did not try to play tennis in the
traffic," Claude shrieked. "I was with you and we were drinking
ouzo in the Queen's Garden"). Unlike most lovers, they didn't
recount their exploits as adults or their exploitation as children nor
did they exchange compliments or pledges. They were always either bored and seeking a new pastime or quibbling. Daniel would
move the varnished pearwood dressing table with its drawer covered in vellum veneer or shift the block of luminous quartz or the
gypsum lamp.

They'd sit for hours in silence tossing balls of scrunched-up
paper into a shagreen basket or gazing out the window and com-
menting on the passersby. A momentous conversation would con-

sist of Daniel's saying: "I think no more gold for you. From now on, it will be silver, and I'm thinking of changing your perfume too."

One day Mathilda left for her seaside house with her great love, that spotty, skinny oaf Gabriel ("Mater, are you sure you can't do better? People who don't know us will take him for me"). Disgruntled, Daniel sent for Claude. When she arrived, uncoiffed and turbaned, hiding behind dark glasses her unpainted blond lashes and undrawn nonexistent eyebrows, unbathed and smelling, Daniel exploded and slapped her. "You filthy bitch," he shouted at her. He threw her to the ground. "Fat albino," he said. She wriggled out of her panties. He toed her with his boot, then wiped the leather with a cloth. She was quaking with pain or laughter, he didn't know which. He went over to the window, sprawled in a chair and began to read. After a while she crawled to his side and rested her head on his knee. Without a word and never interrupting his reading, he began to stroke her head. The next day she showed him the bruise on her thigh and he shrugged.

He was always giving her lessons, teaching her why the old red velvet and crystal coiffeuse must go in favor of a new vanity table in sanded oak and white leather. He threw out all her genre paintings of slurping peasants and kitschy stags in favor of black-and-white woodcuts of actors. He let her eat only one small meal a day —just shaved carrots and a mushroom fricassee, say (he abhorred meat and only just tolerated fish). Any dish that contained even a suspicion of onions or garlic was banished with a chuckle. When his feelings were under control, his highest word of praise was *nice* and his most damning insult *silly*. If he told her she was being silly she grew cold with fear. He made her wear his vetiver and she felt like a branded animal. He hated Claude to wear one blouse over another (last year's fashion) and would greet her with a sneer: "Cold? Bundling up?" When his mother moved Gabriel into their house,

Daniel threw Claude down the stairs to punish her for wearing the cameo instead of her new black glass pendant. When she locked herself in the toilet he broke the door down. They made love on the floor as he whispered death threats in her ear.

His rages alternated with gentleness toward her during her own attacks of craziness. One evening Claude gave a supper party for ten friends. She dismissed the servants, prepared the exquisitely light dish of three kinds of fish in a saffron broth and served it with her own hands. In fact, she didn't set a place for herself, since she preferred to wait on her guests and not mix those duties with half-hearted socializing. Everything pleased the eye, starting with Claude herself, whose blond hair was long and glazed back flat on one side, clipped blond fuzz on the other, whose face was so powdered it had flattened out except for the thickly kohled eyes and the shining, meticulously painted red lips. Her newly starved body was sheathed in a black taffeta gown and her arms and neck were bare and radiantly pale. The dining room had been walled in big polished squares of padded fawn leather that contrasted voluptuously with the porous white stone fireplace. The clothless rectangular dining table was of black gaboon. The lights were white plaster wall sconces shaped like seashells; the window niches were mirrored in blue. Wine had been banished and champagne was served throughout in milky opaline goblets fitted into black iron bases. The conversation was distinguished by its inconsequentiality, a gift the guests offered as a tribute to such a room, such a hostess.

And yet, despite their compliance and admiration and Daniel's obvious approval of every detail—from the unnourishing eel broth to the "offstage" sound of trapped crickets to the look of a white silk scarf wrapped around a chilled bottle, from the table decorations of lightly painted pale green twigs instead of flowers and the ubiquitous scent of his very own vetiver—despite these smoothly orchestrated details, Claude started acting strange. Something one of the guests had said caught in her mind and began to sprout instantly, rampantly. Her face seemed partially paralyzed, her mouth was working and muted curses boiled up out of her. This suppressed turbulence was like a hectic waltz someone might play on a silenced piano, the noise of nails tapping ivory louder than the chromatic frenzy. Daniel gathered her anguish under his huge arm and led her slowly away. The aristocrats at table admired the way in which he never looked back, never apologized and never returned to the party; "Good show," a young lord said.

When she was well enough, Claude would accompany Daniel and Gabriel when they went out to roam the city at night. Mathilda never reproached "her boys" for the hours they kept nor asked them where they were going. In order to turn herself into an intellectual, she had had to reject every qualm she'd inherited from her conventional parents. Her stance was as wide as she could make it. She'd learned in her philosophical musings to tweezer a crystalline structure into place and then neatly glide the foundations out from under it, reverse it, rotate it to some new angle. Her mode was to view the same proposition from every side and against an always shifting background. Now the only misgiving she had was her fear that in her quest for intellectual suppleness she'd become personally obtuse (Daniel had told her she was the least self-aware person he knew). Could it be that her very flexibility as a thinker had required emotional rigidity, that she had not been as brave, as ready to risk everything as she'd intended?

She longed to set every corner of her mind and heart in motion, to cause every atom to spin, revolve, cycle freely and rapidly.

Her love for Gabriel had forced her to unearth many fears. She came to half-fear him as well. Now she saw that before she met him she'd been preening like a dirty swan in the stagnant admiration all around her. When she slept with a man it was just once. These encounters came at long intervals. She'd grown used to sleeping alone, reading all night, brooding, daydreaming, regretting past loves. Her energy had gone into her reading. Sometimes she and

Daniel would sit up reading in matching chairs. More often she'd fall asleep in a pile of books and wake up in a nest made of crumbling paper and old leather bindings. She'd ring for coffee and sit up only far enough to start reading again. She preferred keeping the blinds drawn so that she never knew whether it was night or day. She forgot to dress, received no one, ate only when hunger forced her to. If the intellectual vision faded for a moment and her very torpor prompted sexual thoughts, she'd quickly dig her way through all the men she could imagine and then toss their images back in the bin and slam it shut.

But with Gabriel she had to start living again. She had to submit to a sort of discipline that frightened her. Her body, her breath had to be clean at all times because she never knew when he would visit her next. At the very least he wanted to make love to her once a day. Even toward dawn, after she'd been asleep for hours, he'd slide in bed beside her. In her dream she was being held captive in a temple from which men were excluded and the priestesses were slowly but insistently helping her to sit down on the ceremonial lingam . . . She laughed and said out loud, while still asleep, "I can't take it all," but Gabriel knew that she could. In her sinking, sweet defenselessness she saw her body go transparent and light up from within. A radiance condensed into hot spots on both breasts and her left ear.

The next morning she noticed that her face looked tired but happy. Her muscles ached in unusual places. When she read, the lines of type widened as her focus shifted to Gabriel's face. She could feel him in her even when he was far away. And this sensation got translated first into affection and then panic (he's too close, I'm losing myself, I'll never read again!) and back into a devotion still more extravagant since it had had to overcome these very anxieties.

She didn't want to speak out in favor of mindless ecstasy. But she also dreaded the tendency to treat every new experience as an instance of a familiar principle. In art, in love and in thought, principles should be secondary to style, if style meant *rubato*, a lingering for significance. The way her hopes swirled around her fears, twirled slowly on point before rushing to catch up with the beat, the way she leapt high, held aloft by Gabriel's strong hands, his closeness beneath and behind her, until finally she sank slowly, gracefully down into his embrace . . . She felt she was a shell he was prying open.

Daniel and Claude invited Gabriel one afternoon to a "tea-cruise," the latest fad among the Peers. Everyone was in white boating cashmeres. The young men and women sat in small group-ings of white wicker chairs beside green glass-brick tables on the deck as servants circulated with trays of tea and biscuits. Gabriel, always such a success these days at Mathilda's receptions, kept striking the wrong note here. He'd mention an unusual word he'd discovered or bring forth a bizarre juxtaposition of thoughts—and everyone smiled queasily or coughed.

He who'd exchanged his original dream-wracked innocence for a new manner, itself ornate, could just as easily pick up yet another one, he thought. Almost as easily, surely. He'd learned that the "intellectual" manner of Mathilda's salon (so shamelessly par-odied by Walter) consisted of striking one attitude after another. A visiting scholar, for instance, would be trotted up to meet Walter. First, Walter would establish his knowledge of the man's field ("As a geologist myself . . ."). Then he'd praise this particular man's contribution ("You've said the last word on granite"), although in startling terms ("So touching, so elevating—I read your mono-graph on granite as moral philosophy"). The scholar's most childish aspirations toward grandeur were massaged with plenty of oil: "You should be much better known. Our leaders would be well advised to memorize your texts. Your observations on schist . . . ! Forgive me, I can't go on, I'm so overwhelmed by the very thought of you on schist."

On a second meeting the granite-and-schist man would be

expected to have a thought about today's somewhat different topic, the evolution of cult images over the last five centuries. If the geologist smiled with arrogant modesty and protested, "But I know nothing of such things," Walter would say with grim primness, "I'd rather hoped that there would be a wider relevance for your some-what . . . narrow concerns," and the geologist would see his status sink. To recover, he'd be forced to make his first awkward venture into art criticism: "It couldn't have been much fun for them to sculpt this malachite . . ." Nodding approval and looking signifi-cantly around at the other members of the chat box, Walter would murmur, "I knew he must have a *collegial* side," by which he meant a willingness to appear foolish in the service of his own vanity.

Less grotesquely, the "intellectual" manner Gabriel had mas-tered consisted of several milder tricks easy enough to learn. The intellectual never said of abstractions "that" but always "this," to indicate his physical proximity to ideas ("This is a fascinating hy-pothesis you're advancing"). Nine times out of ten the intellectual could be counted on to be a sympathetic and encouraging listener ("Quite . . . exactly . . . brilliant!") but on the tenth, by way of demonstrating his integrity, he'd suddenly become obstinate ("Not at all, I cannot endure this sort of category mistake you're mak-ing"). The intellectual cheerfully confessed his lack of worldliness ("I'm afraid I'm hopeless when it comes to money") but vaunted his *mondanité* ("We did manage quite a spread for His Lordship's breakfast"). One constantly paraphrased the interlocutor's ideas ("Now you seem to be saying that in the modern world—if by modern we mean the last ten centuries") not in the interest of making sure everyone understood everyone but as a way of flatter-ing the speaker.

Despite all the buffoonery, a kindness did reign at Walter's or Mathilda's or during the chat box sessions; a common assumption prevailed that each life was a lonely project, patient, scrupulous. If people were clumsy or crazy, at least they were well-meaning. The evening get-togethers were offered as a time to burn off the daily residues of poison accumulated during solitary study, just as midnight suppers enabled Edwige to calm herself after an electrifying two hours on stage. In both cases the hosts recognized their own minor roles as masseurs to the sore spirit. If one of the celebrated guests simply sat in the corner not talking and wearing a smile, then Walter or Mathilda recognized that the studies of this goofy genius had turned him into a holy fool. They'd let him grin and eat his dinner and shuffle home, his head still echoing with the angelic voices of music or mathematics. Similarly, if Edwige dozed off between courses after a performance or suddenly scooped up her white fur and made for the door, ready to go home even before the fish, her doting host would never protest. Thinkers and actresses were all workers and one was permitted to feed them and talk to them only if one recognized that their spirit was sand passing through an hourglass. While each artist or intellectual drained away as a living presence, daily becoming less and less distinct and defined, his or her achievement piled up correspondingly.

Among the conquerors, everything was otherwise, as Gabriel had to learn. For them a salon was not the green room but the theater, the illuminated cube in which society's most conspicuous players could make love, fight, stage a coup, fall from favor. To be sure, the conquerors also trailed a legend when they made an entrance, but it was one of family history rather than personal accomplishment, hence it was invariable. A prince could do no wrong, a servant no good. Of course some middle-class people could rise. A great rider who maintained a choice stable, who lived in jodhpurs and decorated his rooms with antlers, fox paws and hunting prints, who attended auctions, frequented veterinaries and talked feed would rise effortlessly, no matter what his origins. Or a dashing tennis instructor with a faultless dinner jacket and a conveniently bedridden wife; or a witty but homely woman who was willing to travel anywhere at a moment's notice and could pay her own way; or a generous and boundlessly rich couple with large social appetites, acceptable manners and no complicating sexual tastes—these were specimens of the middle class who could penetrate the world of the grand salons even without a pedigree.

What Gabriel had to realize was that aristocrats, unlike intellectuals, had no desire to improve or prove themselves. In the world of the salons there was no future, only the present. One looked at a painting, one consumed a lime ice, one played a round of cards, one talked, walked, shopped, rode a horse, cooked up a practical joke. The absence of time was paradisal, if paradise is conceded to be splendid but dull. No one struggled to memorize the names of foreign painters, to question the meaning of money or society, to talk amusingly, to stand at a viewing distance from the moment.

As a result, in society such talk as there was had no coherence. Each remark set off a minor fuss followed by a silence. Then a new comment would bubble up, only to drain away a moment later. For someone as serious and sensitive as Gabriel, such conversational inconsequence was exhausting. For him who brooded on the appropriateness of speech, who knew the outsider's fear of the social blunder, the hundreds of separate initiatives every hour in society demanded was nightmarish.

Nor could he dismiss these salons as worthless. He loved the atmosphere. He sat nursing his drink and listened to the thrilling voice of a woman beside him as she stroked her tiny, trembling dog and addressed a friend; "She's like a monkey, really. One wanted to offer her a nut." Later, she said, "But all those people are wonderfully absurd. When George insulted me last week, I sulked. The next day he sent me marvelous flowers, a kilo of love letters, a beautiful doll and this note: 'Have dinner with me. I am the King of Fools.' When I took him back I decided to give him a new name, to make our reunion less painful. Now he's *Hank*. Yes. Hank. When people call him George I feign confusion." Still later Gabriel heard her discussing the eternal carnival, a subject more acceptable here than at Mathilda's. This woman, terminally thin, said, "How could I wear such a costume—I who have to take off my rings during dinner if my hands are not to be too utterly exhausted." Her friend replied, "But do come. Your 'Hank' has promised to come as a convalescent in a cyclamen dressing gown of crackling silk and a shirt with a pleated jabot. He'll probably wear my shoes—he's so proud they fit him."

These voices were so rare, so expensive that even when they pronounced an ordinary word such as *marvelous* it sounded cryptic, exotic. For days afterwards Gabriel seized every opportunity to say *marvelous,* even when it didn't apply.

When they went into luncheon they were surrounded in the ship's cabin by gaunt iron statues and on the walls the cartoons for a suite of religious paintings long since lost. The sculptures and drawings were piercingly beautiful, but no one seemed disposed to acknowledge them. It even seemed to be a breach of manners to look at them. Gabriel felt as though he was sitting in a circle of ordinary mortals but surrounded by a company of gods. The one condition for having these divine guests to dinner was that no mortal could look at them.

Whereas intellectual women prided themselves on their imperviousness to scandal and liked to throw in wicked remarks of their own, social women were far more easily shocked. One of Gabriel's waggish ways, picked up at Walter's receptions, had been to purvey off-color stories to feminine ears that resolutely refused to blush. But now that same habit caused the young woman who'd been seated beside Gabriel to cough, to put down her soup spoon, flush and stare into her lap. Gabriel was titillated by such a violent response—and chagrined by his own bad taste. Soon he steered the conversation back to the more pleasing subject of the lady's spaniel. She readily provided answers to his questions, although she was looking around for rescue and seemed to resent being "interviewed" even on this agreeable topic. Mateo had taught Gabriel that one need never feel shy with strangers. One could always grill them about every aspect of their lives—their hobbies, career, birthplace, love life—and sit back and nod. But this rule, infallible until now, didn't suit the style of the salons.

Here everyone who counted could be counted on to know everything about everyone else—wealth, lineage, power. Since conversation did not serve to establish credentials, since it did no work, it was given over to pure play. Gaming, dancing, boating, hunting were noble pleasures because each required money and leisure and they all forbade sustained talk. Or so Gabriel told himself. His speculations were only partially true, since he knew too little to be accurate (but not so much he'd be incapable of any evaluation whatsoever).

After supper Edwige was brought in on the arm of a high government official. Even later, when the whole party had moved to shore, Edwige was still the center of attraction. She attracted around her a circle of blue and grey military uniforms. Gabriel studied her and felt the same awe as when he'd first seen her on stage. Could this be the joking, casual tomboy he so often saw at home as she lounged about in her white chemist's smock waving perfume testers in the air, interrupting her stream of banter to sniff her latest blend, her forehead wrinkling slightly, the wings of her delicate nose contracting? Here she'd put aside her coarse jokes and was playing what she called her "dollface" routine. Sometimes she'd say, "I went all dollface," and would turn on Gabriel or Mateo her sweetest, most innocent expression. The odd thing was that at such moments she really did look innocent, so innocent that for an instant Gabriel would feel his own features melting in sympathy—until she would mutter out of the side of a pinched-lipped mouth, "It drives them wild every time."

Today her dollface was glowing. The men standing around her felt their chests swell, their shoulders bulge to form a protective barrier against the world. She who could shout down the wind when she was cursing her maid for wrinkling her blouse was now so helpless, so breathy she could scarcely be heard and the men all stepped fractionally closer until they touched and became half aware of their collective force. Under their imperial uniforms they were shaggy, muscled brutes. Nothing would have been more natural than a free-for-all to determine which brute could rape this seductive child. But those urges—legible in the wet eyeteeth of one officer, the dilated pupils of another, the tensed jaw muscle of a third and the clenched fist of a fourth—were so inhibited by convention that their force, audible in their ever louder and deeper voices, held the room in suspense like a wave that keeps gathering but refuses to break.

Gabriel looked at Edwige as though she were an older sister pulling a fast one on all these morons. She winked at him over the gold epaulette of a short, square captain. But so much attention focused on her also made her seem . . . desirable. He remembered he'd desired her often in the past, before their encounter in Mathilda's toilet, but then Edwige had still been his uncle's mistress and he'd been just a drowsy, unhappy kid lurking about, blinking into the light and making shadows. He'd gawked and gawked at her and then carried off the way she looked printed on the insides of his closed eyelids, a faint impression that a sudden bright light could have erased. But if he could keep the picture of her face, her bare shoulders, the gold down on her nape—if he could preserve these images until he reached the toilet, he'd lock the door, drop his trousers with his eyes still shut and sit down to a feast, exactly like a hungry servant who carries off a nearly untouched plate from the master's table.

The party had moved to an unusual house and grounds. There were few gardens in the capital since land was so scarce, but this house, although unimpressive in itself, was situated in a walled garden that took half an hour to explore thoroughly. Today children were playing ball at the end of one of the symmetrical walk-ways. Suddenly a huge, oceangoing ship, ten stories tall, glided past just beyond the far brick wall—a delirious shift in scale, as when one peeks into a dollhouse, becomes absorbed and then sees, through the miniature French windows on the far side, part of a real child's enormous pink face and her cow-catcher eyelashes, blinking ominously. Gabriel and Daniel were ambling down the path, both of them enjoying the mild and ambiguous satisfaction of having attended a fashionable but not particularly gay social event. Gabriel felt a bit of pleasure only when he recalled how many people wanted to be here in his stead. He wanted to work up some enthusi-asm for the salons, since Daniel liked them so much—since, indeed, so many of these people were Daniel's friends from schoolboy days. "I love the conversations these people have," Gabriel said. "They don't go anywhere. They merely circulate, disperse—like clouds, but clouds with platinum linings."

Daniel leaned his hand heavily on Gabriel's shoulder as they strolled. A weird wheezing sound was escaping from some part of his anatomy, his lungs, possibly, as though his chest contained a small, self-operating bellows. "Ah but no, my dear boy, where you imagine you're seeing some supremely decorative nullity, what one is actually witnessing is the extinction of all individuality under tyranny. The conquerors live under an ancient dictatorship that has always worked through spies, informers, anonymous tattlers against any sort of individualism. That's why the conquerors love us and fear us. We have opinions. We have ideas. We have scruples. What you consider to be aristocratic *désinvolture* is slavish submission."

Gabriel could scarcely concentrate as Daniel went on, pointing out that the pleasures and pastimes of the conquerors had been designed to eliminate all reflection or even sequential thought ("Continuity itself would be too dangerous, since a pursued idea is already a threat"). All Gabriel could think about was Edwige, who was moving down an adjacent pathway trailing her guard of soldiers. She was laughing. Her long hair, which on stage every night spilled over her naked body, was now pinned up in some paradox of seductiveness under her tricorne. She didn't walk smoothly forward but stopped frequently to turn, address one of her escorts, point up at a cloud, stifle a laugh, act out a little scene between two disputants, taking each role by turns.

Gabriel remembered that evening last fall at Mathilda's house when Edwige had stripped herself and shown herself to him, although they'd never touched. Now he wouldn't be so stupid as to obey her. Now he would never agree to come so near (yet remain so far from enjoying) her favors.

It dawned on him that he'd gladly exchange Mathilda for Edwige and the patriots for the conquerors. He'd be willing to lose his uncle's love and to face the hatred of the citizens of the capital. He knew he might have to make such a choice. It was unlikely he could have it both ways.

He and Daniel walked up and down the garden pathways and listened to the sounds of the canals, which they could not see, although the waterways were just on the other side of the brick wall.

He knew there was this thing they called *morality* that might cause him trouble. Most of the time, ninety-nine times out of a hundred, people ignored morality and peacefully, predictably pursued their own interests or submitted to prior prejudices, although naturally they did so with all the usual little nods to modesty and rectitude. But every once in a great while someone took it into his head to behave morally or, even worse, to mention morality. Gabriel had noticed that once morality was mentioned people started sitting up straighter.

His mother, as best he could remember, had never mentioned morality when he was a child. Perhaps she had, but the lesson hadn't taken hold. Never, as he sailed through his days, did he feel he was navigating past a treacherous coast of morality. He simply never thought of morality unless its name was invoked—and then suddenly he remembered that everyone else had been consciously keeping quiet about it until now. Conversely, the zest other people knew when they flouted morality passed him by as well. Sometimes he thought he was like a color-blind person in a world he knows so well that he's found sufficient clues to fill in for the absent sensations; he had no need of morality to understand his world. He was simply curious to know what it would feel like.

But he suspected he was better off without morality. He knew his uncle did exactly as he pleased, but so often felt bad about it. Mathilda appeared to waste a lot of time pondering the moral aspects of other people's actions. Since her theoretical resourcefulness was joined to a powerful but naïve egotism, her moral researches always ended with a conviction of her enemies, an exoneration of her friends and a sort of ethical perfect attendance pin for herself that she smilingly accepted with a shrug.

Daniel's responses were harder to predict. Mathilda and Mateo had stripped themselves down for action and were, finally, endowed with avid appetites they knew how to quench; their moral scruples were never allowed to interrupt a flow of satisfaction. But Daniel, one could say, liked impediments that stood in the way of desire, even his own desire. At least he liked impeding any sequence of agreeable events or mutual congratulations by saying, "Now, wait a minute . . ." In that minute he gained in importance. As a dandy, he didn't have accomplishment as his goal. Indeed, he didn't have a goal. He wanted to make the people around him more beautiful or at least more conscious. Their reeducation began with his inhibition of their habits. He was like a swimming instructor who tries to undo an inefficient crawl by isolating first the kick, then the breathing, finally the stroke. Morality—bringing it up, creating a silence with it—was his way of making people freeze, flinch, doubt themselves. Because he so often acted against his own interests, he thought his own morals must be pure. He didn't notice that he liked the role of arbiter better than anything he might gain through arbitration.

He and Gabriel strolled into "the potting shed," as the hosts called it. No one minded that the house attached to this resplendent garden was so small and inconvenient. It actually did serve as a greenhouse in the winter, and during warm weather it was the repository of tools, discarded clay pots, cuttings, sprouting bulbs. It smelled of wet earth and dried straw. The hostess, apparently, had laughably bad taste, but she was the first to laugh at it. She was the daughter of an old conqueror family (the bad taste), but she had been born here long before the conquest (the ability to laugh). She seemed something out of a fairy tale with her bonnet and work apron and mud-caked hands and weather-beaten face. She looked worried under the lock of false black hair curling across her forehead below the bonnet's rim.

And then, with all the ease of a dream, Edwige had taken Gabriel's arm and was saying, "Don't worry, I won't haul you off to the toilet again," and he was blushing and smiling with a great stab of cayenne heat inside his stomach and talking, using words that little successive laughs were leapfrogging, "I sure wish you'd give me a second chance, I wouldn't be so docile this time," and she was spreading her fan over her face in what was at once a parody of coyness and its most seductive expression.

And then they were together in a boat on the water with just her crew, three sulky bronzed tribesmen who went shoeless whenever possible and whose feet were long, flat and hammertoed. Now the men were creeping smoothly, silently over the polished mahogany decks in their spotless white uniforms, but their trousers were in each case too tight and too short, stopping high above the knobby ankles and huge, deformed, nimble feet. The captain had full lips, almost purple, surmounted by a plucked black mustache. With his depthless black eyes and greased-back black hair he would have looked murderous except that when he spoke he revealed his teeth, which were comically bucked; his smile softened the impression made by the burst blood vessel in his left eye. When he spoke his voice was agreeably burred from having smoked too many cigarettes.

They, Gabriel and Edwige, went below deck where everything was efficiently stowed, where the galley was all polished chrome and multiple function, where a brass wall clock ticked pedantically within a silence enfolded by the slaphappy turbulence of wind and wave outside, where a new novel and sunglasses were tossed alluringly on a bunkbed dressed in virginal sheets and a blue-and-white seersucker spread. As Gabriel followed Edwige down the seven mahogany steps, all he could think about was kissing that downy nape or the way her body would feel inside. He remembered she was hairless. He'd seen her naked a dozen times on stage and once "in person," that time at Mathilda's. Later, when he'd visited her in her apartment, she'd sometimes asked him to help her lace herself into one of her long-waisted gowns. Or if he'd stopped by between the matinee and evening performances he'd see her, exhausted, step out of her heavy skirts and their crinolines, leave them abandoned in the hall like a lobster's shell as she squirmed, defenseless, toward bed and a twenty-minute nap ("No, no, Gabriel, don't tax your poor old workhorse of a mom now, not now, for pity's sake, just rub my shoulders and—" gleeful parody of severity—"and no monkey business, got it? You can let yourself out, can't you, if I doze off, and no fair telling my fans I snore").

And now, here he was, helping her out of her gown, but she wasn't tired at all, she wasn't pretending to be poor old mom, the dazzling porthole behind him was revolving its reflection into each of her pale blue eyes as she turned around and looked at him. He thought the crew members must be hammertoed from having always gripped slippery decks with their bare feet. Were they still pacing the decks above, silently? Why did she need him, when she already had three such men under livery? Her mouth tasted salty from the nuts she'd been gobbling in the potting shed. She had a low, throaty murmuring sound she kept making, and he kept echoing. All through the tangled timing, the intricate positionings of their love-making, they kept murmuring back and forth to each other. It was a sound that reassured Gabriel, that made him know that they were still together, that convinced him he hadn't lost her, that oriented them. Then she began to whisper, again and again, "You're the best" over and over. "You're the best."

At a certain moment she pulled herself firmly out of his embrace, turned over, knelt on all fours, reached back with a hand full of white cream, grabbed him, deftly introduced his penis into her anus, held up her hand to signal him to pause for a moment until her muscles adjusted to this intrusion—then she salaamed forward with her shoulders touching the mattress and her exquisite rump raised, deckled across the hips by the diamond pattern of her panties. Gabriel liked the snugger fit of the anus but missed the way the muscles of her vagina had gripped the entire length of his penis like a milkmaid's hand.

Her very acquisitiveness in pursuing a specific sexual quest excited him, made him harder. He no longer needed to fear repelling her with his own insistence. He stood on the floor beside the bed, turned her until she was athwart the narrow mattress. He was merely the perpetrator of their mutual pleasure; he would rape them. The porthole cast a stripe of white light down her spine, contouring with gleam above, shadow below each delicate knuckle of bone, stirring in the wispy cotton candy of her hair collecting at her nape. A tiny sigh of a fart escaped from her, the nasty smell rose to his nostrils, she seemed to cringe with shame—and he was thrilled to have tapped this corrupt gas out of such a perfect vessel. She sensed that her humiliation had excited him and she pressed back with new greed. There were no more pretensions between them; they were both vulgar, greedy. His right hand snaked down between her legs and reached up into her vagina; he hooked his thumb over her clitoris and circled it gently as he drove deeper and deeper into her anus. She began to moan so loudly that she grabbed the pillow and bit it. Gabriel licked the fingers of his left hand and applied them to the nipple of her left breast. Her combs fell out and the lavish fortune of her gold hair was spent on the pillow.

Gabriel could feel his own body changing, expanding, growing more forceful. He'd once again found the one corner of his thoughts that tunneled away from the sunlit world of caution and courtesy toward this obscene wrestling match between two laborers he scarcely recognized. If his thoughts scurried back up the tunnel —if he thought, Will she see me again, does she like me, will she tell my uncle—then his erection wilted and he was reduced to becoming again a brooder and skulker.

But right now they were far from such pale, tense realities; they'd grown into these larger selves, blacker and simpler. Gabriel was nothing but a flat chest sluiced in sweat and he restrained a leashed animal whining to be let go, to shoot off in pursuit of the one prey it was born to hunt. And Edwige was no longer the arrogant dispenser of favors but this gleaming white rump (the deckling had faded) and its smell. He loved the smell of her shit because it smelled of the most shameful act of the day, the one no one dared to share. He knew she was fearing a further loss of muscle tone and it was there, exactly over that ambiguous noodle of shame, that his thumb kept circling as he tempted her into relaxing, into surrendering. His own pleasure required her humiliation. Not that he himself was repelled by the odor; far from it. It was the smell of a stable, of huge standing horses shifting their weight in the stall, of his own long-ago lonely stings in the thunder box back at Madder Pink, the smell of steam lifting off those black sacs of roe he'd produced, that pair of blood sausages on a frosty morning in the echoing immensity of yet another day, as though time were a freezing mansion and he its caretaker bravely rubbing a fire into life with hard black and fluid white emissions, the *demi-deuil* of being human.

Edwige moaned louder and louder; the waves were slapping the hull; Gabriel's hand was slapping her hip, not with hard purpose but in a disorganized reflex. He wondered if the crew was listening. Or had she hired deaf sailors somewhat as pashas buy eunuchs to guard the harem? Gulls were flickering in the sunlight far away, the visible ash from an invisible fire. And now the ship was listing, Gabriel was staring straight down out of the porthole into pale green water and white foam. Edwige's head was pressed into the corner of the bunk, her rump was tilted still higher, Gabriel was standing over her, green bubbles, gull cry, creaking mast, salt spray, he exploded, Edwige's muscular wetness contracted around his hand, she shouted, and his body, disassembling, diminishing, discovered a dozen separate aches as his soul, which only seconds before had been a pulsing red nimbus, dwindled into a small brown crick in the neck.

She laughed. "What a caution," she said, coming up for air, darting into a peignoir, putting an arm around Gabriel's waist, wrinkling her nose as she looked at his dunged and still erect penis. She said, "There! I told you not to sneak into mother's fudge!" She guffawed, then slapped a hand over her mouth. She was playing the outrageous scamp and making him into a stuffy old man. "Here, love, right this way to wash up," and she shoved him into a tiny, sparkling toilet, having switched comedies to the daytime one in which she played the motherly nurse and he the lovable and bumbling patient. Gabriel didn't like the way their sexual combat of a moment ago had been switched into a vaudeville turn. Once again he sensed the nasty, cheapening part of Edwige so at odds with the sterner part, the annunciating angel, feathers tipped in flame.

Until now Gabriel had known nothing but the dowdy, talkative and serious world of Mathilda's and Mateo's friends. He'd seen a few courtiers brush past, like swans gliding through a backwater, but he'd assumed Mathilda had been right in assuring him they were to be pitied. "How they long to live out lives! At court, of course, one's nothing but a high-paid valet who can't quit but who can and will be fired. They lose fortunes gambling since etiquette permits them to sit only over cards. Those minutes of being seated can cost millions. At court all comfort has been sacrificed to grandeur, all wisdom to wit, all honor to vanity and revenge—and at any function an observer would naturally assume the courtiers hold the lowest rank, below the servants and the dogs."

Now, of course, Gabriel could see that Mathilda had exaggerated, carried away by the temptation to make her own circle look good. To be sure, hers was a strangely solitary notion of society, since her irritable honesty caused her to reject all groups as self-promoting, all public intercourse as theatrical, all covenants as dangerously numbing to skepticism. But if the moralist in her required gloomy solitude, the aesthete required company, for the aesthete adheres to art, which is public. If in any actual group she sank deeper and deeper into her armchair until she was nothing but enraged eyes and ruffled feathers, when she contemplated some *future* group she became confidently utopian.

In actual groups Mathilda was bored when attention wavered away from her, offended when it returned to her, always dismayed by the vulgarity of the tone and the lassitude of the intellectual level. But at the prospect of a new "colloquium" or "seminar" she was gleeful, even though her fame and snobbism had made her so distrustful of outsiders and newcomers that she could only imagine forming such seminars out of the people she already knew, as though a capricious officer of an oasis garrison were to keep casting his handful of besotted soldiers into ever more sprightly roles in ever less likely operettas.

From the vantage of a polished and self-assured court society, Gabriel could see how molting Mathilda's plumage appeared to be. The airs she assumed, the petty games she played, the devotion she exacted seemed only slightly less ludicrous than her claims to universal knowledge. "She's the best argument against female literacy I know," the general himself had once remarked. He'd met her at a reception soon after he'd been appointed commander of the capital. She'd been ready to grace his viceregal court and steer his reign. She'd sent him flattering notes about his wisdom-travel books and his search for the original Ur-plant from which all later plants had derived. She sauntered confidently up to his side at his matinee, as though she were a local monarch welcoming a foreign cousin. And then she'd asked him, dimpling with anticipation, "What sort of woman do you admire most, General?" and he'd growled, "The sort that breeds the most babies." He'd so insulted her she would have left the capital altogether except, as she remarked to Walter, it was the only city where you can do without happiness, since its distractions divert your attention from all thoughts of the past or the future.

One day Edwige, who could never remember Mathilda's name and always referred to her sweetly as "your brainy friend," passed along a scrap of anonymous doggerel to Gabriel:

> Of politics and poetry and God
> She spoke; of love and food, then gave a nod
> To riddles apt to tease, torment, perplex,
> To sex, philology and the best pets
> For laps, the hunt, fun, fur, profit. And then
> She paused, rhetorically, to gasp for air
> Before she braved death, deficits, the law,
> The press, free trade, lace cuffs, the cooked, the raw.

"I don't think that's a bit nice, do you?" Edwige asked. "I'm sure if I looked like her I'd be knowledgeable, too." Later Edwige sought another compliment for Mathilda but couldn't come up with one.

Gabriel saw Edwige as often as possible. He longed for her

play to end so he could be with her every minute; he longed for her play to continue so that he would know where to find her every evening. His uncle had once told him that Edwige was a bored troublemaker between engagements. It was then that she acquiesced to every man's attentions. "She never pays for a ride, in a hired vehicle," Mateo had said, "or rather the payment never involves money." Even now, when her strenuous role required her to submit to a life of "discipline" (one of her favorite words), he kept catching her eyes appraising passing men—a waiter, an usher, a tradesman—in a way he had never noticed in another woman except Angelica. But in Angelica lust and curiosity were unconscious. Her eyes would grow enormous and her lips would part; if something suddenly made her aware of herself, she'd lower her eyes, swallow, even blush.

Edwige, however, knew the effect she was producing. Her glance would dart from the male eyes she'd engaged to her own legs as though assuring him that, yes, all this loveliness, this delight, was being offered him. During the run of a play she had a superstitious dread of quick encounters, as though they would sap her energy. Moreover, since she had to appear naked nightly before hundreds of eyes (some of them minutely watchful through opera glasses), her skin had to be flawless and she shivered at the thought of a bruise from a love bite, a mauled nipple, or on her thighs a lash mark, however delicate. Her allure was based on a sophisticated manner and a naïve body—and that innocence had to be all the more assiduously cultivated when her blond beauty was on constant public display.

Any man who "slept" with her (an inaccurate euphemism, since she almost always slept alone and had ten memorized excuses to send men packing after they'd served their purpose, all ten excuses designed to conceal the truth: that sleep for her was more intimate than sex and her loins offered less resistance to invasion than her dreams)—any man, then, who *coupled* with her could only admit how experienced she must be, but her body betrayed no sordid signs of her past. No stretch marks, no stitches, no scars, no calluses, nothing except her hairlessness could give a clue to her adventures or intentions, and even that precaution only served to strip her of any disfiguring evidence of adulthood. This combination of innocence and experience, her "naughty virginity," which afforded an almost "period" taste of the piquant, worked its charms on men with remarkable efficiency, since in the realm of the senses time does flow, to be sure, but much more sluggishly than elsewhere, and we see as the painters of the last century taught us to see, enjoy the music our great-grandfathers found cacophonous, and hope to marry the erotic ideal their mistresses invented. Other women found Edwige ridiculous; men found her irresistible.

By nature she was secretive, as Gabriel was discovering, even when the secret wasn't worth the bother to dream up or keep. When Gabriel asked her where she was born, she said, "Nowhere interesting." If he asked where she was dining after the theater, she merely gave him a cryptic smile, even if (or especially if) she would be eating at home alone. She didn't like to introduce her friends to each other. She wouldn't reveal her age, her parents' religion, her real name, when or if she'd ever been married. Because she was so free with other people's secrets, no one realized at first how morbidly discreet she was about her own.

Both she and Mathilda rushed to the looking glass after a sexual encounter—Mathilda hoping to see she'd been transfigured, Edwige fearing she might have been changed. Of course Edwige followed many, even most of the current fashions. Edwige adapted her disguise, even her dialogue, to the changing modes, but as the only way of staying the same: eternally young, chic, available, perfect. As with an eye test, the revolving styles dropped slightly different lenses—sharper, vaguer, darker, brighter—into the frames the perceiver wore, but the perception remained the same, capital *E:* Edwige.

And yet as Gabriel drew closer to her he saw the elements that made up this image—the passion beneath the surface calm. Her greatest passion was for vengeance. She never forgot an insult. Her brain performed daily an integral calculus of slights and favors, of courtesies and chastisements. Now that she was the star of a popular success, she wriggled in the warmth of her fame and sank into delicious daydreams of retribution.

There was another Edwige, the wild kid who found the burden of fame exhausting. If each person is granted one moment in life most suited to him or her, a single instant that feels snugly appropriate, then for Edwige it had been her days as a camp follower. Each morning she had awakened in a new bed or haystack, and by evening she'd found a new campfire and sometimes someone new to share it with. She and Skeets had squabbled over rations, bandaged each other's powder wounds. She'd worn a drummer boy's uniform and half the time passed for male. Her male freedom—and the freedom of the general chaos—had been unbounded, and if she'd found it to her taste, that was because her taste had been formed by this very freedom.

Some nights Gabriel told Mathilda that he felt he'd been neglecting his uncle and wanted to sleep at his palace. Mathilda didn't mind particularly because she was involved with the premiere of a new opera she'd commissioned. Then he'd go home, ignore Mateo and curl up in a window to look down at the smaller, second courtyard outside Edwige's door, a courtyard that had been built and rebuilt so often over the centuries that discolorations in the stone walls revealed that the ancient wishbone-shaped windows had been bricked over to make way for fewer, bigger, nobler rectangles. Here and there a ghostly stone sill under such a canceled window broke through the plaster like an emerging wisdom tooth. On the courtyard stairs the stone pots received so little sunlight that the plants crawling out of them were spindly and pale. Tonight only a single lamp glimmered over the stairs. A shadow blackened, lengthened, ran: a cat. A stone warrior in the niche stared calmly at his spear, as though he were about to put down his favorite horse rather than slay a dragon. Water was seeping through a wall, invisibly, but its culpability revealed itself in a velvety zone of moss.

Then the gates were flung open, loud voices rang out, lights swam. Edwige turned on the stair, pushed back her hood, her hair starred by the night mist, and she gave her hand to her escorts. Gabriel watched them each incline over this fragile offering, as though it were a fountain they were drinking from. They left. Edwige called out her last merry farewells. The gates groaned shut. She leaned against the wall for a moment, stunned by exhaustion, then trudged up the steps like an old woman, muttering to herself.

Half an hour later Gabriel tapped at her door and she opened it as someone else. She had shed her rancor and heavy skirts, squeezed into trousers, tucked her hair up under a cap, scrubbed her face clean of makeup, donned a formless jacket. They stole out into the night together. Gabriel was instructed to introduce Edwige as Piet, his kid brother from the sticks, too shy to utter a word but mean as hell in a fist fight. Every fortnight Edwige needed to resurrect her career as a drummer boy, and she was a good enough actress to carry off the impersonation.

Neither Gabriel nor Angelica had known about love. They'd never even heard the word, and their feelings had frightened them. Mathilda loved him, without meaning to, and she had taught him love's taste. She who lived so publicly, so stridently, craved the shelter love offered, the shelter of silence and intimacy. Her habit of skepticism, like a design of oblique lines, needed to be placed against the grid of love's credulity. She would wander through her rooms, picking up books and discarding them and, like so many people in the capital who kept themselves warm before the glow of their own chafed egos, she'd freeze when alone and without controversy, at least until she lost herself in reading or writing a new book. Until then disjointed phrases from past or possible arguments flickered through her mind, the unlit kindling of future fires. Love—its blind affirmation—released Mathilda from contentiousness. From Mathilda Gabriel had learned the doctrine of love as salvation, but learned it without feeling it.

Now with Edwige he was in love for the first time; he loved Edwige and until now he'd been incomplete. Again and again he told Edwige that he loved her. He went to her play every night, dug his nails into his palms during her big scene and glared at a woman who dared to untwist a candy wrapper. He stood in a corner of Edwige's dressing room after the performance, listened as her fans filed by and tried to judge each of their remarks from Edwige's perspective. He touched the letters of her name on the printed program.

When they were alone at last he rubbed her neck and shoulders and told her funny stories, short enough to catch her wandering attention, none too long or complex, since he knew she was replaying in her mind scene after scene from *The Priestess*. When he held her and kissed her he wished he were twice as big and strong, since he feared he had nothing to offer her but strength, and that was in short supply. He bought a bottle of her special perfume, doused it on his handkerchief and sniffed it from time to time, never too often; he had to ration himself lest his nose come to accommodate the scent.

He told stories about her to acquaintances just so he could mention her name, dull, even false stories. "Funny you should mention that kind of furniture. A friend of mine collects it—Edwige, the actress . . ." He would say that, even though Edwige collected nothing and could pack all her belongings into two suitcases and one hat box. Everyone more or less seemed to know who Edwige was, just as everyone might know the name of a small city several kingdoms away, but no one greeted the mention of her name with the excitement or respect he thought it merited. "Oh yes, Edwige," they'd say, "the actress, and what about her?" Sometimes people, perhaps finding strange the intensity this young man brought to a pointless anecdote about a popular boulevard performer, divined he must know her, be related to her or enamored of her, and then they said, "She's so *eternally* youthful," an observation thrown in to warn the boy that his idol was by no means his contemporary. Gabriel ignored the warning and registered the compliment. He loved her, he loved her talent, he couldn't bear to have her treated merely as an acknowledged but unimpressive feature of the cityscape. At last Edwige had found someone to help her bear all her grudges.

From the beginning of their affair Edwige denied that they were having an affair. When he embraced her, trembling, and told her all the thoughts he'd been hatching while they were apart, she'd feel his head with her palm and say, "It will feel better if mom kisses it," and she'd laugh. Sometimes she said after one of his outbursts, "You poor kid, you must be bored if you had time to think all that up since this morning." Most of the time she treated him as a sick puppy.

Since he'd never loved before, he thought the problem must be a simple failure of communication—a thought that spurred him on to ever more explicit and involved avowals of his passion.

"Phew!" Edwige would exclaim, "you must really be randy," and if they were alone she'd sit staring straight ahead but like a spy passing a note she'd slyly reach over—and grab his crotch. If he had an erection she'd laugh and exclaim, "I thought so!" as though his state of arousal invalidated his romantic declarations. Then he'd hear in her voice the cynicism she'd learned so long ago from Skeets.

He came to dread his visits to Mathilda and saw no reason not to break off with her. She was unhappy for other reasons as well, for Daniel was becoming more and more dissolute and had arrived late at her dinner party for the opera premiere completely drunk and accompanied by prostitutes from the dyers' quarter. She'd recently thrown herself into new research, and her library was filling up again with piles of books she'd bought or borrowed, more and more of them carted in by servants and functionaries, caps in hand.

The green desk lamps burned all day and night; she never opened the curtains or arose from her bed, but slept fitfully and worked deeply under ever heavier blankets of books and writing paper. When Gabriel came to her door he might catch her rummaging through the latest stack of books, her nightgown stained with coffee, sleeves soaked in ink, penwipers in her hair, and she'd look up at him with the faint reproach the long dead direct toward the still living.

Yet even as he was preparing to leave Mathilda, he feared he was already losing his hold over Edwige. Edwige didn't take him seriously. Or so he feared.

The truth was that she'd *meant* to love him. An affair, even a real union, with Gabriel struck her as an attractive idea. Such an alliance would wound Mateo, which was what he deserved; he'd been neglecting her recently and rumor had it he was keeping a preposterously young and pretty tribal girl. Gabriel wasn't handsome, but he was highly sexed. Romantic in a crepuscular way by day, at night he was a hyena in bed, a combination suited to her penchant for being worshiped until violated. Because he was homely he was terribly grateful to her and could be counted on to stay constant. Besides, his looks set hers off to advantage and his certifiable youth made her appear young as well, since he was young but haggard, scrawny, pale, whereas she was blooming at . . . at whatever age people chose to assign her. Mathilda loved Gabriel and it was always amusing to defeat a rival, especially one whom other people, at least, took so seriously, although Edwige found Mathilda rude, sallow, incapable of small talk. People said she couldn't even play cards.

A high-ranking official at court had encouraged Edwige in this affair with Gabriel. Apparently the authorities liked the idea of this boy, the youngest, most susceptible member of a family the rebels revered, being brought over to the side of "peace and order" (Claude's father had formulated the slogan). Such a conversion seemed particularly desirable given the growing rumble of discontent and a few hints here and there of organized opposition.

But Edwige had never been able to love wisely. The rest of her life was wise. So much, perhaps most, of her activity was purposeful, directed toward fame or vengeance, and every day she rotated with monastic discipline from the wig-maker to a dance lesson to the masseur, slept with her hands in cold-cream gloves and never forgot to apply rubber suction cups (the "snake-bite kit") to her nipples half an hour daily; she'd already managed to make her nipples much plumper, as though she'd soaked two dried raisins in rum overnight. But in her choice of men she'd always been wildly impractical, inevitably drawn to virile poverty, handsome insignificance. She'd usually ignored the little duke, with his high voice, active hands, and frequent but always unfinished remarks, in favor of his footman, silent and two meters tall.

She liked the idea of Gabriel as a lover. He'd amuse her, flatter her, make love to her whenever she wanted, and he was eager to adjust to her peculiar schedule. Ordinary men, especially important ones, needed to sleep at night, which was always a nuisance. A working actress can enjoy herself only during the hours from noon to two and midnight to three; most of the men rich enough to afford her favors didn't want them at those awkward times.

When Gabriel first began to tell her how much he loved her, Edwige had fancied the challenge of this sort of courtship "scene." What would her action be? Her objectives? Her *plastique?* Her subtext? The young man draws near, palms sweaty, voice out of control, then erupts without prelude into the most unlikely speech. "I can't believe you're here," Gabriel said one day.

"Here, in this room?" she asked.

His eyes grew wider, he touched her as though she were a mirage, he said, "No. Not that. It's so . . . Oh God . . . *this*. It's this *this*, don't you see?" He kissed each of her fingers slowly and separately and she felt confused and oppressed by such ontological naïveté. Another time, when she touched his erection and said cynically, "I can just feel how much you missed me, big boy," he burst into tears and sobbed and sobbed until his mouth and nose were flowing unattractively.

Her problem was that she could never figure out who she was meant to be in these scenes. Sometimes she played the motherly older woman, worldly, disabused, already sad at the prospect of losing her young lover. But Gabriel, who'd just had precisely that sort of relationship with Mathilda, saw Edwige as his own age and refused to feed her the right lines. Next she played her favorite part, Clara the credulous, randy country girl who's tricked into bed every time by the city slicker, but Gabriel was in fact a bit of a bumpkin himself and preempted that role. She even tried to play Piet and greeted Gabriel's declarations with embarrassed silence or by socking one fist into the other palm while muttering, "Damn!" but Gabriel, hallucinated by the simple reality of Edwige's being, didn't pick up on this excursus, so irrelevant to his own.

Unable to find her character, Edwige began to resent Gabriel's love. One day it even occurred to her that what she saw as a thorny acting problem was what other people meant when they said someone was "incapable of loving." For a moment she even considered staying with Gabriel and learning from him how to love. At least she could play devotion, who couldn't, which actress wouldn't?

But then Douglas, her old admirer, the one who liked to give her after-theater suppers, one noon sent her a minor fortune in flowers and chocolates, and she liked the delivery boy, whose shiny black hair swept over his cool white neck, whose calves bulged as thickly as his thighs, whose breath smelled of beer and youth, who'd missed shaving just below his mouth a haze of hair that glowed in the crosslight, who must have paid extra for the fourth feather in his uniform cap (florists only provided three feathers), whose big brown eyes were quick city eyes, free of the melancholy love that veiled Gabriel's gaze. The idea of rolling naked with this boy (who said his name was Massimo, an almost comically promising name) excited her, especially if he kept his peach and khaki uniform on. That Douglas had unwittingly sent her this floral tribute also amused her, as did the realization that a patient, devoted Gabriel was sitting just outside the door waiting for her to complete her toilette.

Gabriel heard the gasps, the sound of rustling silk, of one shoe dropping heavily to the floor, Edwige's own rhythmic moans, but higher, more urgent than ever before. He struggled to interpret these clues—a heart attack, a robbery, her sudden blinding immersion into despair—and because he loved her he threw the double doors open. He was standing above Edwige's face, she was biting her pearl necklace, her peignoir foamed all around her slender naked body, and a trembling gold arrow of light, bouncing up from the canal below and ricocheting off the mirrored ceiling, fell across her neck like the mortal blow he longed to deliver. Her legs were wrapped around the bared buttocks of her partner, who looked up with the accidental prettiness and intended nastiness of a mudlark just as Edwige said, "Gabriel, can't you see your mom is tipping the delivery boy?"

A shout was pushed out of him, he clambered away, stumbling down the steps and into the fetid courtyard exposing its shameful stripe of moss, through the gates and out into the blinding treeless square with its sealed-over well, its full-figure statue, its pedestrians looking as though they felt conspicuous. He didn't know where he was going, he just had to get away from the thing he'd seen. Sounds —loud, urgent—came out of him, fragments of sound, and he listened to them, as one might listen to an oracle. What did he mean, this *he* within him?

So often Gabriel, who had no ambition, few friends, fewer habits, suffered from the emptiness of the day, from the arbitrariness of existing under such slight pressure, as though some casual decision had lightened the atmospheric force and he was slowly seeping outwards, growing fainter, dispersing. Ordinarily, as he idled across town, stopped to glance at the traffic, strolled toward his own bemused face approaching him in a storefront mirror, smelled roasting chestnuts, looked at the dozing waiter with his feet up on a green metal chair, Gabriel feared his own substance was flickering away, the last glimmer sputtering and dying above the empty jets.

But today he was carrying this antique burden of his grief, an absurd thing, hot, holy, as though the rule of the world could be reduced to one scroll and it had been confided to him. His usual weightlessness and coolness seemed somehow "modern" to him, since they assumed the anonymity of the city and the mild interchangeability of people. But not now. No, not now, when he had this pain within him, as though in a tribe of only five thousand people he was the chosen one and his suffering was unique.

He was surprised. He'd been surprised by Edwige's wantonness (when he called it "wantonness" in his thoughts he felt comforted for a moment). He was even more surprised by this pain he felt, the way his eyes had grown enormous, the way he'd moaned, staggered, staggered away, exactly like the noble witness of a royal murder. Again and again he saw himself in antique robes, his head tilted forward, his leg stretched out behind him, the perfect pleats in the robe flowing away from him to indicate motion, the whole body so eloquent that the face could afford to be blank.

He wandered the city, feeling like the only ancient hero, heavy under gold, in an insubstantial world of modern men and women almost spectral with indifference.

Edwige's cruelty shocked him. When they'd made love, she'd told him more than once that he was the best. She'd chanted it like that, "You're the best, you're the best." But now he could see it was just a litany she recited to excite herself, she was probably telling the delivery boy, "You're the best," she'd probably said it in every room in the dyers' quarter, probably all along she had been addressing the compliment to herself.

Now he crumpled and sat on the steps of a public building. Tears spurted out of his eyes. He didn't even wipe them away. Strange, he thought, that in a world of so many people, just one of them should be able to hurt me so much.

Edwige regretted what she'd done. She blamed Gabriel for being so thin-skinned and suspected he had no sense of humor. She'd been just like him—so serious, so sensitive, so devoted—until Skeets had toughened her up. She was grateful to Skeets for his lessons, painful as they'd been at the time.

She thought Gabriel had grown too attached to her. She was a working actress, not some sprightly hostess eternally at home to love. If Gabriel could treat her in a simple, comradely way, pay her his strange compliments but only half mean them, give her some thrill with his intense sexual energy, then fine. But if he was going to go pale with reproach every time she grabbed after adventure, *please*—he was trying to interfere with her talent! Her nurturing of her talent. Other people, men not in the theater, didn't realize that she was *always* acting, even when she least seemed to be doing so. Always, always. She was *never* offstage. Her clothes were an aspect of her career, as was her walk, her smile, her diet, her exercise, as was the cultivation of her taste through looking at paintings or of her wit through civilized conversation. She was always acting, especially when she was out on a sex spree, for it was precisely with these strangers that she was able to try on new selves. Not lying, as some bores and spoilsports called it, but acting; really, it was acting, the purest form. She'd invent a new accent for herself, a new age to be, a new past, a new look. Just the smallest change—a slight limp or lisp, a slight deafness and the consequent raucousness—could lead her in unexpected pathways. For instance, with the flower delivery boy she'd played the kept girl, recently imported from the provinces. Gabriel she'd explained away as her monstrous, greedy brother who'd sold her into slavery and who would surely punish her later for this romp, bad for business, risky. And could she see him again?

"No," Massimo had said, buttoning up, "Massimo has a girl of his own. I only go out walking once with any given individual." Edwige liked this trick of referring to oneself in the third person. She liked the idea of having rules about sex and his way of using the fancy word "individual" with the countrified expression, "to go out walking," and she resolved to incorporate all these "bits" into Piet's character. After Massimo left, she strode up to the mirror with her hands buried in her pockets, rolled her shoulders forward and growled, "Piet don't like to go out walking with no individual more than once." She did it again, this time dropping her eyes, making her voice young and frail and stroking her chin—the effect was so droll she howled with laughter.

But much as Gabriel was to blame for presuming on her time and interfering with her career, Edwige took pity on him. She'd already introduced Gabriel to her understudy and said, "Like him? I do. You bet. This time it's for keeps." Now she found him down by the water feeding birds and she wiped his eyes with her handkerchief, the one she'd used as the Duchess in *Bitter Tea,* and she played the whole thing wordlessly, pulling him to her, touching his cheek not with her palm but with the *back* of her hand, much more effective, then framing his face with her palms and looking into his eyes, then leading him home, their arms linked, tears flowing from his eyes and hers, a flicker of dollface, blurred smile . . . curtain! The funny thing was that Gabriel refused to be consoled. Still crying, he left her and went wandering out again through the hot city.

Mathilda almost hated Gabriel for having brought her back to life and love after she'd become reconciled to their loss. She'd trained herself to look away from young lovers along the embankment and to snort with impatience over descriptions of love, young or old. She'd decided love was a trance people gladly went into, although it inevitably brought them anguish. She'd said, "People complain about falling in love with the wrong person. They don't realize that falling in love *means* falling in love with the wrong person."

She'd begun to "take notes" on love, a process far more arduous than it might sound since, in spite of her celebrity, she was deeply unsure of herself and felt obliged to know everything, absolutely everything, about a subject before she committed herself to a single printed opinion on it. She read everything on love, underlined key passages, asked herself schoolgirlish questions in the margins ("Do *you* think this?") and quizzed her colleagues at the chat box for days on end about methodology ("Am I being naïvely biological? Can love be analyzed as a simple discourse? What is it like? Art? Etiquette?"). She didn't want to treat love as a ruling-class conspiracy or a male hoax worked on women. She didn't want to deny the intensity of the lover's feelings, nor did she want to accept them as spontaneous or unmediated. She didn't want to reduce *amour* to *amour propre,* though that was surely a temptation. She intended to be especially suspicious of the "naturalness" of love.

Gabriel had interrupted this research by lending convincing weight to the shocking premise that love was exactly what it claimed to be, a communion of souls, a seamless blend of the physical and spiritual, a humming of the ideal struck upon the actual, as when a new wife's voice or laugh awakens sympathetic vibrations within her dead predecessor's harpsichord in a sun-filled, dust-filled, long-locked room. With Gabriel she'd been happy again and felt the two feelings that for her had always been essential, gratitude and shame, and that, because she was an intellectual, she insisted were essential to everyone else as well. She'd been grateful because he'd loved her without wanting anything from her except what she thought no one would take: her body. She who'd coached herself into believing that love was behind her now felt so young, so passionate that she was taken aback whenever she noticed the ropey veins in her hands or her flabby upper arms. On other days she'd feel so old, so bloated and stiff, that she had no desire to impose something as unsightly as her body on such a young man, even if he was deluded about its worth. She knew that only beauty merited love. As a student of literature, ancient and modern, she knew that when old men or women court the young they are invariably figures of fun—every standard author said as much and couldn't *comedy* be defined as the pathos of the inappropriate? That was the shame she felt.

And yet Gabriel had convinced her he loved her. He'd said he admired her mind, but surely such admiration was only good nature and better faith since he had no grasp of and little interest in the contents of her mind. No, it was on the level of the creature, of dailiness that they established their rapport. As creatures, they suited one another. If they'd been pandas in a zoo, they would have slept curled up together in the same corner of the cave. They each had a passion for chocolate; they shrank from tobacco and alcohol as though, in their panda way, they recognized these substances as poison. They could sleep ten hours and awaken more exhausted than ever. They each liked to create a mess—then they would panic and become frantic in cleaning up. They both worried all the time about the smallest details of everyday life—the laundry, a leak in the ceiling, a cold—worried and did nothing. They liked to shop for food and improvise funny little meals, cold water biscuits and caviar and cold spiced green beans. They snuggled into a litter of teacups and toast crumbs.

By living at such close quarters with her, Gabriel saw how often she dared herself to action. Left alone, she'd have vegetated; she was shy, slovenly, melancholy. A single afternoon of worrying and being isolated could age her alarmingly. But then, just at a critical moment, she'd urge herself forward and make a resonant (sometimes disastrous) remark—and in rising to the occasion she became tall, historic. Once again she was fully alert, her sallowness gave way to a fresher tint, her cheekbones emerged handsomely, her whole body became lighter. If Edwige knew how to imitate other people and could mime a whole range of emotions becomingly, she nevertheless lacked Mathilda's innate sense of drama. Mathilda enjoyed scandal, needed it, as though a yearly crisis were necessary to her metabolism. Edwige sneered at Mathilda's clumsiness, at her way of talking with a hand over her mouth, at her dowdiness, but Edwige didn't understand that in life the actual delivery of a line is less important than the timing and content of the line itself, not to mention the simple decision to appear or not appear in this particular scene. The brute fact of an entrance or a speech, now rather than sooner or later, was all that counted in life, not its execution.

But now Mathilda was suffering and she had no recourse. She'd been left for a pretty blond actress. Gabriel's very indifference to the life of the mind, at first such a refreshing change, now placed him beyond her reach. He was silly, distractable. Someday he'd recognize that he would never again find such shelter as he'd found in her arms. He was safe with her. When he slept she could run her hands over his funny face and the pale defenselessness of his body and cherish them. When he coughed, she could wrap him in flannel, protect him from draughts. When he couldn't sleep, she could sit up with him all night, the two of them on "nerve alert" as she called it. "Mister Pine," she would whisper.

He'd left her. It was all too predictable. She almost pitied him, for he, too, was alone, cast out into the servile world of the salons. She could have forged him a career. She would have trained his mind. Not a village where she didn't know the one intellectual, not a noble family to which she wasn't related, not an artist who hadn't taken a handout from her or a stand for or against her pronouncements, not a government bureau where she didn't have her informers. She sat over this magnificent, amplified instrument, so expertly tuned, and she had nothing to play on it.

"You took him from me," she said to Daniel.

"I *what?*" he exploded, hoping to intimidate her and frighten her off.

But her gaze was unfiltered as she sat at the reading table in her room, her hands in the yellow light, her grief-stricken face green from the milk-glass shade. "You took him from me. When you introduced him to the court, you knew he'd be too weak to resist—"

"Mater, dearest," Daniel said, ominously bored, leafing through a new book of actor prints, methodically pressing back each new page and never looking up. Mathilda's body, heavy with suffering, offended him. "You ascribe far too much power to me. Can I help it if the twit has lost his head over his uncle's mistress? Rather disloyal to Mateo, I would have thought. *Messy Lives,* that's the name of the book I'm going to write. *Messy Lives,* good, what?"

"You were jealous, you were afraid of losing me, you took him to the dyers' quarter, led him into dissipation." She whose manner was usually so weary with irony whenever she spoke to Daniel, so that they both felt like offended but not surprised customers sorting through the world's shoddy goods, now let her voice drop to its deepest, malest register as she stared levelly at him through the green light.

"*Dissipation?*" Daniel snapped, pressing back a fresh page. "That's a word out of a novelette."

"I always choose my words accurately. I take a pride in the accuracy of my words. And then, after you had softened him up with drugs, you dazzled him with the splendors of the court."

"You ascribe great powers to me."

"He might have gone that way on his own, Daniel, but you led him there. You took my lover away from me."

"Mathilda," he said, standing up and fiddling with his boutonniere as he studied himself in the mirror, "you flatter yourself even in your grief. I would have been delighted to have unloaded the maternal burden onto his bony shoulders but he, clever thing, wriggled out from under. Frankly," he started down the stairs, "I've gotten rather used to the freedom and don't want my old job back."

Mathilda couldn't run to anyone except Mateo. She hesitated before contacting him. But after two more days of looking at food without touching it, of staring at books without seeing them, she decided to visit her old friend. Oh, Gabriel had been wrong to bring her back to love, to have awakened all these desires that had so humbly held themselves in sticky suspense and dozed; now they were wheeling sightlessly in the unsealed cavern of her heart, thousands and thousands of them wheeling.

In the streets a summer haze clung to everything, irradiated by a queer amethyst light. High above, two golden-pink cirrus clouds hung motionless in an otherwise empty sky, two notes a strong thumb and middle finger had plucked out of a harp and then allowed to go on humming indefinitely, never damped. For some reason the streets and squares were empty—ah! it was dawn.

She'd forgotten time.

Then she'd have to awaken Mateo. Surely she couldn't go back to her house until she'd accomplished her mission. The smell of her unchanged sheets, the sight of the brown apple core, of her own handwriting . . . She'd started taking notes again on love. But now she had neither her cultivated skepticism nor her more recent lyrical optimism to guide her. While Gabriel had loved her (she was walking up a bridge, crossing a canal, even this despised fat pigeon had an iridescent necklace to flaunt), while Gabriel had loved her, her notes had been inspired by a perusal of classic love poems ("Note that here the *age* of the couple is never mentioned since love invariably erases time"). She'd recorded the anguish and happiness of each of love's devotions (she saw love during this period as the residue of religion and its devotions as stations of suffering); the Broken Date, the Giving of Nicknames ("Mr. Pine" for Gabriel, for instance), the Linking of Love to Death (as in "If you left me I'd die").

Now that Gabriel no longer loved her (two girls, tourists, each hauling an enormous valise, passed her; one of them was saying, "I can smell bread; I tell you, there's got to be a bakery near here"), now that Gabriel no longer loved her, her own passion for him could not be erased. It was enormous, threatening, a servant summoned by magic who keeps growing until he fills the entire room, whose turban jewel glows an ever more sinister red. She stopped in the dry square where old clothes were sold to read a piece of graffiti scrawled in blue chalk: "The bears are coming out of hibernation." Mateo's family name was a homonym for *bear* in the old regional dialect. Did the patriots still look to Mateo's family for leadership? Did she?

He had her brought into his study while he performed his toilette and dressed. The usual disorder reigned. Coffee without sugar and toast without butter were brought in by a servant Mathilda had never seen before. Her cup wasn't clean. And then Mateo himself strode in enveloped in a preposterous yellow silk robe. Mathilda—who'd grown used to Daniel's dandified fastidiousness, with his adherence to dull colors and almost invisible variations on classic forms (buttoned jacket sleeves that could actually be unbuttoned)—found the childish exuberance of Mateo's garment almost touching in a man whose taste in the realm of language and manners was so refined.

She recognized she was in a dangerous state of shock. The proof was the way in which each element of her self had broken away from all the others. An automaton that resembled her had been able to dress itself and cross the town, find this door. Another part stood coolly aside and affectionately observed the follies of her old friend. Yes, this part thought, the gaudy clothes of a literary man represent his first fresh attraction to the flashy—a primitive attraction that, at least in books, is soon obscured by a cultivated style, just as a composer's original affection for a cheap mountain air is transformed into the thirty-two variations on it he writes over the years. The author's sequined slippers, grotesque meerschaum, houndstooth vest, shantung tie are the *données* of the sober, cerebral stories not yet written.

And as these observations flickered through the still-sensitive part of her brain, in the numb part certain physiological crises were being monitored but not interpreted—the tightness across her chest, the pounding of the heart, the dryness of her mouth, the early warning signs of tears detected in the prickling of the skin around her eyes and the constriction over the bridge of her nose. She knew that behind a soundproof glass partition all her suffering was crying aloud, but she couldn't hear it or feel it—she could only observe it, and this silence imposed the mysterious dignity of being ordinary on what she was undergoing.

Mateo began by humbling her. He forced her to eat raven (at least something more ceremonial than mere crow) for having ignored him for so long. "Mathilda dear, I'm delighted to have you here even if under what I can only gather must be extraordinary circumstances—delighted that your demons have driven you to remember our old friendship which, though a sturdy enough plant (a *perennial,* I'd judge), had nevertheless begun to wilt."

"I'll water it with my tears," Mathilda said. When she smiled she recognized that these particular cheek muscles had gone unused for weeks. Her face felt loose and rumpled, as though it were one size too large.

"You shall soon enough weep, and I shall dry your tears. This hydraulic exchange will no doubt comfort us both, as you have obviously anticipated with your usual shrewdness." Mateo had begun to pour out thimblesful of black rich coffee; all of Mathilda's sadness suddenly struck her as pity for those liver spots on the back of Mateo's hands and his overnight growth of white stubble. She'd known him forever but now this boy had grown old. He'd always masqueraded as her *cher maître* and now he'd become that figure.

"I recognize, Mathilda, that I'm merely your equal, once even your mentor, if I may be so bold as to flip back to that strange page from our past."

Even as Mateo tilted his head back and eyed her through narrow lids, even as he allowed honey (gathered by killer bees) to enter his tones, Mathilda could tell he was ready to forgive her, that, in fact, he was ravished by her return, and his chastisement and her submission were purely symbolic.

"The company of equals is an acquired taste," he said. "A subtle, sometimes sour taste, easily replaced by the stronger, naïve salt or sweet flavors of sycophancy or arrogance."

"You're seasoned to perfection, Mateo," she said, thinking, How absurd I am that even this lunatic wordplay at seven on a Tuesday morning soothes me—if only mildly, the tricky needlework Penelope is proud to display even as her tears fall.

"Mateo," she said, "I have come because I'm worried about Gabriel."

"And so I was foolish in assuming you were belatedly acknowledging your obligation to me?"

She smiled a ghostly smile, her pale lips flickering. "On the contrary, precisely that obligation has brought me to the side of the boy's uncle. Precisely the sanctity of our old friendship" (now Mateo was smiling) "sanctifies our parental concern."

Mateo's left eyebrow, remarkably independent of the other one, was raised eloquently. "I believe you, for your part, have given considerable *body* to your conception of parenthood."

This sally, with its cruel emphasis on *body,* made her picture her own as though in one of those dreams in which the dreamer walks naked through a disapproving crowd. A moment ago, she'd felt buoyed up by Mateo's obvious vexation over her "defection," since she knew he begrudged her her fame and wanted to share it vicariously by being seen with her wherever she went. Over the years he'd attacked her for forgetting her old friends and cosseting herself with worthless sycophants; his merest allusion now tapped that corpus of complaint. He who'd once been her mentor, her lover, and whom she still respected, now envied her—and envy was a sort of compliment.

Old friends need not state their points. Like a paleontologist who can reconstruct from a single footprint the size, height, carriage and diet of a vanished species, in the same way an old friend can hear echoes of a hundred earlier conversations in a single word. In the play on *body,* Mathilda could pick up the amplified rumor of all Mateo's past lectures to her about "realism." Too often she'd heard him remind their contemporaries that they should not forget that their bodies were an aesthetic burden on everyone, most of all on the young lovers expected to box these old bags. Mateo detested middle-aged men (and women) who ceased to feel gratitude to their young lovers, who became so foolish as to imagine that youth and beauty *owe* sexual favors to age and experience. If one remained a realist, one knew the reverse was true, and one would leave the most lavish tip for even the most miserable service. Mateo counseled his contemporaries to treat the young as a separate species—nervous, easily flushed from the nest, hard to lure back. The body—this shameful body of the no-longer-young—was what she was concealing now beneath her rumpled clothes.

Her shame irritated her. Unlike Mateo, she had not been obsessive in her pursuit of love. She hadn't needed love. She'd lived on her own for years and liked it. Whereas he relished the submitting to the asceticism of unblinking self-contempt and living day after day under its stinging lash, she wanted either to renounce love altogether or have it back in its original glory.

Or so she thought. What she didn't know about Mateo was

how Angelica had revolutionized his feelings. Just as Gabriel had restored to Mathilda her first youthful longings, in the same way Angelica had convinced Mateo that all his cynicism, his "realism," had been misplaced.

He now believed that love, mutual love, was possible, and what it required was an abandonment of secrecy and guile. Now, whenever he lay beside Angelica in the dark and inhaled her clove scent, which emerged only after the day's residue of jasmine perfume had burned off in love-making, he told her of all the things that troubled him in their affair. He was afraid of repulsing her with his fatty breasts, his balding ankles, his desert-dry elbows, vagrant hairs and the adipose cummerbund he never ceased wearing.

She lay in the dark, her eyelashes pulsing as slowly as moth wings, and said, looking up at the ceiling, "But I don't think that way. I never loved you because of your looks. Not that you're ugly. This is all so delicate, I'm afraid of hurting your feelings no matter what I say. I know how sensitive you are. No," she paused, sorting out her thoughts. They were both staring at the ceiling, not touching one another, as though touch would be a handicap favoring her in a game that required them to be equal. "No, I fell in love with you because of your kindness, because I like myself when I'm with you, because you see everything about me and still like me, because I have the feeling you need me and no one ever needed me before. It's strange, you'd think someone as . . . as *poor* as I am would want a man who could give her things. Of course you have, you've given me everything—"

"I'd give you more, much more if I could."

"You've given me everything, but I love you because you're poor and I'm rich. You need me and that makes me—" She stretched and yawned. A silence installed itself in the little bedroom with its delicious disorder, the discarded costumes and scattered paillettes of a life now nearly entirely given over to carnival. In the distance, on the more touristy side of the hill, late-night revelers were carousing. Someone was even trying to harmonize, with disastrous results. The restaurant downstairs was closing. He'd settled his head on her shoulder and even though there was no way to guarantee they were thinking the same thoughts, at least their bodies had surrendered to the same rhythm of yawns, of sighs, the same pattern of breathing. A diagram would have shown their pulses slowing at the same rate.

In this comfort and village silence (except now that the revelers had moved on her quarter was even quieter than a village, since no roosters were crowing) Angelica had added "You see? I didn't fall in love with your looks. I came to love your looks later. I would never have—" another yawn, which made her hold her breath for two full seconds and struggle to fit her mouth around this morsel of eternity "—I would never have said you were my type, but now you are." She laughed. "If you leave me, I'll look for someone just like you."

Mateo could scarcely judge what she was saying, so grateful was he that she'd brought such gentleness into her consideration. As her teacher he was proud of her eloquence. More deeply, he was touched by her kindness. All his life he had been a seducer, and a seducer shares his delights but not his misgivings, unless they can be turned into a tactic. He'd never before confessed his fears to a woman. That he had taken this risk—and that Angelica had responded with such kindness—made him feel closer to her than he'd ever felt with anyone.

Of course her beauty almost made his devotion suspect. He regretted now that Angelica was so beautiful, that she had such a profusion of black hair, such full breasts, such narrow muscled hips and fat lips too large for beauty but perfect for love, a long sleek back, so long one suspected the artist of having added extra vertebrae solely for the suave line they described. He knew he loved her in the way he would have loved a homely old wife he'd spent thirty years with, someone who gossiped with him under the quilt half the night, clucked over the price of eggs, checked to see if he'd shared her impression of the visitor's manners and told him of the maid's way of inventing ever more exotic religious holidays to take off—oh, Angelica was so wise, so wifely that only when she spoke with fevered excitement about the next carnival event did he remember that she was still just a kid. Recently he'd backed out of a costume contest he had earlier agreed to go to with her. She became hurt and angry and muttered, "Sometimes it's not so easy to have an older lover." He said, "I prefer not to be tested, but if I must submit to a test I intend to pass it." And he went in triumph to the ball as a frisky satyr with shaggy cotton haunches, a red taffeta phallus, pink satin buttocks, patent leather hooves and matching horns and a wonderful floss silk tail that was, perhaps, more equine than capricious. Angelica went as a nymph in a cloak the color of water on startled thighs.

When he was away from Angelica or when he couldn't find her (she seemed to be spending more and more of her time in the carnival throngs), he felt her absence as both a joy and an ache. Joy because he could think about her, about the perfect calm and warmth of their love. Ache because when she wasn't with him he felt her absence as a physical loss. Joy because he needed only to rub her name in order to see her face, which was never static, not even in memory, but a dawning smile, a widening glance, tossing hair. Ache because he recognized that his addiction to women, to seduction and conquest, had narrowed to an exclusive need for this one woman, no other would do. At last he was willing to leave behind his career as a gallant. He could certainly imagine sleeping with other women; not a moment of walking through the streets went by without his spotting a missed chance. But he preferred to miss it rather than risk losing the serenity of his attachment to Angelica.

He had no reason to doubt her, but the depth of his love for her frightened him.

This mixture of profound happiness and faint anxiety was stirred up in Mateo as Mathilda poured out the story of her suffering. "He's left me. I didn't want a lover. If I had to have one," she looked up as a startled bystander might watch a horse thunder past, "he should have been handsome at least. I'm someone who admires beauty." She sniffled. "If he had to pursue me, he should—" here the dam began to crumble, the restraining rocks buckled, worked free, shot out in the flood "—at least he should have made sure of his own feelings first. I'm not someone to be tampered—" but her voice cracked and she hit "tam" on a high note, almost a shriek, and dissolved into her handkerchief as Mateo watched. His instinct was to rush to comfort her, but he felt a trace of repugnance before such pain. He knew he'd entered into the period of life when he should expect nothing but overcast pleasures and bleak pains, but Angelica had brought him this Indian summer of golden contentment, and he wasn't ready to let it go just yet. He knew he was selfish not to share Mathilda's anguish, but he also knew that to share it would mean to surrender to it. When he'd been a young man he'd sought the general happiness and had denounced a singular pleasure one man might enjoy while another was suffering. His outlook had been based on the idea that happiness can be universal if only society would be decent. Now he saw they were all on a liner that was sinking. Third class was already submerged and this watery shroud would soon enough engulf him, but in the few remaining minutes he reached for another kiss from lips that before long would be cold, coral.

Perhaps Mathilda detected his reluctance. After she honked her nose into a handkerchief, she said spitefully, "You know, of course, he left me for Edwige." Her wet red eyes flew on three slow strokes up to his face to inspect the damage she might have done.

Like every gallant, Mateo felt betrayed whenever he heard that a woman he'd betrayed had found a new lover. He'd seduced as many women as possible to assure himself of countless refuges.

He'd been like the emperor of a newly declared country who smuggles sums from the national treasury into banks all over the world against the day of his own inevitable downfall. Every woman he'd ever loved he regarded as an unnumbered account he could always draw on. News of Edwige's failing him gave him a renewed flurry of anxiety about his future with Angelica. She would continue to love him at fifty when she was twenty, but at sixty when she was thirty? At eighty when she was fifty? His lips moved as he performed these mental calculations. She might insist his disgraceful appearance did not bother her now, but he was not yet old.

"I hope Edwige won't hurt the silly boy," Mateo said. "You know she will. He'll be back at your door before long. Then the question will be, will you sign for the damaged package?" Long ago Mateo had realized that the greatest anguish is the pain of powerlessness and that the best way to comfort unhappy friends is to assure them they still possess choices.

But he hadn't taken into account how long Mathilda had already suffered. "I don't want your shoddy comfort," she said. "Of course, Gabriel has been led over to the conquerors by Daniel. By—" she stared hard at Mateo "—by Daniel, why not say it, by our son."

All spring she'd half-observed her son's dissolution. More and more he'd spent his nights in the dyers' quarter and returned late in the day, haggard and dirty. She hadn't wanted to know too much, but Gabriel had told her bits and pieces. She'd always rejected the shallow common sense that had declared a lack of paternal guidance would ruin the boy. Nor would she accept the banal hypothesis that her attachment to Gabriel might in any way wound Daniel. At first she'd maintained her ignorance about Daniel's decline because she wanted to protect her love for Gabriel; she couldn't bear to hear a reason for giving him up. She'd even overcome the shock Daniel had given her just a month ago when he'd arrived so late at her party for *The Ice Rose* with those gabbling she-devils in saffron.

Now that Gabriel's love for her had ended, Mathilda was even less willing to spar with Daniel. She wanted to hand over to someone else the responsibility for a son she admired when he guided her but feared when he himself required guidance.

*Grief makes us clumsy* were the words that spelled themselves out in Mateo's brain; he stood back and stared down at this revelation, concentrating on it so that he could delay his recognition of Mathilda's more shocking divulgence. Until now, for all these thirty years, Mateo had always been on hand to help Daniel, to introduce him to friends, to listen to his problems and advise him. The unexplored possibility of kinship had always shed a glow over Daniel and Mateo's friendship; they'd each marveled at the perfect ease of their conversations. Mateo had observed the pattern of Daniel's beard as it first grew in and had recognized the dimple at the commissure of his lips.

Because Mateo's paternity had been in doubt, people had whispered that Daniel's father must be someone else, someone powerful or rich or noble; now the myth of such a protector had been blasted and Daniel's prestige would sink. Or would sink if Mateo said anything to anyone.

And yet, even as all these shadowy considerations flickered past in one key, a golden, open octave, in a quite remote key was steadily emerging: my son. He's my son.

The instant Mateo knew Daniel was his son he stopped judging the boy. Like any parent, he now saw Daniel as a lien on the future, someone in the process of becoming something wonderful.

Then the open octave filled in on the fifth with the softly inserted note of Angelica's presence. Without formulating the thought, Mateo dimly felt that she was his wife and Daniel his son (no matter that the son was old enough to be her father). He, Mateo, who'd always sallied forth night after night for decades in search of adventure, who'd heaped contempt on the squalid pathos and pipe-and-pantofle comfiness of marriage, now pressed this secret wife and infant to his heart. He smiled.

In his smile, which enraged Mathilda and made her suspect his sanity, there was even a trace of relief. He'd feared the day when Gabriel would discover his alliance with Angelica; now the betrayal worked both ways and, he assumed, Gabriel's indignation had been defused in advance. By flashing past Angelica's name and face in his mind, Mateo managed to stifle his anxiety about Daniel and reawaken all his longing for her—his need to be beside her, in her arms, to feel the fire in her brown skin and to smell that clove scent burning somewhere within her; he yawned in a funny pantomime of a yawn, smiled foolishly and said, "I'm sleepy." He didn't mean that he was sleepy; he'd merely seized on an expression that signaled his desire to sleep with Angelica. "I'm sleepy" was a discreet way of saying, "I'm so in love."

Dazed, insulted, Mathilda pushed past Mateo as she silently mouthed, "Sleepy," and staggered out into the streets, where the daylight stung her eyes. As she came around a corner, her heavy, limping gait startled a flock of pigeons, which whirred up around her in a calamitous vastation. A strange amethyst glow seemed to outline the grey castellation of the rooftops; up above, the sun—untidily radiant—looked down at the world as a flushed woman might stare into a bowl of steam. She thought, We cloak ourselves in fame but when we die we're bare, all naked.

The thought of death, which always shadows love, as a muscular servant might follow his fragile mistress through the streets, appeared again; love and death are inseparable, whether the love is happy or sad. Happiness in love always brings up the thought of death. Since suffering in love leads even more surely to the contemplation of death as relief, one can only think that love, as a form of beauty, is founded, as beauty must be, on evanescence. Reciprocal love is the apprehension of the perfect passing moment and the fear of an empty future; one-sided love *is* that future. (If only she had her notebook with her; these might be usable reflections.) Just as the happy lover dismisses all his own earlier passions as counterfeit, so he cannot imagine any future love with someone new; nor can the unhappy lover. True love is singular each time, unique if indefinitely repeatable.

An old man with a tray of books suspended by a dirty cord from around his neck was standing on one leg like a sleeping bird in the middle of the shadowless square. Mathilda stopped, but not as in the past in search of a choice item for her library. Now she was thirsting after wisdom. She needed knowledge, know-how, advice. She'd done everything wrong, made the wrong moves, somehow lost her lover, lost him. She seized on an advice book, filled with rules and steps to follow, "musts" in blacker, larger type, "reminders" and "tips," all in the falsely jovial and uplifting lingo of years ago, with a bit of scientific doubletalk thrown in. She paid for it and sat down on the stone steps before an abandoned palace. The square was empty although pigeons sized her up for crumbs, decided nothing doing and took off. Somewhere a baby was crying, a mother was singing a lullaby while on the street below an ethnographer in a black veiled hat and bombazine skirt (part of a team sent out by the conquerors) was feverishly jotting down the words to the song.

Mathilda read and read through her book despite the coldness of the stone seeping up through her skirts. She read about "the second chance" and how to bring it about. She read about what men liked and disliked in women. She read about how to seduce him and make him think he's seduced you (including tips on creating a seductive setting—something that can be done with just a shawl and a simple folding screen if you don't live alone).

She put the book aside and cried in a great headachey neuralgia of grief, nothing decorous but a sickness of grief. She was sick with it. In her intellectual vanity she'd half-fancied that she'd created this whole tirade of love, talked herself into it. Now that she couldn't laugh it away, couldn't laugh at all but only throb with suffering, she had to admit her will was useless. She may or may not have invented this love or acceded to it, but now the contract couldn't be voided. Her ink-stained right hand stirred as though to take this note, too, and then she looked down at it and found such fatuity in her desire to write down her feverish thoughts that her tears of rage and self-hatred redoubled and she actually made noises. When she'd worn herself out she blinked her eyes dry of tears and looked around her.

Sitting under the fountain across the square was Gabriel, also crying. He was crying because he'd just left Edwige.

Mathilda, however, in the egotism of suffering assumed Gabriel was crying over *their* separation. Slowly dragging herself across the dusty, sunstruck expanse of white stone, she approached him. She let the self-help book tumble out of her hand. Her skirt was twisted to one side, her face was streaked with tears and ink, her body was shaking with an unvoiced chuckle. She'd gone through this mortification when all along he'd been anguishing too; there he was, her skinny, ugly boy, perverse child, usually so arrogant, now reduced to tears and because of her, over her, he was suffering over her! She reached down and stroked his hair. He looked up startled. "Mr. Pine," she whispered. Because he had nowhere else to go on a Tuesday afternoon, the emptiest, loneliest, sunniest day of the week, he went home with Mathilda.

That same afternoon Maurizio, the candle salesman, called on Angelica. She'd often wanted him to come by her little room, but he was more and more active with the resistance and she'd seen him only twice briefly at his aunt's. Now he presented her with a candle as a gift for her home. He threw open the windows, stuck out his head and admired all the sights as Angelica stood behind him. She liked the way his bow legs looked in the tight black trousers. She made a pot of tea which she poured out with all the ceremony she'd learned from Flora. She was sorry that Maurizio should have come today of all days when she had started bleeding. She'd always imagined seducing him if they were ever alone, but now she decided to make a virtue out of necessity. "Usually if I like a man I want to sleep with him, but you, I feel—you're more of a brother!"

Maurizio seemed so relieved she suspected him of still being a virgin. Back at Madder Pink she had not known words like *seduction* or *virginity,* but in the capital she'd surrendered quickly to their allure since they gave an idle woman something to worry over and feel important about.

Maurizio praised her for having eschewed the "loose morals" of the conquerors for the "peasant modesty" of the people. She soon forgot her real reason for choosing friendship with him and imagined she was in fact exemplary in some new way. Since Maurizio was so handsome Angelica refused to admit to herself he was a fanatic; since Angelica was so appealing, Maurizio failed to see she was intelligent but lazy, enthusiastic but unable to sustain any one feeling for long, affectionate but self-centered. He would have been surprised to discover how confused she was as well. She dreaded "the people" he praised or at least her own people, whom she dismissed as dull and depraved. But she also regarded Mateo and Maurizio and Gabriel and everyone else she knew in the capital as "outsiders," that is, alien to her own tribe. She even thought of them as inferior, since they didn't belong to her religion. Only Flora was her equal, but since Flora was a woman Angelica didn't take her seriously.

Nor did Maurizio see she had no capacity for abstract thought, which Mateo had discovered early on and considered a defect designed to inspire confidence. Mateo hated ideas; he'd seen so many of his friends succumb to them. He'd heard the shoddiest lies uttered in the name of Truth. And once someone had embraced an idea he became the poorest sort of observer. An idea man no longer smelled coffee or noticed that the part in someone's hair was being worn on the other side tonight. He forgot to ask questions about the kind of bullfighting done in this village. No, now he jabbered away about the art or politics of the capital even on a walk through the oldest, most fascinating provincial town, a place where five languages were spoken, once the port where a king had embarked on his voyage to a distant war, though centuries ago the sea had withdrawn twenty miles south and left the town landlocked. The man obsessed with ideas noticed nothing, asked no questions, repeated the same stale truths he'd always known.

Angelica, by contrast, observed everything around her since she had no ideas to defend. She'd been brought up with certain beliefs (the interpretation of cards and dreams, dietary restrictions, fear of certain animals and draughts) but she'd not abandoned them so much as they'd abandoned her. In the capital no situation reminded her of tribal traditions and slowly she'd stopped looking for opportunities to enact them. She felt no urge toward consistency. Flora had knowingly made references to what men like and women need, to how love always ends unless the right couple make the right compromises . . . these flat notions had been injected with effervescence by the illustrated romances Angelica and Felix had read day after day. Her childhood taboos gave way to a smaller but more flexible repertory of romantic tips, but at no point had she formally renounced one set of beliefs for another. Everything was inconsistent and overlapping in her mind, and since she judged every case according to the appeal of the individual presenting it rather than by a set of rules, she never noticed her confusion. Indeed, she wasn't confused. She liked someone or she disliked him and her estimation of people didn't change. In her world things had been accomplished by powerful individuals.

Maurizio she liked. When he asked her if she'd introduce him to Gabriel, she said yes before he'd explained why he wanted to know him. "Gabriel is just now ending a romance with the actress Edwige," Maurizio said. "You may recall I knew her slightly when I was a boy. It was she who cured my stammer. Edwige has always liked me and although she'd despise my politics if I told her about them, she's always filled me in about the men in her life. I'm her confidant."

Angelica pretended to be nipping dead leaves off the basil plant on her sill so that Maurizio could study her profile. Actresses usually showed their profiles in pictures; did he think of her as someone suitable for the stage? she wondered. And how had he discovered she knew Gabriel?

"Edwige, I gather, is afraid of unrest in the capital," Maurizio continued. "She feels, quite rightly, that the patriots despise her and that she wouldn't fare well in a takeover. She is leaving Gabriel and heading off on a tour among the conquerors. Now is the exact moment for you to reappear in Gabriel's life. He needs you and the patriots need him."

Although Angelica would have preferred being presented at court to joining the resistance, Mateo had never introduced her to anyone. Driving out the conquerors, in any event, seemed as important and amusing as joining them. She also liked the way Maurizio talked of her as the embodiment of the People, almost as though she were the mascot of a carnival dancing society, but a big one, as big as the city itself. She wondered if he'd be put off if he knew she wasn't an ordinary tribal girl but a sort of princess (she didn't know exactly how to translate her title). The thought of being a patriot princess appealed to her.

Even though Maurizio had denounced the carnival and saw it as a conqueror conspiracy, Angelica knew better. For her the long, drunken nights of carnival, the spontaneous processions and dances, the feeling of being passed from one group to another, of assembling and discarding her costume from bits strangers gave her or snatched away—these exuberant encounters, warm and anonymous, had taught her everything she knew about the people. If she was willing to fight for the patriots she'd been convinced by the carnival—by the sight of a dancing bear in blue silk and silver lamé or by the experience of sleeping in a narrow bed one night with the circus strong man, whom she'd just met in a samba contest. Actually she'd never really slept that night, since she'd had to synchronize her turns in the single bed with the strong man's, but she'd dozed and listened to a guitarist in the next room who'd sung all night about his old home and the moonlight beside the bed that looked like frost on the ground, about fishing in the mountains and shooting birds, about fleas in blankets and burrs in a dog's withers. She'd drifted in and out of sleep beside the kindly strong man who, when they'd made love, had so feared he might crush her that he'd borne all his weight on his elbows. His skin had the puffy feel of skin that's always sweating inside flannel clothes. The narrative song and the big innocent body of the strong man blended to become in Angelica's mind the voice and the smell and the feel of the People. When Maurizio talked about the "broken body" of the People, Angelica imagined cradling the strong man after a barbell had slipped and broken his back.

As Maurizio was recruiting Angelica, Claude was dismissing Daniel from her life. He'd come for her fitting but in the midst of it he halted everything, announcing that as of today he despised leather, anything leather, especially black leather. "Really too queasy-making, Claude," he said. "You know it's not hygienic. There's no way to clean it. The idea of walking around in some other animal's skin is horrifying and *dyed* skin is still more nightmarish. The sight of a woman sitting in a stiff black leather skirt is about as appetizing as lipstick on teeth. Leather is the *bad breath* of fashion, we might say."

His tirade was punctuated by the whine of bullets in the square below. The tailor had sewn these leather garments with his own hands to Daniel's specifications and had worked all night with his wife and younger daughter to have the clothes ready for today's appointment. His right index and middle fingers still ached from the bite of the big needle being forced again and again through the resistant leather. Little spells of dizziness kept giving him the sensation of falling an inch forward. Exhausted and irritable, he heard the gunshots with pleasure and even as he smiled at Daniel's caprices he pictured him felled and bleeding, each shot another black dot on the white domino of his immense body.

Claude, too, was in a dark mood. She dismissed the tailor and picked up a nail file. Last night she'd argued with her father about her "future," that cheerless fate that always sounded like a deformity, something no one would have chosen but that now must be dealt with. To the degree he was vague and exalted with his readers, the general was coldly precise with his family and other subordinates. No one would ever have surmised from the pantheistic raptures of his books—with their espousal of the brotherhood of man and animal, of "hand, fin and claw" as he not only phrased it but had had it emblazoned on pins he gave to admirers, the three elements gruesomely entwined—no one would ever have surmised from such grotesque fancies that he was as narrowly dynastic as any plump merchant who'd never scaled a mountain nor trapped a snow leopard. Indeed he was so determined to have Claude marry properly that he was even willing to meddle with her always fragile sanity.

From his informers he learned how constantly and violently Daniel harangued Claude about her taste. Even he had noticed how his plump, homely daughter had been starved, bleached, bound, shod and gowned into submission; he had even heard her deliberately vomiting a nourishing and highly traditional dinner of venison in rabbit sauce seconds after he'd excused her from the festive holiday table. Whereas in the past she'd been as docile and colorless as any respectable woman should be, now she was always making a moue in the mirror, cutting out fake fingernails for herself, dangling barbaric trophies from her newly pierced ears and slouching into a room with a taloned hand on a bony pelvis or, in full view at public gatherings, slowly repainting her mouth with two different brushes and blotting the patterned grease with a grey ducal handkerchief soaked in Daniel's own vetiver.

Claude's father thought that her susceptibility to this petty despot was due to her lack of a proper musical-ethical formation (he considered music to be the ultimate source of his own morality, the very breath of the World Soul as squeezed through the ocarina of individual genius). But he knew his irritable daughter, so busily worshipping and adoring the totem her body had become, could never be reached through Harmonic Discipline, much less nature hikes. Only her fears shaped her behavior. Since that was so, he would have to shape her fears. But indirectly. Indirection, the lesson of the Beaver, would be his method, joined to the stealth of the Badger.

A campaign orchestrated by her father soon enough convinced Claude that Daniel was gossiping about her all over town, bragging about his power to make her submit to any whim he dreamed up, regaling whores in the dyers' quarter with choice idiocies straight from the "albino's scarlet mouth." Claude's mother, prompted by her husband, warned her against Daniel, as did her sister. Another friend also had a heart-to-heart talk with her.

"I'm afraid you've forgotten your place," Claude announced to Daniel, her eyes trained on the nail file and her lower lip protruding.

"My place?" Daniel exclaimed. He stood back to regard Claude's insolence and made a low, insulting whistle as he doffed an invisible cap. He knew that Claude liked to needle him so that he'd slap her all the harder, but he was wearying of so much violence so close to home—even *in* the home, now that he'd declared war on his mother.

"Yes, your place. Which is away from here. You're not one of us. I'm tired of your rudeness, your lectures—"

"I suppose you prefer looking like a plump white shoat all decked out in pleated organdy, a juicy pork chop complete with a pink paper shaker at one end so the diner can eat without getting his fingers greasy." He laughed, but a moment later the vision of the chop faded. "Perhaps you think I treasure your conversation?

Or your high spirits? Generosity of soul? Generosity?" Since his code as a dandy, although it encouraged impertinence to other men, forbade rudeness to women, Daniel looked out the window and imagined he was addressing Claude's father.

Claude's father was planning to send her back to the fatherland, which he always referred to not by its name but by a word in their language that could only be pronounced with tears in pale blue eyes and that signified a cluster of meanings ranging from "homeland" to "cradle of the spirit." She stood beside Daniel. They were both looking down at the square below. "I'm leaving you," Claude said. To say the words cost her the greatest effort, but the instant she heard them a great anger against him overwhelmed her. She only wished someone else was in the room, because she was afraid Daniel would strike her.

He was surprisingly docile. He even seemed apologetic when he asked for another cup of tea. He had a fever blister on his upper lip, and she knew how such blemishes upset him. She was relieved at the prospect of being rid of his inspection of her clothes, remarks and manners. Even if she learned nothing more from him, she'd already acquired enough sophistication to last her a lifetime in the dowdy fatherland. She knew that soon enough, of course, she'd miss his attacks on her and the wisdom of the world he imparted to her, but just for now she welcomed the respite. They talked some more and then he left. At the door he offered her his little finger and looked away.

When she was alone she smoked something he'd given her and lay down on her bed and felt emotions storm through her like hostile armies, banners flying, advancing in waves across a field. She experienced a small thrill when she remembered she'd said, "You're not one of us."

That was right. They didn't even speak the same language, or rather when she spoke his she never felt sincere. Among the conquerors everyone teased friends for not working hard enough; in his world, one had to pretend never to have worked at all. In her circle people had a good sense of humor and laughed a lot and razzed each other in amiable fashion; his people were just nasty. They don't know how to be silly in our splendid, lighthearted way, she thought. But of course they *are* stylish. She wondered if a revolution really did break out whether new styles would continue to evolve in the capital. Thirty years ago, when the patriot leaders were being guillotined, their women had worn their hair up *à la victime*.

She dozed off for a few minutes and then woke, jostled slightly by the chemicals filtering through her. She remembered when she'd been a little girl and played "it" in hide-and-seek. While all the other children had looked for her she'd hidden. She remembered two boys had whispered just outside the closet door and then moved on; their whispers had played all over her body, as though she'd been a flute they'd been breathing into. Funny, but Daniel's badgering had been like that. Now she felt lost, as though the searchers had given up and left her crouching in a dark closet.

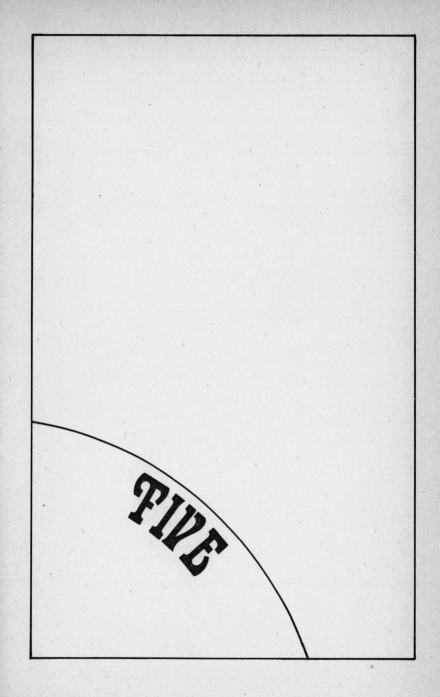

FIVE

TWO days later the violence in the streets seemed to have become part of carnival and revelers didn't know whether a giant was walking on concealed stilts or stacked explosives or whether a moment from now the flame eater would turn into an incendiary. The *Little Gazette* had suspended publication, the banks had closed and a curfew had been imposed on the city, but no one observed it. Every time the police asked to see the people's documents an angry crowd gathered. An army of soldiers in civilian dress had infiltrated the city. Wherever one looked one saw clusters of three or four adolescent men in regulation raincoats, sometimes going through the motions of window shopping or examining chipped soap dishes at the flea market, sometimes just sitting vacantly in a café, looking too muscular, their sideburns too long and shaggy to be convincingly urban. Like supernumeraries on stage, they stood about trying to look "typical."

For Mathilda the sound of snipers became confused with her migraines; she scarcely noticed the collapsing city. When she did she rejoiced in this public amplification of her personal distress. The morning after her jolly, sinister reunion with Gabriel she'd begun to suspect he had not been crying over her. The second morning he roused himself enough to confirm her suspicion. He spoke of Edwige's cruelty (and her beauty and her charm and her humor) with such enthusiasm he seemed to have forgotten that Mathilda could not share this particular obsession of his. He'd grown so used to drawing for her each of his neural doodles, over which she exclaimed with delight, that now he failed to see why she didn't find this motif equally inspiring. Ten times a day she'd observe him smiling to himself or wiping away tears and each time she knew that his invisible visitor was that actress.

When Gabriel took a shower she saw the flash of his skinny white body through the open door and she thought, This will be the last time I'll ever see him naked. When he brewed his own tea and carried it to the window seat with that peculiar deliberate gait of his—that robotlike slowness and jerkiness that made him look as though he had been fabricated before the inventor had smoothed out the kinks—Mathilda watched him and knew this was also the last time she'd ever see him lift the lid and stir the tea, forget the strainer then remember it, tilt the pot with maddening inaccuracy, exactly as though he'd grown up on another planet where objects weighed less than here. Whenever he read a book, his face went cold as a judge's. He reached blindly for his muffin, raised it but put it down again without taking a bite, read on and on. Their long, peaceful, domestic evenings, the way he'd lent a peculiar emphasis to the word *comfort* and would say, "I feel so comfortable," as though by achieving comfort he'd reached the highest wisdom, the snuffling and padding about, his habit of reading in the bathtub until the soles of his feet puckered like seersucker—all of these signs she'd mistaken for love.

In her bitterness she calculated exactly how much she'd spent on that robe he was wearing, those slippers, that silly gold bracelet he'd asked for, although it was more suitable to a shop assistant than an—she started to say "intellectual," but now she acknowledged he wasn't an intellectual at all, nor even someone as predictable as a shop assistant. No, he was just this half-shaped half-baked kid from the provinces she'd decided to love, but why? Had she found him to be a sweeter, less bristling stand-in for her first love, Mateo? Had he been for her an emblem of her own sense that she was a stranger in her world, despite the fact most people assumed she ruled it? Recently someone had said, smiling, "You are the real spirit of this city, Mathilda. If people are discussing the latest intellectual fashion, they say, 'It's great, but will Mathilda buy it?' You're their criterion."

At the time Mathilda had fled the room, panicked that this unsuspected thing had happened to her, that unwittingly she'd become a password. Now she thought that Gabriel remained unknown—to her and to everyone else. Again and again she'd tried to understand him, and she'd always assumed he was hiding the truth from her. But now she thought he didn't know the truth about himself. He was both confused and stubborn. He didn't know what he was feeling. His savage childhood had deformed him, pushed him toward isolation. She pictured him wandering the woods on his stick horse, his face a riot of spots, his eyes flashing shiftily from under a dusty mop of hair. Her mistake had been to offer too much love, too much indoor love, to a desert plant. No, she'd drowned her cactus with too much water. Just a few drops a month, that was all he could take. That actress—silly, selfish, cruel—she gave him what he wanted: nothing.

The thought of Edwige sickened her. Mathilda looked at her

own clothes hanging in the closet and hated each dress, the day she'd bought it, the places she'd gone in it, the person who'd worn it. She looked at her piles of books and the flurry of notes around them, stale chips off old blocks, and she felt the same sense of futility she would experience whenever she'd wander through the city archives, that rubbish heap of history. In some ideal world where people led tranquil lives that lasted two hundred years, there would be time enough to ponder the theory of love, to find the aptest classical quotations about it, to untie the knots between private desire and public order. But now more than ever she could see the random desperation of living. She was too driven to think clearly. She pictured herself as someone who stumbled from errand to chore, interruption to lapse, mistake to mischance, who alternated between sloth and pride, whose vision of the truth was occluded by spite and who, in fact, had no need of the truth. What she needed was this skinny boy to make whimpering sounds in his sleep and without ever waking hug her for comfort. But he wouldn't. Never again. That was the stubbornness. He didn't know what he felt and he insisted on feeling it.

She recognized that she, a woman who'd brought down one cabinet with a single snort of disapproval, who'd remade herself from a vacuous deb into the high priestess of the mind, had at last encountered an obstacle her will couldn't budge, this quite inconsequential child.

She sighed a great sigh that was like shifting a sack of bricks from one side to the other, a clattering sigh that exhausted her. She sat down and became aware of this big, unlovely body of hers and sighed again. She looked around her rooms and, sighing, hated them; she'd fouled her nest. She thought of going to her house overlooking the harbor, but that only reminded her of the happy days she'd spent there with Gabriel. She sighed.

Without even brushing her hair or cleaning her teeth she went to the opera, wearing a rumpled dress and a sweater over her naked shoulders, because she couldn't tolerate anyone looking at her body and evaluating it. She didn't want anyone to have an opinion about her, not even a favorable one. She marveled that for so many years she'd put her stale charms on display, that all the ladies at the opera did, as though each box were a whore's room in the dyers' quarter and each duchess a "specialist" proffering something a little "different" for clients with unusual tastes. For instance, in this box one could get salacious conversations; in that one a glimpse of big breasts; in this *baignoire* one could be sure a feminine hand would keep tugging at a glossy male lapel; over there one could get a cold glass of champagne and a canapé freighted with right-wing politics. But Mathilda's shop was closed and nothing, nothing, was for sale.

At the beginning of the second act, when the a cappella chorus of slaves sings a soft hymn to their country in chains, the students in the top balcony stood up and bawled out the old national anthem. Although the conductor angrily beat the air with his baton, the orchestra refused to resume playing. Finally the fire curtain was slowly lowered to indicate the performance would not go on, and the house lights came up. Operagoers in the dress circle, perhaps more vexed at missing the rest of the evening than inspired by rebellion, started a round of catcalls and hoots.

A shot rang out. Inexplicably the overture to the first act was played doubletime by the half of the instrumentalists who still remained in the pit. The lights dipped mysteriously and then came up. Some women were sobbing and several were shrieking. The ushers had vanished and in their stead three frightened-looking soldiers had entered the viceregal box. They were pelted with fruit and programs. Even someone's walking stick came flying through the air. A stampede convulsed the stalls, where a fistfight had broken out.

Mathilda withdrew to the cloak room adjacent to her box. The outer door to the corridor was locked. Only the usher could open it with her key, and she had undoubtedly fled. As Mathilda sat in the twilight of the velvet-lined antechamber, a locked door on one side and a closed curtain on the other, she smiled. She smiled at the shrieks, the angry buzzing, the ragged music that kept playing on and on even though one performer after another was slipping away —there went the trumpet-player in mid-fanfare! Another shot rang out, and an instant later an implausibly stagey voice said, "Good lord, he's dead. Oh, no. No . . ." And Mathilda smiled.

She returned home through the violent streets, which were thronged despite the ceaseless tolling of the old curfew bell, the one they called "Mother" in dialect, that flat sound of a wood spoon thudding against a skillet. As soon as she entered she knew the house was empty. She could feel its emptiness, hear it, while she was still ascending the stairs. On the long refectory table was a note from Gabriel: "I'm only making us both miserable. I hope you believe how much I love you, how unhappy I am that my heart has rebelled against my head."

What head, she wondered. "They never miss a chance," she said out loud, not knowing what she meant. She threw open the windows and stepped out on the balcony. "Mother" rang and rang, like an old peasant woman calling her menfolk from the fields to the noon dinner. Although the conquerors had picked it to be the curfew signal, "Mother" now rang out as a call to arms. Down one dark street a flame spurted and a moment later Mathilda heard the report of a gunshot. "Vulgar," she murmured; she despised the style in which Gabriel had written his letter.

An old servant, apparently the only one who hadn't rushed out to witness or participate in the fighting, called Mathilda to a midnight supper. When Mathilda waved a hand in refusal, the old woman crouched to put her arm around Mathilda's waist and said, "Come, my darling, come with me. There may not be anything to eat tomorrow. Come, Mathilda, come," and she led her away to the table as though she were her daughter. To be addressed by her first name, to be touched, to be fed moved Mathilda so much that tears sprang to her eyes. All her life she'd known this old servant, a tribeswoman now so feeble she did nothing but dither around the kitchen and annoy everyone. Brought up in the country, she'd never learned how to address nobility in the third person (as in "Would her ladyship be so kind as to . . ."). Although she had a true peasant's reverence for her superiors, she also intuited their humanity—their need for company or solitude, for a cool palm or a second blanket. No amount of time spent among brisk, citified servants had changed her ways. Her strong old hands moved surely and fearlessly right to the pain in her mistress's side. "Eat something, my darling," and she seated Mathilda before a bowl of steaming barley soup, which for the moment seemed the only possible dish to eat.

After obediently lifting the spoon to her lips Mathilda looked up to see, at the other end of the table, her son. He was eating soup, too. "The Darling," she thought. His eyes, his puffy face and long, dirty hair were a mirror image of her own distress. Mother and son slurped their soup. A white flare trembled luridly outside the window and Mathilda didn't know whether it was fireworks or a bomb. Far, far away men and women were singing the anthem out of tune, the strophes beat out by "Mother's" tolling. In the doorway the peasant woman was watching her lord and lady eat the barley soup she'd made them.

"What's wrong with you?" Mathilda asked.

"Claude just gave me the gate."

"Claude? That girl's only drawback is her total stupidity. Surely you don't mind losing her?"

"I do, actually. I mind terribly. I'm afraid I love her. I just discovered that. Yes, she's stupid. Yes, I mistreated her terribly. Yes, she's the enemy, but I love her." He put his spoon down. "There you are."

"There we both are," Mathilda said.

For a few minutes Mathilda took some feeble comfort in sharing her suffering, but then the soup made her nauseous and she decided Daniel's failure proved that her own was fundamental to her nature, not an accident; suddenly she disliked looking at him. She rose from the table without a word. Daniel stood, too, and she could see how dirty he was, his boots, trousers, linen. Grief, it seemed, had turned him into a vagabond.

There was something in Daniel that made her afraid, a dissoluteness and craziness she didn't share. She wasn't addicted. She never let herself become attached to . . . medicines. She didn't have habits. She traveled too much to have them, she changed her friends too often. She changed herself as well; she'd changed from an innocent girl to a social leader to a radical intellectual to a skeptical critic to—a foolish old woman addicted to an unpromising boy who no longer loved her if he ever had.

Daniel came close to her and she feared she'd snarl at him if he touched her because she saw him as more of herself and she hated herself. When he asked her if he could sleep in her room tonight, she said, "No."

"I don't have anywhere else to go," Daniel said.

"Yes, you do," Mathilda said. "Your father, Mateo."

She left the room before he could question her. Her decision to clarify his identity had been a move to push him away, he felt certain. Until now she'd been all at once his lover, friend and mother but slowly she'd been cutting each of these ties. She'd made Gabriel her lover. Then Daniel's friendship with his mother had dwindled away and now Mathilda was choosing to relinquish her parental responsibility for him to Mateo.

Mateo was his father. This certainly was belittling. If Daniel had drawled, condescended, sneered, snickered, yawned and more than once threatened to horse-whip a cad or cane a scoundrel, he'd behaved as he thought the son of a great noble should. Never had he asked his mother to tell him his father's name because he'd secretly feared it might not begin with a *particule.* In his reveries he'd fancied his father now as one man he knew, now as another, and in their routine courtesies to him he'd detected an intimate pressure, as a handshake in a reception line might seem to convey a special warmth to someone in need of it. Sometimes he'd see the original of his nose and arrogance in one lord or detect in another the source of his own sure taste and bistered eyes. He'd often imagined he'd already been designated as the heir to a great fortune —and he'd spend accordingly. At other times he felt his mother had concealed his father's identity because she'd been embarrassed to name a conqueror duke—the genetic source, no doubt, of Daniel's conservatism and the inspiration of Mathilda's circular meditation on imperial culture, its creepy will to power and appalling gigan-tism (four-day operas, twelve-day plays, two-year histories—two years to *read,* that is, if the reader also hoped to maintain a normal life).

Now the warm vagueness of his speculations was blown away. Daniel could no longer daydream of some day inheriting northern keeps hung with stag trophies, of mint-sauce lawns rolling down to the copper beech, of chill, dimpling trout streams and fields cropped by a flock of sheep on a distant hill, the last sunny spot since everywhere else the sky was filling up with white and grey clouds.

He remembered all the times he'd chuckled at Mateo. He'd said that Mateo had lots of manners but no manner. Mateo was too eager to please. Daniel had always assumed that several of his fellow students at the Peers School knew who his real father was and treated him with appropriate if covert respect. Now he saw that their respect had been owed to Mathilda alone, and Daniel felt all the more depressingly linked to his mother. He'd often attributed his own antic wit and black moods, his insomnia and addictiveness, his extravagance and bad temper to a mysterious father; he'd even felt that this father was thinking for him, pumping him full of virtues and failings, as an unborn baby lives off its mother's blood, food, breath.

Now this exalted, imprecise destiny had been annulled. Nothing stood as an alternative to his mother. A companion, his big, forceful father, immoderate as a tycoon, had been taken away from him and in his place was Mateo, compromised by familiarity, worn by use.

Claude had said, "You're not one of us," with no conviction. She'd merely been repeating what her father had dictated. But in retrospect the words took on an unaccountable rightness. Certainly a prescience. Now that he knew who his father was, he had no more access to Claude. She was being sent off to the homeland next week, after the old governor's ball, the only social event of the summer, yet one the conquerors favored since it coincided with the height of the tourist season and the visits of their countrymen.

At first, after she'd dismissed him, he'd laughed at her, as though a cow could dismiss its herdsmen, as though beef could give orders to the butcher. In the dyers' quarter he'd slipped through knots of angry men and women plotting rebellion and he'd grinned at the prospect of a bombed viceregal palace—the inexplicable, then explicable sound of the explosion; the instantaneous bloat of the walls; finally the teetering of everything on the edge of everything as the facade dissolved into cataracts of stone.

After a week of dogged dissipation with the girls of the House of Negative Assent, Daniel's contempt for Claude turned to anger. She'd fed on his imagination, stolen his taste, cannibalized his style. For three nights running Daniel roared his rage to the girls, keeping them awake, shouting out all the ways he planned to get even with Claude. In their language her name sounded like the word for spoiled milk, so as they attended him through the night and into the first fresh moments of dawn they consoled him for this lactic mishap.

Daniel decided that the first of the many revenges he would wreak on Claude would be to dress his mother in the same gown he'd selected for Claude to wear to the governor's ball. He was sure

Claude would wear the dress. She lacked the courage to choose another garment and the moral sense to know she ought to. He told Mathilda that he would be selecting her dress, but he didn't explain to her why. She who right now found the smallest act overwhelming felt grateful for his offer. She had her own reasons for wanting to go to the ball, but she had no idea how she'd get there. Of course, it was purest folly to hold the ball this year, she thought, given the political unrest, but she'd been told the general refused to be intimidated. In his books he'd always counseled the young to act ahead of their sentiments. He'd written: "Pretend to courage and you'll be courageous. Do what you know to be right and your feelings will measure up." In the present crisis he was determined to follow his own advice, not his instinct (which was to break and run). He delegated that baser urge to his wife and daughter, whom he would soon be sending home with visiting relatives on the pretext they had to attend a family reunion, which he'd convened to validate the excuse. At least Claude had broken off with that degenerate fop of hers and seemed willing to go home. Although the general had hoped his daughter would pick up some of the sophistication of the native women of the capital, he abhorred her apprenticeship to that insupportable cicisbeo, the son of a local bluestocking.

Claude never went hiking now or joined in merry athletic competition or campfire singalongs with girls of her own class. Her father doubted if she could survive even a day in the wilderness, so etiolated had she become, a scrawny clotheshorse—and what frightful clothes! A rag nag. How strange that he, who'd wrestled the killer turtle to death, who'd set the broken wing of the man-o'-war and scaled the highest, coldest mountain in the world, should have spawned this bloodless girl who only became animated when she discussed nail varnish.

At least she'd have a chance to wear her choicest shade to the governor's ball, to unveil another bizarre gown to the excitable and vacuous people fate had given him to rule.

Everyone who hadn't fled the besieged city attended the ball. Although on the mainland the industrial district of the capital seemed to have been "liberated" by the patriots, who apparently had declared a new republic, most of the old nobility doubted this government could prevail against the imperial troops and half-feared what might happen to them if it did. They'd grown used to conqueror rule. Some of the best families had married into the ruling nobility. Others had sent their sons to the best imperial schools abroad. Some collaborationist nobles had risen higher than ever before under the republic, whereas many resistance families had sunk. The unreasonably vast holdings of old endowed institutions had been broken up. New bridges had been built, public transportation improved, charities consolidated, weights and measures standardized. Despite their superior technology the victors freely admitted their inferior culture—and that admission flattered their subjects. Little did they realize that among the conquerors culture itself was at once revered and mistrusted, even regarded as an enemy to rectitude.

Maurizio had decided that Gabriel would become suspicious if Angelica sought him out. Gabriel would wonder how she'd found him, wonder who had told her of his whereabouts and why. Better for them to meet "by accident" at the governor's ball, which in any event was expected to touch off a general insurrection. Patriot spies had reported that the general's daughter had recently broken with Gabriel's friend Daniel. Daniel, of course, was too unstable to be predictable, but common sense would suggest he might be wounded deeply enough to lose his sympathies for the court. The patriot cause would undoubtedly triumph without any of them, but if circumstances led Mateo, Mathilda, Gabriel and even Daniel into the ranks of resistance, their names would lend a dignity, an orderliness, an inevitability to the reestablishment of native rule.

What no one knew was that Mathilda had decided to murder Edwige at the ball. The passions that decades of reading novels and attending operas had instilled in her would finally be released. As soon as she made this decision she regained her happiness—not a true joy in living but the gaiety of a strictly provisional mandate to finish a job.

She went out into the streets and found a gun shop and there bought a pistol. As she walked home she smiled at this comfort in her pocket. She felt light-headed and the daylight hurt her eyes just as the air hurt her lungs, as though she were an aquatic animal unable to sustain oxygen in this form.

Her ironic self snickered at the preposterous melodrama she was instigating, but her tragic self moved with gravity toward her goal. Primitives did things—attacked, killed, struck back—and sobered up later to regret their impetuosity. Civilized people did nothing and prided themselves on the self-consciousness that had tranquilized them. They didn't understand that their inaction, far from proving how highly evolved they were, actually demonstrated they were suited only to belong to the chorus. They could comment on the deeds of the principles but not step out to become one. Of course every educated person found anything bold ridiculous; and of course every action of any sort creaked with the awkwardness of the discernibly real. Yes, how wonderful that we should exist; how hilarious that we should do or make. But someone worthy of being a protagonist finally steps forward and, no matter how stylelessly or inopportunely, plants the axe in the stomach.

Mathilda knew that sculptors liked to contrast Contemplation with Action, the one musing over books and astrolabes, the other girded for battle. But she would fuse them: she'd become an artist, for surely that was the high destiny of art, to do something in full knowledge of its meaning. A soldier marches or kills: a thinker reflects each act in the angled mirrors circling his mind. Her accomplishment, her synthesis would set a deed into the surround of understanding.

That night, the eve of the ball, she dreamed that a sad but smiling Edwige gave Gabriel to her. Gabriel was singed with shame —his edges were literally charred and crinkled, as though he were a page rescued from the hearth. And she, Mathilda, was opened up like a big fiddle case and her real body, the slender lovely one, was lifted out, held to the light, tuned. Gabriel held her.

Then she woke to discover Daniel had flung himself across her bed and was crying. She blinked into the darkness and lay there listening and wished her boy had someone to kill. His grief seemed so irrelevant now, even to his own predicament. But she smiled and acknowledged that she had been lucky; she'd found her solution without much fuss.

She felt no more responsibility toward her son. How could she, in the light of her decision? Nor did she have much sympathy for what he must be feeling; she could scarcely imagine it. Nonetheless a certain playful charity prompted her to stroke his head and to say, "You've lost that girl and I've lost Gabriel, but we must be brave." She could hear her own breath and his in the dark. She went on, remotely amused: "Did you ever really think you and I would know how to impersonate lovers? Don't worry. We'll go back to reading all night. Or you'll explore the city and tell me about it the next morning."

"Mother," he said. He always called her Mathilda; not since he'd been a little boy had he called her Mother. By the time he was seven he'd already been shocking guests by pouring out the wine for them and aggressively correcting "Mathilda." Now he called her Mother and he said, "You will wear the beige silk dress I've chosen, won't you?"

"Yes, my love," she said. She wondered if she'd be able to do everything neatly at the ball. History, like some importunate monarch, had summoned her and she hoped her curtsy would be accurate and deep. When she stood to go to the toilet the bed under its heap of lights and shadows seemed to shrink and slide away.

Suddenly Daniel looked tiny on this piece of dollhouse furniture. When she chose she could restore everything to its normal size, but distancing and diminishing things (right now the sink, her hands under the water) made her laugh, and only her resolution to pull everything off tomorrow night persuaded her to stop fooling around with dimension. When she went back to the bedroom Daniel, poor thing, began to tell her how important he was—important in having "finished" Claude, important in leading the revolution to calm. Mathilda bounced him up to man size for one of his sentences and reduced him down to gnat size for the next. It crossed her mind that this was craziness, but the word meant nothing if there was to be no future. Craziness was a scandal, but nothing without repercussions could be scandalous. In any event, among the people she knew, fear of scandal inhibited whatever impulses hadn't already been silenced by irony.

Daniel meant nothing to her now. She'd dragged him around with her as though she were a king and he her exotic gift, but the casket upon presentation had turned out to be empty.

The next morning she was sitting on her balcony looking down into a square that was forming in the first light like a sandbar surfacing at low tide. A lamplighter who had one leg shorter than the other was rocking his way along the edge of the square when a shot rang out. The man staggered and fell. Gunsmoke drifted gently away in the cool dawn breeze. After a bit someone entered the square, saw the body and quite comically backed out. Did he hope to avoid the nuisance of contacting the police? Or was he afraid he'd be the next victim?

Mathilda went in. She'd been satisfied with the look of dying and pleased to discover her heart wasn't faint, not faint at all.

Weeks before Angelica had asked "Teddy" to take her to the governor's ball, but he'd turned her down—in his most charming way, of course. Mateo's love for the girl made refusing her anything difficult. He emphasized the onerousness of his duty to escort Edwige, whom he didn't name but called "this lady who rents an apartment in my building and insists I take her."

Mentally Angelica smiled at such a description of the glamorous star, who she knew was the great love of Mateo's life. Flora had told her of their "torrid affair," as the city gossip would have it, but Angelica had detected the cruelty of this rival in Teddy's gratitude to her, Angelica, for the smallest kindness. He'd been damaged by Edwige. Often he spoke in late-night whispers to Angelica of her generosity, by which she could infer Edwige's meanness. If Angelica had been more worldly she might have feared her kindness would bore a man so habituated to pain—but such a fear would have been misplaced, for Mateo had not been drawn to Angelica's coldness (which was hidden and would reveal itself only in time, when it was too late) but to her vulnerability (which was apparent from the start because she'd cultivated it as an aspect of her appeal).

Maurizio convinced Angelica to go to the ball as a boy in a costume and mask that would match his own. "We'll be brothers," he said hopefully. She readily agreed, since often she'd concealed her gender and moved mysteriously around town in search of adventure.

She knew Gabriel would be at the ball. What would he say to her when he saw her? He'd be in costume and mask as well. Would she recognize him? In all the time since they'd come to the city she'd seen him only once and that had been at the opera. She'd gone with the pharmacist and sat in the highest balcony. At the intermission she'd hurtled down the stairs to mix with the gentry. She had been wearing her emerald necklace, the costume-jewelry Teddy had bought her. At one moment she'd glanced up to a box where she thought she saw a skinnier, sadder Gabriel standing in evening clothes behind the chair of a striking old woman. But Teddy had begged her not to "upset" Gabriel, who certainly looked peculiar, and she'd ducked behind someone then crept back up to the balcony and that darling druggist with his fun pills and droll sex fantasies . . .

And yet, all along, she'd been curious about Gabriel, almost as though he were a twin, a brother—or her husband, as indeed he was by the lights of her people. She'd felt him somewhere nearby, waiting, dangerous.

She loved making Teddy happy. She thought it strange that he who'd lived in a milieu devoted to pleasure had known so little happiness. The men of her tribe—scarred by the tusk of the wild pig, hunted by irate farmers whose chickens they'd stolen, paralyzed by directional taboos that kept them pent up for days on end —they'd never talked about happiness at all. It wasn't something they thought about. But these men of the city, overstimulated by talk and art and drink and sex, complained so much about the happiness they were missing that Angelica soon came to think they deserved it—and was thrilled that she represented it to Teddy.

On some days she'd go to a picture dealer with Teddy and look soberly at one painting after another. She really didn't know what he was seeing, what was taking so long, nor could she imagine why people would spend such demented sums on inscrutable daubs. Nor could she ever predict which one he would like—why he'd find this one "strong" or "courageous" while another he declared to be "weak" or "merely decorative" or "a step backward." But just as all this concentration and money had authenticated "art" for her as something real, a real thing, in the same way Teddy's and Flora's insistence on "happiness" had also brought it into being for her. Happiness was a legitimate commodity, like art. Just as her own people made cult figures the city dwellers called "art," in the same way the tribesmen often experienced an elation which they called "wild high spirits" but Mateo's friends might call "happiness." And yet "wild high spirits" or "going over the top" (depending on how the word was translated) was given as a proof of pleasure at an elaborate banquet, an acknowledgment of the host's generosity, a demonstration of the greatness of one's own soul—whereas "happiness," as she discovered, described private moments as well as public demonstrations. Yet Angelica thought that even for Mateo "happiness" must have its banquet origins, for often he'd look up from a book or hug her in bed and say, "I'm so happy," as though he were toasting the world.

Maurizio came to dress and mask in her room at ten. She'd prepared an elegant cold supper of cucumber soup, chicken and champagne, just as Flora had suggested to her. Angelica greeted him at the door in the costume he'd provided; it matched his. They did a turn before the mirror, singing and dancing the current hit, "Brothers." Maurizio blushed when Angelica kissed his cheek and murmured, "Incest, anyone?" The costumes only emphasized their differences, Angelica so dark and female, Maurizio so fair and masculine. He was almost a foot taller than she.

The ballroom was the old Council Chamber still graced with its allegorical ceiling of the Marriage of City and Sea and their preparation of a crib for their infant, the Republic, from weeds and seaweed, grass and eelgrass, the national flag (now suppressed, of course) held up by angels and angelfish ("The only two kinds of patriots they could find," went the quip among the conquerors).

To reach this august chamber—lined on all four sides with carved wood thrones, the former seats of the patriarchs—one followed a devious route. Through the gates, across a courtyard assembled out of spoils from many centuries and countries, up the marble staircase, through a pair of antechambers and the former Senate, then the Star Chamber, the Treasury and the High Court (one low, barred door led directly down to the dungeons). Finally a narrow hall zigzagged into the most recent wing and the Council Chamber, the only room large enough for a ball. The lack of a properly grand or direct entrance had always caused criticism, but Angelica liked the adventure of such a long, delaying, funhouse route. The very narrowness of the last corridor had always prevented women from wearing bustles that were too wide and had enforced the sumptuary laws that otherwise were so gaily flouted.

The general and his wife and daughter were enthroned on a dais in front of a wall covered with a red velvet curtain, newly installed to conceal a fresco that narrated the most important victories of the Republic—*not* an acceptable theme for the ball, given the present unrest, although hiding the wall had only focused attention on it.

The July night drew Angelica and Maurizio to the open doors giving onto the balcony. A breeze touched Angelica's right cheek, slipped behind her, then caressed her left shoulder and brushed her exposed neck with its lips. Angelica pictured the breeze as a dancer gracefully performing a game of tag. Like Mateo toasting some unseen banquet, Angelica said to Maurizio, "I'm so happy."

Yet she was a bit disappointed that her boy's clothes, which at home she'd thought of as outrageous, had caused no stir and seemed dully conventional beside the shocking or gaudy costumes on every side. She hoped she'd recognize Teddy and his actress. She half-hoped and half-feared Teddy would recognize her. Would he think she was spying on him? He'd often explained he couldn't take her to various parties and receptions because of his "work," whatever that was. She hoped she wouldn't be annoying him if he was at work again tonight. Like "art" and "happiness," "work" was another one of the invisible but recognized realities of the city. Something like a buttonhole, work seemed to be useful precisely because it was a carefully defined absence.

Walter was standing near a table of refreshments, wearing a pink dress. Angelica had never met him, but she'd seen him at the opera in Mathilda's box. Now she backed up to him in the crowd and lingered next to him, listening to his conversation. He was saying that he saw much that was good in the revolutionary leadership and no reason not to anticipate the success of "our" cause. For a moment Angelica was confused until she realized that Walter considered himself to be a revolutionary. "After all," he said, "I was a Septembrist and I've always remained loyal to that movement." Although Mateo had often complained to her of Walter's lies and pretensions, she liked his way of talking, so lively and entertaining. He seemed so eager to please and so afraid of losing his turn to speak that Angelica was touched. If she lived with him she'd listen to him all day, just to make him feel better. She hoped for his sake that he would outlive his brilliant friends, who teased him so much, and survive to rework the story of their lives so that he'd emerge as the hero.

A wonderfully ugly boy in a cheap blue gown, too small to fit him, sidled up to her and asked her to dance. His entire side was exposed where the snaps refused to close. Even so, his ribs were protruding and he was terribly gaunt. She in her smart but dull boy's suit and this ugly boy in his garish gown, with a big blue cloth rose sewn to the bosom, twirled across the floor. She felt comfortable in his arms. She wondered what he looked like under his mask. Did he know she was a girl despite her costume? Many men had obviously been fooled and she missed their lingering looks.

She was revolved out onto the broad dark balcony. She and the boy waltzed more and more *lentamente* between potted palms in stone vats. He was suddenly kissing her and moving his hands all over her. The taste in his mouth awakened memories, as did the little clicking sound he made when he cleared his throat. He raised her mask and pushed his own back.

"Gabriel," she said. "How did you—"

"The man dressed in the same costume you're wearing pointed you out."

They kissed in the shadows. She remembered how he hadn't liked to kiss her at Madder Pink, how he'd never told her he loved her; she dimly recalled that no one had talked much about "love" back there so long ago.

His hand seemed annoyed with her boy's tunic—it wanted to get to her breast. To torment him she put *her* hand down his bodice and squeezed *his* nipple. When his fingers finally gophered up her tunic, she lowered her hand and found his big erect penis muzzled behind the sleazy fabric—just where she'd known it would be; a black drool mark was seeping up through the blue silk.

The sound and smell of the forest on a summer night came back to her and she felt they were in their hollow again, thrashing about on the ground—a vivid scene conjured here on this shadowy balcony behind the indiscreet palm tree pretending to hide its eyes but peeking at them through spread fingers.

"Mother" stopped tolling. The silence, after two days of clangor, sounded ominous. Down below masquers dressed as dukes and duchesses were laughing the hearty boisterous laugh of the conquerors as they drifted across the piazza. They probably were dukes and duchesses.

An unlit ship gliding through the harbor blew its baritone foghorn and slid across the illuminated face of Mateo's palace, hiding it for ten long seconds as a magician might lightfinger something under his silk square.

Gabriel and Angelica sought privacy. They crept down corridors and up stairs, Gabriel holding his open lady's fan over his aching erection. Once when they thought they'd found a perfect corner, a soldier helmed in darkness stepped forward, clicked his heels and saluted.

Finally they returned to the ballroom and ducked behind the red velvet curtains covering the insurrectionist fresco. Here at last, in a hot passageway only two feet wide, separated from thousands of dancers by just a thickness of fabric, Gabriel hiked up his skirt, pulled down Angelica's trousers and plunged into her. They couldn't so much as whisper or sigh; every sound would be heard through the curtain. On the other side, only a few inches away, a woman was asking her husband who everyone was, and Angelica, even in her delirium, could tell the man knew no one. At least his voice didn't inspire confidence.

Angelica loved Gabriel. He was her husband. This "love"

they talked so much about, as real and invisible as "art" or "happiness" or "work," now seemed so full and present within her that she looked and looked into Gabriel's eyes—did he feel it too? Surely anything so strong must be shared. She couldn't be hearing so much love unless he was saying at least some of it to her. She reworked their past so that every tough, animal grappling followed by aversion now seemed to have prefigured love and the promise of happiness. What had been all silence and shame now became talk, the eloquence of love.

"But do you think that can be Mathilda in the beige gown and black mask? She certainly has the mature figure, doesn't she—and how odd of her to have chosen the same gown as Claude. At least I assume that's Claude—no, here, here—" the woman's murmur switched to a hiss "—next to the general. See?"

Gabriel's woman's wig was askew and his lipstick smeared as he poured himself into Angelica. He felt as the sun must feel just before it sets. As they uncoupled with the pain of sensations too acute to be pleasurable, Angelica sneaked a worried look at Gabriel. She wondered if he'd become as remote as he used to after sex, but no, he winked at her and helped her pull her trousers up and hugged her then tugged his own dress down after playfully slapping at his half-erect penis as though it were an overeager dog. Now the same woman on the other side of the curtain was saying in a bored voice, "They claim that men like tribal girls because their skin is cool in the summer."

"Come now, my dear," the man protested.

"No," she went on, "it's supposed to be as cold as a toad's. Quite a blessing in this heat, I'm sure."

Gabriel touched Angelica's arm, shrank back, made a silent "Woo-o-o" with his lips and pretended to tremble from the cold of her skin. She wept with suppressed giggles, stood on tiptoe to kiss his lips with a mouth bubbling over with laughter, stared him right in the eyes, crossed her own, pushed her wild hair back up under her schoolboy's cap, then stroked his lapel, helplessly, confidingly, as she'd seen Flora do.

"I feel like such a moron in this outfit," Gabriel said as they slid out from behind the curtain and melted into the crowd. "But, Angelica—" and he stopped her in the midst of the multitudes so that people looked at them with the sort of apprehensive pleasure with which one is led into an unfamiliar game "—where have you been? I could scarcely wait to finish renewing our intimacy—"

She audibly sighed at his choice of words, for with them he gave their childish "stings" a grown-up name, "intimacy." Apparently he was going to let them go on with the fiction of being civilized adults.

"—scarcely wait until we'd, uh, embraced so that I could talk to you, ask you a million questions. Oh, Angelica," he lowered his voice and brushed his painted lips on her forehead, leaving behind a smear that startled him when he saw it and made him break out in an elated laugh and rub it away, then drop in quick descents back into the tenderest solemnity, "I've missed you so much. I've suffered so much without you. Have you suffered, too?"

She hadn't, of course, at least not recently, but politeness required her to hang her head in mute testimony to her trials.

Gabriel's arm was around her waist, squeezing her to him as he glared into her eyes: "Who hurt you? Who did it?"

"But Gabriel," she said, "you mean you don't know I've been living all this time with your uncle?"

Gabriel smiled, shrugged, closed his eyes patronizingly as he started to set her straight when a smart blow of truth tapped him hollowly on the back of his skull and made him stand fractionally straighter. "Mateo?" he asked in an awed voice.

She explained everything that had happened to her since they last met, and his groans of outrage, his rapid intervals of flushing and paling, his cries for revenge cast her in such an appealing light as the victim that she couldn't help exaggerating the indignities she'd endured and suppressing all mention of the joys she'd known. "Yes, he begged me not to contact you because of your unstable health, although I did send you a note—"

"My health! Angelica, that man broke my health, for without you I was so alone, so frightened, whereas if I'd had you—" and he minimized the consolations he'd managed to find along the way in order to dramatize his desolation.

Although they did not see him, Mateo spotted Gabriel and Angelica in the crowd. As they talked they were leaning into each other and scanning the throngs with such unconscious ease that he knew they already took each other for granted. His heart sank. He'd lost her. Just as she'd given up her past and never looked back when she came to the city, now she'd merge without a qualm into a new life with Gabriel. The boy's smeared makeup and horrible dress only pointed up his acrid manhood. He was someone Mateo had saved and now feared. He knew that if his nephew ever had the power (if he became a patriot bigwig, for instance), he was quite capable of exiling his uncle to Madder Pink, where he would molder, as forgotten as Gabriel's own mother.

But it was Angelica whom Mateo couldn't bear to lose. In spite of himself he'd come to see love as ludic, not agonistic, but if love was a game it was one he was about to lose.

A new murmur swept over the crowd. Gabriel and Angelica broke off their delighted lament long enough to hear a neighbor say, "Looting. That's right. Some tribal servants have started looting the palaces," until his companion jabbed him in the side and gazed significantly at Angelica, who looked around and noticed for the first time how few of her own people were present at the ball.

When Gabriel said he wanted to find Mateo right now and challenge him to a duel, Angelica feared things had gotten out of hand. What if the looting and pillaging reached her quarter? Who would protect her, feed her? She knew Gabriel owned nothing but what he'd received from his uncle and that woman, Mathilda. Angelica wanted Gabriel's love and sympathy, but she didn't fancy surrendering her room. She said, "He could be very useful to us, your uncle; we musn't offend him."

"My dear Angelica," Gabriel said with just a hint of his old superiority, "Mateo is a nobody."

"I know," she hastened to concede, vexed that Gabriel was taking this tone. Didn't he realize how stylish and sophisticated she'd become? But how could he, when she was dressed in this lackluster costume?

She spotted Mathilda and said, aggressively, "There's that nice old friend of yours, what's she called?"

Mathilda stood inert, masked, swollen in her unflattering beige gown. Her son was dressed as a brigand in black cape, tricorne and half-mask pushed up on his forehead, where the eyeholes gleamed brightly with the white skin beneath. He was a good foot taller than everyone else around him; he was rolling his eyes, tossing his head back, his smile coming and going as though it were a cold, evaporating medicine being painted on his lips again and again. He was searching in vain for general hilarity over the "fashion coup" he'd staged, but only a few people had idly noticed the similarity between Claude's and Mathilda's gowns.

"But that woman means nothing to me," Gabriel said.

"Wasn't she your lover?" Angelica asked.

"Only in the sense Mateo was yours—she was forced on me."

They squeezed each other's hands in unfelt sympathy.

Just then the crowd parted to let a woman go by with her honor guard of imperial soldiers. She was in a dress sparkling with brilliants, although she wore not a single jewel on her arms or neck and only a crescent of emeralds in her blond hair, which she'd let down. It was extraordinarily long and it flowed over her bare shoulders. "Who's that?" she asked Gabriel.

The sound of his voice, so pinched and small, made her turn, her mouth open. "Edwige," he said.

"You know her? Isn't she the actress who broke your uncle's heart?"

Gabriel thought Angelica suddenly looked too small and ethnic and he felt as though he'd awakened from a glorious, terrible dream that sadly had left no marks on his appearance. He was being stripped of everything that had happened to him—his suffering over Edwige, his hope and his despair. Like a traveler who returns home after a long trip but can find no one to listen to his adventures, Gabriel thought he was being reduced to the present, that Angelica was making him look at himself through the wrong end of the telescope.

He was about to say, "She's the actress who broke *my* heart," when a shot rang out, the emerald crescent fell from Edwige's head, she staggered forward to pick it up, and then she was falling, turning her head to one side like a swimmer searching for air, and like a swimmer she lifted one arm over her head as she fell, her hair a thin wash of gold over her face behind which Gabriel could just see her eyes filling up with blood and a trickle spilling from her nose down toward her lips. And then she'd fallen and in falling turned face down. Gabriel could see that the whole back of her head had been blown away.

In the midst of the general panic, Gabriel was hopping from one foot to another in a dance of pain, his hand weirdly autonomous and clapped over his mouth, and he was whimpering, "No, no," but he knew that if someone pulled his hand away they'd discover he was grinning. When the smoke cleared he saw emerging out of it the forlorn, stubborn figure of Mathilda, her black mask like the muzzle of a pointing dog. Her hand was open; she'd dropped the gun.

Standing near her, in the identical dress and mask, was Claude, seemingly eating the knuckles on her right hand except she was screaming, not eating. And then someone somehow had swooped up the gun from the floor and forced it into Claude's hand. When she saw what it was or perhaps when she felt the heat of the metal, her scream became more intense, as though all the rainbow of her horror had been squeezed into a pure white noise, and this unearthly sound, even more shocking in a sullen girl who seldom spoke above a whisper, served to draw every eye to her. She gripped the gun tighter and tighter.

Everything was confusion—the maelstrom of masks and costumes, the jovial tinkling and whining of the dance orchestra, still obliviously playing pretty banalities even though the moment required opera not operetta, while outside every bell in town except "Mother" was clanging, including the fixed bell in the campanile next to the palace, which some unseasonably triggered mechanism had set into motion. One after the other a procession of life-sized figures, each representing another tributary people the capital had once ruled, flipped up and clicked past on rusted chains, each grasping a mallet to strike the resonant bronze cavity. In the overhead glare of fireworks and bombs these revenants (one nude and broad-nosed, another bearded and robed, a third revealing his kinship to Angelica by his particular mallet, a boar's tusk in hand) twitched from side to side as they were trolleyed along, their jerky motions catching different lights and lending a ghoulish liveliness to the metallic faces. Far away an army of insurgents was singing the anthem; in the opposite direction, toward the Grand, shouts of "Fire!" and "Thieves!" were getting louder and louder.

Angelica was staring straight at the gun; she'd seen that it had been spirited into Claude's hand by Maurizio and she feared she'd be blamed, since she was more or less his double, just as Mathilda (who'd vanished) had been Claude's.

Without realizing it, Angelica had grabbed Gabriel's arm for safety, but now he plunged forward and knelt beside the gold and gore stew of Edwige's blasted head. He was shivering all over and his hand, which reached out to touch her, vibrated with the radiant indecision of a grave robber held off by the magic inscription over the tomb. Maurizio had suddenly materialized. He pulled Angelica aside and through his mask he whispered, "We must tell everyone that Claude murdered the great patriot actress Edwige. She did it because she loved in vain the great patriot leader Gabriel. Gabriel, naturally, repelled her advances and remained true to Edwige, supreme artist of the people."

Angelica realized how much she'd learned about the capital because with every one of Maurizio's assured phrases a new objection rose to her lips. Edwige was no patriot, but rather the plaything of the conquerors. Gabriel was a patriot only because the people had always looked to his family for leadership or at least a sign. Claude had never been involved with Gabriel but with Daniel. And Mateo, not Gabriel, had surely been Edwige's lover.

And yet, and yet . . . She turned the puzzle to one side and saw how neatly the pieces could be made to fit Maurizio's version of events so long as people agreed to seek not the truth but a battle cry. "PATRIOT ACTRESS SLAIN BY JEALOUS OPPRESSOR" the headline in the *Little Gazette,* might read; and in smaller type below: "People Rise Up to Avenge Beloved Idol. Her Grieving Partner, Patriot Gabriel, Leads Revolutionary Attack."

Would Gabriel play the role fate or Maurizio had assigned him? Angelica, who had gained so much experience in quickly orienting herself to unexpected changes, felt a professional kinship to the equally nimble Maurizio, so clever in grasping how to profit from a crisis.

With the simplifying grandeur of destiny, she knelt beside Gabriel and began to explain to him what he must do and who he'd become.